D1293559

Woodbyrne:
The Fallen Forest

by James D'Arienzo, Jr.

The Fallen Forest is James D'Arienzo's first of three books, retelling the adventures and lessons learned in the dark forest of Woodbyrne.

In The Fallen Forest, young Prince Aaron defies his father's wishes and enters the forbidden forest on an adventure of his own. He soon learns why the forest is forbidden and that his actions and choices have serious consequences. While in the forest, Prince Aaron rescues a young lady named Quinn who is being held captive by Isidore, an evil demon. The rescue and escape lead to a friendship with the peaceful native elves. As the tale unfolds, readers learn with Aaron and Quinn the value of friendship, honor, and family.

Woodbyrne:

The fallen forest

James D'Arienzo, Jr.

Published by Moo Press, Inc.
Warwick, New York

This is a work of fiction. Names, characters, places and incidents are either the product of the author's imagination or are used fictitiously, and any resemblance to actual persons, living or dead, business establishments, events or locales is entirely coincidental.

WOODBYRNE: THE FALLEN FOREST

Copyright © 2003 by James D'Arienzo, Jr.

Cover design and art by Jill Lindner.

Map of Woodbyrne area by Megan D'Arienzo.

Editing by Gina Maria Kleinmartin, The Sounding Board
Proofing by Laura McCarthy, Silk Purse Editorial Services

༄

The Library of Congress Cataloging-in-Publication Data
D'Arienzo, James Jr. 1974 -
Woodbyrne: The Fallen Forest: a novel/James D'Arienzo, Jr.
— Warwick, NY : Moo Press, 2003.
p; cm.
ISBN 0-9724853-1-7 (alk. paper)
Summary: Prince enters forbidden forest, saves damsel in distress and together they wage a battle against evil.
1. Fantasy Fiction
PS3604.A75 W66 2003   2002114003
813.6—dc21   0305

Published by Moo Press, Inc.
P. O. Box 54
Warwick, NY 10990
info@moopress.com
Press room & ordering available online at www.MooPress.com.

First Edition May 2003

PRINTED IN THE UNITED STATES OF AMERICA

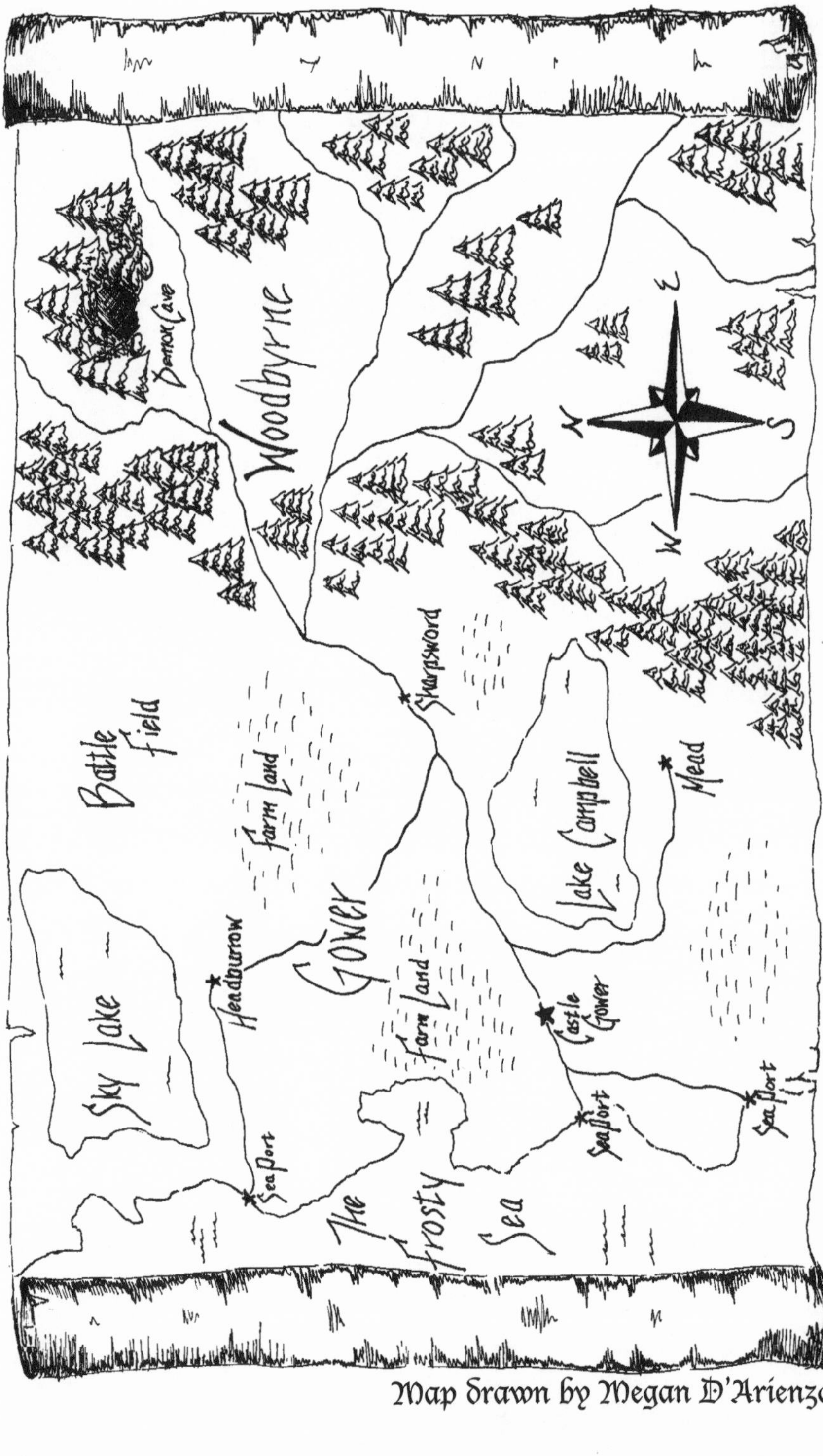

Map drawn by Megan D'Arienzo

Dedication

This book is dedicated to my wife, Megan.
Thank you for believing in me. I love you.

Cast

Main Characters In Order of Appearance.

Wynn.. Wizard's Apprentice
Salomon.. Wizard's Apprentice
Senthll Moonglow... Wizard
Isidore.. Demon Master
Aaron Gower.. Prince of Gower
Byram Edelmar... Master Archer
Sir Bickford Browne.. Head of Archers
Dermot Gower.. King of Gower
Audrey Gower... Queen of Gower
Lady Allison Churchill..................................... Head of Cavalry
Sir Henry Goodwill... Head of Infantry
Delwyn Westbrook.. Master Wizard
Brother Frewin Romney................................... Priest/Healer
Gertrude Stonegully.. Dwarven Barmaid
Dusk.. Trader
Damek.. Demon Scout
Quinn Brainard... Daughter of Robert
Ulric.. Demon Lord
Helinda O'Shan.. Farmer
Cathmore Stardust.. Elven Scout
Lennox Softfoot.. Head of Scouts
Forrester Silverbow... Elf Lord
Kemp Hethington.. Foot Soldier

Prelude

The small flame pierced the darkness of the cave, forcing Wynn to allow time for his eyes to adjust to the dim glow of his lantern. When he could see, the elf looked over his surroundings and smiled in approval. Three days before, the magic user had been out exploring his homeland in hope of finding a place where he and his friend could practice their craft in solitude. His exploration had taken him far away from his village, and the peace and solitude would ensure that nobody would disrupt his studies.

As he waited for his companion to return, the elf dreamed of the day when being a magic user would actually mean something to his superstitious people. Wood elves did not trust anyone or anything outside of the forest. Wandering humans in search of secrets and rare spell components had originally brought magic into Woodbyrne. Using magic was not illegal, but those who dabbled in magic seldom received the respect and trust accorded a scout or warrior. Wynn, however, planned on changing his people's perceptions tonight.

❧

"You're late, Salomon!" Wynn clenched his sweaty fists so that his green knuckles turned white. "Time is not our ally this evening! We have to get things started right away!"

"Sorry, but it took me longer than I expected to grab one of these and not hurt it." Salomon opened up a box that he had safely tucked under one arm and pulled out a rooster by its feet.

"It doesn't matter," Wynn sighed. "We have what we need so let's get ready before the moon hits its climax."

Salomon gingerly placed the squawking rooster back into the box and grabbed a piece of chalk. Together, the two novice wizards drew an intricate pattern on the floor: a circle filled with runes and other magical symbols. In order for the spell to work, the circle must be perfect.

"Be sure not to mess up the pattern!" Salomon scolded. "One mistake could be devastating."

"This is going to be great!" Wynn responded. "All of Woodbyrne will speak of us until the ends of time!"

"If this works," Salomon added. "Are you sure you stole the right spell?"

Wynn stopped his laboring and looked at his friend with a smile. "Very sure. Senthll himself showed it to me." Their master, Senthll Moonglow, was one of the most powerful wizards in Woodbyrne, and an excellent teacher of the magical arts. Five years earlier, the seasoned mage had agreed to take in Wynn and Salomon as apprentices. Overall, he was pleased with their progress but felt Wynn was a little too eager to learn, regularly getting into trouble by casting spells he was not ready for. Usually, nothing more than a burnt hand and a wounded pride would result, but the young mage never seemed to learn from his ways. In the case of a wizard, that could prove treacherous.

"But didn't you say that this spell has never been used?"

"Never used by Senthll," Wynn corrected. "It must work if he kept it locked up in that box all these years." The stubborn elf pointed to a corner where a pile of splinters and a mallet lay. "Enough talking. Let's just finish this pattern before its too late. If the moon passes its climax, we will have failed before we ever began."

The two friends went on with their work for hours without saying a word. Occasionally, they would refer to the spell book in order to make sure that the intricate pattern was correct. All the while, Salomon was beginning to have doubts about their abilities. Still, not wanting to hear his stubborn friend curse him, the younger wizard went about his business as best he could.

᠊ᢒ᠊

The long dagger sliced the neck of the rooster with ease. Wynn made sure that its blood covered all of the right patterns in the circle of power while Salomon lit the many candles that surrounded the sacred area.

"This looks great!" Salomon was truly impressed with the work that he and his friend had done. The pattern on the floor was finished and looked perfect.

"It's time, my friend," Wynn announced, tossing the dead rooster in the corner next to the broken box.

"I'll just say a quick prayer to honor the soul of the rooster." Salomon felt bad for stealing the rooster from his father and hoped a quick prayer in memory of the poor beast would lessen his guilt.

Again, Wynn's anxieties got the best of him. "We have no time, Salomon! Your guilt is merely the price of a higher magic!" Not wanting to turn things sour, Wynn took some deep breaths in order to calm his nerves. "I promise we will say a prayer once we are done. Will that suffice?"

Salomon nodded in agreement and nervously picked up two scrolls, carefully handing one of the ancient parchments to his friend. He still wanted to go through with the spell but the butterflies in his stomach were telling him otherwise. "What's going to happen again?"

Wynn turned to his nervous friend and laughed. "Relax. We're going to get through this just fine. By this time tomorrow, everyone will be speaking of us."

"I hope so, Wynn." Salomon swallowed hard. "But what if something goes wrong?"

"We are going to cast a spell that will allow us to speak and see beings from a different plane than ours. Creatures that nobody has ever seen before! Not even Senthll!" Wynn's adrenaline pumped fiercely through his entire body. "Salomon, I really need your help with this. I truly believe in our art and I want the rest of our people to do the same. If we succeed, the others will have no choice but to show us some respect. And maybe my son will finally warm up to the idea of becoming a magic user, and not some boring warrior with a steel blade. And, one day, you may even be able to open your own school of magic. How many times have you spoken to me about that? We both want this to work, my friend. Our lives depend upon it. So, are you ready or not? The moon is near its climax."

3

After a few seconds of serious contemplation, Salomon looked up at his friend and grinned. "I'm ready. Let's get this started."

Wynn and his partner cleared their throats and began to recite the ancient spell. The writing on the paper was old but legible and they hit all of their cues perfectly. The spell had begun without a flaw.

From out of nowhere, a small clap of thunder echoed through the cave and a light breeze entered from the forest outside. A storm was heading toward Woodbyrne.

Both Wynn and Salomon were now in a trance. The words of the spell flowed from their mouths like water and the entire cave began to glow red. The spell was working! After a few minutes, the two apprentices opened their eyes to see that a small, black sphere had formed in the middle of the circle of power. The strange formation grew with every word uttered by the two wizards and it stretched out to the size of a large doorway. The spell was complete, yet nothing could be seen. All was black and cloudy.

Salomon looked at his friend with both fear and excitement, for it was time to call upon the creature.

Wynn, covered in a thick sweat, looked at the parchment in order to make sure he could pronounce the name correctly. After mumbling to himself several times, he placed the scroll on the floor and pointed a slender finger at the mystical doorway. "Isidore!" he shouted, but nothing seemed to happen. "Isidore, come to me! I summon you!"

Another clap of thunder shook the ground and the doorway began to glow deep red.

"It's working! It's working!" Salomon hopped from foot to foot.

Wynn, on the other hand, was paralyzed. His eyes never left the magical doorway and his finger remained pointed forward.

The storm outside had quickly grown deadly. Monstrous hail and fierce bolts of lightning were shooting out of the sky at an alarming rate, splitting trees and rocks alike.

Wynn turned his head very slowly toward Salomon. His almond eyes were still glazed and his normally green skin looked white. "He is here."

"Who is here?" asked Salomon. "Who? Isidore is here?" The young mage looked at the doorway and frowned. "The spell failed, you fool! Nothing is here!"

Wynn, still under the effects of the casting, simply gazed at his friend. "He is here."

"Look!" Salomon walked through the circle carelessly and pointed at the doorway. "Nothing is happening, Wynn. Why are you acting so strange?"

Wynn's eyes rolled back and foam slowly began to drip from the sides of his mouth. A strong gust of wind blew out all the candles and the peculiar red glow began to intensify. Soon, the entire cave grew incredibly hot and the walls seemed to be bleeding profusely from every crack and imperfection.

Salomon looked into the doorway and cursed as he thought of the trouble he was going to get into. How could I have let this idiot talk me into this?

Suddenly, a huge red arm decorated with long black claws shot out of the darkness of the doorway and grabbed Salomon by his skinny throat, almost popping his head right from his shoulders.

Wynn violently snapped out of his trance and desperately shouted for his friend. "Get away, Salomon! Get away from there!"

Black smoke suddenly poured out of the mystical doorway and a pair of large yellow eyes looked down at the frozen elf. Salomon tried to break free, but the creature had the strength of twenty war-horses. He could only pray that his friend would help him before it was too late. Before his neck gave way beneath the might of his assailant.

Wynn stepped back in horror and leaned up against the cave wall. The red blood that oozed from the cracks burned like acid on the elf's tender green skin. "What have I done?"

A loud laugh bellowed from inside the black smoke and the yellow eyes turned toward Wynn. With a quick snap of its wrists, the summoned creature crushed Salomon's neck and threw him to the ground at the feet of the young wizard. Wynn stared into his friend's lifeless eyes that seemed to ask why his best friend would simply let him die.

Wynn looked up just in time to see the massive creature leap out of the black smoke. Out of sheer panic, he ran out of the cave and into the forest where he was greeted by one of the worst storms ever to hit the beautiful woodland. Fearful of the consequences, he decided not to head back to his village. Instead, he would seek shelter in the woods until the beast he conjured returned to its own world.

The creature stood in the center of the circle of power for only a moment. As he made his way toward the dead elf, the evil black smoke still clung heavily to his massive frame. "Thank you," it muttered mockingly. "Thank you for calling me to this plane of existence. And thank you so very much for crossing the circle and breaking its hold on me." The evil beast began to laugh as it thought of the chaos that would surely follow in the days and months ahead.

Isidore, demon master of the lower planes, had come to Woodbyrne.

Chapter 1

An arrow streaked across the sky and slammed into the bull's-eye with pinpoint accuracy. Prince Aaron Gower had been honing his aim for quite some time, and his instructor had taught him well. After congratulating his own skill, the prince lost himself in thought, something he was rather accustomed to.

"All I do is *practice*," the young man said. "I have never seen a real battle, nor have I ever had to rely on my own skills to survive." Glumly, Aaron threw his weapon to the ground and huffed. "What good are skills if you can't put them to any use?" How he desperately wanted to leave the safety of his father's kingdom in order to see what the rest of the world had to offer. He wanted a life of excitement and danger. No trainer or tutor could show him such things. There were lessons in life that could not be taught through books and paper. Upset with his situation, he turned and looked at Castle Gower and thought about the two people who lived within its magnificent walls. The two people who had sheltered him since the day he was born.

King Dermot and Queen Audrey were kind, loving parents that would do anything their son asked. Anything but let him go off and explore the very kingdom that he would one day rule. They were very protective and the fact that Aaron was their only child did not help the situation.

Aaron brushed back his blond hair and turned his head toward the sky. It was the middle of summer and the weather was typically hot. The land was alive with sounds of beautiful songbirds and the smells of exotic flowers. Aaron always enjoyed the wild animals and birds that roamed about in search of food and shelter. He adored the beautiful trees and flowers that decorated the countryside. Deep in his heart, the young prince felt he was meant for a life more exciting than the one he had.

"Heads up!" someone shouted from across the target range.

Aaron, having been through the ritual hundreds of times before, threw himself on the ground and smiled as a deadly arrow whizzed past where his head had been and hit the bull's-eye, splitting his own arrow in two. Once the shaft had stopped vibrating, Aaron dusted off his clothes and rose to his feet to greet the person who had forced him to "eat grass."

"I think your warnings are getting shorter," the prince said to Byram Edelmar, his cousin and best friend. When Byram was four years old, bandits had killed his parents. The king and queen had taken him under their care. A year later, when Aaron was born, Byram had watched over his younger cousin with a loving eye. Despite their age difference, they had become close friends, sharing each other's dreams and ideas.

"Not bad," the prince continued as he wiped clean his polished boots and made his way to the target.

Byram also walked over and relished the accuracy of his shot for a moment or two. "I see you have been practicing," he said with a wry smile. "Your skills are improving every day."

One of the biggest differences between the two young men was their lifestyles. Byram, unlike his unfortunate cousin, was not held down to the responsibilities of royalty. Ever since he was able, the young archer had traveled the world and had many adventures, both fun and dangerous. Byram's exciting lifestyle was what drove Aaron's spirit, fueling his dreams and desires. Over the past two months, the cousins had developed a plan that would allow the prince to experience some of Byram's world.

"Are you sure you want to go through with this?" the archer asked, breaking his cousin's train of thought.

"Yes. We leave tonight. Once the party has ended, we'll depart. Nobody will know we are missing until late in the morning. By then we should be long gone. We'll leave a note explaining our 'trip' so no one will worry." The prince, satisfied with his answer, drifted back into his dreams. The party he spoke of was being held in his honor and the entire kingdom was going to be there. The very thought of having to sit

8

around all night while the kingdom's elite bowed before him and show-ered him with gifts made the young man sick. *Nobody ever knows what I really want anyway*, he thought.

"The big twenty, eh? My dear cousin, you are catching up to me. I sometimes forget that there are only five years between us." Byram hated to see his cousin in such a foul mood and was determined to make him smile. "So, what do you think you'll be getting this year? A brain? Some common sense? A bath perhaps?"

"Each year it's the same old thing! Robes, jewelry and clothes that never fit. I never even know half of the people that show up anyway! Useless baubles, that's what I get."

"Hey, if you don't want them, I could use a bauble or two. My room is looking rather dull these days."

The prince looked at his cousin and smiled. "*I* know what I want, Byram. Since no one else is going to give it to me, I'll just have to give it to myself."

"And what was that again? A nice blow to the head?"

Aaron looked back to the sky and watched as small white clouds passed effortlessly through the air. Nothing held them back and no-body knew where they were going. He also saw three falcons flying over Lake Campbell. How he wished that he could be with them! He wanted to soar in the air and be free and wild. Nothing was going to stop him this time, he swore. Not even the king. "Freedom," he said. "I want to live, my cousin."

"We all do, my friend. It's an urge embedded deep within even the smallest creature." Byram could only imagine what it must be like for the young prince, always under the watchful eyes of the entire king-dom. Never able to do anything by himself. Never allowed to breathe the air of other realms, to taste the foods of the wild, or to rely only on skills and senses for survival. Those thoughts made Byram shudder. Being a bit older, he had seen more of the world. Not being the sole heir to the throne helped a little too. "I want to do this with you, Aaron. I under-stand your pains more than anyone else does. Together we will see new lands. Together we will have the adventure of a lifetime." Byram put a comforting hand on the prince's shoulder.

Aaron simply smiled and wiped the tears from his eyes. After a moment, he took a deep breath and picked up his bow. "I bet you can't hit that bull's-eye again, you beggar!"

"I believe that was a challenge."

Quickly, the two friends readied their bows and took aim.

♪

"Nice game. Next time we'll play for ale," Byram declared after he had won the accuracy challenge. He was an extraordinary archer and King Dermot himself spoke of the day when the young man would be head of the Royal Archers. For now, he was a recruiter for the army's archery division, second only to the venerable Sir Bickford Browne. It was a good job and everyone in the kingdom respected him.

"I don't think so," replied the prince. "Even I have limited funds." Aaron knew deep down that he would never beat his cousin in such a game. He had only made the challenge because he wanted the company. "Besides, what good is a drunk archer?"

"You'd have to ask the fair ladies about that one, my friend."

Together, the two cousins shared a good laugh and fetched their arrows from what was left of the bull's-eye.

"Aaron!" a voice boomed from across the target range. King Dermot made his way across the well-groomed grass with great strides, sporting a big smile across his bearded face. Dermot stood a solid five inches over six feet and was more than capable of fighting off three giants at once. He had the face of both ruler and warrior. A very large scar that ran from his left ear to the side of his mouth was the result of fighting mercenaries sent to loot and destroy Headburrow, a small town located on the northwest side of Kingdom Gower. He had only been eighteen at the time, and had since tried to cover the wound by growing a beard, but it was still visible to all who looked at him.

Dermot walked up to the two young men and laughed. "Mr. Birthday Boy, did you let this street thug win yet *again*?" Aaron's face turned red. His father liked to embarrass him whenever possible.

"Good afternoon, sire," Byram said bowing in respect to the king. "I was unaware of the prince's mercy on me." He said, turning toward Aaron, "So, it is for my own well being that you always throw the match?"

"Yes, I don't want to see you cry like a baby. I know how important it is for you to one day lead the archers into battle, my cousin." Aaron played along with the little game.

"And lead it he shall," the king answered. "Once, of course, the good Mr. Browne has resigned from the position." King Dermot turned to Byram and sighed. "I am going to be honest with you, my boy. I didn't come over here to speak about archery. I came to speak with my son in private." The king looked at Byram and gave a quick nod.

"I'll see you later," Byram said as he headed off to the castle.

"What do you want to talk to me about, Dad?" Aaron looked nervous. Did his father find out about his plot to leave the castle? Did Byram leak the plans to his family?

"Relax, Aaron. This isn't of any importance." The king pulled out a piece of paper from inside his jacket. "Your mother found this in the garbage this morning."

The crumbled paper was his "assigned" speech for this evening. Aaron *hated* giving speeches. Every year, they made him speak to the guests and thank them for attending the festivities. "I was hoping that this year I wouldn't have to speak like a trained dog to a room of people who really just want to eat, drink, and be left alone."

The king frowned. "Aaron, you are the prince of this kingdom and it is expected!" Dermot took a moment to calm down and put a hand on his son's shoulder. "You have to face the fact that there is a great amount of responsibility that comes with being royalty. You are the next in line to wear the crown. You have to start acting like royalty."

"But I don't even want a party. Do you think these people really care about me? It's the food and wine that they're after."

Dermot looked upon his only son with great sadness and disappointment. "Is that how you feel about the people of this land? They are hard working and deserve better than that. I gained their trust through battle and honesty. I will not have you or anyone else speak poorly of them!"

"Father, I don't see what the big deal is. I stay behind these walls every day and learn about being proper. It drives me crazy! Why can't I go anywhere by myself? Do you doubt me so much as to hide me and shelter me like a puppy?" The prince turned around and looked over the horizon. The sun was quickly setting and it cast a red glow across the land. "I've been so busy these past few years that I couldn't even find the time to hold a meaningful relationship with a woman. It's all just so pathetic!"

The king understood how his son felt. He was the same way when he was a young man. However, since his parents were not as strict, Dermot had been allowed to go places and see the world, despite the fact that he was the youngest of three sons. As he grew older, Dermot realized his responsibilities to the kingdom and to his family. His two older brothers, unfortunately, did not. Daniel, the oldest of the three, died at the hands of pirates while out at sea. His other brother, Henry, had set out to explore Woodbyrne, the dark forest that bordered Gower on the east, and was never seen again. Dermot was left as the only heir to the throne. He had to make sure the Gower name survived. Aaron was the royal family's only son. King Dermot and Queen Audrey would have loved to see him go off and explore, but they could not afford to take the risk. It was a hard choice, but it seemed to be in the best interest of the people.

"It's because of your brothers, isn't it?" accused Aaron with a sharp tongue. "Because they both died young doesn't mean I will, you know! Well, they are better off dead than having to spend the rest of their lives trapped in this castle like me!"

"I will not have you speak of my brothers like that!" A very hurt and angry King Dermot stormed away toward the Royal Gardens.

Aaron stood very still for some time after his father's departure. He simply could not believe what he had said. "How could I speak of my uncles like that?" he asked himself, disgusted with his actions. His two uncles had passed away before his parents married and he knew very little of their lives. Apparently, his father still grieved their deaths and the prince felt awful for bringing up such bad memories. But why were their lives always kept secret from him? What really happened to them? Determined to find the truth, Aaron ran as fast as he could toward the castle. He knew exactly who to ask in order to learn the truth.

᠅

"Place the flowers over in the corner," instructed the queen to the decorators as she prepared the ballroom for the night's festivities. Not long before, she had spoken to the chefs about the dinner. The menu's main course was roast duck with a strawberry sauce, and for dessert vanilla cake topped with honey-coated pecans, the prince's favorite.

"Your Highness," one of the servants called out. "Prince Aaron is here to see you. He wants to speak with you in private."

"Show him to the library, if you please. I don't want the guest of honor to see the hall until tonight." Before she left the ballroom, Audrey took one more glance at the decorations. "I wanted the flowers to be *next* to the punch bowl, not in front of it!" she shouted. In an instant, the flowers were pushed to the correct location. "Thank you."

Prince Aaron sat in the library looking through some old books when the queen arrived. "Hello, mother," he said. "Where were you just now?" A smile cracked across his face because he had a good idea what his elusive mother was up to.

"I was just arranging things for the party tonight," the queen said. She sat down next to her son and smiled. She placed a hand on Aaron's knee and looked him in the eyes. "What's on your mind? You know you can talk to me."

The prince searched for the right words. It was not every day that he asked about his two dead uncles. "I'm curious," he stuttered. "I never learned how my uncles died. I know that each of them died adventuring, but that's all. What were they doing? Where did they die?"

"I think your father should talk to you about that," Queen Audrey explained. "I only know bits and pieces of two very long stories."

"Then tell me what you do know. Dad is out in the garden and not in the mood for talking. I mentioned his brothers while we were arguing and he got very upset. If I had known the truth, I would have held my tongue. The last thing I want to do is hurt Dad's feelings like that." Prince Aaron looked into his mother's eyes and pleaded. "One story, then. Why did Uncle Henry go into the Woodbyrne forest?"

The queen stood up and walked over to a very old painting of the king's family. They all seemed so happy and carefree. Swallowing hard, the queen looked back to her son. "There is nothing in Woodbyrne," she said. "Nothing but evil. Once, a very long time ago, peaceful elves ruled the Woodbyrne forest. The elves were a kind and friendly race."

The prince sat and listened to his mother's description of the mystical people of the forest. He could almost see them walking around the forest. Their tall stature and olive green skin blending in with the trees while their brown hair flowed gently in the wind. He saw a set of pointed ears jutting out of their heads like small peaks of a mountain.

"The elves had lived peacefully in Woodbyrne since the dawn of time," his mother continued. "Then, two hundred years ago, a great evil overtook the forest, destroying the good that once lived there. Most of the elves were killed, and even the trees turned wicked. Men and women have both journeyed there never to be heard of again. Nobody has ever come out of Woodbyrne alive." The queen became silent and looked off into the distance while her son digested what she had told him.

"What of Uncle Henry?" Aaron asked. "Why did he go into Woodbyrne? Why didn't he come out?" The young prince desperately wanted to know. His heart was beating fiercely in anticipation.

The queen looked back to her son. She took a deep breath and continued the story. "Henry Gower was known as one of the fiercest warriors in all of Oneira. People would come from distant lands to train with him, and Henry never turned down anyone who was willing to learn. One day, he was out at the training grounds when a messenger came calling for him. Apparently, there was an argument at one of the inns at Sharpsword. Someone was saying that your uncle was not up to the challenge of a lifetime."

"What was the challenge?" the prince asked.

"Your uncle also wanted to know what this challenge was. The very next morning, he saddled up his horse and raced toward Sharpsword. When he entered the inn, Henry saw a man sitting at the head of the bar, smoking a very long and twisted pipe that looked like a serpent. After a small greeting, the challenge was given. Your uncle was to enter Woodbyrne that very night and spend two evenings behind its dark walls. If he made it out alive, the man agreed to pay him a thousand gold coins for his bravery and his report on the mysterious woods. Henry thought for a moment and agreed to do it."

"Why did Uncle Henry take such a challenge?"

"You see, since Daniel died, Henry wanted to prove that the Gowers were a strong family. Henry felt that, by taking the challenge, he was honoring the name of his older brother."

"But didn't Dad try to talk him out of it?" Aaron was completely compelled by the story of his uncle.

"He never got a chance to," the queen explained. "By the time Dermot arrived at Sharpsword, Henry had already left for Woodbyrne. Witnesses reported that Henry lit a torch before entering the woods and it could be seen slowly fading into the woods." She turned to Aaron and looked him in the eyes. "Your uncle was never seen nor heard from again." Queen Audrey got up and walked out of the library.

Aaron sat alone for many minutes and played back the story in his head over and over again. He had many more questions to ask, but he knew no one had the answers. Before he left, Aaron looked at the same painting his mother had stared at and an idea flashed into his head. "I must go and explore Woodbyrne! That will be my adventure!" he whispered.

Excited, Aaron rushed off to his room to prepare for the evening ahead. It was now dark outside and the guests would be arriving shortly. However, it was not the party that was on the prince's mind, it was Woodbyrne. The mysterious woods that bordered his father's kingdom had invaded his thoughts, digging a deep and impenetrable trench.

Chapter 2

The Royal Ballroom was filled with over two hundred people. Some of the guests were the lords and ladies of Gower's three main towns—Headburrow, Sharpsword, and Mead. Others were either close friends of the Gowers or lucky citizens who had been picked out of a lottery to attend the party.

The prince greeted all who walked through the elaborate double doors. Although he hardly knew any of them, Aaron still made the effort to act sincere. After the proper greetings, the agitated birthday boy grabbed a tall tankard of ale and found a dark, quiet corner in which to hide. He took in a nice mouthful of the potent brew and surveyed the massive party. Byram, as always, was busy drinking and getting to know the females of the kingdom a little better while King Dermot and Queen Audrey sat at the main table and kept busy by answering the guests' many questions and comments. In a small corner, the king's war council sat and debated with one another over politics and war strategies—something that they always seemed to be doing. The three elite members included Sir Bickford Browne, head of archers, Lady Allison Churchill, head of cavalry, and Sir Henry Goodwill, head of infantry. These three noble and honest soldiers were the king's personal assistants during a crisis. All but Bickford Browne, a sixty–six–year–old veteran, were in their mid-forties.

Aaron noticed that, just as Byram seemed to get the attention of a beautiful woman, she threw a glass of wine into his face. The young archer sheepishly looked around the room and prayed that nobody saw the humiliating scene. However, Aaron saw everything and found it most amusing.

"Always the charmer," Aaron whispered to himself. The prince took another sip of ale and turned his attention to the aging wizard, Delwyn Westbrook, as he entertained the children. The venerable man was creating small glowing balls of red and purple that popped into confetti over his audience's head. Delwyn was always a favorite among the guests at any gathering. He had a very good sense of humor and was patient with the young ones. Nobody knew for sure how old the wizard was, but Aaron guessed his age to be near seventy. Delwyn was also the wisest man in the entire kingdom and always had an important role in any major decision King Dermot made. The old mage had even been asked to join the members of the war council but had declined, stating, "There is too much to do in this world without spending all day worrying about war." Delwyn made his home on the beaches west of the castle overlooking the Frosty Sea. Many people traveled to Delwyn's home to ask the wizard questions and advice. Most visitors left with valuable knowledge, more than just answers.

After a few uneventful minutes, the Royal Brotherhood politely approached the king and queen and presented a gift for the prince. Aaron enjoyed watching the priests simply because of the strange way they acted. The Brotherhood was a very solitary group of men and women who lived in small chapels scattered throughout the kingdom. They rarely spoke and never asked for anything in return for the prayers they said and the healings they performed.

Among the priests, the prince recognized one of them to be Brother Frewin Romney of Sharpsword. He was only twenty-one, but it was rumored that he wielded the powers of a great priest. Frewin was also considered a rebel in the eyes of his peers since he liked to speak, often giving as much advice as he possibly could. Aaron had spoken to him on many occasions and was glad to see somebody he knew at the party. Quickly, the prince made his way over.

"Brother Frewin, thank you so much for coming tonight!" Aaron called as he crossed the giant room. He gave the priest a hug and a handshake. He picked up the gift in front of his parents and examined it. It was a pipe, carved from solid oak with etchings of the moon and stars around the entire shaft. "Thank you, my friend. This is truly a work of art. I'd like to share a smoke with you one of these days. If it's okay with the Brotherhood, of course."

"I would like that very much, Prince Aaron," Frewin replied with a smile. "Please be reminded that all of us took part in making the pipe." The priest gestured to the brotherhood and they bowed in recognition.

Prince Aaron bowed in return. "Thank you all for the gift. It is a remarkable piece of artwork. Please, make yourselves at home this evening. Drink and eat all you can handle, and more." With that said, Aaron seated himself next to his parents and thanked the rest of the guests who placed their gifts on the table. Afterwards, the prince ate his meal in relative peace.

"My dear Prince Aaron," Byram said, as he sat himself next to his cousin, his breath smelling like a barrel of mead. "How goes the party?"

"It seems to be going better for me than it is for you," the prince hinted. "Tell me, cousin, do you actually *drink* your wine, or do you prefer various women to throw it in your face for you? It seems easier to do it your way, but it must ruin your clothes."

Byram's face turned red. "You are lucky it's your birthday, or I would be forced to put you in your place."

"So, are you ready for tonight?" asked the prince. He had looked forward to the journey for a long time yet he did not know how to tell his best friend that he had changed the final destination of their trip. "After the party, meet me in my room. I want to go over the details before leaving."

"You can count on me, cousin," agreed Byram with a smile.

With that said, Prince Aaron and Byram finished their drinks and tried to relax.

The rest of the party was uneventful at best. The guests danced and drank all through the evening and Aaron even made the time to share a dance with his mother and some of the kingdom's beautiful ladies. Though he was a handsome man, Aaron never found time to meet anyone suitable for marriage. He always dreamed of meeting a woman from a far off land who could bring some excitement into his dreary life. Though tempting to say the least, the women of Gower—especially the spoiled daughters of the nobles—had nothing substantial to offer. They were all so superficial.

When the party was at its end, the king decided to speak. "My good friends," he began. "Thank you all for coming to my son's birthday party. I pray that you are having as good of a time as my family and I am." The room sounded with cheers and applause for the generous hosts. The king continued. "I would now like to turn the floor over to our guest of honor, Prince Aaron Gower." Again, everyone cheered and shouted for their future leader.

Aaron's face was covered in sweat. How he hated speaking in public! Forcing himself in front of the room, he addressed his guests. "As my father said, thank you all for coming tonight." As bad luck would have it, a drop of salty sweat fell into Aaron's left eye, causing a very annoying sting. He tried to ignore the discomfort but it only forced him to blink and squint spastically. "The gifts I received are beautiful, and I will cherish them all." Aaron decided to end the speech quickly, while it was still going well. "I thank you and wish all of you the best that life has to offer. Have a good evening." He quickly picked up a cloth and rubbed his agitated eye while the guests clapped accordingly and made his way out of the ballroom.

Queen Audrey stood at the door and said a few parting words while King Dermot spoke with some of the remaining guests who had not gotten their chance to speak to the king. Byram left the castle to take care of some last minute chores. Prince Aaron, as silently as he could, made his way up to his room where Byram would meet him later. As he ascended the castle's stairs, the prince cracked a smile. "That speech went off without a hitch," he said to himself. "I think I'm improving with age."

⋙

Aaron paced around his room like a caged tiger. He checked his supplies at least a dozen times in order to make sure he did not bring anything that would make him stand out. The prince knew it would be detrimental if anyone outside the castle recognized him, so he made certain that no reminders of his royal status accompanied him on the journey. He would be a regular person, like everybody else.

Everything seemed to be going as planned, except for the fact that Byram was late.

"Where is he?" the prince asked, nervous because it was fifteen minutes past midnight. Had he been caught bringing the horses around the back of the castle's north wall? Maybe the king and queen knew about this little trip all along and had Byram sent to the dungeons for going along with it.

A light knock came from the prince's door and snapped him out of his miserable trance. The young man ran across his room and flung the door open.

Byram simply walked in as if there was nothing wrong. "Hello, cousin. Are you ready? The night is lovely with not a cloud in the sky and the moon is full."

"Where in the name of all that lives were you? You should have been here almost an hour ago. What happened? Did you get caught or something?"

"Your shouting is going to wake up your parents and that would spoil this little trip real soon." Byram explained, "When I got to the stables I found that your horse was not saddled properly. I had to do it myself. In order to fix your saddle, I had to remove all of the supplies. That took some time." Byram sat down on his cousin's bed. "Now, what details did you want to review?"

"Nothing really," Aaron shrugged. "I just decided that I no longer want to explore the neighboring kingdoms of Gower." He got off his bed and slung his pack over his shoulder. "I want to explore Woodbyrne."

Byram jumped to his feet and looked directly into Aaron's eyes. "Aaron, have you gone mad? Nobody has ever come out of those woods alive!"

"That is exactly why I want to go into them!" Aaron's blue eyes lit up like wildfires. "We can do it! Together, you and I will uncover the mysteries of Woodbyrne."

"But the stories, the warnings—have you heard nothing?" Byram was at a loss for words. "Nothing *ever* leaves Woodbyrne! Nothing!"

"Yes, I've heard all of the rumors and tales, my cousin. All of the stories are how one person tried to prove himself to the rest of world by going into the woods alone. I want to enter the forest with you so I can see what lies behind its thick borders. I don't care about my reputation as a man. If that were the case, why am I being so secretive? Why am I traveling in these clothes?" Aaron pointed to his rough breeches and homespun shirt.

"How far will you go for the thrill of adventure?" Byram asked.

"As far as I have to." Aaron gave one quick look to make sure nothing was forgotten, and headed outside.

Byram reluctantly followed his cousin out the door. He did not want to go to Woodbyrne, but he saw no way out of the situation. If he let Aaron go on alone, the king and queen would never forgive him. On the other hand, if Byram woke up the king and queen now and told them Aaron's plans, his cousin would hate him forever. At least if Byram went with Aaron, he could protect his cousin. And maybe tomorrow, after some adventuresome traveling Aaron will come to his senses and change his mind.

"This is going to be fun," Byram murmured. "A nice trip into one of the most feared places in the kingdom with a young man bent on living dangerously. A recipe for success I'm sure." With that said, Byram headed out the door to catch up to his crazy cousin.

Once outside, the two men had to make their way toward the north side of the castle wall, the least guarded section. Aaron and Byram studied the situation from behind a patch of large trees. As expected, tonight only two guards kept watch from the north tower and they seemed to be caught up in some sort of conversation.

"This'll be easy," Aaron whispered to his cousin. "Where did you put the horses?"

Byram moved in closer. "They are fifty yards to the northeast of the wall, behind a small group of trees."

Positive the guards were not aware of their presence, the two friends shifted through the shadows to make their way to the large, stone wall. Once there, Byram reached into his pack and pulled out a rope with a grappling hook attached to it.

Aaron made sure the guards were still busy chatting. Satisfied, he gave his cousin a sign and threw the rope over the wall.

The prince climbed first while Byram kept an eye on their surroundings. The archer followed soon after Aaron gave a whistle that he had safely scaled the stone wall. When the friends were safely on the ground, they packed the rope and ran off into the night. The two guards never heard a sound.

The horses were relaxing near some trees and eating fresh grass when the escapees arrived. All provisions and equipment were tied neatly onto their saddles. After a brief check on supplies, the horses were led out of hiding.

"It will be best to stay off the road for a couple of miles so nobody will see us leaving," Byram said, as he walked his horse away from the trees.

"How far should we go tonight?" asked Aaron, unsure if they were going to ride all night. He had hoped for a rest before the long journey in the morning.

"We will lead the horses through some farmland until it is safe to take to the road. Then we should be able to travel for a couple of hours before resting." Byram wanted to travel all night, but understood the prince's need for rest. He, too, had drunk more than his share of wine and ale at the party and his stomach was not in the mood for a long ride tonight.

The partners walked for several hours without saying a word. The night was pleasantly cool and it seemed that every star in the sky was out. The moon was at its fullest and shed a soft, blue light onto the land.

All the while, Prince Aaron thought of his Uncle Henry. I wonder how he died? What could possibly be so deadly in those woods?

Byram was also enjoying the evening. He had a very good time at the party and the night was beautiful. He too thought of Woodbyrne. Although it promised to be an exciting adventure, common sense told him to stay away from the mysterious forest. Perhaps Aaron would see the evil woods and decide to turn around. No matter what his foolish cousin decided, Byram knew that he would follow Aaron. He loved Aaron like a brother. And, he owed a great debt to King Dermot and Queen Audrey for taking him into their home when his parents were killed. He owed it to them to protect Aaron at all costs. "I would follow him to the pits of existence, if need be," he said to himself.

❧

"Let's look for a place to spend the rest of the evening," Byram said after several hours had been spent on the long, dusty road.

"How about over there?" suggested the prince, pointing toward a patch of trees. "It should provide us with enough shelter for the evening."

Byram agreed and headed for the trees. There they found a clearing where they could set camp. The horses were tied to a tree, given some oats, and the sleeping blankets were unrolled.

"Tomorrow we'll ride all day," Byram said, as he tucked himself under his blankets. "If all goes well, we should make Sharpsword by late afternoon." The exhausted archer fell asleep in a matter of minutes, dreaming of the beautiful woman who had thrown wine in his face at the party.

Aaron took a little while longer to fall asleep. He was excited about visiting Sharpsword and he hoped to get some information pertaining to Woodbyrne there. "We should get a map," he thought lazily as he gazed into the night's starry sky. He smiled as he thought that he'd given himself the best birthday present ever.

❧

The two men woke up rather late in the morning. The sun had risen three hours before and the birds were already singing. Byram rose from his blankets and pulled out some bread and dried meat from his pack for breakfast. Aaron remained hidden under his blankets while his cousin prepared the small meal.

"Get up, you lazy bum, and eat some food."

"I am a prince. Make me my breakfast, you slob. I'll take scrambled eggs and ham."

After Byram poured cold water on his head, Aaron thought better of his approach and ate the meal before him without complaint.

They ate fast and cleaned up even quicker. Sharpsword was still far off and they had a lot of ground to cover. Once everything was put away, Aaron and Byram mounted their horses and sped off down the road.

Along the road they passed some farmers and merchants; but they paid little attention to the men on horseback. Aaron actually enjoyed the attention he was *not* getting! Byram was also pleased that the people did not notice them since the king had probably sent scouts out to find them by now.

The further they rode from the castle, the fewer people they saw, and they began to relax a little. If the king's scouts were really looking for them, they would have a hard time tracking them down here.

The prince was thoroughly enjoying the trip. The day was beautiful and the landscape was breathtaking. After a few more miles, they passed through the vaste farmlands of Gower, covered in wheat and corn crops. Quaint farms were scattered over small hilltops and nestled between gentle valleys. The air was clean and fresh, not full of the poverty and congestion that usually accompanies a larger town. All sorts of birds and insects were out that day, and all of them seemed to be singing their own song. Aaron was in all of his glory.

Byram looked at his blissful cousin and smiled. "Are you enjoying yourself, Aaron?"

The prince snapped out of his daydream and laughed. "Byram," he said, "I am having the time of my life! I never knew how gorgeous the kingdom was. There are so many sights to see, places to visit, and people to meet. Best of all, I am on my own. That is what makes this so special for me. I am not under my parents' thumb."

"Enjoy it while you can," Byram added, "there will be hell to pay when we return." He began to chuckle. The young marksman was very happy to see his best friend act like a little boy again. It had been a long time since the two of them shared such a private moment and he began to think that the trip was vital for the prince's very existence.

As Byram looked ahead, he saw Woodbyrne, the place where they may meet their end if all went wrong. Maybe, he thought, Aaron will forget about the forest once they arrived at Sharpsword. That thought brought a smile to Byram's face.

"I can't get the forest out of my mind," Aaron said suddenly, completely bursting Byram's bubble. "I want to visit Sharpsword, but I only want to stay there for a night. Woodbyrne is our destination and nothing is going to stop me." The prince gave his horse a light kick and galloped down the road.

"Why is he being so foolish?" the archer asked his horse. "Doesn't he realize the dangers of entering that evil forest?" He just shook his head in disbelief, nudged his mount into a trot, and caught up with his cousin.

As the day went on, the vast countryside took on a more settled appearance. It was still just as beautiful, but the signs of an active town were evident. The people they passed were mostly merchants and traders instead of farmers and herdsmen.

"We're getting close to Sharpsword," Byram announced. "It's less than two miles from here. When we get over the next hilltop, we'll be able to see its flags blowing in the summer breeze."

"*If* I make it there," Aaron responded bitterly—almost pathetically. "I haven't had a bite to eat since this morning."

Byram was also hungry, but he wanted to keep on moving forward. Feeling that they were behind in their travels, the two young men decided to eat their lunch on horseback, which consisted of water and some bread with honey.

A short while later, they reached the top of a small hill. Byram got off his horse and called for his cousin to join him. Just a few minutes away, their first destination awaited with eager yet dangerous arms.

"So, we have come to Sharpsword," the prince said, as he dismounted his horse. "I am not that impressed."

Sharpsword was not as decorated as Castle Gower, but it had a quaint, cozy appearance. Its small buildings were neatly arranged in rows and alleys. They were not elaborate structures, but they held a certain charm.

Quaint taverns and inns were littered throughout city where a weary traveler could always find a hot meal, warm bed, and good conversation. The local government made sure its shop owners gave everyone equal attention in order to ensure return visitors. The cottages that outlined the city were small and wholesome. Their clay roofs reflected a dark orange off the sun's rays. Although there was no moat or wall to protect the friendly city, it did have a military presence to ward off any trouble. Fortunately, there had not been any war since before Aaron was born. The people of Sharpsword were very friendly folk, yet they liked to stay to themselves. They worked hard and lived well.

Byram turned to his cousin and took a deep breath. "Aaron, there are some things that we have to go over."

"Sure, what are they."

"First of all, keep your mouth in check. Secondly, tell no one of our destination. Woodbyrne is not very far from here and these people are very superstitious. That name will never be spoken of! Finally, tell no one your name. If anyone asks, you will be Stephen Willows."

"Do you take me for a fool? I know what to do, Byram, so you don't have to treat me like a little child."

"Listen, I just want this to go smoothly. We need to gather as much information as we can and leave for Woodbyrne in the morning without incident." Byram could not believe what he had just said.

Aaron jumped to his feet. "I knew you wouldn't let me go in alone! I will do as you say, I promise. If anyone asks, I am Stephen Willows. We will get as much information as possible and head out first thing in the morning."

The young archer looked at Aaron and smiled. He thought to himself, I *must* be going crazy.

Chapter 3

One of the guards that kept watch at the main entrance of Sharpsword stopped the two cousins just as they approached the gates. He was a tall, muscular young man wearing brand new armor and holding a shiny war axe which showed no signs of wear. The smile on his face exposed his inexperience.

"Dismount your horses and come forward!" he demanded. "You will not be allowed into Sharpsword without the approval of the king's men!"

The two friends dismounted their horses and approached the guard. Prince Aaron made sure that his cousin walked ahead of him because there was the slight possibility that the guard would recognize him as the prince of Gower.

"Greetings," Byram began with a warm smile. "We are two travelers who have been on the road for many days. We are weary and in need of a hot meal and a warm bed."

"What's your business in Sharpsword?" asked the guard.

Slowly, Byram held up his hands in peace. "We have no business inside your lovely town, good sir. We just want to spend the night. If you like, you may hold onto our weapons until we are ready to leave in the morning."

The soldier looked the two men over and decided they were not there for trouble. Happily, he put his axe back on his belt and smiled. "Welcome to Sharpsword, gentlemen. Our inns are warm and our people are friendly." The soldier moved aside and let the strangers pass.

Aaron put his head down as he tried to walk past the guard, but the soldier stopped him.

"Excuse me good sir, but do I know you from somewhere?"

The prince turned to see that the guard was asking him the question. "I don't think so, my friend. I am not from around these parts."

"What is your name then? I am sure I know you from somewhere."

This guy is starting to get on my nerves, thought Byram. "He is Stephen Willows and my name is Byram Edelmar. I think you have gotten us mixed up with some other people." The two friends turned around and headed into town without saying another word.

"Oh, I guess you're right," the disappointed soldier called back. "I see so many people each day that even I get mixed up every once in a while." The young man took his position and waited patiently for his next visitor to arrive.

❧

The town was busy with people running about as they tried to finish their work before the day was through. It was almost time for supper and everyone wanted to go home for a nice meal.

Aaron was overjoyed to see life outside of his castle. Sharpsword was quite different than the castle area. The streets were much more crowded and the buildings were taller. Everyone seemed to be shouting at once and there were many activities being performed on every corner and in every alleyway. A burly blacksmith could be heard as he pounded shoes needed for a farmer's horse. Local merchants peddled their goods by trying to out-scream their competition. On the sidewalks, stands had been erected where one could purchase anything from a piece of fruit to a dress for a ball. There was an energy there that Aaron had never felt before.

While his inexperienced friend absorbed the sights and sounds of the small city, Byram looked for a nice inn for the two of them. His search led them to a quiet corner of the town where a small building sat. The sign outside read *Lantern Inn*. Darkness was slowly approaching and the inn's lights spilled onto the street along with the noise of conversations and laughter, welcoming the weary and the hungry alike.

"I think we've found our place of rest," Byram said happily. "It's been a long day and I am more than ready to kick off these smelly boots and drink some ale."

When they walked inside, a few patrons glanced in their direction, but no one cared enough to stop drinking and eating. Aaron quickly spotted an open table in a dark corner against the wall. Quickly, the two men sat down and waited for service.

"What can I git for ye?" came a voice from a rather odd looking woman. She was no bigger than four feet tall and she had a beard that would put King Dermot's to shame! Her beady eyes and barrel chest waited patiently for the two patrons to speak.

Aaron didn't know what to say so he just looked at the floor and hoped for the best. The barmaid had the largest feet he had ever seen and they too were covered in fur!

"Don't tell me ye ain't never seen a dwarf before?" the barmaid asked. She was indeed a dwarf. It was not common to see the people of the mountains in those parts of Oneira. Dwarves were a solitary race and liked to live inside the mountains, pounding away at the stone walls for precious gems and metals. Until then, Aaron had only read about the strange race in books and poems.

Byram was quick to reply. A good thing, since dwarves were known to lose their patience rather easily. "Please excuse my friend. It's just that he has never seen such a beautiful dwarf as yourself."

"I bet he ain't," she said gruffly, giving Aaron a quick wink. "So, what's yer poison?"

"We'll both have a tankard of your finest ale and the venison stew," said the hungry archer.

The barmaid gave Aaron one last playful wink and huffed away to place the order. "Hey Frank! Two brews and two bowls of that steamin' deer dung ya call food!"

Aaron blushed and sheepishly looked at his cousin. "I never—"

"I understand," Byram cut in. "Just remember that we are going to see a lot of strange things along the way, so try not to act so stunned. You don't want to insult the wrong person."

"Agreed. I'll try to conceal my expressions the next time I am—"

"Here's yer ale, good sirs," the barmaid shouted. "Nice and cold for ya." She slammed the tankards on the table, sending some of the ale's thick head onto the prince's face. "Now ye'll just have to wait a bit until the stew's ready. If ye need me, my name is Gertrude. Just give a yell." Gertrude stomped back into the kitchen to grab orders for the other patrons. "Frank, what in the blue blazes is takin' so long in here?"

Among the crowd that night, Aaron noticed an old man looking his way from the bar. He was leaning on a crutch and holding a full tankard of beer. Devouring the potent drink, he limped over to their table. "Do you mind if I sit down?" he asked in a scratchy voice. "My leg could use the rest."

"Please, make yourself comfortable," Byram said, as politely as he could. "Can we get you some food?"

"I am curious, what brings two strangers such as yourself to the Lantern?"

"We are just passing through," Aaron answered. "We needed a bed for the night and this seemed as good a place as any."

"You speak quickly, stranger. No need to worry, though. I don't really care why you came to Sharpsword. We all have our reasons and they usually aren't for sharing."

"Well, sir, if you aren't interested in our business, why don't you tell us about yourself?" Byram asked. He knew the man was out for something and he was not in the mood for games.

The old man leaned forward and gestured for the two travelers to do the same. "You can call me Dusk. I can provide you with anything you need. *If* the price is right, of course." He sat back in his chair and ran his slender fingers through his pepper-gray hair.

"Who said we need anything?" the prince asked defensively. "We're just here for a meal and some sleep."

Dusk smiled and looked at Aaron with pity. "When I see two strong young men with a look of caution on their faces walk into a tavern and sit in the most secluded seat in the house, I think that they have something to hide."

"And if we do?" Byram asked, his hand slowly making for a concealed dagger in his shirt.

"Then I become interested."

"What can you offer us?" Aaron asked. Thoughts of Woodbyrne

entered his mind, but he made sure to keep quiet.

Dusk looked around to make sure nobody was taking an interest in their conversation. When he was satisfied, the old man spoke. "Weapons, magic, armor, maps, information, and anything else you might need."

Byram quickly put a hand on Aaron's wrist. He knew his cousin wanted to ask about the forest, but it had to be done right. "What if we were in need of a map? How much do they cost?"

Dusk smiled and let out a soft chuckle. "That will depend on the type of map you want, of course. The rarer the map, the higher the fee." He leaned back on his chair and waited for a response.

"Woodbyrne," Byram said flatly, not wanting to tell the con artist anything more than he needed to know. He didn't enjoy having to reveal their destination to such a shady character, but such adventures were not taken without some risks.

Dusk's eyes widened. "Woodbyrne," he repeated, scratching his cleanly shaven face. "A fitting place for a hardened adventurer, but a foolish one for an amateur warrior who has fought only padded men and shot at bull's-eyes from a distance." Dusk paused for a moment longer. "I have the map you seek. It is very old and will cost a sizable sum. Twenty gold coins. No less."

"We have money," Aaron said as he spilled a bag full of gold and gems out on the table, causing more than a few people to take notice.

"I see," responded the old man with a chuckle. "Meet me in the alley behind the inn at midnight. I'll be there with the map. You be there with the gold." Dusk got up from the table and hobbled out the front door.

Byram looked at his companion in utter disbelief. "Are you crazy?" he whispered. "Why don't you just put on a jester's hat and shoes if you're going to act like a fool? What were you thinking just now?"

Aaron didn't know what to say. Part of him wanted to find a hole and hide in it while the other part wanted to go back home to the castle. Defeated, he put the coins back in his pouch and drank his ale.

Gertrude came out of the kitchen a short while later with two big plates full of stew in her hands. "Here's yer stew. Nice and hot."

"Gertrude, we'll be needing a bed for the night, if you have room?" Byram was so angry with his cousin that he almost lost his appetite.

"Not to worry, my dear," the dwarf assured. "We got a few good ones left for ya. I'll go and have a room made up for you." The gruff little dwarf stomped away and left the two men alone.

Supper was eaten in total silence. Aaron was busy pondering how foolish he acted with Dusk. He knew he should have been quiet and learned how to handle men like that by watching Byram, but he got too excited. He vowed to try and be more relaxed and in control the next time a situation like that presented itself.

Byram was also busy thinking of how foolish Aaron acted. His cousin should have shut up and let him do all of the talking. That would have allowed the prince to learn how to deal with conniving men like Dusk. The archer only hoped that the old man didn't read Aaron's anxiety as a sign of an inexperienced fool. That hope, Byram knew, was not the case. "He *is* an inexperienced fool," he muttered as he took in a spoonful of the stew.

"What, Byram?"

"Oh, nothing. Just thinking out loud."

The black demon soared quickly into the night sky, his leather wings cutting the clouds in half as he flew through them with reckless abandon. The moonlight reflected the evil off the black scales that covered his reptilian torso as his red eyes scoured the land for signs of trouble. Damek was in a hurry; his master had beckoned him to return to the caves immediately. The evil demon was not sure why his lord had summoned him that evening, but he had no choice but to respond. The vile beast was rather upset because he had just cornered a rather large deer and was going to slaughter it for dinner. Damek's stomach growled at the obscene thought of going hungry for the evening.

"Maybe Isidore will have some leftover swine for me to feast on," the creature whispered. Thinking of sweet pig's blood made Damek drool. He beat his wings faster, soaring over Woodbyrne at a remarkable speed.

The two demon guards that kept watch at the cave's entrance were tall, lanky creatures with the body of a furry human and the face of a wolf whose fur had been burned clean off. Their clawed hands held onto small swords and shields in case of an intruder. As usual, however, neither one of them looked very alert. The woods were quiet that evening, just like the hundreds of other evenings they had to stand and watch for intruders.

Suddenly, a force with the might of a falling tree slammed into the clueless demons, knocking them clear off their feet. "What was that?" spat one of the unfortunate creatures in its unearthly tongue.

Damek simply flew past the guards without hesitation. His master had called him and all else would have to be put on hold. Quickly, he flew through the twisted corridors that headed downward, deeper into the lair where his master could be found.

Isidore was not a patient leader.

⌘

Damek tried to calm himself as he stood in front of the huge double doors which led into Isidore's main chamber. No matter how many times the demon scout saw the magnificent doors, he was taken aback by their intricate artwork. The doors were made out of the bones of the victims who had been slaughtered over the past two hundred years. The bone doors evoked an image of death and despair. Most of the bones were from the elves of the forest, but some came from Isidore's former companions.

The demon master rarely held meetings in his private quarters simply because it made all who were with him uncomfortable, understandably, since few who entered left in one piece.

Damek took a deep breath and knocked. The doors flew open and a black mist poured out of the room, concealing what lay ahead.

"Come in, Damek," a voice boomed out of the darkness. "I've been expecting you," said Isidore, demon master of Woodbyrne.

Damek simply shrugged his shoulders and ignored the dark mist as he walked inside the chamber, the doors slamming shut behind him.

The nervous demon found it quite impossible to see in front of him, even with his night vision. "Where are you, my master?" Usually, the room was lit by thousands of candles and the air was clear.

"I am over here, you fool," Isidore responded. His yellow eyes glowed bright, making it easier for Damek to approach him.

Damek walked to his master and knelt before him. "What do you ask of me, Isidore?" He still could not see more than two feet in front of him, but his master's eyes acted as two burning torches.

"Sorry about the mist," the demon master apologized, "but I was speaking with our demon lord, and this always seems to be the outcome of such meetings." The eyes rose into the air and floated around the room like fireflies. Apparently, Isidore had been sitting on his throne when Damek entered the room. "I have grown tired of my previous companion and I was hoping you could find me a new one."

Only then did Damek know why he was called. Isidore was bored. The master's companions were merely female prisoners brought in by Damek to serve their master for as long as he desired. They were not treated poorly, but once Isidore grew tired of them, he showed no mercy. It seemed that the last woman was no longer in favor.

"Are you bored? Another victim to adorn your walls, my master?" the scout asked with a smile. Damek actually enjoyed the search because it allowed him to travel over Oneira. "What have you done with the last lady I captured for you?"

Within the evil gloom, Isidore smiled wickedly. His servant knew all too well what he did with his last companion. "If you like, Damek, I could do the same to you."

The smirk fell from Damek's chameleon-like face as quickly as it appeared. "That won't be necessary, I can assure you." He rose to leave the room, but Isidore grabbed him by his neck and slammed him to the ground.

"I *never* said you could leave!" the demon master hissed.

Once he regained the nerve, Damek got on both knees and pleaded for forgiveness. "I didn't mean any disrespect, my lord." His answer was simply a kick in the face so powerful, it sent him flying ten feet across the room. Blood dripped from his cut lip.

"Never insult me like that again!" Isidore roared, still concealed within the nasty mist.

Damek could only prepare for another brutal strike. "I apologize, Isidore," he begged. "I acted foolish and deserve death. Please, spare my life!"

"Go now, and find me a maiden," the rotten master barked, tired of Damek's presence. "Return as soon as possible or your pathetic soul will be the next to adorn my walls." Isidore handed the scout a flask filled with an orange liquid. "Take this and leave."

Damek took the flask and headed out of the chamber. Once in the hallway, he opened his wings and flew for the exit.

The two guards were well out of the demon's way this time, as he raced up into the night's sky. The sneaky lizard did not intend to return as fast as Isidore demanded, however. He knew that time would make his master calm down.

Damek left Woodbyrne's borders and headed toward the tiny kingdom of Galahan, many miles to the east of the forest. "Maybe I should just stay there for a few centuries," the demon snickered as he licked the blood from his face. "I'd be treated better, that's for sure."

❧

It was a warm, humid evening in Sharpsword. Mosquitoes and other nightly insects made their way about in the dark alley behind the Lantern Inn in search of scraps of food and water. There, Aaron and Byram patiently waited for Dusk to deliver the map. It was not yet midnight, but the two friends wanted to arrive early to check for any possible traps.

"Do you think there'll be any trouble?" Aaron asked nervously. The longer he stood there, the darker the streets grew, and more sinister. The voices that came out of the inn sounded like the cackles of witches. "I feel very far from home right now."

"Just relax, Aaron. We're going to exchange the money for the map and go straight to bed." Byram knew that any odd movements from his cousin would make Dusk edgy, which could make the old man leave or turn on them. Neither scenario seemed too inviting.

The prince took a deep breath and wiped the beads of sweat from his brow. Aaron moved his sword to where he could draw it faster. "He *is* just an old man. What could possibly happen to us, right?"

"You are right to be nervous, my cousin," Byram corrected. "Dusk may be old, but there is a reason why he has survived in his business for so many years. You must be sure to never underestimate anyone, no matter their age, size, or sex."

Aaron absorbed every word. "Then what can we expect? Are we in any danger?"

"Yes, we are in some danger right now," the archer quickly answered. Dusk will not be alone. We will see only him, but be assured that the alleys and rooftops will have eyes watching our every move." Byram unbuckled the strap that secured his sword. "We have to be on alert. Don't let your guard down. My job is to get the map, yours is to watch our backs."

Aaron nodded in agreement. He felt a little more relaxed, but his stomach was full of butterflies. "It's not going to be an easy night," he muttered under his breath.

Just as an old clock tower rang its heavy bell, light footsteps began to echo from down the alleyway. Although they grew louder with every passing second, neither man could see anyone in the dark shadows. Eventually the noise ceased and nothing was heard for the next few minutes. Nothing except the prince's thunderous heartbeat.

Byram unsheathed his sword.

Aaron, thinking the whole thing a trap, took out his blade as well. "Show yourself, you scoundrel," he shouted into the gloom.

"Nervous, are we?" came a call from behind.

Aaron and Byram spun around to see Dusk standing less than five feet behind them. He held a rolled up piece of yellow paper in his right hand. In his left, he held a silver sword that gave off a soft orange glow.

Oddly enough, the old man was no longer using his crutch, and his voice seemed a bit clearer than at the inn.

Both men put away their weapons as soon as they realized that Dusk was not attacking them.

Satisfied, Dusk did the same. "I have what you came for," he said dryly. "Did you bring the money?"

"Yes," Byram answered, "Twenty gold pieces, just like you said." He pulled out a small sack from underneath his shirt, and opened it in front of the old man. "First, I want to see the map. You get the gold when we are satisfied that you delivered what we need."

"I warn you, young man," said Dusk as he handed over the map, "neither of you will get very far if you decide to run." The old man's threat sounded far from hollow. The way he said it made the hair on the back of Aaron's neck stand on end.

Byram cautiously unrolled the map and looked it over. It was indeed a map of Woodbyrne! It showed ancient trails not traveled by man in ages. The paper was very worn but still in good shape. The archer handed it over to Aaron when he was finished. More than satisfied, the prince gestured for Byram to pay Dusk. Byram tossed Dusk the sack of coins.

"Here's what it came in." Dusk tossed a black wooden tube to Aaron.

Aaron gently rolled the map and placed it in the wooden cylinder.

"We want to thank you—" the archer began, but when he turned to face him, Dusk was nowhere to be seen. So the two young men headed back to the inn.

As they made their way out of the dark alley, two figures began to walk toward them from the street. Their faces were covered by the darkness, and they carried long dirks.

Aaron put his hand on his sword. "I am not about to lose this map so soon," he swore through gritted teeth. Byram, more confident in his skills, remained calm.

"Hand over your gold now and we'll spare your lives this fine evening," the first brute chided.

Aaron pulled out his long sword and took note of his surroundings.

The alley was wide enough for the two cousins to fight next to each other but their movement would be limited.

"I'm sorry to disappoint you, you fool," Byram said with a seething bitterness, "but we are not in a charitable mood tonight. Doesn't your mother bring in enough money?"

Byram casually removed his hand from his sword and folded his arms across his chest. "Well? I'm waiting."

The two thieves raced forward, their weapons leading the way.

The prince swallowed hard but remained levelheaded. He was more than ready for the fight. Let's see just how good my lessons have trained me, he thought, as a smile cracked across his face.

Wanting to end the fight quickly, the first thief took a wild swing at Aaron's throat. The agile prince was able to duck out of harm's way and deflect the clumsy attack with the hilt of his sword. As the assailant passed by, Aaron reversed his momentum and took a powerful swing at the thief's back. The seasoned thug anticipated the move, however, and tucked into a roll, causing the prince's blade to go wide, leaving him vulnerable.

The second thief came in low with a wild swing of his dirk. Byram, though, was not as vulnerable as the thief had hoped. The archer quickly grabbed his assailant by the hand and dropped back toward the ground. The confused thief fell forward while the more skilled fighter lifted both of his legs and placed them on the thief's stomach. As he hit the ground, Byram kicked out and sent the poor fool flying into the side of the inn. The thief hit his head so hard that he was completely unconscious by the time he fell to the filthy pavement.

The first thief went to stab Aaron in the chest but his dirk was no match for the prince's armor. Instead of piercing his heart, the rusty blade deflected upward and sliced the young prince across the face, leaving a thin line of blood in its trail. The wound was harmless but Aaron was enraged. He swung around and smashed the thief in the face with the back of his fist. Five teeth bounced off the ground along with a nice mixture of blood and saliva. Not phased by the blow at all, the thief charged at Aaron, aiming for the throat.

As soon as the prince saw the opportunity, he brought around his sword and slashed the thief's neck in self-defense. The dying man fell to the ground. In a matter of seconds, he passed into darkness.

Byram walked over to the remaining thief. He was alive but unaware of his surroundings. Blood oozed from a gash on his forehead and he was breathing heavily.

Aaron wiped the sticky blood off his sword and joined his cousin.

"He'll survive," Byram said, pitying the poor fool. "Should we allow him to live?"

It took less than a second for Aaron to answer. "Yes, let him live. This one no longer poses a threat to us."

"But when he recovers, he'll surely go back to his life of villainy," Byram reasoned, testing the prince. He did not want to kill the man either but he had to know how his cousin felt. He wanted to know how merciful the prince was in such a situation.

Aaron walked over to the delirious man and took away his weapon. "Now he won't be able to hurt anyone." The prince grabbed the fool by the collar with one hand and dragged him to his feet. "I know you can hear me, scum. If you ever take from people again, I will destroy you! Do you hear me? I will break your useless body in two!" Aaron's face was red and little veins streaked across his forehead like bolts of lightning.

The thief moaned in response. He heard everything loud and clear, and truly believed every word. His days of evil had just ended.

Aaron stood up and put his hand into a small pouch tied to his belt. "Here, take this," he said, flinging a gold coin to the startled man. "Use it to clean up and get a good meal. Find a job and live a life of peace. A good, honest man is truly rich. Remember that, and you will live longer." Satisfied, the prince turned and walked away.

Byram was impressed with his younger cousin. He had never seen such an act of mercy before, he thought as they headed back to the Inn.

An hour later, the two friends were cleaned and ready for bed. Aaron had placed a small bandage on his face in order to stop the bleeding from his wound. His cousin, of course, had mentioned that he looked better with the nasty cut and should let it fester a few days.

"If all goes well, we should make it to Woodbyrne by late afternoon tomorrow," Byram said, as he tucked himself under the sheets. He still did not want to go into the forest. "Are you *sure* you don't want to go home?"

"Another day, another scar," Aaron replied before falling to sleep.

A few hours before dawn, Damek reached the kingdom of Galahan. There, he saw a small town situated on the eastern side of a large mountain range. He knew the place to be Stovia, a small community where people minded their own business. The demon smiled wickedly. He was sure he could find a woman there that would appease his master. "First, however, I need to rest my weary bones." The demon scout found a small farm not two miles away from town. There, he silently flew into the attic of an old barn and made his bed in some hay. "All good things to those who wait," he said before falling to sleep.

Damek dreamed of killing Isidore and ruling Woodbyrne on his own. Then he would have his own servants to scour the countryside in search of beautiful women and endless riches for Damek.

Chapter 4

Damek awakened close to midday, refreshed and almost ready to visit Stovia. "First, I must feed my empty stomach," the grotesque demon said to himself. Damek looked out from the top of the barn and spotted a small flock of sheep grazing quietly in a grassy meadow. After a quick check to make sure the owners of the property were nowhere to be found, the demon swooped down on his prey and grabbed the fattest sheep he could find.

After his breakfast, Damek headed toward the lonely town of Stovia. Upon arrival, the demon scout was surprised to see the small community bustling with activity. The cobblestone streets were crowded with farmers and traders showing off their goods to needy customers; merchants tried to haggle with buyers for extra money, women were busy shopping for clothing materials; food was being inspected for supper, and children were playing their usual games of tag and mouse hunt. Everyone was busy in that remote area of the world, too busy to notice a dark form drop stealthily behind the local bakery.

Damek looked around to make sure nobody was aware of his presence. Satisfied, he quickly pulled out the vial Isidore gave him and popped the cork. The liquid inside smelled awful, reeking of rotten flesh that had been in the sun for too long. The odor assured the demon that his master had given him the proper potion and not some form of poison. "How I love these missions," Damek said to himself before drinking the magical fluid.

A burning sensation quickly engulfed the demon's body, sending his muscles into a violent spasm, and causing his head to feel as if it would explode. If not for the fact that he had done it before, Damek would have thought the potion to be lethal. As best he could, the demon tried to control the pain and wait for the magic to take effect. That was always the hard part.

A short while later, a tall, thin man walked out from behind the baker's shop. He was clad in a well-tailored black suit with a wide-brimmed hat to conceal his face from the sun. The young gentleman needed but a few minutes to gather his surroundings. Since nobody was screaming in horror, he graciously made his way into the hustle and bustle of the crowd.

The demon wondered where to find a suitable companion for Isidore. After only a few seconds of deep thought—too long for the likes of Damek—the demon decided that a local tavern would be as good a place. Pausing only to ask directions to the nearest tavern, Damek strolled down the street in complete confidence in himself and his magical disguise.

ॐ

"That's five you owe me!" Robert Brainard shouted as he threw down his pair of aces. It was well into the afternoon and the frustrated old man had been at the Empty Mug since the night before. Robert loved to gamble and his heart lay in playing cards. It was not uncommon to see him spend days at a time gambling away his meager earnings. Unfortunately for him, he always seemed to lose.

"I think not," said Gromp, as he laid down his cards and showed a straight. "That's five *you* owe *me!*" The fat man had come in for a lunch break and saw Robert "The Sucker," as he liked to call him, waiting to play a game of cards. Knowing the old man was pathetic at the game, Gromp couldn't resist. "How about this?" he asked with a chubby smile, "I'll settle for you picking up my tab." Satisfied, the plump man made his way over to the bar and ordered himself another drink.

"Robert, why don't you just go home to your daughter?" suggested the bartender, tired of seeing the poor loser decorate his tavern every day. "I'm sure Quinn would like to know her father is still alive, ya know?"

"Why don't you just leave me the hell alone?" Robert, tired of the mockery, headed to a lonely corner where he could gather himself together for the rest of the day. He swore that he would not rest until he at least broke even. "I'll get them the next time around," he promised, something he said on a regular basis.

Suddenly the tavern door swung open and a stranger walked into the Empty Mug. The tall gentleman paid little heed to the barflies and ruckus as he walked across the room and sat himself down at an empty table.

Quickly, foreseeing a generous tip in her future, one of the barmaids made her way over to the patron. "What can I get for you, sir?" she asked politely, brushing her sweaty red hair from her green eyes.

"I'll have wild boar, potatoes, and some mead, if you don't mind." Damek surveyed his surroundings and came to a disappointing conclusion. The entire inn was littered with low-life ruffians and trash. Even the barmaids wouldn't meet Isidore's standards.

"How would you like your boar?" the young woman asked uneasily. She sensed something strange with her customer, something unwholesome.

Damek looked her straight in the eyes. "I like it rare, please." He could tell that she was getting nervous. Although the potion easily covered the demon's hideous appearance, it did little to hide his aura. Even the most naive of people would get uncomfortable and unexplainable anxieties after spending just a few minutes with him.

※

Damek cut through his wild boar with the vigor of a starved child. He had become so involved with his bloody meal, he found it hard not to tear at it with his bare hands. Although the demon's mood had lifted, the scene in the bar improved little. The people who entered through the rickety old doors were just ordinary men and women in search of ale or food. Damek began to think that this was no place to find a suitable female for his master. He would finish his meal and leave.

Robert noticed that the stranger was almost finished with his lunch. Not wanting him to eat and leave, the poor fool got up and headed toward the table. Besides, maybe the stranger wanted to play cards.

Suddenly, the doors of the inn burst open and two very large men walked in. They were dressed like common folk, but brandished weapons of war. One wielded a warhammer while the other held an impressive looking long sword.

Robert Brainard, I believe you owe Mr. Luntz three hundred gold coins," one of the brutes said with an evil grin. "We are here to collect his fee. I hope for your sake that you have the money."

Noticing the bartender and the barmaids were heading behind the bar for protection, Damek decided to stay a while longer. The patrons either walked out the back door, or sat silently with their heads facing their tables.

"I haven't gotten it just yet," the coward answered. Robert looked as pale as a ghost. "I'll try to get it for you by next week, I swear."

"You said that last week!" the larger of the two men shouted as he walked forward, his warhammer slung casually over his massive shoulder.

Seeing no hope in talking his way out of the situation, Robert drew a dagger from under his cloak and attacked the approaching enforcer. His first strike did not even come close. Instead, the large brute deflected the dagger with the head of his weapon and kicked out with his leg. He sent Robert flying across the room into a table full of food and wine.

Just as the old loser lifted himself off the floor, the second assailant was by his side, arms crossed and wearing a big smile. He waited until Robert turned to face him and struck out with his large fist, knocking Robert off his feet and back onto the floor.

"Please, I can get the money by next week, I promise." Robert knew he would never be able to scrape up five copper coins, let alone three hundred gold ones! Still, he had to try.

"Mr. Luntz is through dealing with you, you vile scum!" The second brute pulled out his long sword and raised it over Robert's neck.

"Please," cried a woman from the tavern doors. "Stop this!" One of the most beautiful women Damek had ever seen ran into the Empty Mug and knelt down next to the old man. "Please, spare my father's life. He's all I have left in the world."

Damek saw promise in the young beauty. She was a stunning indeed! "Early twenties, long auburn hair, lovely voice, and sweet smelling," the evil creature muttered as he looked the woman over. Isidore would be very pleased with this one, he thought, strong in character, and full of life. Damek's only dilemma was that the two assassins were about to cleave her in two.

"Out of the way, wench!" ordered the bully with the warhammer. "We have business with your father, not his little girl!" He went to push the young lady out of the way, but was stopped with a sharp dagger to his belly.

Indeed, Quinn was no ordinary woman. She had been saving her father's life ever since her mother died. Over the years, she had become quite efficient with the blade and was not afraid to use it. Quinn had often pretended to be a harmless little girl in front of her enemy, only to jump into action at the last minute, killing or wounding anyone in her way.

Holding onto his bleeding belly, the wounded man dropped to his knees in disbelief. Never would he have guessed that one so fragile could be so deadly.

Quinn realized that the other attacker was right behind her. Sensing a strike, she dove to her right and rolled out of harm's way, allowing the clumsy hammer to hit the ground with a tremendous boom. So enraged was the attacker, he didn't notice Robert slip out of the main entrance.

Satisfied that her father was safe, Quinn wanted to end the battle before she got hurt. But, the enforcer with the hammer would not oblige.

Damek was truly amazed by the woman's prowess. "Beautiful and deadly," he hissed to himself. "Isidore will have his hands full with this one." The scout realized that he *had* to take the woman back to his master. The trouble that she would cause would be sweet revenge for the abuse he had taken over the years. "First," he said, "I had better make sure she survives this encounter."

Before the demon scout could react, the remaining fighter had pinned Quinn into a corner. He had small lines of blood on his face and forearms from her dagger, which seemed to have enraged the big bully. "It looks like your luck has ended, missy," he hissed as he raised his weapon. "I hope you know that your father is going to follow you to hell just as soon as I am done smashing in your skull!"

Quinn, however, was not ready to die so soon. Taking advantage of the hammer's slow speed, she kicked out with her leg and planted her foot deep within the man's groin. The would-be assassin dropped his hammer to the ground and squealed in pain.

To make sure the fighter would not follow her home, Quinn sliced his throat as she ran for the exit. The big man was dead before he hit the ground.

Damek could not help but laugh aloud. The smaller female had killed two heavily armed men with just her dagger and wits. The demon was determined to capture the temptress. Visions of Isidore clutching his groin after a swift kick danced in Damek's mind as he left the tavern and followed the father and daughter back to their home.

❧

"How could you be so stupid?" Quinn asked her father, after all of the doors and windows were locked shut. "Why didn't you tell me that you were in so much debt?"

Robert could not answer his daughter. He could not tell her how he blew away all of his savings over a silly card match with one of the most famous, and powerful, players on Oneira. He thought that he had been taken for a fool, but had no way of proving it. Mr. Luntz had a very respectable reputation while he, a poor laborer with no money or power, certainly did not.

"Well, they shouldn't be bothering us for a while," Quinn concluded with a sigh. The young woman looked at her father as he sat there with his eyes aimed down at the floor. She had to think of a way to come up with the money, or leave town very quickly. "While you just sit there and pout, I'll make us some food." Quinn went the fireplace and lit some kindling. "All we have is some soup from last night," she said in disgust. It seemed that soup was all she and her father ate anymore.

"I'm getting tired of the same old thing all the time." Robert put his head in his hands and yawned. "I sure could go for some venison."

Quinn had heard enough. It seemed like her life was in a horrible tailspin and there was nothing she could do to stop it. Angered, she threw the pot of soup on the floor and screamed, "Maybe if you weren't such a loser, we would be able to eat a nice meal every so often!"

"It's hard these days to make good money! Do you think I like living the way we do? I was meant for something more than this, Quinn! It's not my fault the entire world is out to get me!" He got up and kicked over the table. "I can't help the way I am, Quinn! I can't help it! All I seem to do is lose! Even my own daughter has no faith in me!"

Quinn simply looked her father in the eyes and began to cry. Having no sense of hope for their situation, she ran into her room and locked the door so she could be alone for the rest of the day. How she so desperately wanted to be with her mother! Quinn remembered the days when she and her family would go out for a nice picnic on a lazy afternoon, or just sit by the fire on a cold night and tell stories to one another. "Where have those days gone?" she asked. "When will they ever come back?"

Back in the kitchen, Robert was busy cleaning up the mess he had made. He felt horrible for the way he had just acted toward his only child. His wife would have never allowed him to act like such an animal. "Please forgive me, my Quinn," he whispered, "Please find it in your beautiful heart to love your father." He continued to clean the floor even as he cried. It was the first time the downtrodden fool had wept since his wife's death, exactly two years ago to the day.

A few minutes later, Quinn heard a loud thump on the roof, followed by a creaking noise as if something was making its way around the house. Seconds later, a window broke and the sounds of a struggle came from the kitchen.

When Quinn came out of her bedroom, she screamed in horror. A tall, dark creature with leathery wings and the face of a lizard was holding her father by the throat. The terrifying monster turned his head and smiled wickedly. "Excuse me, my dear, I will be with you in just a moment." The demon threw Robert across the room and into the wall.

"Quinn, get out of here!" Robert shouted, blood oozing from a fresh cut on his head. "Get away from her! Leave us alone!"

Damek took a few large strides forward, his long claws glistening in the moonlight. "Quinn, please don't make this any harder than it has to be. You are coming with me tonight."

Robert stumbled back to his feet and ran at the demon. "I said get away from her!"

Damek slashed out with one of his hands and sliced open Robert's face. With his other hand, Damek thrust his claws into his neck.

Robert dropped to his knees and grabbed his throat, trying to breath, gasping for air. Before he died, the failed father looked his only daughter in the eyes and mouthed, "I'm sorry."

"No!" Quinn screamed as she watched her father hit the floor with a lifeless thud. Enraged, she held up her sword and ran for Damek; all fear in her body was replaced with anger and venom.

"Silly girl," the demon snickered, "I am not just some thug sent out to collect money." Damek quickly stepped to the side and let Quinn's jab pass him. He grabbed her sword arm and knocked her into unconsciousness. "It's time we go, my dear. Isidore is waiting," Damek commanded. He secured her wrists and ankles with rope, and gagged her mouth with her father's scarf.

Damek held Quinn in his muscular arms as he flew into the night sky, back toward Woodbyrne. As he flew back, Damek fantasized again about the day when he would be a demon master. Then he would be able to send servants out on errands like this.

Chapter 5

The sun had been up for nearly an hour when Byram awakened his sleeping cousin. "Hey, get up, you handsome fellow," he said sarcastically, referring to the bloody bandage that adorned the prince's face. Once he was sure that Aaron was awake, Byram headed down to the kitchen to fetch some breakfast.

Aaron sat up in his bed and tried to yawn, but his injury had dried up overnight and made his morning routine a very painful experience. Why does this hurt so damn much, he wondered as he got out of bed and walked to a small mirror. It was clear to him that the bandage needed to be removed, but the pain that would accompany such an act made him cringe. Reluctantly, Aaron poured some cool water on the bloodied wrap in order to loosen its hold to the torn flesh, and readied some new bandages that would replace the old one. Once he was ready, he counted, "One...two...three!" The pain was excruciating, and it took all of his will to stop from screaming. After he cleaned the wound, he applied new bandages along with special salves.

A few moments later, Byram walked in with some bread, honey, and fresh juice in a small basket. "Breakfast is served," he said, as he lay out the meal on a nightstand. "I paid for the room and got breakfast while you were busy ripping your face apart. I suggest we eat fast so we can reach Woodbyrne by this afternoon."

After breakfast, the two young adventurers packed their goods and left the Lantern Inn. "You know what, Byram?" the prince asked while trying to ignore the pain from his injury.

"What's that?"

"Although I kind of messed up last night, I have to admit that I enjoyed my stay here. I think I actually learned a valuable lesson last night and I wouldn't mind stopping here again on our return trip home."

Byram turned toward his cousin and smiled. "It is only a lesson learned if you don't repeat it. Remember, not everyone in this kingdom is trustworthy. I think you found that out the hard way last night. If we are going to make it through this little adventure of yours, you are going to have to curb your tongue and your emotions." The archer gave his companion a playful wink. "Still, you handled the battle like a professional. I was pleased to see you control your anger like that. Mercy is not easy in a situation like that. I commend you on your good judgement. Now, let's be on our way."

Once the horses were readied, Aaron and Byram rode out of Sharpsword with their mind focused on the east, toward Woodbyrne.

"We'll eat lunch along the road so we waste little of our precious daylight," Byram explained. "I don't want to set camp outside of the forest because I fear its borders will be protected by spirits at night." Byram let the last sentence hang in the air for a while. He was trying to plant a little fear in his companion and knew that he was running out of time to do it.

"I'd like to see these spirits you talk of," Aaron responded with a smirk, aware of his cousin's intentions. "They probably look better than you anyway."

"I think not!" Byram snapped angrily. "Either way, we are to make haste this day and enter the evil woods before sundown."

⟩⟩

"Master, I've returned," Damek announced as he waited outside Isidore's chamber. He knew that the demon master had to prepare himself before being introduced to his new love so he had a demon guard watch Quinn in another room as he went over the details with Isidore.

"Enter, Damek," called Isidore while the two huge doors swung open on their own accord.

Cautiously, the demon scout stepped inside. No light shone from inside the huge room since Isidore extinguished all candles before meeting his new harem girls. He felt that a meeting in pitch darkness helped break down his captive's spirit and bestow a good deal of fear.

"What have you to report?" asked Isidore, his yellow eyes piercing the darkness.

"I have returned with a new servant for you, my master."

Isidore relaxed and sat himself down in his throne, placing his sword back into its scabbard and telepathically sending away his unseen servants. "Excellent. Where is she?"

"I have placed her in the hands of one of the guards while we go over some business," answered Damek, getting ready to ask for his due reward.

"What is it you wish?"

"To be left alone for one week's time," answered the scout. "I want to be able to roam these woods free of any beckoning and demands from anyone."

Isidore thought the request was rather large for such an easy task. Usually, Damek asked for some gold or a nice banquet to fill his ever-empty stomach. "Why should I grant that kind of freedom to you? Was this not a simple mission?"

Damek knew that he asked for a lot, but Quinn's beauty alone was worth a week of solitude. "Because this time I have truly outdone myself, Isidore. The beauty I have returned for your enjoyment is not only lovely to look at, but will be an even bigger joy to tame."

Isidore could not help being a little intrigued by his servant's words. "Bring her to me," he demanded, eager to see his new toy.

Damek opened one of the doors and called for the prisoner to be brought in.

Quinn, gagged and blindfolded, was led into the chamber by a large demon guard who eagerly handed the woman over to Damek and fled. "May I present Quinn," Damek said as he led the young woman closer to Isidore.

The young woman felt the evil that lurked inside the hot, arid room. Although she was blindfolded, she could sense that no light was present and her very soul shook inside of her slender body.

Isidore was indeed impressed with Quinn's beauty and he could detect an inner strength that he had never seen before in any of the thousands of slaves he had. "Welcome to my lair, Quinn. May my home be your home for as long as you live." His deep voice boomed, sending terror all throughout Quinn's body. Isidore motioned for her gag to be removed.

It took Quinn a moment to catch her breath. "Where am I?"

"In my home,"

"Who are you?"

"Your new master."

"What do you mean 'master'?"

Isidore sent Damek off with a snap of his fingers. "I mean you are now my property and I am your new master, of course." How the rotten demon loved his little games.

"Am I a prisoner here?"

"No. You are free to serve me without bondage. However, you may never leave, Quinn. You are mine now and I am very hard to please, so, if I were you, I would come to face the fact that you are here for the rest of your life."

Quinn could tell that Isidore was not making empty threats. His confidence was overpowering and she could feel his iron will trying to bend her own. But, she would not give in so easily. "What will I call you?"

Isidore was amazed by Quinn's willpower. "You may call me Isidore, my lovely." He cut her blindfolds with one of his black claws.

Quinn thought the darkness of the room to be even darker than her blindfold, as if she were in a void of some sort. The air around her was warm and thick. No noise could be heard, and she felt very vulnerable. Suddenly, Quinn saw a pair of yellow eyes no more than two feet in front of her and at least three feet over her. Unable to control her fears anymore, she shuddered and fell to the ground.

Isidore kneeled down next to her. "Relax, my pet," he whispered, "I am not a harsh master, just a strict one. I am allowing you to live and in return, you are to serve me as I wish. Do not worry, though, I will treat you with *some* respect. Your flesh must be untouched if you are to be sacrificed to Ulric one day."

Quinn suddenly spit in the direction of his voice. To her surprise, though, no retaliation was made.

"I like your attitude, Quinn, but you had better be sure to refrain from those sort of actions in the future, or I will be forced to tear your little throat out and feed you to my minions!" Isidore's voice boomed across the chamber like an earthquake. He grabbed Quinn by the neck and raised her off her feet. "I am sure you understand, don't you?"

Quinn was full of rage, but decided to not be killed just yet. "Yes, Isidore. I understand."

"Good," the demon replied and dropped the helpless woman to the ground. "Now, look at your new master." Isidore spoke a small word of command and a few candles burst to life, giving off an eerie glow to the massive room.

Quinn looked up at her captor in horror. His features were too much for her to take in at once, and the vulnerable woman thought she would faint. As she averted her eyes from the demon, Quinn looked around the giant room and took notice of the thousands of small flasks that adorned every section of wall from floor to ceiling. Each one of the jars reflected the candlelight giving the room an eerie orange glow.

Without warning, the double doors flew open and Damek walked back in with a big smile spread across his ugly face.

"Take Quinn to her new room," Isidore commanded.

"With pleasure."

This was all too much, even for Quinn. Thoughts of her father, Isidore, Damek, captivity, and death all made the normally strong woman grow very ill. She tried to get up from the floor, but became dizzy and passed out into unconsciousness.

"You may have your week of solitude, my friend," Isidore decided as he walked out of his chamber and down the hall.

"Thank you," Damek replied. He looked at Quinn as she lay on the warm stone floor and smiled. Already she was worth the effort. Damek had been watching when Quinn spit in Isidore's face. How he marveled at the spectacle! The demon scout had fantasized about doing the same thing thousands of times. With a sigh, the winged demon shrugged off his joy and picked Quinn up onto his shoulder.

✂

The clear, warm morning passed by lazily, giving way to a very warm and hazy afternoon. Aaron and Byram rode along the dirt road with little conversation between them. The prince kept busy reviewing the ancient map they purchased from Dusk. It was intricately designed, but worn with age. He tried to figure out where they would enter the forest by tracing back to the road they were traveling on. It seemed that the main road went directly into and through Woodbyrne, cutting the evil forest into two sections. There seemed to be another way into the forest, but they passed that road many miles ago. Once in the forest, however, Aaron would not be able to navigate too well. The road into Woodbyrne continued eastward, but there were dozens of side roads, and even they branched off into more secluded trails that Aaron dared not think about.

Byram was busy studying his surroundings. The land around them was once again farmland, but not as open as it was before Sharpsword. Few people lived out in those areas and their proximity to Woodbyrne made the archer a little more cautious.

"I see no definite path to take," Aaron said, talking about once they entered the forest. "The paths seem to go everywhere and nowhere at once."

"I think we should worry about getting to Woodbyrne before walking through it."

Aaron did not answer his sarcastic cousin that time; he was too interested in the map to argue with anyone.

"I see a small farm coming up on our right," Byram suddenly announced. "We should be cautious. Put the map away and be on the look out for trouble."

As the road wore on, the trees cleared a little and gave way to a small, quaint farm. As they drew closer, the two cousins saw a petite old woman tending to a flower garden that surrounded a small quaint cottage. She seemed to have taken an interest in the two travelers, and rushed up onto the road, waving her hands for them to stop.

"Good-day to you," Aaron said as he and his partner approached the farmhouse. "Is there a problem?"

The old woman had the sweetest smile that Aaron and Byram had ever seen. Although old, she seemed to be full of life. "No, no problem at all, my young lad. Except for some boredom, I am quite fine. Tell me, did you come all the way out here to have lunch with an old lady?"

Both friends did not know how to answer the woman's generosity. Actually, the thought of a good meal seemed like a good idea.

"Yes, I do believe we could have a quick bite to eat with you, good lady," Byram replied. He looked at Aaron and shrugged his shoulders. "We might get some information from her, besides I'm hungry," he whispered.

"Oh, excellent," the farmer cackled. "My name is Helinda O'Shan and I am the owner of this farm."

Byram jumped off his horse and introduced himself. "My name is Byram Edelmar," he said.

"And I am—uh—Stephen."

"Do you have a last name, or should I just call you Mr. Stephen?"

"No, no. I do have a last name, but it's a secret."

Byram just shook his head. Aaron would never make it as an actor.

Helinda eyed Aaron suspiciously. "I do not like secrets, Mr. Stephen," she scolded. "Especially from someone who is about to enter my house for a good meal!"

"Please forgive my friend," Byram apologized. "He is but a fool and doesn't know when to stop joking. His name is Stephen Willows, and he is very thankful for your hospitality, Mrs. O'Shan."

"All right, follow me," the old lady instructed.

Aaron and Byram followed Helinda O'Shan up the front porch of the house and into the kitchen.

࿊

After a hearty meal of various meats and cheeses, Byram was determined to pull whatever information he could out of their lovely host. "So, Helinda," he began," where is Mr. O'Shan, or do you tend to these fields by yourself?"

Helinda finished cleaning up before answering. "I get along with some hired help. My husband died many years ago, Mr. Edelmar. He and I were scouting for new land to farm when our search led us to the borders of that nasty Woodbyrne forest. It was the most vile-looking place I had ever seen. Its trees and shrubs are so twisted and thick that there is little place left for sunlight to shine through. There is a great evil there that consumes you—makes you cold."

Helinda needed to take a moment before continuing her tale. "Roland, my husband, was just fooling around, running behind trees and trying to scare me, when, all of a sudden, I heard him screaming for help. I thought he twisted his ankle or hurt something, but I was very wrong." Helinda drifted off into memories past and briefly forgot about her two guests. After a few moments, she snapped back into reality and continued her story. "I saw a creature holding my husband up against a tree and pressing a nasty looking blade to his neck. My husband began screaming again. It was then that I realized he wasn't screaming for help. He was screaming for me to run away."

"What did this monster look like?" Aaron asked.

"The creature was built like a human, but he had huge wings and his hands had long claws. He had black skin that reflected light in a horrible way, I'll tell you. Almost like a lizard's scales. To tell you the truth, I don't even remember what his face looked like, I think I blocked that out. I knew there was nothing I could do to save my husband, so I rode my horse as fast as it would go in search of help. When I returned with a few workers, there was no trace of my Roland."

Byram and Aaron sat in silence. Helinda held back her tears as best she could but could not hide her grief. After a long while, Aaron rose from his seat. "We are truly sorry for your loss, Helinda O'Shan. Your husband was a valiant man." The prince bowed his head.

"I do believe it is time for us to be going," Byram announced and got up too. The day was still young and he wanted to get to the forest as soon as possible. He was hoping that Mrs. O'Shan's story would have a sobbering effect on Aaron and cause him to reconsider his decision to enter Woodbyrne.

"Thank you both so much for keeping me company," Mrs. O'Shan said as she showed her guests to the door. "Please, if you are ever in these parts of the kingdom again, stop by and stay a little longer."

"We will do just that, good lady," Byram insisted. "Thank you again for the meal. It was excellent."

After the brief good-bye, the two warriors headed back out on the road. Once out of sight, they sped up their pace and made for the woods. All the while, Prince Aaron was busy in his thoughts. Byram took his cousin's silence as a good sign. Perhaps Aaron would realize that Woodbyrne is an unfit place to have an adventure.

What Byram did not know, however, was that Aaron was seething with rage. The picture of a young Mrs. O'Shan watching as her husband was killed lingered in his mind for a very long time. Revenge for her loss is what he desired. Aaron's decision to enter Woodbyrne could not have been more definite.

"Let us speed up our pace," Aaron said. "The sooner we enter the forest, the sooner we get to seek out this creature of destruction."

A stunned Byram replied, "Haven't you heard anything this day?"

Aaron had a determined look on his face that reminded his cousin of King Dermot when he had reached a non-negotiable decision. His eyes were completely focused on the road ahead and his jaw was tightly clenched. Byram realized that there was no way he could stop Aaron from entering Woodbyrne. He was just too stubborn, like so many Gowers before him. Like King Dermot's two deceased brothers.

◦⁀

Quinn woke up on her cell floor with a horrible headache. After a few minutes of panic, she forced herself to her feet and tried to examine her surroundings. The first thing the disoriented woman realized was that she was no longer wearing her regular clothes, but white robes. The loose fitting garments revealed just enough to make her feel vulnerable.

The cell that held Quinn was not a pretty sight, by any standards. The walls were dark gray stone covered in dirt and filth from centuries of neglect. Small spiders and other little creatures made their way in and out of tiny cracks while a rusty pair of cuffs bolted in the wall reminded Quinn about the penalty for disobedient behavior. Underneath the restraints lay a small pile of bones, which did little to make the young prisoner feel at home. At least the cell door had a small window, which allowed some light in the otherwise gloomy cell. The blood-covered steel bars that adorned the window, however, told Quinn that she had little chance of escape.

In addition to the filth and decay, there was a tiny cot in the far corner where Quinn could rest, and a nasty hole in the floor that made her sick from even thinking about what it was supposed to be. The only good thing about the dank, dark cell was that it allowed the young woman private time away from her captors, for a while anyway.

Quinn cautiously walked up to the window and peered out. Many candles on the walls lit the filthy hall outside where many other cells, much like her own, sat in ruin and decay. The hallway connecting the cells was wide and the floors were dirt-littered with bones and food scraps. Little furry creatures could be heard, not seen, scampering about in search of food. Some of the cells were apparently occupied, given that eerie noises seeped out of them every so often. The soft, moaning sounds echoed off the stone and delivered a new sense of fear to Quinn's heart.

"Hello? Who's out there?" Quinn's voice echoed loudly off the walls. "My name is Quinn. Can anybody hear me?"

"Help me," a faint voice answered. The dialect was foreign to her, but she could make out what the person was saying.

"What is your name?"

"Help me. Help me. They are going to get me."

The voice definitely sounded male, but his voice was so weak and faded that Quinn could not tell how old, or which cell it was coming from. "Where are you?" she asked desperately.

"I'll show you where he is!" another voice boomed.

A rugged demon guard marched down the hallway and stopped at Quinn's cell door. His burnt, dog-like features frightened the woman and she jumped back in horror. "What's the matter?" he asked, "I thought you wanted to talk so I came all the way over here to listen to you."

Quinn did not answer her tormentor. Instead she prepared herself for a fight, if need be.

"Oh, you were talking to someone else, weren't you?" The demon walked over to a different cell and knocked on it with his rusty axe. "Anybody home?"

"Help me. Help me," the voice responded again. "They are going to get me."

The guard opened the cell door and walked into the dark room. "I'll help you, you smelly elf!"

Quinn tried to listen in on what was happening, but she could only make out mumbles and the sound of someone getting beaten without mercy.

"I think he wants to see you, Quinn," the demon shouted from inside the cell. "You'd like that, right?"

Quinn was horrified when she saw the guard drag out the beaten body of an elf! She had only seen them before through pictures, but never in person. This elf, however, did little to represent his usually vibrant, charismatic race. Without the dignity of clothes to adorn his body, Quinn could see that his pale-green skin was covered with sores and blisters. He looked starved and reeked of rot.

"Well, what do you have to say to Quinn?" the rotten guard asked the delusional creature.

The elf opened his eyes and looked at the young woman. His lifeless orbs told a story of sorrow and pain. "Help me, Quinn," he answered before passing out.

Mercilessly, the demon kicked the fallen elf with hatred and bitterness. "C'mon you fool! Speak to her! I thought you two were best of buddies."

Quinn could not take it anymore. "Leave him alone, you scum! Why don't you try that on me?"

The demon stopped his fun and dragged the poor elf back to his cell and locked the door. "Believe me, sweetie, I'd love to teach you a lesson or two. Once Isidore tires of your attitude, I'm sure I'll get my chance!" The guard walked up to the door and shot Quinn a look that sent shivers down her spine. "Remember, Isidore will protect you from us only for as long as you please him."

The unfortunate woman realized that the guard was telling the truth and that she had better change her attitude before she was killed. "My apologies."

"That sounds better, sweetie. Isidore is hungry and has asked for you to serve him his meal. I suggest you act like a lady, and serve him well." The guard unlocked the cell door and led Quinn to get Isidore's food.

⤳

Woodbyrne loomed over the two cousins like a wall of terror. It was a menacing looking place, with dark trees that stood hundreds of feet in the air. A powerful evil was present and it seemed to emanate from all over the forest.

Aaron and Byram arrived at the woods a few hours before sundown. Now that they saw the fabled woods first hand, doubt and fear washed over them like a swarm of bees.

"So, this is Woodbyrne," Aaron said with a slight crack in his voice. He began to question the logic of entering the forest with his cousin. All of the warnings and descriptions of Woodbyrne had done little to deter the prince from his goals. Now that he saw the forest first hand, Aaron realized that those tidbits of information might have been correct.

"Yes, this is where you wanted to go," Byram spat, angry that they had not returned to Sharpsword. "Happy birthday."

Aaron, however, swallowed his fear and thought of the stories of his uncle, and Helinda's unfortunate husband. Again, a look of steel found its way onto his face and his blue eyes peered forward into the gloom. The bandage that covered his wound had fallen off miles ago, and the scab left behind made him look more like the king than he had before.

"I am going in, Byram. You can follow me or head back to Castle Gower. Either way, I *must* enter this dark domain."

Byram knew that moment was coming. He owed it to the King and Queen to protect their only son. His loyalty to them was only over shadowed by his loyalty to Aaron. He knew that he would follow his cousin to hell and back if he had to. There was nothing else to do. He had to go. "Let us go then, Prince Aaron. May the evil in this forest tremble at our feet!"

Prince Aaron smiled. "Entering Woodbyrne, or telling King Dermot that you allowed his only son to enter the most vile place on Oneira alone. I think you just picked the lesser of two evils, my cousin. Come, let us see what lies in this forest together."

With that said, Aaron and Byram marched into Woodbyrne with only an ancient map and some rumors to guide them.

Chapter 6

The trees in Woodbyrne were enormous, towering over Aaron and Byram like huge giants ready to strike with heavy, wooden limbs. The thick canopy that they formed allowed very few streaks of sunlight to pierce the otherwise gloomy forest. A few small animals could be heard deep within the tangled brush, foraging for whatever food they could find, but no signs of any recent travelers could be seen on the main path, where large roots and small plants made their homes.

"What a wondrous place this is," said an amazed Aaron. "It's so quiet and peaceful in here."

"This forest reeks of evil," corrected the archer. "I can almost hear the trees demanding our immediate departure." Byram studied the forest with great care. "I suggest we keep our eyes focused on the land around us. These trees are good cover for an ambush."

"An ambush from what?"

Byram's horse began to act spooked as if it could smell something foul in the air. The beast seemed to calm down a little when Byram patted it on the neck, but not as much as its rider would have liked. If he were able to read the horse better, he would have figured out that the sensitive beast had sniffed out a spy.

High above the ground, concealed by the treetops, an elven scout named Cathmore Stardust watched as the two intruders traveled through the forest. His keen senses made him aware of their presence the second they entered the woods. Since there had not been any visitors in Woodbyrne for more than a decade, the two travelers gained the attention of the entire forest.

Cathmore was amazed at the humans' boldness; their horses could be heard miles away, and the larger of the two companions spoke loudly, as if he were in the comfort of his own home. Normally, the wry and silent elf would have run off and informed the rest of his clan, but the uniqueness of the two characters touched the elf's curiosity. Cathmore decided to follow them a while longer to see if he could find out what their purpose was, and if they posed any threat to his home.

Unaware of the pair of eyes above them, Aaron and Byram pressed on without incident. They rode for over an hour without spotting any of the side roads that were so clearly labeled on the map. Both partners were beginning to doubt the accuracy of Dusk's resources.

"I hope that old man didn't trick us into buying a false map," the prince said.

Byram, however, had a logical explanation for the confusion. "Remember, that map is extremely old. Most of the trails it describes are probably overgrown with trees and bushes by now."

Aaron agreed, but wondered if they were going to find anything at all. "What kept *this* road in such good shape? Shouldn't it be overgrown with nature by now?"

The question was a very good one, and Byram simply did not know the answer. "It'll be dark soon, I think we should keep an eye out for a secluded place to set camp." Byram's voice seemed nervous.

Aaron agreed wholeheartedly. He could actually feel the darkness slowly closing in around him as the creatures of the night began to make their mournful calls. Wolves could be heard in every direction welcoming the night as owls awakened and sang their nighttime melodies. Even the little insects' noises bounced of the trees like wails from a banshee. It was dusk, and Woodbyrne was just beginning to awaken.

Another fifteen minutes had passed before a fork in the road was spotted. Aaron tried to find the split on the map, but became concerned when his search ended in failure. "I cannot find this place anywhere."

Byram remained silent; something felt wrong. "I think we should leave our horses here and scout the road ahead."

Cathmore watched patiently in the thick canopy.

⟳

Quinn walked cautiously into Isidore's main chamber with a tray full of raw meats and vintage wines. Although she was alone, she knew that unseen eyes followed her every move. Even if she could escape, the shackles around her ankles would retard her mobility.

A small band of demon guards broke Quinn from her daydream, some of the nasty creatures spitting on the poor woman as they passed by. Still, despite her submissive behavior, Quinn made sure to take notice of the soldiers' direction. She knew that they were heading toward the outside of the cave for their patrol duty.

"Where is my food?" a thunderous voice bellowed.

Quinn hurriedly made her way down the hallway. As the slave approached the main doors that led into Isidore's chamber, the doors swung open.

"Enter, Quinn," Isidore called from inside the room.

Quinn could not see the monster because only one small candle was lit in the far corner of the large room, letting off an eerie red glow. She stepped into the darkness and the doors closed themselves behind her, sealing her off from the rest of the cave, and any hope for escape.

"Put the food down," the demon demanded, and Quinn followed his orders. "Approach me, my sweet." The nervous woman slowly made her way toward her caller, all the while using Isidore's yellow eyes as beacons to light her way. "Kneel before me!" the demon howled as Quinn reached the bottom of the stairs. He made his way down toward his petrified slave, making sure to slam the heels of his boots into every step. "I think you fail to understand why you were brought to me."

"I was brought here because you had my father murdered, you vile beast."

Isidore smiled wickedly and sat down on the last step. "I see my fair warnings did little to change your attitude, my beauty. How unfortunate for you." With lightning speed, Isidore grabbed Quinn by the neck and dragged her closer to his fiery eyes. "I guess you will just have to learn your mistakes through the sufferings of others! Bring in the elf!"

The double doors opened and the demon guard in charge of Quinn's cell block walked in holding a rope that was tied tightly around the neck of the sickly elf that he had beaten earlier that day.

Isidore's grimace turned into a wide evil smile. "You see, Quinn, I have many ways of getting my slaves to obey my every command."

Quinn gave the demon master a horrified look as she tried to figure out what games he had in store for her and the elf prisoner.

⌇

Three demon soldiers hid silently behind two massive trees that lay in the middle of the two trails. They had heard the clatter of the horses and quickly readied themselves for an ambush.

Aaron and Byram walked as silently as they could toward the fork in the road. It seemed that the main path continued to stretch to the east, while the second, a smaller and more rugged looking trail, broke off to the south, where the trees seemed to get larger, as did the plethora of roots and rocks.

"I think we should get off of this road and take the path to the south," Byram said with a little bit of confidence. "The way we are heading now has led us nowhere and —"

Suddenly, three axe-wielding demons crashed out of their hiding place and attacked the humans. Two of the beasts headed for the prince while the third attacked Byram.

Cathmore instantly pulled out his bow and readied an arrow but waited to see if the two humans were worth the risk of being spotted.

The demon attacking Byram swung violently at the archer's head, but rage had caused him to take poor aim and Byram quickly dove out of the blade's path. When he rolled to his feet, the archer unsheathed his sword and began a deadly parry with the vile creature.

Aaron, horrified by the very sight of the beasts, acted purely on instinct, drawing his sword and taking a defensive stand. Unaware of the prince's capabilities, the two demons charged in with their axes poised above their heads, their rotten smiles assuming a quick and bloody kill. Aaron, however, would give them no such pleasure. In a flash, he ran toward the closer of the two demons and rolled on the ground. When his move had brought him close enough to his foe, he kicked out with his legs and sent the closest creature crashing backwards and gasping for air, snapping a few ribs in the process. The second demon swung wildly with his axe at the prone fighter, but only struck dirt as Aaron leapt back to his feet.

Byram was not having much luck with his fight. The demon he was up against apparently had some skill in the ways of battle and was able to deflect all of Byram's cuts and jabs. However, the archer knew that the demon's huge axe weighed much more than his nimble sword and it would eventually wind up being the creature's downfall. He only hoped that his horribly strange attacker tired before he did.

The second demon attacking Aaron was not as good a fighter as his commander, who was busy with Byram, but he did have a few tricks up his sleeve. Aaron, on the other hand, continued his flurry of attacks and looked to capitalize on any mistakes. After a few well-placed thrusts by the skilled human, the demon lost its balance and fell to one knee. Aaron thought that his moment had come and led in with a killing blow.

Unfortunately for the prince, the demon had feigned his slip-up and tripped Aaron with a powerful sweep. Aaron fell on his back and was suddenly overcome when two hundred-pounds of demon came crashing in on his chest. The vile creature tried desperately to sink his fangs into his adversary's neck, but the human was stronger than he had expected.

Out of the corner of his eye, Byram noticed that his cousin was in great peril as the first demon got up off the ground and ran to help his comrade, who was busy rolling on the ground with the powerful human. The clever archer had to move quickly in order to save his partner from certain death. He began to act as if he was tired from the brutal melee, letting each parry with the demon knock him back further, and further until, finally, he was pinned against an enormous tree.

The demon commander saw that his enemy was vulnerable and leaped in with an arching swing aimed at the human's neck. Byram defiantly jumped out of the axe's path a split second before it connected with his head and the heavy weapon dug itself deep into the giant tree, forcing the demon to tug wildly to get it free. Before the demon could free his weapon, Byram jabbed his sword deep into his back, slicing through his ribs and biting into his heart. Black blood spewed forth from the open wound and the demon crashed to the ground in a gory heap. Byram left his sword in his victim and quickly pulled out his bow and took aim at the demon heading toward his cousin.

Through the corner of his eye, Aaron saw the first demon heading toward him with an evil smile. He knew that his life was on the line and that he had to get back onto his feet if he was going to have any chance for survival. "Get off of me you wretched beast!" he shouted.

In response, the demon bit down hard on Aaron's skull, his razor sharp teeth tearing flesh and scraping bone. The prince howled in pain but used his rage as fuel to knock his enemy off his body. Just when the prince thought his life to be over, he heard the whistle of arrows streaking through the air. One of them slammed into the side of the closest demon and lodged itself deep within his chest. Aaron jumped back onto his feet and desperately picked up his sword. While the demon fought to remove the deadly shaft, the enraged prince charged over and sliced his neck, spilling more dark blood onto the forest floor.

"Well met," called Byram as he dropped his bow and ran over to his injured friend.

Aaron let go of his sword and tore off some rags to place on his bleeding head. The bite wound was painful but not incapacitating. Once the bandage was in place, he examined his dead enemy. The monster he felled was far beyond anything he had ever seen. It even made the gruff barmaid, Gertrude, look pleasantly normal. "What in the world is this creature?"

"I wish I knew, but I have no clue as to what these fiends are."

"It is a good thing that you killed that other one when you did," Aaron added. "I was certain that I was going to die here today." Another brief pause made the prince think harder. "Tell me, Byram, how'd you shoot so many arrows at once, and with such accuracy?" Aaron pointed to the four arrows that protruded out of the chest of the second demon he had been battling, and the one that was protruding out of the first creature.

"That's the problem," the archer said, "I never got a chance to take a shot. When I finished off my enemy, I grabbed my bow and turned to shoot, but it was already on the ground, dead." Byram looked up into the trees.

"But I heard arrows go whistling by my head! Are you going to tell me that you did not make the shots? Maybe you did shoot but forgot now that your battle rage has passed?"

"No, I never took a shot. Look at those arrow shafts. My missiles are quite different."

Aaron believed his cousin, but could not bring himself to face the fact that there were eyes following him as he walked through the strange forest. Unable to answer his own questions, the prince went back to his wounds. The bleeding had stopped but the pain was very much present.

Without warning, night crept into the woods while the two friends recovered from their battle. Aaron felt alone and vulnerable. Byram did not want to spend the night standing in the middle of the road and decided that they had better find a campsite soon before it was too dark. When they retrieved their horses, the two warriors noticed that their saddlebags had been opened, and their supplies thrown on the ground.

"Everything seems to be here except our rations and water," concluded the prince, after picking up his belongings. Again, he looked around the forest, trying to find what had stolen their goods.

"No footprints have been made," said the archer. "It seems that our rescuer is very adept at stealth as well as archery. We should make camp and take turns keeping watch."

The two men dragged the dead demons to the side of the road and covered them with leaves and bark. Satisfied that the bodies were concealed, they set up a small camp fifty yards from the side of the road. The horses were tied up close to them and no fire was lit.

Byram instructed his cousin to get some sleep while he took the first watch. After only a few minutes, the archer felt dozens of eyes peering into his very soul. However, despite his fears, he considered himself lucky that the unknown kept its distance.

⁊

Cathmore leaped from his perch without a sound and sped off into the forest. In his right hand, he held the food that the two strangers carried in their bags. Although the wood elf knew the men were not allies with the demons, he had to report his findings to his superiors. How deadly the two humans were, he could not guess, but his race had many ways to capture even the most dangerous of creatures.

⁊

Quinn awakened with a very large headache many hours after Isidore's attack. Her wrists and ankles were shackled to a stone wall with sharp, rusty clamps and chains that cut into her delicate skin. Although she was blindfolded, the hideous stench of rot and decay told her that she was in the dungeon.

"Welcome to my favorite part of these halls, Quinn," greeted Isidore, who stood dangerously close to his prisoner. "I was hoping that you would be awake to witness tonight's lesson. Unfortunately, I cannot be present for the ceremony, but, I assure you, what you will see is a direct consequence of your actions."

Quinn felt the demon's hot breath, followed by a long, forked tongue, slide across her exposed cheek. She held back from reacting strictly out of fear of what would be done to her if she did.

"Don't disappoint me again!" roared the demon master, before storming out of the room and slamming the door shut behind him.

"My, my," came another familiar voice. "It seems to me that you still don't get all of this, do you?" The creature removed Quinn's blindfolds with a harsh tug that almost snapped her neck. The evil guard in charge of Isidore's personal slaves simply smiled and walked toward a large cage set in the middle of the room. Various torture devices lay scattered throughout the dank chamber, each one seeming more evil than the other. Many of the devises still held their victims, either long dead or barely alive, but all were wood elves unfortunate enough to have been captured. A large pile of bones and rotting flesh stacked neatly in a corner told a grim tale of pain and suffering.

"However," the guard continued, "I do love these kinds of lessons so I urge you to keep up your attitude with Isidore." The demon lit a few candles on top of the large cage, exposing a small figure curled up in the far corner of the metal prison. It was the elf that had been horribly beaten for speaking to Quinn!

"You vile scum!" Quinn shouted. The hot-tempered woman began to curse at the demon with a rage unlikely from such a lovely creature.

The demon guard paused for a moment only to savor her anger. "My dear Quinn, you are the reason this one is going to die."

"Let him go or I'll kill you!"

The guard walked into the cage and grabbed the elf by one of his puny arms.

Quinn, no longer able to hold back her tears, began to weep. The elf never flinched and took the beatings stoically, silently.

When the guard had finished, he left the cage for just a second and returned with a large bucket filled with a crimson fluid. Flies flew over the thick vile liquid, and even the guard swayed from the stench. "Kneel!" he commanded, and the wood elf fell to his knees more from exhaustion than obedience. The guard proceeded to pour the vile substance onto the elf's head and body.

Quinn had no clue as to what was going to happen next, and she really did not want to. "Please let him go," she whispered. "He did nothing to you."

The guard, satisfied with his handywork, smiled at the sobbing female with his wolf-like face. "Remember, this is your fault, wench!" he shouted as he locked the cage. Then the demon proceeded to pull on a large rope that hung from the ceiling. A small door on the opposite side of the cage opened up, as did a hidden doorway that lay directly behind it. Two sets of yellow eyes appeared out of the darkness, and low growls echoed off of the chamber's walls.

"Please, no," Quinn whispered to herself as she said a silent prayer for the elf's soul. She knew what was about to happen and she only hoped that it would be fast.

Two wild dogs rushed out of their holding pen with madness and starvation visible on their faces. Saliva poured from their mouths as soon as their keen senses caught the scent of rotten blood. The elf just knelt in the middle of his cage with as much dignity as he could muster.

Quinn could not bear to watch the gruesome scene take place before her and turned her head just as the wild dogs got to the elf.

"Thank you, Quinn," the elf said, just before he was overwhelmed by the ferociously hungry canines. "You have freed me."

Quinn was filled with rage, but she knew she needed to plot an escape rather than get more innocent elves killed over her actions. "I'll remember this," she swore. "I will remember this forever."

"Do we understand each other?" the demon guard asked the seemingly broken prisoner.

Quinn knew that she had to pacify them and wait for the most opportune time to make her escape. However, such a thing would not be an easy task. "Yes, I will obey from now on, my keeper."

The demon smiled with glee, convinced that the killing of the elf had finally broken the spirited woman.

⁊⁊

The night passed uneventfully for the two adventurers. They awoke to a misty morning and empty stomachs.

Aaron, sore from the battle with the demons, could have used a nice meal to reenergize himself. His injury had scabbed over but he had a headache and his eyes burned.

Byram was also hungry and thought that they should scavenge for food of some type. "This forest is full of roots and insects if we are hungry enough," he said, trying to sound positive.

Aaron, on the other hand, was not as optimistic. "I wouldn't even know where to begin," he complained. "Besides, the last time I tried to live off the land, I came down with poison ivy."

"I remember that well," Byram replied with a bit of a chuckle. "Did you remember to pack the proper supplies this time?"

Aaron blushed, it had taken weeks before the itching between his legs subsided. "Like I said," he retorted, trying to muster up some dignity, "I wouldn't even know where to begin."

A short while later, it was decided that the prince would hunt for game while Byram scouted the area and searched for edible fruits and berries, if that was possible. Just as they were about to split up, Aaron caught site of the largest rabbit that he had ever seen nibbling on some thick grass. As silently as they could, the two cousins made their way closer. When they had halved the distance between themselves and the rabbit, Byram pulled out his bow and loaded an arrow.

The keen ears of the rabbit heard the archer long before the shot was taken and it ran off into the woods. Immediately the two friends chased after their potential breakfast as fast as they could.

"It went into that bush!" Aaron shouted.

Before the creature could escape, Byram and his cousin were on their bellies grabbing to get a hold on the speedy creature.

"I think I got it!" Aaron shouted with glee, and yanked with all his might. Unfortunately, Aaron pulled out some sort of wooden peg with animal hair wrapped around it.

A loud whooshing sound came from a large tree and a thick net shot out of the earth where it had been cleverly buried. Byram and Aaron were easily lifted into the air where they hung in a net and watched as the large rabbit ran off into the deep forest.

"Well, now we're captured and the rabbit is free," Byram lamented.

As the prince and the archer struggled to free themselves, they heard noises in the trees and bushes that surrounded them. Aaron began to speak, but was cut short when he saw dozens of tall, greenish humanoids walk out of the forest's morning mist. Soon, the peculiar looking men and women surrounded the net and waited. Some of them held beautifully crafted bows while others brandished delicate swords.

"Don't say a word," Byram warned his cousin. The archer knew whom he was dealing with, and he knew that he and his cousin had no chances of escape. They would simply have to wait until the elves of Woodbyrne were ready to speak.

Chapter 7

A aron and Byram were led through the forest by the small band of wood elves, which consisted of both males and females dressed for battle and holding powerful weapons. These exotic people tied the humans' hands securely behind their backs but not so tightly that it caused any pain. All the while, the elves were busy speaking to one another in their native tongue, a melodious language that would calm even the most enraged dragon. Aaron guessed that he and his cousin were the main topic of conversation since a few of the elves looked in their direction every few minutes, some smiling and others frowning. Any thoughts of escape were forgotten when the two young men saw even more shadows slipping from tree to tree.

The small group marched through the thick woods for almost two hours before stopping at a small clearing where a well-used fire pit was situated, giving the impression that the area was used frequently by the elves. Aaron and Byram were led to a fallen tree where they were tied to its thick branches. Although the elves were careful not to hurt their captives, they tied a strong enough knot to ensure the humans could not escape.

"What's going on?" asked the prince. He noticed that many of the forest creatures that followed them to the resting spot had vanished without a trace, and those who had stayed behind were no longer paying him any heed.

"I have no idea," Byram finally answered. "We're just going to have to wait."

Suddenly, a slender female marched up to the two prisoners and knelt down in front of them, taking only a second to fix her beautiful brown hair. She had raven-colored eyes and a chiseled face. "Why have you come to Woodbyrne?" she asked in a very thick accent.

"We are on an adventure," Byram replied, not knowing what else he could say. The fact that they were on a stupid mission to make his sad cousin become happy again did not seem like the right thing to say, although the archer thought it to be true.

"Are you on an adventure to see Isidore?" The elf's dark eyes glistened with both intelligence and strength. The two friends just looked at each other.

"Is Isidore your master?" asked the prince. His answer was a hard slap in the face.

"He is not my master, nor is he the master to any of my kind!" she shouted. "We are Isidore's most deadly enemies! We have survived in these woods for over two centuries, our lives ruined by Isidore and his demons. You two are unwelcome visitors that know nothing of our ways!" The young warrior stormed away, leaving Aaron and Byram to sit quietly on the fallen log without a word to say.

⤳

Quinn sat quietly in her cell; the sight of the tortured elf still burned deep in her mind. She felt horrible for the victim of the demon's rage, but Quinn knew that she had to somehow plan an escape before it was her turn to wear the rancid blood. Unfortunately, the usually reliable woman could not think of any way to break free from the heavily guarded caves. The demon patrols were always on alert and she was either at Isidore's side or locked up in her cell. "There must be a way for me to get out of here," she defiantly whispered.

A loud clanging noise snapped the young woman out of her funk. As she ran up to look out of her cell door, she saw the nasty prison guard lumbering down the corridor with a plate full of food. As thoughts of escape raced through Quinn's mind, she noticed the pathetic eyes of another elf looking out at her from the cell door directly across.

"Pay attention, Quinn," the elf suddenly whispered in a strong voice. The prisoner seemed to have more life in him than the one who had been fed to the hounds. His eyes still had a hopeful glow to them. Quinn had no idea what the inmate wanted from her, but was very intrigued.

"Isidore thought you might want some food before he summons

you again," the hideous beast said to Quinn as he made his way over to her cell. As he opened her cell door and slid the food tray into the room, he spit on her food. The tray consisted of a small glass of brown water, a piece of stale bread, and spoiled chunks of cold venison. "You *will* eat this, wont you?" the guard asked in a threatening tone.

Quinn had no choice but to play her role. "Yes, and I thank my master for such a generous meal."

"Good. I see your attitude has taken a turn for the better. I'll be sure to tell Isidore that you are ready to serve him properly." The guard slammed the door shut and headed toward the exit but stopped when he heard a strange moaning noise from the cell across from Quinn's. "What's your problem, scum?" he asked.

Quinn watched as the guard unlocked the cell door and walked in.

"I asked you a question, elf!" The guard walked right up to the vulnerable prisoner and went to give him a swift kick in the ribs.

The elf, however, had anticipated the clumsy move and grabbed the demon's leg before it struck him. Faster than the guard could have dreamed, the prisoner kicked out with his leg and shattered one of the brute's kneecaps. The elf followed up his move by planting his second foot deep in the demon's groin, forcing him to the ground. He proceeded to grab the keys and run out of his cell.

Quinn was at a loss for words when she saw the elf rush toward her cell and open the door with the stolen keys. Once the door was unlocked, the elf gave Quinn the key to her room and ran off with the rest down the hallway.

"Stop him!" roared the demon guard while he grasped his swollen knee in agony.

The injured demon shouted loud enough to be heard by two armed soldiers patrolling a nearby cellblock. The two guards looked over just in time to see the elf flee down the hallways. Quickly, with thoughts of murder and revenge, they drew their swords and gave chase.

Quinn was shocked by the elf's heroic actions. She was not sure when to use the key for escape, but she knew that this was not the right time. After making sure that nobody was watching her, she closed her cell door and locked it. She placed the key under the pile of bones in the corner where it would stay until she could formulate a proper plan.

꒰꒱

The elf tried frantically to get away from the pursuing soldiers. Although he wanted to escape the caves, his main concern was to find a crack or hole in the ground where he could throw the keys in. That way the demons would not be aware of the missing key that he had given to Quinn. Although elves were known for their speed and endurance, malnutrition and harsh conditions prevented the prisoner from living up to his reputation. Blindly, he turned right at a dark corner and came face to face with a second group of soldiers out on patrol. Determined to get rid of the keys, the fatigued elf turned around and ran down another dark hallway with both patrols right on his tail.

"Use your crossbows!" shouted a soldier, his voice echoing off the stone walls. The demons had orders from Isidore to return any escapees alive, so that he could deal with them personally.

"Aargh!" shouted the elf as a small missile tore into his skin, lodging itself deep within his hamstring. The poison that coated the bolt was very powerful, and the prisoner quickly became delusional. Finally, with all hopes of escape lost, he turned to face his enemy. Knowing the demons were about to end his life, the proud elf began to sing. An ancient song that spoke of the days when the forest was a peaceful place and the wood elves were abundant and thriving.

The demon that had shot the elf stopped a few yards away and waited for the rest of his party to arrive. "We'll just see how much you can take," he threatened as he loaded another bolt in his crossbow. "If I had known you could sing, I would have killed you weeks ago and saved myself the agony of hearing your hideous voice." In a matter of seconds, the rest of the soldiers joined in and loaded their weapons.

As his comprehension waned, the poisoned wood elf became silent. He noticed a nice sized hole where the floor met the walls. "I hope none of you were looking for these," he said in his native language. His response was four more crossbow-shots that slammed deep into his chest.

As the poor elf collapsed, he tossed the keys into the crack where only insects and vermin could find them.

"Did you get the little monster?" asked a murderous voice from down the hallway. Isidore turned the corner and pushed the rest of his soldiers out of the way. The sight of the beaten elf answered the master's question. "Good," he congratulated, as he knelt down beside the elf and stroked his brown locks with his long, black claws. In his other hand, Isidore held a small, empty flask.

⤳

It had been almost two hours since Byram and Aaron arrived at the camp. All around them, the wood elves ran in and out of the campsite, relaying messages and informing others of what they saw on their patrol.

After a few more minutes, the female who had struck Aaron returned with some water. She seemed to have calmed down since they last met and even managed to smile as Aaron rubbed his swollen cheek. "I am sorry for the way I acted before," she apologized, "but I have been under a lot of stress lately and had forgotten that the two of you are not from these parts."

"We understand, my lady," Byram replied, interested in the elf's story. "What exactly did you mean when you said 'demons'?"

"I was talking about the creatures you and your friend killed yesterday, before you setup camp." The young elf looked very confused. "You do know what demons are, don't you?"

Aaron looked at his friend with a blank expression. He did not know what those hideous beasts were, but he would have never guessed them to be demons.

Byram, also a bit surprised, took the news in stride. "I am sorry, good elf, but we have only heard of demons in tales and stories used to scare children out of mischief."

The young lady was taken aback for a moment. She had been born only one hundred and fifty two years earlier — elves had been known to reach the age of four hundred — and had no idea that there was a place without the evil that she had to endure every day. "I am sorry as well, but I have only heard of places without evil and destruction in tales and songs sung by our elders."

"Excuse me," Aaron asked, "but what happened to this forest? I was told many stories, but it would seem that your people lived through the events that made this place what it is today."

The young elf began to look very upset. "And what is this place to you?" she asked, trying to control her emotions. "Is it an evil place? Well, what you call evil and dark in stories and tales is my home." The young woman was not enraged, but Aaron could feel her anger and sorrow. The prince truly felt for the wood elves, as did Byram, who was captivated by the sheer beauty of the elf maiden.

"Please forgive me if I seemed rude," Aaron apologized softly, and with as much charisma as he could muster, "but I would love to learn more about your mysterious race. Perhaps there is a way that I can help you?"

"My lady," Byram interjected, "I was told, when I was younger, that elves were a beautiful and wonderful race. I was told they had a light in their eye's that reflected the purity in their souls. They were said to live in tightly knit communities with little contact to the outside world. Elves were supposed to be the most magnificent people on Oneira, and could warm the heart of even the coldest soul. I see now that those were not just rumors, but the truth."

"Thank you for your kind words," the young woman whispered to Byram. "It means much to me and my people to know that those stories exist. One day, warrior, the trees of Woodbyrne will be alive again, and all of the other races on Oneira will hear us singing for joy." The beautiful elf's smile suddenly turned into a deadly stare. "And our enemies will shake when they hear our songs of war." She gave the prisoners water.

"Will you tell us why these demons came to this forest, or why your people haven't overthrown them yet?" asked Byram.

"All in good time, my friend. Cathmore, the head of this patrol and the best scout in Woodbyrne, will return later this afternoon. If he finds that he can trust what the two of you have to say, you will both be untied and allowed to ask as many questions as you like. But," she warned, "you will have to answer just as many from us. I suggest you be honest." She gave a quick wink and sped off into the woods.

"My lady," Aaron called after her, "do you believe us to be trustworthy?"

The elf stopped and turned back toward the young prince. Again, she smiled. "Yes, I believe what you and your friend have to say, but Cathmore is in charge, not I."

"Well, what do we do now?" the prince asked his cousin, who was busy watching the beautiful elf run back into the woods.

Byram snapped out of his trance and blushed as he looked at his smirking cousin. "Wait for this Cathmore, and hope he doesn't decide to kill us."

Aaron did not find any comfort in his companion's answer.

⌁

Quinn stood silently in the cell of the elf that had given her the key. The room was dark, except for one red candle lit in the center of the floor which gave the room a sinister appearance. Isidore was there along with the prison guard and soldiers who helped take the prisoner down. Quinn welcomed the darkness because it concealed their grotesque features. She still felt very uncomfortable being so close to such horrifying creatures. Isidore had not yet revealed himself fully to the young woman and she was more than grateful for that. If he looked as evil as he sounded, Quinn would never be able to sleep again.

The elf, awake and beaten, was strapped to the far wall by wicked ropes that dug deeply into his wrists and ankles, making it very difficult for him to keep his composure. The crossbow bolts that had slammed into his chest drove him wild with pain, but they were not large enough to kill him. It was their poison that delivered the agony.

Quinn did not want to know what was about to happen. She did feel awful since the brave elf had sacrificed himself for her. She could only hope his death would be a quick and painless one.

"My dear Quinn," Isidore began, "you are about to witness what happens to anyone who is killed by my hands. You'll also find out what happened to my slaves before you, and what will happen to the ones that follow you."

"Yes, my master," Quinn answered, and bowed low for the demon master.

"I told you she was changed," the guard reminded his master.

"Quinn," Isidore said, ignoring the fawning guard, "I want you to hold this for me." The demon master placed a small flask in the woman's hands. "It may become warm to the touch so I warn you not to drop it."

"Yes, Isidore."

The large demon walked casually up to the hanging elf and smiled. "Did you really think that you could escape my home?" When no answer came forth, Isidore slowly caressed the elf's slender face with his large, red hands, letting his black claws glide dangerously over the prisoner's gentle features. Still, the elf did not move. "You are a fool, my friend," the demon master teased. "You and all of your kind will eventually wind up as decorations on my wall." Isidore pressed harder against the elf's face with his claws, leaving streaks of red blood behind in their tracks. The elf still did not move. He refused to cry out in agony and give his torturer what he wanted.

Quinn turned her head in disgust. She was no longer able to watch the brutality.

"Watch, my pet, or you will suffer the same fate as our rebellious little friend here!" Isidore continued his little game of torture, raking his razor-sharp claws all across the prisoner's face until there was no more room left to slice. The elf did not flinch. He took his punishment with poise and dignity. Isidore had dealt with the forest people long enough to not expect any response, no matter what form of punishment he thought of.

Quinn looked around the room in horror. She could not believe how much the other demons were enjoying the spectacle. Their hideous smiles and laughter made her sick to her stomach. The more blood that was spilled, the louder their roars.

Finally, when Isidore had enough of his game, he plunged his red hand straight into the elf's exposed chest, causing him to spit up blood and saliva all over the cell floor.

"No, you monster!" Quinn's shouts were made out of sheer desperation, as if her entire world had abandoned her.

The elf began to squirm as the pain in his chest spread like a wildfire throughout his entire body. The world was now a blur to him and he tried desperately to think of better times and better places. Somehow, the elf did not feel like he was dying. Instead, he felt as if something unnatural was tugging at his very soul. Something cold and evil.

"Hold on to that jar, Quinn!" Isidore demanded. When he thought the elf had suffered enough, the wicked demon master closed his fist around the beating heart of his prisoner, crushing it in one quick motion.

The elf knew that his life on Oneira was about to end but somehow realized that he was not going to be freed from his life of pain and suffering. Suddenly, pure dread washed over the elf's body as he felt himself being sucked into a powerful void of despair. "Save me, Quinn! Save us all!" He passed into the darkness.

Quinn could not hold back her horror. The flask she held began to glow bright green and it grew hot to the touch. In just a few seconds it became so hot that it blistered the skin on her hands. However, as fast the heat intensified, the flask cooled down. When the spectacle was over, a strange mist wound its way inside of the sealed container.

"You see, my sweet," Isidore explained, "when I kill another living creature, its soul is captured in a soul-keeper. The more souls I have, the more power Ulric gives to me."

"I understand, my lord," Quinn replied. She would rather die a thousand deaths than spend an eternity trapped inside a small jar like some damned genie.

Isidore spoke a command and the jar vanished from Quinn's hands. "I truly hope that you do not disappoint me again, Quinn," he said. "I would hate to have to make you suffer the same fate as the thousands of other souls." While his threat still hung in the air, Isidore stormed out of the cell, leaving Quinn with only her fears to comfort her.

"I know that I have no chance of a quick death," she whispered to herself.

"You never know when the master will decide to change his traditions," the demon guard answered, although Quinn really did not care for his opinion. "But for now, I think you should get back in your cell and rest up for tonight's dinner." Just as the guard grabbed Quinn's arm, she pretended to faint. "This is only the beginning, my sweet," he laughed, hoisting the woman onto his shoulder. "Eventually, you will become a complacent slave who doesn't care about her life any longer. You will wait on Isidore hand and foot, praying for his mercy." He carried Quinn to her cot and walked out of the room, locking the door behind him. The overly confident guard was so caught up in his little speech that he never even realized that his dagger was missing from its scabbard.

Once Quinn was sure that she was alone, she gingerly placed the long knife under the pile of bones. She was almost ready.

～

Less than an hour after the female elf left, Prince Aaron and Byram saw a tall, slender figure run into the campsite, quickly heading over to two older looking elves and starting a conversation. This latest elf to enter the camp wore a dark brown hooded poncho that concealed his face to the others. The rest of the elves moved away from the new messenger and went about their business.

"I am guessing this is Cathmore," Aaron whispered to his cousin. "See how he and the other two keep pointing at us?"

"I believe you are right," Byram answered. "He seems to receive a great deal of respect from the rest of the group."

The hooded elf gave a quick bow to the two older men and walked over to a large storage area where he picked out two bulging bags. He proceeded to walk over to the human prisoners.

"Why do I have a bad feeling about this?" Aaron asked as quietly as he could.

"Because you are unaware of who I am," replied the elf with a smile. He walked up to the two friends and knelt down in front of them, pulling back his hood to reveal a young, handsome face. "My name is Cathmore Stardust, and neither of you are my prisoners." Cathmore untied the ropes that bound the humans. He opened the two bags and revealed their missing food rations. "I apologize for stealing your food," he said, "but I was not sure if you would come willingly." He handed the bags over to the two men and they quickly began to eat some of their rations. "When you finish, I must ask you to speak with me under the large oak tree. I am sure you will not try to run away, since I have come to the conclusion that the two of you are trustworthy people." Although he did not make any open threats, the elven scout's words came to Aaron as both a warning and a greeting.

As Cathmore stood up and walked away from the humans, Byram noticed that the arrows in his quill matched the ones found in the demons. "I think we could safely say that he was the one following us through the forest," the archer concluded. Although he tried hard not to let his cousin see it, Byram was filled with joy and excitement. Byram Edelmar was having the time of his life.

Chapter 8

Aaron and Byram met Cathmore under the large oak tree once they had finished their meal. The friendly elf was already waiting for them with a big smile. "Please, sit down and speak with me," the elven scout insisted as he plopped himself on the ground.

"What is it you request of us?" asked Byram, trying not to sound too pushy. He figured that Cathmore was testing them, and that the young elf had more in mind than just getting to know them a little better.

"I followed the two of you from the second you entered these woods. Two young men seeking adventure in Woodbyrne is a very uncommon sight in these times, and I was not sure if you had come to the woods to side with the enemy." Cathmore smiled again. "When I saw the demons attack you, I knew that you were just wandering the trails of Woodbyrne without a clue as to what you were getting into."

"We didn't just come to Woodbyrne without a clue," defended Aaron. "We came here guided by an ancient map, and the advice of some of the most noble people on Oneira."

"I do hope you understand that the map you speak of can never leave this forest again," replied Cathmore with a sigh. "Items such as that put my people at great risk."

Byram was a little agitated with the seemingly overconfident elf. "Why is that?" he asked.

"Because, good archer, it is a map of my home. I do not want it falling into the wrong hands. There are many people who would kill for such an item. People with far greater powers than you and me combined." Cathmore saw that he was not getting his point across to the two humans. "Would you like me to sell a layout of your castle to the highest bidder, not caring what their purpose may be?"

Aaron stood up and bowed, a move that had caught Cathmore by surprise. "I am sorry to have offended you, Cathmore," he said. "We did not come to this forest to kill or harm anything that is good."

"Then why did you come to my home, noble warrior?"

"It was my idea to enter Woodbyrne. I am Aaron, Prince of Gower, the kingdom that borders these lands to the west. I talked my cousin, Byram Edelmar, into joining me on this adventure," prince explained.

"And what of you, Byram Edelmar?" asked Cathmore.

"There really isn't much to add to my cousin's story," admitted the archer. "I am an archer in charge of recruitment for the archery division of the Royal Army. I have traveled a long time with my cousin, and I have to say that I was not that happy with his decision to enter Woodbyrne. But, now that I have met such a marvelous race of people, however, I am overjoyed with my cousin's decision."

"An archer, are you?" asked Cathmore, somewhat intrigued. "How good are you?"

"I am a rather excellent shot, if I must say so. I have beaten his highness on many occasions at our target range."

Aaron shot his cousin an angry glare. Apparently Byram had no problem poking fun at him even in front of strangers.

"Well then, let us see how good the humans have become with the bow." Cathmore looked for a challenging target to hit. He finally decided on shooting a small apple that would be tossed in the air by the prince. While the target was given to Aaron, Cathmore gave Byram his bow and arrows back. They had been neatly wrapped and not a scratch could be seen on the beautiful weapon.

"I thank you for keeping my weapon in good condition," said Byram, more than a little relieved. "Not only has this bow been with me my entire life, it once belonged to my father. He gave it to me as a gift. Again, I thank you for showing me respect."

When all was set, Aaron readied himself for his cousin to give him the sign. The prince knew that this shot was very important for himself and Byram. Not only would it prove that the archer was not lying about his skills, the shot would confirm that the two friends were worthy of the elf's trust.

"Go!" Byram shouted as he stood there with his arms crossed, looking rather smug. Aaron threw the apple into the air with all of his might. It sailed high above and was almost lost in the trees. Byram acted quickly, grabbing his bow with one hand and an arrow with the other. After a quick aim, Byram let loose his missile. The arrow whistled through the air and shot right through the middle of the apple, splitting it in two.

"Very good, Byram Edelmar," congratulated Cathmore.

Byram wondered about the elf's ability with a bow. He killed the demon rather quickly, but he had had all the time in the world. "I would like to see how good an elf is with the bow," he said, trying to stir up a little competition with his new ally.

Aaron grabbed another apple and waited for the call. They all seemed to be enjoying the friendly competition.

"Need I remind you which ancient race created the bow?" asked Cathmore with a playful smirk. "Now!" he shouted, and, again, an apple soared into the air. Cathmore pulled out his bow and an arrow so fast that those watching barely had time to blink. In less than a second, an arrow had streaked into the air and sliced the apple in half. Almost immediately following the first shot, Cathmore's arm moved in a blurring frenzy and two more deadly missiles were released, each one splitting one of the halves of apple into two more sections. The four chunks of fruit dropped to the ground right in front of the amazed humans.

"I would like to learn more from you, good elf," Byram admitted, his eyes never leaving the quartered apple that lay on the forest floor.

"And I would be happy to teach you, Byram. Once my people have more time to enjoy life, and not worry about living day to day."

Aaron wanted to know more about their talented host before becoming such good friends. "I do believe it is your turn to give us a story, Cathmore Stardust."

The wood elf's smile turned forlorn. "Alas, there really isn't much to say. I am a head scout for our leader, Forrester Silverbow, and I am also in charge of this scouting party. I apologize for treating you as prisoners, but my people had orders to do so until I decided what your fate should be. I spoke to Forrester himself and he told me to treat the two of you with respect and caution."

"Why did the young elf lady get so upset when I questioned her about Isadore?" asked Aaron, pointing to his swollen cheek.

Cathmore became quiet for a moment as he thought of the right words. "Isidore, is the demon master. It is said that he came to the forest over two hundred years ago, bringing chaos with him. How the wretched demon entered this world, I do not know for sure. There have been tales of wizards foolishly calling him through a portal, but I cannot think of why an elf would want to do such a thing."

"Maybe," Byram suggested, "the wizards were lusting for fame. Where I come from, mages thrive for recognition, especially amongst their peers."

Aaron nodded in agreement. He also heard ludicrous tales of wizards who had been destroyed because of their search for more power.

"First," Cathmore continued, "the demons were sent out to destroy what few mages we had in the forest. Isidore didn't want to risk having one of them find a way to destroy him. But, Isidore wasn't satisfied with the destruction of the wizards, so he ordered the total annihilation of all wood elves."

"How did the elves manage to survive over the years?" asked Aaron.

"Forrester Silverbow showed us how to survive. He had developed the skills to blend with his surroundings so the demons could not see him. As wood elves, we have that ability naturally, but Forrester helped us hone it to perfection. Still, despite the fact that many of the demons now fear us, Isidore knows that we cannot survive for long. Our time on Oneira is limited."

"Where does this monster live?" asked Aaron, a little too interested for his cousin's liking.

"He resides in a cave many miles northwest from here. The roads leading there are small and secluded. It is an easy hike, but the constant threat of the demons makes for a treacherous journey."

"If you don't mind, I would like to see this place."

Byram could not believe what he was hearing. Why was his cousin acting so foolishly?

Cathmore stood in silence for an uncomfortable amount of time. He did not know if he should put the two humans at such risk. Still, sympathy from a powerful ally was hard to find in Woodbyrne, and the two humans would eventually return home where they would spread the stories of the wood elves' plight. "We will talk about that tonight, over dinner. For now, I must go back into the woods and keep watch." Cathmore hurried into the forest where he planned to speak with the leader of the elves about his unusually fortuitous opportunity.

⟿

"Get in there, little lady!" the prison guard shouted. Isidore had ordered his servant to return Quinn to her cell after he decided she was not massaging his hands properly. "I think your time is coming to an end," the dark monster continued, noting the red welt on the side of Quinn's face. "I am going to enjoy watching you die, you little trouble-maker!" Satisfied with his torments, the miserable demon turned away and limped down the long corridor, wincing and cursing every time his broken kneecap shifted under his weight.

Quinn knew the guard's words rang true. No matter what she did to please the master, she was always rewarded with a blow or an insult. There was no telling how much longer Isidore was going to play his little game of dominance, and Quinn had no intentions of finding out. Earlier that day, while she was waiting for Isidore's meal to be prepared, Quinn had watched a small band of soldiers made their way past her. As they ran by, one of the demons referred to weather conditions outside the cave. Quinn had wisely taken note of the passage the demons had chosen and planned on using it for her escape. After a quick check to make sure nobody was watching, the battered woman walked over to the pile of bones in her cell and pulled out the dagger and the key. "Tomorrow," she whispered, "I make my escape."

⟿

Cathmore and his human guests sat in front of a small fire and ate their rabbit dinner. For the most part, the two cousins kept quiet while they ate their meal. They both had a lot on their minds and were in no

88

mood for lengthy conversations.

"Why do you wish to see the lair of the demons?" Cathmore asked, when he finished eating. He had been instructed by Forrester to be blunt with his guests, catching them off guard to make sure they meant no harm to the elves.

"I wish to see this lair because your story was most intriguing," Aaron answered, hoping to win over the elf's favor. "Maybe I can kill a couple of the monsters along the way."

"Do you know of the dangers that Woodbyrne has to offer inexperienced fighters?" the elf reminded.

"Yes, I know of the danger, but I have seen and fought a few of the demons and lived. I believe the three of us can handle more than a handful of those rotten creatures."

Byram exploded. "You have to be kidding!"

Cathmore laughed loudly. "But I never said that I would accompany you on your journey, young prince. I just wanted to know why you want to see the cave." Cathmore's tone turned more serious. "Death lives in that Woodbyrne cave, Prince Aaron. Nobody has ever come out of it alive. I suggest the two of you leave while you can still walk." His was not a selfish race and the thought of sending the two humans into danger without a fair warning would not sit too well with him.

"I have a score to settle with the demons," Aaron finally said. He stood up and thrust out his chest as proudly as he could. "These woods took the life of my uncle when he was just a young man like myself. I must avenge his death for the honor of my family."

"Even if it means killing yourself?" asked Byram. He never remembered the prince vowing revenge for his uncle's death.

"Yes, even if I die trying, Byram. I will kill as many of those demons as I can." Aaron sounded a lot like his father just then. King Dermot was famous for making promises that seemed impossible. However, all the king's vows always seemed to be fulfilled no matter what odds were against him.

Byram was proud of his cousin. Thus far, the journey had some positive effects on the young prince. "Then I will accompany you, my dear cousin," he said. "Even if *you* die trying."

All three men laughed. Cathmore could see the purity and honesty between the two cousins, and was confident that they were worthy of the quest. "Then it is settled," the elf said. "We make for the cave in the morning." Cathmore walked over to the two humans and put a hand on each of their shoulders. "I warn you, this is no laughing matter. I will show you to the cave, but I will not enter if you decide to go in. My people need me and I cannot abandon them. I hope you understand."

Prince Aaron bowed low to the noble elf. "I understand and respect your decision," he replied. "We are honored to have such a mighty warrior guide us."

Byram also bowed. "I just hope we make it out of the cave alive," the archer whispered to himself as he went to check on his supplies.

Cathmore followed, leaving the prince alone.

"Byram," said Cathmore. "I would worry more for your cousin than for me or yourself," he said. "Aaron is noble and just, but his desire for revenge could be his end. Try to deter him from going into the cave when we get there. Nobody ever comes out alive. Nobody."

Byram agreed with the wood elf, but he also understood Aaron's decision. "A man who does not follow his heart's desires is more of a slave than one who is captured by his enemies," he said in the prince's defense. "I serve Prince Aaron, and if he decides to enter the cave, I will follow. We do not ask, or expect, anyone else to accompany us, but I must remain loyal." The archer bowed and ran off to join his cousin.

Cathmore stood silently for a while and thought of Byram's words. Cathmore had always thought of humans as greedy and selfish people. But these two who had aimlessly entered the forest had easily proven the myths wrong. Perhaps it was not by chance that the humans entered Woodbyrne. Perhaps fate had played a hand in delivering Prince Aaron and Byram Edelmar to the elves. Cathmore Stardust sped off into the woods to gather supplies for the upcoming journey, and to inform the other elves of his plans for departure. In his heart, Cathmore had renewed hope for the future of his people.

Chapter 9

Cathmore woke the two humans just as the sun was about to rise. "Our time has come, my friends. This day will require a fast pace through the woods. I hope you are both up for the challenge."

Aaron and Byram sat up in their blankets and yawned deeply. They had a very relaxing night's sleep and they were more than ready to brush the dust off their boots.

"I slept so comfortably, I almost forgot where I was," Aaron said as he got up and stretched.

Cathmore found the way humans awakened very humorous. One would be hard pressed to find an elf that was groggy in the morning unless he or she had been consoling with large flasks of mead and wine the night before. Wood elves welcomed each day as if it would be their last, paying homage to the sun and all of nature's beauty.

After a quick breakfast of dried fruits and berries, the three men sped off into the woods, heading west. Along the way, Cathmore had to make sure that he did not lose his companions. Years of experience had made the naturally agile elf into a creature as nimble as a cat. Aaron and Byram were fast learners and, after a few cuts and bruises, were able to maneuver past fallen trees and thick brush with no problem.

After a while of steady hiking, Cathmore halted his friends. "Stay here quietly while I scout ahead." Before the two humans could react, he slipped into the woods without a sound.

"What seems to be the problem?" asked Aaron. "We have been hiking for most of the morning and we haven't even seen a deer."

"Maybe that's what worries him," replied Byram. The archer listened for the noises that had alerted Cathmore, but his ears could only pick up a gentle breeze that softly rustled the leaves in the gigantic trees.

As fast as he left, Cathmore came leaping back to his friends with the stealth of a cat. "All is safe, my friends. Let us make haste while we still have the chance." He turned around and continued his trek through Woodbyrne as though nothing had happened.

Byram, however, was very interested in the elf's behavior. "Cathmore," he called, "what was it you heard?"

The wood elf paused for a moment before answering. "A demon scouting party was walking ahead of us and I wanted to make sure they were gone before we continued."

"But how did you know they were there?" Byram asked.

"My people have lived with the demons for many years. We have learned how to listen, see, and smell where the vile creatures are." Cathmore finished his explanation and started off down the trail, urging the humans to follow.

⁓

Quinn tried hard to hold back her rage as the guard grabbed her by her hair and dragged her down the filthy corridor. Apparently, the miserable demon still had a lot of pain in his knee and taking his frustration out on the woman seemed the best option.

"Are your pretty little robes getting all soiled?" he teased. "Not to worry, we have plenty of elven clothes for you to wear. By this afternoon, you will be covered in fine silk and linens. Then, by the end of the day, I will make sure that you look like the filthy wench that you are!" When he reached Quinn's cell, he gave her a kick that sent her crashing to the stone floor. The young woman quickly recovered and slammed the cell door shut so as to prevent the guard from beating on her. "What's the matter, Quinn? Afraid I might hurt you?"

Quinn walked right up to the small window and looked the demon directly in his brown eyes. "I am more afraid that I might hurt you, you twisted, fat, nasty freak." She could no longer hold in her anger. Thoughts of grabbing the knife and jabbing it into his eye ran freely through her head, but Quinn knew that she had to wait. She would depart in the afternoon when most of the demon soldiers were out on patrol, leaving many of the corridors unguarded.

"We'll see about that!" the demon spat. He turned and headed down the corridor, grumbling to himself with every painful step.

After Quinn was certain that her tormentor had left, she ran over to the pile of bones and quickly placed them under her bed sheets. Everything had to be perfect in order for her to escape.

꒰Ꙭ꒱

The morning passed quickly for the three travelers, stopping now and then for a quick rest and some water. Still, the entire forest was unusually silent and there was a tension in the air that could not be explained.

"We must be extra cautious from here on," warned Cathmore, breaking his verbal dry spell. "The cave is barely a mile away and I fear that Isidore's soldiers might be on patrol."

"When do you plan on leaving us to rejoin your kin?" asked Aaron. He wanted to have the powerful elf by his side. The forest had become more and more sinister-looking the closer they got to their destination.

"I told you I would not enter the cave long before we ever set out on this journey, Aaron." The elf had become very tense since they came so close to the demon's lair. If he were killed or captured, what would his people do? It was very possible that Damek, the infamous demon scout and second-in-command of the demon horde, would be able to follow his tracks back to the main camp. "Just follow me and I will lead you safely. You must decide, Aaron, if you still want to enter the lair, or if you'd prefer to return safely back to the king and tell him what you have witnessed."

Aaron understood Cathmore's position. After all, his people were on the verge of annihilation and desperate times called for desperate measures. Sometimes, the prince thought, you have to swallow your pride and do what is best for the ones you love.

"When we see the cave," Byram interjected, "we'll be sure to inform you of our decision."

"Agreed," said Cathmore. "We'll have a light meal now before we continue."

꒰Ꙭ꒱

"The damned wench had better be ready this time or I'll murder her myself," the angry guard mumbled to himself as he hobbled down the long corridor. It was midday and Quinn was to serve Isidore's lunch. The demon walked up to the prisoner's door and peered inside. To his surprise, he found her fast asleep in her bed. "Time to serve the master," he called, but there was no response. "I told you to wake up and get dressed!" The demon was fed up with Quinn's attitude and fumbled for his second set of keys. "What the hell is this?" he asked as he pulled open the unlocked cell door. He was at a loss for words when he ran over to the bed and ripped the sheets off, revealing nothing but ancient bones and rubble.

Quinn, hidden behind the door, jumped at the demon with her dagger in hand. The demon saw the wild woman out of the corner of his eye and reached for his own sword. However, he was too slow and fell into shock as the sharp point of the knife poked through his jugular, his black blood spewed forth.

Although the demon knew his wound was severe, rage helped him stay on his feet for a few moments longer. He swung wildly with a closed fist and slammed Quinn on the side of her head, forcing her backwards. Still, Quinn did not release her hold on the dagger, and her momentum helped free the blade.

"How does it feel to know you are going to die?" asked the angered woman, taunting the creature as he had her so many times before. Her response was only a bubbling gurgle from the open throat of the guard, who desperately lurched forward for one final strike. Quinn expected the attack and nimbly ducked under the lethargic swing. She rolled forward and jabbed her dagger directly into the demon's broken knee-cap, sending one final bolt of pain into his dying brain. Pleased with herself, Quinn ran out of the cell and closed the door behind her. She did not have long before Isidore would send more guards looking for her.

꒜

The three companions kept silent, as they peered at the cave from the cover of their hiding place, a thick patch of trees and shrubs no more than fifty yards away. The opening looked ordinary, but a powerful evil poured out of its black mouth. Its stone was as black as night and no light came from the large opening. Fallen trees and destroyed brush littered the large clearing that surrounded the cave, giving the impression that even Woodbyrne rejected the demons' presence.

"Are you sure this is the right place?" asked Aaron, curious as to why there were not any patrols or guards in the area.

"I know for sure that this is the cave," assured Cathmore. "Besides, can you not feel the evil? Just because danger is not physically facing you, doesn't mean it isn't there."

"I agree with Cathmore," Byram added. "He has led us to the cave safely and has done more than his share on this little excursion. We should return with Cathmore to our kingdom and tell King Dermot of the evil menace the good elves are facing. I'm sure he'd lend a sympathetic ear and possibly send some help."

Cathmore, hiding his joy, nodded in agreement. Still, the wood elf saw more than a want for adventure in the prince's eyes. He saw determination and stubbornness.

"I have every intention of informing the king and queen of the elves' misfortunes, once I have seen this Isidore for myself." The prince pulled out his sword and gave Byram a quirky smile. "Besides, I wouldn't want all of the kingdom to think that their prince was a coward."

"You are a fool, Aaron!" Byram scolded. "Entering the cave is suicide. Did you hear nothing of what the elf has said?" He pointed toward Cathmore, but nothing stood next to him except for a few thorn bushes and trees.

"Where did he go? Why didn't he tell us that he was leaving?" Aaron asked.

"Because he knew that you would want to enter the cave," answered the archer. "Cathmore made it very clear that he would have nothing to do with your personal goals. He was going to lead us to the cave and either take us back to our horses, or leave us to die." Byram unsheathed his sword and waited for Aaron to make a decision.

"Let's get closer to the entrance so we can get a better idea of what we are up against," Aaron said with confidence. "Maybe, we'll even get a chance to see Isidore himself."

"I don't think you want to see the master of all the demons of Woodbyrne," Byram whispered flatly. He could not believe how wreckless his cousin acted. He thought back to the story of his uncle who had foolishly entered the dark forest without hesitation. It must run in the family. "Besides, wouldn't you rather return here with the king and the Royal Army?"

"I am going in the cave, Byram. Are you going to follow me or not?"

"After you, my prince."

ɔ⌇

Quinn sped down the hallway as she tried to remember which corridor to take. One wrong turn could lead to absolute disaster.

"Where do you think you're going, missy?" asked a lone soldier out on patrol.

Quinn was not surprised to see the demon soldier. Before he could react, she dove forward and slammed her head into the demon's snout, giving him a nasty nose bleed. While the guard tried to stop the bleeding, the desperate woman slid her dagger into his throat to stop his screams for help. A few yards away, several soldiers heard the commotion and called for backup.

Quinn ran at full speed, letting her long legs take her as far away from her captors as possible. She noticed that the dungeon floors were beginning to slope upwards, and that could only mean one thing — freedom.

"We have ourselves a runaway!" a guard shouted from down the hallway. "Go and inform the master that we are in pursuit and shall apprehend the stupid human in a few moments!" More voices cheered in unison, and it sounded to Quinn that the entire dungeon was in pursuit. She had to act quickly before it was too late.

"Gotcha!" cried a hidden demon as he lunged for the fleeing woman from a dark niche in the wall. He had heard the cries from his kin and decided to ambush the prisoner as she ran past his section of the cave.

Quinn had to react quickly. Her enemy was closing in behind her, and the demon in front of her had the upper hand. A weaponless upper hand, she noted.

Although the claws of the demon could slice through flesh like a hot knife through butter, they were not that long and did little to match the sheer power of a steel blade. Quinn let the overconfident demon know that by slicing deep into his wrist as she ran past him.

By then, the entire dungeon was aware that Isidore's slave was trying to escape. Many demons ran around desperately trying to find her before she found daylight. They knew that their master would unleash his wrath on the entire army if she were allowed to break away.

One clever soldier decided to take a more subtle way of capturing Quinn. While his fellow demons were busy running around like fools, he hid in the space under a trap door by the only passage that led to the surface. There he waited with ropes and a good sized club for Quinn to run over him so he could pull the lever, causing her to fall through the floor.

Quinn began to feel the breeze of fresh air wafting through the hallway as she ran in search of an exit. All around her, cries from the demons echoed off the walls like thunder. The light of the red candles along the corridors bent and swayed with each passing of the gentle forest breeze. Quinn had to stop and take a short breath of air; she had been running for a long time. Quinn knew once she got out of the cave, her escape would be far from over. Finally, when the voices in the hall were dangerously close, she continued her sprint for freedom. After a few more bends and turns, a dull light could be seen at the end of a long corridor. Quinn picked up her pace; freedom was not far.

Once the demon heard the soft footsteps patting against the hard stone, he tightened his grip on the lever that would drop the trap door. The demon smiled wickedly as he thought of beating the helpless woman unconscious with his club. As the footsteps grew nearer, he began to smile.

Aaron was still debating how he should enter the cave when a woman's scream came piercing through the darkness.

"What the hell was that?" asked Byram.

"Whatever it was, it came from inside the cave." Aaron was no longer thinking of himself. "It sounded like a woman's voice."

"It sounded like a scream to me, but how do we know if it was a human's scream or the sound of some sort of demon?" Although the archer did not want to enter the cave, his conscience would not let him forget the sound of the shrill cry for help.

"I got her!" came a call from inside the cave.

"Save a piece of flesh for me!" shouted another unearthly voice.

"Tell Isidore to make her scream some more before he does her in!"

"Maybe we should go back and inform the elves that there is a woman involved in all of this?" asked Aaron, feeling a little overwhelmed by the situation.

Byram, on the other hand, was calmer than his cousin and knew what had to be done. "Aaron, by the time we find the elves again, *if* we find them, the demons will have killed the woman. Besides, you wanted me to go into the cave with you, and now you are having doubts? It is time you start acting like the man you want to be. You can't spend the rest of your life running away from your responsibilities."

Aaron knew that his cousin's words rang true. "I am not a coward, my friend. I am a man of honor and courage. Let us attack these villains and put an end to their miserable lives. We'll rescue the woman, or die trying. I am Aaron, Prince of Gower, and, like my father and uncles before me, I am a warrior who shall never bow down in the face of evil."

"Well spoken, my prince," congratulated Byram, full of admiration for his cousin. He looked at the cave for a moment, and looked back at his cousin. The archer's smile turned to a frown. "How should we do this?"

The prince laughed and said, "Follow me."

The two men silently made their way toward the entrance of the cave and before long, they were standing at the front of the cave entrance. An uncomfortably warm blast of stagnant air bellowed from inside the darkness and the opening seemed like the mouth of a sleeping beast. From their closer vantage point, the cousins could see a soft, red glow coming from deep inside the unholy structure.

Aaron had become frightened to the point where he could not feel his hands and feet. Although he longed to experience such dangers, doubt flooded his mind and overtook his ability to reason. Still, he knew he had to go on.

With a quick nod and a deep breath, the two virtuous warriors readied their weapons and walked into the cave. Once they left the forest, all was black.

Chapter 10

The intruders' eyes adjusted quickly to their new surroundings. Although they were no more than a few yards from the entrance of the cave, it seemed as if they had traveled to another dimension. Aaron was appalled at the interior of the cave. The stone walls were poorly built and unkempt, giving the feeling that the whole structure could collapse at any moment. Armies of spiders, ants, and other insects crawled around searching for food, while rats and other vermin scampered about their business. Small red candles, randomly placed on the walls, gave an uneven glow. As the two soldiers pressed forward, fragments of bones and dry blood could be found in every corner and crevice of the cave.

A few hundred feet into the cave, a fork divided the main passage into two sections. One path seemed to stay level, while the second sloped downward, deeper into earth. A warm gust of air crept through the second corridor giving the impression that some large source of heat would be found if one was brave enough to travel the eerie path.

"Where should we go?" asked Aaron. He was a good fighter when he had to be, but the aura of the cave unnerved him, making him feel weak and vulnerable.

"I guess we should go down," answered the equally frightened archer. There were too many hiding places, which did little to calm his nerves. "The lower levels would have more privacy than the ones closer to the surface. I'd guess the demons would want to keep their prisoners as far away from temptation as possible."

The two men made their way down the cave slowly, trying to listen for any clues as to where the woman had been taken. As they got closer to the end of the long hallway, they heard voices coming from a new passage toward the left.

"If we are seen, our entire effort will be blown," Aaron whispered.

Byram, with his deadly bow already in his hand, understood what his cousin was hinting at and gestured for him to stay put as he crept slowly toward the end of the hallway. When he arrived, the archer saw two demon guards, armed with crude swords and crossbows, standing with their backs toward him, talking to each other in their native tongue. Apparently, they were too busy conversing with each other to hear the infiltrators. Byram smiled and waited for the right moment to spring.

Aaron had his long sword drawn and ready. He knew that his cousin was planning a surprise attack, and made sure he was well hidden within a large crevasse in the cave wall. Anyone in a hurry would pass him by, thinking him no more than another shadow cast by the thousands of imperfections in the cave's structure.

ॐ

A demon soldier had seen the two humans enter the cave from the forest while he was returning from a hunt. Before they drew their swords, he thought them to be foolish travelers in search of shelter. The soldier knew that Isidore would reward him well if he took care of the situation. Silently, he made his way toward the one fool who had jammed himself in a cave wall crevasse with nowhere to run. Fools, he thought, as he unsheathed his sword and advanced forward.

ॐ

Byram glanced back to make sure his cousin was ready. To his surprise, Byram did not see Aaron at all, but a large demon with a huge sword drawn and ready to strike. "Aaron!" he called. "Behind you!"

Aaron turned around to see a very large soldier heading toward him with a deadly looking blade. Since he was packed in so tightly, the prince had very little room to maneuver and was certain that his days of adventure were over.

Two arrows slammed into the chest of the demon soldier, knocking it back a few feet and giving the prince enough time to get out of his hiding place and join in the melee.

101

Byram knew the two other demons had heard his calls to his cousin. Before the two guards came running around the corner, however, Byram readied two more arrows and knelt low in the shadows.

When the unsuspecting soldiers entered the hallway, the archer wasted no time in disabling them. He let loose the two arrows, hitting each of the demons in the kneecap and sending them to the floor. The archer dropped his bow and pulled out his sword.

The demon fighting Aaron swung wildly with his weapon, spitting blood out of his mouth with each labored breath. Fortunately for Aaron, none of his attacks had much strength behind them and the young warrior knew that he would gain the upper hand quickly. The demon came in high and fast, but the trained fighter was able to duck under the clumsy attack with ease. Aaron followed up his move with a reverse swing of his own. The steel blade connected evenly against the throat of the unfortunate demon and severed its canine head clear off its shoulders.

Byram also had his situation well under control. The awkwardness of the demons gave the dexterous fighter the upper hand. He quickly jabbed forward with his sword, puncturing a large hole in the gut of the closest beast and sending it to the ground.

The remaining demon was not as hurt as it made out, though. Cunningly, he grabbed Byram's arm just as the archer struck with his sword. Byram tried desperately to free himself, but the demon held strong and snapped out with his fanged maw, sinking his sharp teeth deep into Byram's shoulder.

Aaron charged in from behind and stabbed the demon in the back of the neck with his sword, snapping its vertebrae and severing the spinal cord. The paralyzed creature released its hold on Byram and collapsed to the ground.

After the fight, Aaron grabbed his cousin by his good shoulder and carried him to a darker section of the hallway where they would be safe. "It is a nasty bite, but I think you'll make it," he teased, trying to make light of the matter. "I doubt you could use your bow."

"I'm afraid that it hurts much worse than it looks," Byram replied as he tried to work the pain off by rotating his shoulder. The skilled warrior hoped that the demon's saliva was not poisonous. "Still," he grimaced, "I can walk and my right hand is good enough to swing my sword. I think we should get going before more demons come to aid their friends."

⟫

The long hallway gradually became large enough for the two humans to walk side by side in relative comfort. The ceiling had also risen many feet, giving Byram the impression that they were heading toward a more occupied section of the caves. A strange odor began to make its way into the air as well. It smelled like rotten meat that had been left out on a hot summer day for too long and it got stronger as the path went on. Eventually, both men found it hard not to vomit.

After a few more minutes of descending, the corridor opened into a large circular room. It was at least fifty yards in every direction from its center and dozens of doors and hallways could be seen all around.

"I think I found the source of the foul stench," Aaron announced, pointing to the ceiling where hundreds of rotting corpses hung from thick ropes.

Both Aaron and Byram had to stop for a moment to catch their breath. From the looks of it, all of the bodies seemed to be elves. Some of them were even elven children!

The prince began to murmur little prayers for the dead while making holy signs with his hands. His cousin turned away from the gruesome sight and found a corner to empty his stomach.

When the shock wore off, Aaron surveyed his surroundings. One door, located on the opposite side of the massive room, caught Aaron's eye. It was no larger than the others, yet its appearance was completely different; it was made of gold.

As the two friends crept forward, they were able to notice dozens of engravings in the magnificent door. Small, demonic creatures with spiked tails and huge fangs were intricately carved into every gold panel. Some of the carved figures had huge wings and reptilian bodies and looked

103

like the demon creatures that roamed Woodbyrne. Amongst the menagerie of evil, a lone figure stood at its center. It was a demon to be sure, but it had a more human-like appearance to it, albeit a slight one. Despite the arms and legs, the creature had some major characteristics that set it far apart from mortal men. Huge ram horns jutted out from the beast's head, covering its skull and forming large spirals at the very end of the cranium. The demon's face was a cross between man and goat.

"I am guessing that one is Isidore," Byram decided.

Aaron swallowed hard. "Where did these monsters come from?" the prince asked in disbelief.

"We are dealing with creatures who came from another dimension and set up camp in our world. It's obvious these fiends are not natural. They are evil and strive to bring chaos wherever they go." The archer looked at the ground and sighed. "I only hope one of us lives to tell the king what we saw. This is a horror that has no place on Oneira."

"Leave the master alone!" cried a deep voice from behind the door. "He must perform his ritual with only his most senior servants!"

"But we want a piece of the action, too!" shouted another voice.

"I think we should be leaving," Aaron said.

Byram ran over to the closest door and smiled when he found that it was not locked. Quickly, he and his cousin ran inside and locked it behind them.

The two intruders entered a long, wide corridor that had many doors on either side. The floors were disgustingly filthy and the entire room reeked of decay. While Byram kept watch on the activities going on outside, Aaron began to search the corridor for an escape route.

Byram looked through a hole in the door and held his breath as dozens of demons passed. They looked disappointed; apparently, they were not going to participate in whatever fun Isidore had planned.

"We never get to have any fun these days," one of them barked.

"It's always what Isidore wants," another replied. "The master thinks little of us as of late. I wonder if he even cares about ruling the forest anymore."

A larger, more powerful looking demon that wore bright plate mail armor and a large metal helmet broke up the conversation with a booming voice. "How dare you question Isidore's rule, you pitiful excuse of a soldier!" The two demons fell to their knees in dread. "Isidore is the sole reason why we walk in Woodbyrne! He has brought us here and we have killed many victims over the centuries. The blood we drink and the flesh we feasted on is not good enough for you?"

"Then why has he let Damek leave without any consensus from the rest of us?" asked another demon from behind the large crowd of soldiers. He was small in comparison to the others, but no less hideous, with his dog-like face and deformed torso. "I say that a new master should be chosen!"

The rest of the demons became very quiet. Although many complained, none had ever suggested a revolt against the ruler of Woodbyrne. Isidore was one of the most feared demons in the Lower Planes, but in Woodbyrne, his domain, none came close to his power and rule. The angry crowd turned to face the traitor with vehement bitterness.

Byram could not believe what he saw. "Aaron, come and watch this," he whispered, but got no answer. The prince had discovered that the corridor was some type of detention block. Each door led to a cell. Aaron was busy looking in the cells, trying to find a passage that led away from the very real danger that lurked outside their door.

"You only have one chance to ask for forgiveness, my brother," threatened the demon.

Knowing that his life was on the line, the lone protester walked up to his superior and got down on one knee. "I ask for forgiveness. Please allow me to renew my status in the mighty ranks of Isidore's army."

The large guard looked down at the pitiful soldier and smiled. "No," he said with a slight chuckle. "You may never see the light of day again."

Without delay, the savage crowd jumped on the traitor and tore him apart. When the frenzy had ended, there was nothing left but a bloody, wet spot in the middle of the floor. All were howling in their victory.

"Let that be a lesson to all who doubt Isidore's rule!" shouted the leader of the guards. "Now, all of you, get back to your duties!"

Byram breathed a huge sigh of relief when none of the demons headed toward his door. "That was a close one, my friend." The archer turned to face his cousin and saw that Aaron was several yards down the hallway standing in front of a door with his head hung low. "What's wrong with you, Aaron?"

The prince did not answer. He motioned for Byram to come and look. He pointed at a small window in the cell door.

Confused, Byram went over and looked through the small opening. "My god! How can one person be so rotten?"

"Isidore is not a person," replied Aaron. "He is a demon."

In the cell sat an elf, naked and beaten. He had apparently been left unattended for weeks. Its pale green skin was covered in bloody sores and fecal matter. The stench was almost worse than the hall where the dead bodies hung. The elf, so beaten and tortured, did not make any sign that he was aware of the intruders' presence. Instead, he simply sat on the cold floor and looked at the ground with his deep brown eyes.

Tears began to roll down Byram's cheeks; he did not understand how anyone could mistreat a such an innocent being. Frustrated, he grabbed the door handle and shook it violently, but the door was locked tight.

"We can't be discovered," warned Aaron afraid that Byram was making too much noise. The noise did break the elf's trance and he looked up at the two men. Their curious expressions made the prisoner smile a bit. Unfortunately, the welcomed emotion was too much for the unhealthy creature and he began cough. Streams of blood and saliva coated his lower jaw and he became woozy.

"There must be something we can do for him," Aaron insisted.

Slowly, the archer lifted up his bow, and showed it to the elf. Bile began to build up in the back of Byram's throat at the very thought of what they were about to do.

Understanding the human's intent, the elf stuck out his chest and patted the area where his heart lay. Then, as if he were getting ready for bed, he closed his eyes and waited for all of his suffering to end.

"I am afraid that my shoulder is hurt too bad for me to make a clean shot, Aaron. I don't want to make him suffer unnecessarily."

Aaron held back his tears and took the bow from his cousin, who turned away in disgust. He took aim and let off his shot, sending the deadly arrow into the elf's heart.

To their surprise, the elf did not show any signs of pain, nor did he look saddened. Instead, he looked at the arrow shaft that protruded out of his chest and smiled.

After a long moment of grief, Aaron finally broke the silence. "I want Isidore's head to decorate the castle's walls."

"We will have our revenge on this demon, my cousin, but our mission now is to save the woman and report back to King Dermot. I just hope that we haven't wasted too much time already."

"Quickly, I'll go check to see if it is safe to go back outside." Aaron ran to the door and looked out. Apparently, the demons had gone back to their daily activities.

The two humans left the cell area in a hurry and opened the golden door. Aaron made one last check to see if anyone had spotted them before closing the hideous structure behind him.

"Let's get this over with," the nervous prince insisted. "My father needs to know of this hell as soon as possible."

Byram nodded and moved forward.

Chapter 11

A few worn-down candles hung on the side of the walls, barely lighting the long corridor. The floor, made of black stone, was cleanly swept and polished, giving off a sinister glow from the meager candlelight. On the far end of the eerie passage, very large double doors stood in defiance of any unwanted visitors. The double doors were made entirely of bone. It was the artwork of an evil mind.

"I think they're real bones," the prince said, truly disturbed by the gigantic doors. "I fear what lies ahead of us, my friend," he continued.

Byram gave his noisy cousin an angry glare. He knew Aaron was nervous, but the fool was putting them both in danger. "Would you just shut up?" he urged. "If we are discovered in this hallway, it'll be the end of us for sure. I'm not ready to die today and I was sort of counting on you having the same feeling. Now open the door so we can get out of here."

Aaron shook his head in defiance. "I'm not touching those," he said.

"Why not?"

"You touch them. They're disgusting."

"Well, I am not asking you, you blockhead. I'm telling you to open the damn doors. This was your idea, remember? So you have to touch them."

"I have grown tired of you and your disobedience, Quinn!" said a very loud and unearthly voice from behind the doors. "It is time for you to feel the pain and suffering that you have caused me!" A slap was heard followed by something very large crashing to the ground.

"Please, stop it, my master," begged the woman. "I promise to be good from now on! I swear it!"

"It is *far* too late for that, Quinn. You should have thought of the consequences before you killed my men and insulted my intelligence!"

Another slap echoed through the hall. "It is time for you to join the rest of the wenches that I have collected throughout the years, along with the thousands of elves, for whom you seem to have such a deep affection."

Knowing that time for the woman was dwindling, Aaron and Byram opened the large doors together and crept inside the room. All they knew was that a woman needed help and they were her only hope.

꙰

The circular chamber inside was much brighter than the rest of the dungeon, with large candelabras hanging down from the ceiling. The magnificat room was decorated elaborately, with dozens of demon statues, paintings and etchings. The stone walls were carved out to form deep shelves all around the room. On the shelves where thousands of small flasks. In the center of the chamber, a huge throne, also made of bones, stood atop a black dais. But otherwise, the room was empty. Isidore must have left just before the humans entered.

"What do you think is in those jars?" asked the prince, gesturing at the large number of glass flasks that lined the chamber.

Byram did not hear his cousin; he was busy inspecting the eight pillars that circled the innermost part of the chamber. They seemed to be made for support, but the fact that all of them were carved in the likeness of canine demons holding up the ceiling concerned him greatly.

"Byram, look at this," whispered the prince, as he made his way past the creepy statues and toward the large throne.

Byram ran over to join his cousin. "Touch nothing. We are not here to explore."

Once they were sure that the throne room was empty, Byram and Aaron desperately searched for another passage. When the prince made his way to the back of the room, he heard noises coming from the other side of the wall.

"I hear something but I can't figure out where it's coming from."

"It sounds like someone is talking," Byram answered. "There must be a secret door or something."

Frantically, the two men searched every crack and crevasse on the wall, hoping to find the secret lever which would allow them entrance. Unfortunately, after many attempts and scraped knuckles, the two friends were at their wits' end.

Suddenly, the sound of someone approaching the wall from the other side sent the humans scurrying to find a good hiding spot. In seconds, a section of the wall slid to one side and a robed creature came shuffling out of the darkness. Mumbling loudly, the aggravated demon ran about the throne room trying to find an item that he had apparently forgotten.

"There you are, damn it," the evil priest swore as he walked toward a small flask on a side table. The glass jar looked like the thousands of others, except that it was clear and not clouded. Satisfied, the demon walked back over to the wall, and spoke a command. Instantly, the wall shifted again and the priest walked through.

When they were certain that they were alone, Aaron and Byram came out from behind the huge pillars and approached the wall. Aaron, feeling confident, cleared his throat and spoke the command word as best he could. When the door slid to its side, the two cousins walked through and made their way down the passage.

༞

The secret passage way emanated a red glow and ended at a black curtain that separated them from another room.

"How does it feel to know that you are about to die?" asked a sinister voice from the other side of the curtain.

"As long as I never have to look at your foul face again, I'll be glad to meet my end!" answered the defiant woman.

"I think we should make our entrance," Byram whispered.

Aaron nodded and quietly opened the curtain with his sword. What the two men saw when they entered the strange room took them completely by surprise.

The antechamber was approximately fifty yards in every direction, covered completely in polished black stone. Black candles and crimson drapes decorated the sinister room and all were covered in red and gold runes. The room itself was mostly empty, with the exception of a dark pool placed in the far corner. What unnerved Byram and Aaron more than the decorations, however, was the sight of the room's occupants.

"I think the larger one is Isidore," the archer whispered in a shaky voice, speaking of the incredibly large creature that stood menacingly over a woman who was strapped to an altar. The beast was at least seven feet tall, and wore black and red ceremonial robes. Muscles and veins bulged out from every inch of the massive creature's red body. As in the etchings, very large ram horns protruded from his skull, which wrapped around his head and spiraled just inches behind his pointed ears. Tiny runes could be seen on the bony masses.

"What about the rest of them?" asked Aaron. As if Isidore alone was not enough, Aaron winced as three demon priests circled around the prisoner, two of them holding huge maces while the third carried a flask. In unison, the three evil beings began to chant as they danced around the altar.

As the priests finished their prayers, Quinn became overwhelmed with a loud humming noise in her head. It was a horrible sound that promised an eternity of pain and suffering. Suddenly, before she screamed in agony, all went quiet.

"I hope you've had a pleasant stay in my home," he teased, as he lay his large hand over her heart. Like a bolt of lightning, waves of pain seared up and down the woman's body.

Quinn struggled desperately to free herself but to no avail; the ropes that held her were too strong.

Isidore had just begun to recite the final prayers to the lords of the Lower Planes, when two arrows slammed into his massive back, breaking his concentration as well as his hold on Quinn. When the demon master turned to see what had disturbed him, he spotted the armed humans standing in front of the black curtain. One of the men was holding a long sword while the other sported a longbow. Isidore smiled wickedly at the two foolish mortals. "I see we have guests," he said to his priests. Quickly, the unholy demons raised their maces and waited for Isidore's command.

Aaron did not know what to say or do. He had hoped the arrows would have put the demon out of commission. Instead, it seemed that they did little more than irritate the giant.

"Well, do either of you boys have anything to say, or will you just continue your merciless attack on me and my men?" Isidore's words dripped with sarcasm. "I think you will have to come up with a new plan, good fellows," he said as the two shafts that stuck out of his back burst into tiny flames.

"I think we're in big trouble," Byram whispered to his cousin.

"I demand that you release the woman or I will be forced to kill you!" ordered Aaron.

Isidore's smug smile quickly turned into a deadly glare. "And who are you who dare to demand such a thing from Isidore, Demon Master of Woodbyrne, killer of elves, master of the human will, and destroyer of all that is holy?" Isidore's voice shook the very walls of the room.

"My name, foul beast, is Aaron, Prince of Gower. I am a killer of demons and all that dare try to control the good in my land. I am friend of the elf, and enemy of evil. I demand that you release this woman or a force much greater than you could possibly imagine will fall down on you like a landslide!"

The powerful demon smiled again. He was amused that Aaron had an answer.

While Isidore was being entertained by the two humans, Quinn tried again to break free of the ropes but to no avail. She prayed that the prince and his partner would be able to free her from Isidore and his minions before it was too late. Prayer was all that she had left.

Byram, positive that he was going to die, slowly went for more arrows while his cousin went word for word with the powerful demon.

"I was unaware that such nobility confronted me," Isidore mockingly apologized. "All the more fun for me." He turned to the three demons that knelt loyally beside him. "Kill them both."

Byram acted as quickly as possible, letting loose two more arrows before dropping the bow and unsheathing his long-sword. Due to his injured shoulder, one of the arrows slammed into a priest's thigh, forcing him into a limp. The second arrow bounced off the wall.

The limping demon called for one of his partners to help him with the archer while the remaining, and largest, priest put down the flask and took up his gigantic mace. As he ran toward Aaron, the deadly weapon began to glow as its wielder chanted an ancient and deadly prayer.

Aaron was faster than the demon had planned, however, and easily dodged the heavy weapon with a simple roll to his side. Still, the clap of thunder the mace made when it hit the floor threw the young warrior back, rocking his bones and stunning him for a moment. The powerful demon took advantage of his fortune and sent his mace into Aaron's ribs. Fortunately for the prince, his armor was made by the finest smithies in Gower and was able to take on the powerful blow, although a few ribs were bruised in the process.

Aaron became enraged. With lightning speed, the skilled fighter swung down hard with his deadly blade, severing the demon's forearm from its body. Blood spewed all over the floor as the evil wretch howled in rage. Aaron wasted no time in finishing the demon with a deadly strike to his neck.

"Excellent!" shouted Isidore, thoroughly enjoying the slaughter of his most powerful priest. However, he knew that his men were outmatched and he had to act quickly. Silently, the demon master spoke the words to a spell and a small black globe began to form in the furthest corner of the room.

Byram was having a tough time with his foes, but the seasoned warrior was still able to put up a valiant effort, hoping to wear out his opponents and strike when a weakness could be found. Since he could only use one arm, the archer doubted his stamina and luck would hold out.

Although Byram had scored a couple of solid hits that forced his enemy to the ground, his success opened the way for the second demon. Howling in rage, the demonic priest rushed in with his powerful mace already in motion.

Aaron saw that his cousin was in trouble and threw down his sword and picked up Byram's longbow, which was slick with blood. He took aim as fast as he could and fired one arrow. The missile whistled across the room and slammed into the demon's chest, dropping him to the ground. Satisfied with his work, the prince grabbed his sword and ran to his cousin's side.

"Stop!" roared Isidore, causing the combatants to freeze in their footsteps. "I think my guests had better look around them. I fear their little charade has come to an end."

Aaron and Byram turned to see a score of demons standing behind Isidore, waiting for their master's command. A feeling of panic washed over the cousins like a giant wave of doom.

"Please do not fear my minions," called Isidore. "They are only permitted to attack when I give them the word." The angry demon took off his ceremonial gown, revealing his bare chest and black leather pants. He wore high boots, polished to a glimmering black that reflected every light on every candle. Although he held no sword, Isidore's long claws did little to comfort the two humans. Menacingly, he stepped forward. "Which one of you has the courage to attack me?" he asked. "I am unarmed and quite vulnerable." Isidore closed in on the two men.

"Free the girl!" Byram shouted, as he intercepted Isidore.

Aaron didn't hesitate; he ran straight at the altar and began to untie the woman. "Remain calm and follow me."

Once she was free, Quinn jumped off the altar. The demons that entered through the gate simply waited; fear of disobeying the master far outweighed any gains from killing the wench.

"Take this and use it!" Aaron said to Quinn, handing her a mace that had belonged to a dead priest. Quinn snatched the heavy weapon with surprising ease and readied herself for an attack. When she and the prince turned to face Isidore, they saw Byram rush in on Isidore with blind fury.

Isidore stood still with his hands at his side waiting for the human to get closer. "Come and kill me, my friend," he egged. "I am unarmed and one stab with your blade might destroy me."

Byram never questioned the demon master's lack of caution. He ran up and drove his sword so deep into Isidore's chest that only the hilt could be seen. Black blood slowly oozed out of the horrible wound, but Isidore never flinched. Suddenly, like the arrows, the sword hilt burst into flames from the inner heat of the mighty demon. When it could no longer support its own weight, the once-perfect blade fell to the floor in a twisted heap of metal.

Once the spectacle was over, Isidore reached out and grabbed the archer by the throat, lifting him clear off the ground. "I think you will serve me better as a decoration on my wall!" the evil creature spat. Then, with little effort, Isidore threw Byram against the far wall, slamming his head against stone.

"Byram!" Aaron called out, as his cousin lay on the floor, his head bleeding profusely. He turned to Isidore. "I am going to kill you, you dog!"

Isidore stood there and smiled.

Quinn looked back at the rest of the demons but, to her surprise, none of them was even preparing to attack. They knew that their master was more than capable of handling the weaker humans.

"Quinn," Isidore called, "if you come to me now I promise to make your death much less painful than our two little heroes here." Isidore cracked his knuckles and stepped forward.

Aaron was filled with rage. When he was close enough, the wild prince lunged forward with his powerful sword but Isidore easily smacked the blade out of his hands. The vile demon took a swing at Aaron's exposed throat with his razor sharp claws, but was foiled when Quinn pushed the prince to the floor and out of harm's way.

Isidore walked up to the two humans and smiled. "It is a shame that you chose to disobey me, Quinn. When you were first brought to me, I had planned on letting you live for as long as your health would allow. Unfortunately, you chose to fight me and I am in need of a more submissive wench. Maybe, like your dead father, you are just a stupid fool?"

Quinn's hatred boiled over and she rushed up to Isidore and smashed him in the face with her mace. Isidore never even attempted to defend himself and the heavy weapon did no more than cause a small puffy bruise to form on his cheek. The demon master grabbed the woman by the hair and exposed her tender neck. "I guess you go first!" he shouted as he raised his clawed hand.

Byram, bloodied and beaten, jumped on Isidore's arm and prevented him from killing Quinn. He continued to climb on Isidore's back and, with his good hand, repeatedly stabbed the demon in the face and neck with a small dagger he carried in his boot. Black blood and red skin fell to the floor and sprayed in the air while Isidore struggled to reach for the manic human.

"Run!" Byram shouted, knowing all too well that his little moment of victory was close to an end. "Run, my prince! Take the woman and get out of here!" A clawed hand grabbed him by the face and five long claws dug painfully into his flesh.

Quinn desperately pulled on Aaron's arm. "We have to go!" she cried. "We have to get out of here while the other demons are staying put!"

In a matter of seconds, Byram was being held over Isidore's head. The demon had one hand dug into the archer's face, while the other was holding up his legs. The open wounds on his face and neck had already begun to heal and he smiled wickedly. "Your friend here is quite the warrior," he said. "A pity that he should end up like this." Isidore turned to his soldiers and arched his back, ready to toss Byram to his horde like a cheap piece of meat.

"Run Aaron! Now, before it's too late!" Byram was out of energy. He felt a cool breeze glide across his bloody face as he sailed through the air, into the waiting horde of demon soldiers.

"Feed," was all that Isidore said, and he watched in ecstasy as his minions began to tear the heroic human to pieces.

"No!" Aaron cried, as he watched the savagery unfold before him.

Quinn turned away; horrified by the scene.

Byram tried to break free of the barrage of claws and teeth, but he was too weak. Through the crowd of demons, he saw his cousin and the woman still standing in the room. He had to try one last time. "Run, my cousin! Tell everyone of Woodbyrne!" Byram fell back into the frenzied demons as a sharp set of fangs grabbed hold of his neck and started to sink in. The famous archer was about to die.

Isidore was enthralled by the gory spectacle he had created. "Feed well, my pets," he whispered. "There is plenty more where than came from."

Quinn knew it was time to leave. "Now is our chance to escape!"

"I deserve death," Aaron replied. "I should never have come here."

"Then you stay here to die a coward. Nobody shall ever hear of the sufferings of the elves. And no one shall know the heroic deeds of that fine warrior who just sacrificed his life so we could live." Quinn turned to leave.

Aaron understood the woman's logic and got up off the ground. How could he let his cousin die in vain? "Wait for me!" he called as he ran toward the secret corridor.

"Fast! We have no time!" Quinn replied.

"I know how to get out of this rat-hole," said the prince. "Follow me, and be wary." Just as they reached the secret door, the sound of hundreds of feet shook the ground.

"Get them!" roared Isidore, his voice reverberating off the walls. "Bring them to me!"

The two humans had no time to waste and ran as fast as they could. Behind them, the small horde of demon soldiers gave chase, shouting and screaming all the while.

Isidore stood alone in his secret chamber holding a glass flask in his hand that glowed from the inside. "Welcome, Byram" he greeted. "I have just the place for you."

Chapter 12

"Faster! We're almost there!" As Aaron and Quinn ran through the dark corridors, the howls and shouts of demons reminded them of what lay ahead if they were captured. Aaron's luck had returned; he and Quinn had widened their distance from Isidore's troops. After many dangerous twists and turns, they were finally at the wide corridor that led to the cave's entrance. The hazy mist that separated the dark underworld from the forest outside swirled in its unnatural motion.

"Quickly, before it's too late!" Aaron shouted, but Quinn grabbed his arm before he could begin his last charge. "What's the matter with you?"

"There's a large trap door not ten yards from the exit. A large demon is waiting underneath there for us. Believe me, I know. That's how I got caught the first time I tried this."

"They went this way!" a voice from down the hall shouted.

"Isidore is gonna be mad if we let them go!" cried another.

Aaron grabbed a burning torch from the wall and started to run down the corridor. He had an idea. Quinn was about to object, but the fast-approaching demon army had her following the prince right into the trap.

◦৵৹

The demon that had captured Quinn before sat in his little hiding place and waited for his prey to show up. The loud sounds of heavy boots hitting the stone floor followed by the soft sound of bare feet made the beast smile. "I am waiting for you again, my sweet," the vile creature murmured to himself as he readied for the attack. When the humans were close enough, the slick demon pulled the lever and dropped the floor. To his dismay, nobody fell through. "What's this?" he asked as he stuck his head out of the trap door. His answer was a burning torch jabbed into his face, blinding the creature and igniting his clothes. In seconds, the demon was completely consumed by fire.

Aaron and Quinn went around the trap and ran for the exit. The gray mist that mysteriously swirled around the opening gave way as they barreled through and fled into the cover of the trees.

"Quickly, we must get further away from the cave!" Quinn shouted, knowing that the demons would continue their pursuit throughout the forest.

Aaron could not go on any longer. Overwhelmed with grief, the heroic prince collapsed to the ground in a pile of tears. Thoughts of his cousin's face ran through his head, as did Byram's warnings and cautions.

"We have to move!" Quinn insisted. "There will be plenty of time for mourning after we get out of this alive!"

"Leave me here to die," Aaron said miserably. "I killed my cousin, my friend, and my mentor. I shall stay here and accept my fate." He pulled himself free of Quinn's grasp and went silent.

Quinn sighed, "It is foolish to stay here. Lets go." The brave woman pulled out her stolen mace and stood alert. The sounds of a dozen demons could be heard from inside the cave. Aaron seemed to be frozen in shock, starring blankly at the cave.

The gray mist that covered the opening of the cave suddenly disappeared, revealing evil eyes that pierced through the darkness. Quinn swallowed hard and said a small prayer to her fallen mother and father. In a matter of seconds, a large horde of demons stepped out onto the forest floor. The creatures looked hungrily at the two humans. Many had swords and axes while others just clicked their sharp claws.

"Isidore demands the surrender of the prince and the woman!" said the large gnarled demon who was in charge of the pursuing party. "Your death has been promised to be quick and less painful than the other's."

"You will have to take me dead!" Quinn shouted, willing to accept her fate and take out as many demons as she could before she fell.

"Have it your way, Quinn."

The demons had just started to run forward when, from out of the trees, a flight of arrows cut into their ranks and halted them. A small party of elves readied their bows and prepared for another assault.

The leader of the demon party spotted the elves and decided to run and live to fight another day. "Retreat! Retreat!" he shouted, as he turned and headed back to the safety of the cave. Unfortunately for him, the elves were much faster than the confused demons, and only two of the foul beasts made it back alive.

Aaron snapped out of his trance and smiled when he saw elves hop out of their perches. He was even happier to see a familiar face among the quiet men and women. "Cathmore! You've returned!"

Cathmore looked around for Byram. It did not take long for the elf and his kin to figure out that the archer had not made it through the caves. The understanding wood elf placed a sympathetic hand on Aaron's shoulder. "My people have always said that a person who dies an honorable death is honored forever." The rest of the elves nodded in agreement. "Ah, my prince, I see that you and your cousin scored a major victory today." The tall, handsome elf bowed low in front of the brave woman. "My name is Cathmore Stardust. I am an elven scout of these woods. Tell me, my lady, what is your name?"

Quinn blushed; it had been a long time since someone so charming had treated her with such chivalry. "My name is Quinn," she answered. "Quinn Brainard from Stovia in the kingdom of Galahan."

The elf put his hand to his chin and thought for a moment. "Ahh, Stovia," he finally said. "I *do* know where that secluded town lies. You are a very long way from your homeland, Quinn Brainard. You do not live far from the dwarven mining communities, unless I am mistaken."

"No, you are quite correct, Cathmore Stardust," Quinn said, excited to know that someone was familiar with the place she called home. "The dwarves are a secluded bunch of people and I am afraid we humans don't interact with them as much as we'd like. They make the finest pieces of jewelry in all of Oneira."

Cathmore smiled at the energetic female. She reminded him of a young woman he used to know. The two of them had plans to be married. The stoic elf winced when he thought of what the demons had done to his fiancée. "Dwarves are a strange bunch at that," he continued, as he cleared his head of bad memories. "One can never tell if they like you or if they would like to use you as a pickaxe."

"I believe we should be leaving," suggested the prince. Although Aaron could not see into the cave, he could feel the demons lurking in the darkness, waiting to strike out.

"Yes, let us leave this cursed place once and for all," concluded the elven scout. He led his people down one of the many hidden trails that mapped Woodbyrne's twisted landscape. Once he thought they were safely away from the cave, Cathmore slowed his pace. A while later, as the afternoon was close to its end, the small trail split in two directions.

Another elf soldier was waiting for his companions to return on a trail that led west, out of Woodbyrne. With him were Aaron and Byram's horses, cleaned up and fed properly. Their saddle bags were filled with new supplies so the travelers could last for many days without having to worry about food or water.

"My people of the woods," Cathmore announced, "I thank you for returning with me to the evil cave. Your unselfish attitude toward our friends is commendable. I give all but two of you the right to head back to camp."

Two elves, a married couple, stepped forward while the others quietly said their farewells and condolences to the prince and his new companion. Cathmore's demeanor quickly changed from optimistic to diplomatic. "Aaron, I only ask that you tell the king what you have seen here and that he consider our plight in these once-peaceful woods. It is hard for my people to accept the help of outsiders, but in this case, we ask for all of the assistance that the Kingdom of Gower can offer."

Aaron took the hand of the elf and placed it on his heart. "I promise to you, Cathmore, and to your people that I will speak to my father and ask for his aid."

Cathmore smiled once again. "It pleases me to hear those words, Aaron. For that, I am ever grateful." The two allies stood for a moment in silence. "These two fine warriors will see to it that your departure from Woodbyrne is as peaceful as possible. It is my belief that Isidore will not strike out at us anytime soon." The elf's face became sullen. "I fear that he will have bigger plans for all of us."

Quinn walked up to Cathmore and kissed him on the cheek, causing the green-skinned elf to turn red. "Thank you for all that you have done for us," she said. "I will never forget your people's beauty and grace. Unfortunately, the horror that I have seen in the depths of the cave will also never leave me. I promise to you that I will return one day and fight by your side."

"Thank you, Quinn. It would please me greatly to see you again."

Quinn approached Byram's horse nervously. The magnificent beast acted a little odd at first but the gentle touch of an elf quickly put it at ease. Satisfied that she was not going to get trampled, Quinn got up in the saddle.

"The horse said that he was not used to having anyone else on his back," said the elf. "I had to tell him what had happened to Byram, and that he was now responsible for your fast departure from these woods."

Aaron noticed that Quinn was still dressed in her ceremonial gown and would be quite uncomfortable riding the horse for the long journey home. "Quinn," he called, "there are some extra clothes in one of the bags that would suit you better than your gown."

The young woman got off her horse, grabbed the saddlebag with the clothes and ran off into the woods. In a few minutes, she walked out of the bushes dressed in Byram's second set of traveling clothes and a pair of elven boots that belonged to a generous female soldier.

Aaron thanked Cathmore again, and mounted his horse. Tears welled up in his eyes when he thought of never being able to race Byram through the lush fields of his father's kingdom ever again. That was just one of the many things the prince was going to miss about his cousin.

"Farewell, good humans," called Cathmore as he and his soldiers disappeared into the thick cover of the forest. In mere seconds, all of Woodbyrne was silent.

"My wife and I will follow the two of you from the trees," explained the male elf. "From up there we will be able to scout ahead and make sure that you have a safe journey." The young couple raced up a giant tree with the agility of a cat.

"Let's be on our way, Quinn," Aaron said, as he gave his horse a gentle kick. Together, as they tried to comprehend their fate, the two battered humans shared the silence of the forest.

The ride out of Woodbyrne was uneventful, as Cathmore had promised. Hours passed and not even a bird could be heard singing. The silence of the forest made Quinn nervous, she had never been in Woodbyrne before and she was unsure of what horrors it held.

"Don't worry, Quinn," Aaron said to his new partner. "Woodbyrne has been silent for two hundred years, since the demons came." They still had a long road ahead of them and the prince wanted to put the young woman's concerns to rest.

Quinn sighed. "I see. Still, it would be nice to hear some sort of life. A bird or even a cricket would be nice."

Eventually, late afternoon gave way to dusk, and it was agreed that camp should be made. The elven couple told Quinn and Aaron to relax and enjoy a peaceful night of conversation and food while they kept watch. "You may start a fire if you like," the female elf said. "We are far from any demon patrols and our scouts would see them coming long before they smelled the burning wood."

The small amount of light from the campfire did little to comfort Quinn. In truth, the constantly moving light cast frightening shadows all around the tall trees. It seemed that Isidore would charge out at any moment and rip her to shreds.

"Why did you decide to enter Woodbyrne?" the prince asked, hoping that a conversation would help calm Quinn's nerves while taking his mind off Byram.

Quinn almost laughed out loud. "I did not *plan* to enter these woods," she replied. "I was captured by a demon who flew me from my home to the cave. I never had anything to say about it. What about you? Why did you choose to enter Woodbyrne?"

"Dozens of reasons," mumbled the prince, as he drifted off into memories that seemed decades old. He remembered practicing his weaponry with Byram in the private fields of Castle Gower. He remembered the two loving parents that he constantly disobeyed. "Dozens of reasons that seem empty now." The prince lamented as he recalled all of his cousin's warnings. Why hadn't he just listened for once?

"Well, I'm very happy that you decided to come," Quinn said, causing her hero to blush. "If it were not for you and Byram, I would have been enslaved for all eternity." The proud woman took another drink of water.

After their small meal, the two companions went to sleep under the protection of their escorts. They had a long road ahead of them and a good rest would be needed. The world around them, forever silent, also slept and waited for the first lights of morning.

❧

The elven couple sat next to each other and held hands while they kept watch over the two humans. Together, they discussed the possibilities of having the king's army on their side.

"If King Dermot sends troops," said the husband, "we should be able to destroy the demons easily."

"We would be able to start a family of our own," added the wife. "*If* King Dermot helps us."

That night, while his wife slept in his strong arms, he gave her a gentle kiss on the lips. Although he never let his guard down, the tender elf played with his wife's long brown hair just as he did when they first met. Dreams of a family kept him company until it was time for his wife to take the second watch.

❧

Despite the chill and clouds of the day, Quinn awoke in good spirits. Her sleep under the fresh sky had done much to make her forget the evenings she had spent in the rank dungeons with rodents and other creatures she did not want to remember. After some light rations, the energized woman quickly washed her face and packed her supplies.

Aaron, on the other hand, awoke in the same foul mood. Dreams of his cousin being torn apart by demons had dominated his sleep. Still, despite his demeanor, the stubborn man forced himself out of his blankets and ate some food.

"Our elven friends took good care of us last night," Quinn commented. She knew that Aaron deeply mourned the loss of his cousin but he still had a large responsibility ahead of him.

"Yes, they did at that." Aaron sat in the damp morning mist and ate his breakfast of flat bread and dried berries.

Once Aaron and Quinn had packed their supplies and the elven couple had eaten, the small party of four made their way through the morning gloom. Ahead lay the borders of Woodbyrne and Gower.

The mist and fog that hovered overhead in the morning burned off as the sun broke through the clouds. Surprisingly enough, Woodbyrne did not seem as intimidating in the sunlight. Soon, the prince was in a much better mood and the thought of leaving the forest made him smile.

"You never said how you were captured and brought to this desolate place. Were you traveling, or did you fall into a trap?" Aaron asked.

"To tell you the truth, I can't be sure. My father was always known for his poor decisions. I guess my capture was the result of another blunder." Quinn was still full of mixed emotions about her father and the last thing she wanted to do was make it sound like he was an evil man. "He had been a loving father at one time and tried very hard to make his family proud if him. When I was younger, my father would come home and tell me stories of how he had been out all day battling dragons. Tears swelled up in Quinn's eyes. "I knew he wasn't some famous warrior, though. But I listened to every word he said."

"Do you think he is looking for you?" Aaron asked. "Maybe the king can send a messenger to Stovia for you?"

"The creature that kidknapped me killed my father before my eyes." Quinn remembered that horrible evening through a fog, as if it had happened years ago. Her trials in the dungeons must have aged her substantially. She continued, "My mother is also dead, but by the hands of humans, not creatures from the depths of hell."

Aaron did not ask anymore questions. He could see that Quinn was still not over her losses, and wondered how long it would take for him to get over the loss of his cousin. "I'm very sorry, Quinn. When we return to Castle Gower, I promise you that King Dermot will find the safest and fastest way for you to return to your homeland."

The eerie feeling of Woodbyrne lifted with every step forward and soon the wicked trees would be behind them.

Quinn thought of returning home. She wondered if she would ever be able to go back to Stovia again. Surely, her father's "friends" would still be there. Maybe, she thought, it would be best if the people of her town thought she was dead. Besides, what life would she have there? "I'm alone now," she mumbled to herself. The words hurt her more than anything else had.

❧

As the morning turned into midday, the last row of trees that made up Woodbyrne thinned out as the lush fields of Gower grew closer. Like a long tunnel, the last section of the narrow trail led to an opening filled with the light of day. Even the overcast sky could not hide the fact that freedom lay ahead.

The two humans stopped their horses just before they crossed the boarder in order to pay their farewells to the two elves that so generously watched over them.

"I promise that I will never forget the hospitality and the heroism that the elves of Woodbyrne have shown me." Although Aaron tried to act stoic, he could do little to hold back the tears that slowly formed in his eyes.

"Even if no other help arrives, I will return and do my best to fight by your side." Quinn bowed her head.

The elven female stepped forward and gently kissed Quinn on her forehead. "Thank you for your kind words, Quinn. I, too, look forward to the time when you bless us with your presence again." The beautiful elf turned to Aaron. "Prince Aaron," she began, "I know that you think of Woodbyrne as a place of evil and horror. But I ask you to remember that my people live under Isidore's shadow, suffering every day knowing that our home may soon become our grave." The elf rejoined her husband, who hugged her and kissed her on the forehead.

"Farewell," he said, before he and his wife turned and ran off into the forest. "Never forget Woodbyrne!"

Chapter 13

The landscape became more familiar to the prince as he and Quinn got further from the forest. Although he was unsure of their exact position, Aaron knew that they were north of the original trail that he first used to enter Woodbyrne.

After a few short miles, the two companions came to a fork in the road. Aaron knew that if they remained on the same trail, they would have no choice but to spend the night under the open sky. However, the dusty path that led to the southeast would take them to Sharpsword.

"I believe I know where we are," Aaron said. "We are not far from a friend that we met on the way here."

"Will your friend give us shelter for the night?" Quinn asked, realizing that the afternoon was past its peak and night would be falling sooner than she hoped. "I don't believe we'll be safe on the open road so close to the forest."

Aaron looked back at the dark forest and thought of his options. Even from their distance, Woodbyrne looked menacing. Spending the night under the open skies was definitely not an option. "I'm positive that Mrs. O'Shan will be more than happy to take us in for the night, as long as we arrive before the sun has set."

"Then let us make haste," Quinn urged, as she kicked her mount into a run. In an instant, the two friends were racing up the long hill.

❧

Towards the latter part of the afternoon, the spotty clouds gave way to a setting sun that turned the gray overcast into a wild blend of bright oranges and reds. Aaron's mood lifted even higher when he saw a small column of smoke rising from the familiar cottage's chimney.

"I hope she remembers you," Quinn said. "If nothing else, I guess we could at least sleep in the barn."

"I doubt Mrs. O'Shan would forget me," Aaron said. "She is very kind and giving. Besides, she has much in common with us."

"How so?" Quinn asked, hoping that she could learn more about Mrs. O'Shan before she met her.

The prince answered his friend with a sad smile. "Like the both of us, Mrs. O'Shan lost a loved one to the demons. Many years ago, a demon took her husband, leaving her to live alone." Aaron swallowed hard. Would he ever be able to appreciate life again without his cousin? How would he survive without Byram there to watch over him and protect him?

By the time the prince had finished his short tale, he and Quinn were only a few yards from the cottage. Mrs. O'Shan could be seen in her kitchen, preparing a meal. When she heard the sound of the horses trotting up on the road, the kind lady dropped her utensils and ran for the front door, flinging it open and running up to greet her guests.

"Welcome back, my boy! I was beginning to get worried about you and—" Helinda stopped in her tracks when she saw the woman sitting on Byram's horse. "I don't even want to guess," the old woman said, as she approached Quinn, rubbing her horse's neck. "I hope he died for a just cause."

"Byram sacrificed himself in order to save Quinn and me from a horde of demons," Aaron explained, after clearing his throat and pushing back his grief.

"You went out to fight demons?" Helinda asked, her tone mixed with anger and surprise. "Are you a fool or did my story fall on deaf ears?"

Aaron got off his horse and tethered it to the fence post. "I did not enter the woods to fight demons," he began. "I wanted to explore it when I met the—"

Aaron was cut short by a wrinkled old hand held out in the air. "Speak no more out here in the open, Stephen Willows. Quickly, both of you, come inside and get ready for supper."

"I didn't know your name was Stephen," Quinn whispered to Aaron when Helinda was out of hearing range.

Aaron could not help but smile. "I was using a false name because I didn't want the whole kingdom knowing who and where I was."

"Why is that? Should I make up a name also?" Quinn asked, half joking with the prince. Aaron avoided her gaze as they walked up to the cottage.

Helinda smiled at her two guests as they entered her house. "I would also like to learn about your name, Mr. Willows."

Aaron's face dropped in disbelief. As they sat down for dinner Aaron wondered if she heard him speaking to Quinn. Or, if there was more to Helinda than met the eye.

~

The ample dinner prepared by Mrs. O'Shan was more than enough for the weary travelers. Starving from being on the road for so long, they said nothing during the meal. After the dishes were put away, and after the cherry pie was cut and served, their conversation began.

"I guess we both have some explaining to do, my dear," Helinda said to Aaron, trying to calm his nerves. "Why don't I go first?"

"If that's what you wish, then by all means," responded the prince, wiping his sweaty palms on his pants.

"I know that I appear to be a harmless old woman, but I am actually something a little more." Helinda got out of her seat and started to pace around the kitchen. "When my husband was killed those years ago, I was terrified that those monsters would seek me out and murder me for what I saw." The old farmer took a small drink of tea from her mug. "I went to see some priests and asked if there was someone who would be willing to teach me how to protect myself. In my search, I came across Brother Henry. He was a very old man and had the kindest smile." Helinda's memories of the loving priest brought a smile to her worn features. "Brother Henry said that he would make sure I'd never have to worry about demons again. Three times a week, he would come to my cottage and teach me the rules of being a priest. After I learned the basics, he taught me some protection and detection prayers." Mrs. O'Shan sat down next to Aaron and placed her hand on his shoulder.

"That's how you knew that I was not Stephen Willows?" asked the blushing prince. Helinda responded with a nod. "Then why were you so kind to my cousin and me?"

"Because," Helinda answered, "I could also detect that your cousin and you posed no threat to me or my farm. I could tell that you were good at heart, so I decided to allow you your privacy."

"Did you know that we were coming from Woodbyrne to visit you?" Quinn asked, referring to the full meal that was ready just minutes before she and Aaron arrived.

"Yes, and no. I have the power to detect the presence of beings that are close to my land. Woodbyrne is far out of my vision, although I would like to be able to see there someday. However, I knew that you were coming when you entered my sphere of sight and both of you looked like a mess. A hot meal is a weary traveler's best friend."

"I would say so." Quinn got up from her seat and kissed Helinda on the cheek. "It has been many years since I have had such an excellent meal. I thank you for it Mrs. O'Shan."

"I'm afraid that I haven't learned your real names yet." Helinda gave the prince a friendly wink.

"Quinn Brainard from Stovia," replied the spirited young woman. Quinn was happy that the old lady did not ask her for anything more than her name.

"I guess it's my turn to do some explaining," the embarrassed prince announced. "I am Aaron, Prince of Gower, son of King Dermot and Queen Audrey." Aaron went on to tell his entire story, explaining why he had decided to run away from home without saying a word to his parents. He also explained why he lied about his name, and why he had entered the woods, despite everyone's warnings. Finally, though it was not easy to do, Aaron explained how Byram died. When he had finished his story it was nearing midnight.

"That was a tale that could be heard hundreds of times and never grow stale," replied Mrs. O'Shan, who was completely enthralled.

Aaron would not admit it, but speaking about his emotions to another person relieved some of his stress and anguish.

"Mrs. O'Shan," said Quinn, no longer able to hold back the hundreds of questions that were flooding her mind, "how have you survived for so many years living so close to the borders of Woodbyrne?"

"As I said, I have the power to detect any being that comes into my small section in the world, especially those that are evil. My powers for detection are everlasting and I am very glad of that."

"What protection do you have if an unwelcome visitor attacked?" asked Aaron, now equally curious about the priestess's powers. He remembered Dusk from his adventure in Sharpsword. The old thief had looked like an ordinary person, but his appearance was just camouflage for a deadly killer. Aaron could see the similarities in Helinda.

"All of my workers have some basic training. My house also has some secret chambers where I can hide until the trouble has past. Brother Henry had very good connections with the dwarves from the mountains, and they came down at his request to construct the necessary precautions in my home. I have traps and secret doors that even the eyes of an elf could not find." The tired woman yawned long and hard; her weariness had overpowered her energy to speak. "It helps to have friends in high places," she assured her guests, finishing her tale. "You are both welcome to stay up as late you like, but I am off to bed." The kind woman yawned deeply and shuffled over to her bedroom. "I'll wake you up nice and early for breakfast."

※

The next day welcomed the companions with blue skies dotted with white, puffy clouds. The smell of a hearty breakfast wafted heavily in the air and the strong smell of hot tea helped open the traveler's eyes.

"Rise and shine, my friends!" Helinda called from the kitchen, as she prepared the table with a freshly cooked breakfast of eggs, ham and bread.

Quinn was the first to rise. She had slept well the night before and was looking forward to the open road. Aaron, on the other hand, took a little longer to get up since he had slept on the hard floor, which had done little to ease his weary bones.

"I hope you all like ham and eggs." Helinda said. It seemed that the long night of story telling did little to drown out the everlasting spirit of Mrs. O'Shan.

"I haven't had this good a breakfast in a very long time," Quinn admitted as she spooned a generous serving of meat onto her plate. Her father would usually be off at work or gambling when she got up in the morning, leaving her to fend for herself. With such a small amount of money available, Quinn was often left with day old bread and honey.

Breakfast went more quietly than dinner had. Aaron sat and ate while he tried to figure out the best route he and Quinn should take in order to get back to the castle. He knew they would make Sharpsword long before the day would end, and he wanted to take no part in the city's chicanery. The memories of dealing with Dusk plus the fight in the alley did little to comfort him. When he was with Byram, Aaron needed only to follow his partner's lead. Now, however, he was in charge, and that thought was a frightening one indeed.

"What are you thinking about?" Quinn asked, snapping Aaron back into the real world.

"I was contemplating how we should conduct the rest of our trip."

"I would say it's safe to spend the night out on the road," advised Helinda. "Staying in Sharpsword would delay you longer than you would like." The friendly woman cracked a wise smile. "Besides, I am positive that none of the demons are out of the forest. Whatever trouble you get into on the open road would pale in comparison to what you can get yourselves into in the town."

"I agree," said Aaron. He too was sure that the road would be the best choice, but he was having a difficult time following his gut instincts.

After breakfast, the two guests packed up their supplies and headed for their horses.

"I have blessed the both of you with a simple prayer of protection," said Helinda, "but I truly hope that you won't need it."

"Me, too." Quinn laughed as she mounted her horse and waited for her companion to join her.

Aaron was soon at her side, eager to return to a more familiar place. "Bless you, Helinda O'Shan!" he called as they made their way down the long, dusty road. "May we meet again under more favorable circumstances!"

Mrs. O'Shan waved the adventurers good-bye until she could no longer see them. All the while, the prince's last words hung heavily in her mind. "I don't think so, my prince. I don't think so. I have a bad feeling that the worst is still to come."

⤳

The morning passed on without incident while the two companions spoke to each other about their pasts.

"Why were you having such a hard time in deciding our course?" Quinn asked. "You should know these lands better than anyone else. After all, you are the prince."

Aaron simply shrugged his shoulders. How would she react to him confessing his weaknesses? How could she respect him if he was not even sure where they should sleep?

"Well," Quinn continued, expecting no response, "I think that you chose correctly. The road'll be much safer than a large town. Besides, Helinda blessed us both."

"I just want this entire trip to end," Aaron huffed, not taking his eyes off the road. "The hell that I have been through on this journey is more than I ever want to experience again."

Quinn could not take her companion's self pity any longer. "Prince Aaron!" she shouted. "Do you think you are the only one in the world who has suffered? I lost all my family and friends! Where am I to go? What do I do now? At least you still have a home waiting for you to return. At least your parents will be there with open arms." Tears began to roll down the young woman's cheeks as her emotions got the best of her.

Aaron just stared at the ground as the words of his partner hit him like a bag of stones. "I'm sorry for the way I'm acting, Quinn. It's just that I feel like the world is crushing me under its weight. Byram was my crutch, the answer for all of the dilemmas in my life." Aaron had a deep sense of hopelessness in his eyes. "What am I to do now that he is gone?"

"You are to get over it and be strong, Aaron," Quinn barked. "Did you plan to rule an entire kingdom one day with Byram hiding under your chair? I think the future of Gower is a grim one indeed if their future king cannot even decide if he should sleep out on the road or take a room in a stupid inn!" Quinn's words struck hard and deep. "I hate to alarm you, but Isidore is still alive and I doubt that he's going to let this incident go unavenged. Mrs. O'Shan knows that there is still much more ahead of us! Even if she did not tell us directly, I could see it in her eyes! We need to get back to the castle and tell the king, Aaron! I only pray that he is more of a man than his son."

"Don't you dare question the courage or the authority of the king!" the prince shot back. "He is more powerful than anyone in all of Oneira! People bow in his presence! You will be well advised to do the same, or he is likely to cut off your damn head!" The last sentence was a complete lie and the prince knew it.

"My head?" asked the fiery young woman, as she began to laugh.

Aaron also cracked a smile as he thought of how silly it would be if the king simply beheaded Quinn just because she did not bow. Suddenly, he joined in on the laughter. "I thank you for your directness, Quinn. I promise that I'll try to act more responsibly, but it's going to take a while for my sorrow to blow over. Byram was like a brother to me."

"I believe you, Aaron. Just remember that there will always be someone there to help you. Your cousin will never leave your heart as long as you don't forget he is there."

Aaron liked the way Quinn spoke to him. She reminded him of a mix between his mother and Byram, both caring and very strong. "We should make Sharpsword in just a few hours, but we will only pass through. If we leave the main road to go around the city, it will make our journey that much longer. Tonight, we will sleep under the stars. For now, I think we should set some sort of plan for how we are to get past the guards without raising unwanted curiosity."

The two friends made their way to Sharpsword, leaving behind them a little bit of their anger and frustrations. Aaron felt more like an adult than he ever had before. He still wished that Byram were around, however, and it would be a long time before he could stop grieving.

Quinn was relieved to express her feelings of losing her family. She still mourned the loss of her mother from years ago, but she had never been able to speak to her father about the matter. Robert was more like a baby-sitter to Quinn than a father, and that made it difficult for her to reach his inner emotions and feelings. Quinn found comfort in Aaron, though, and she was glad to use him as a target for her emotions. A large weight lifted from her shoulders that day, and she rode almost happily next to her new companion.

Chapter 14

I t was well into the afternoon when Quinn spotted the flags of Sharpsword blowing in the late summer's breeze. Although there was plenty of light left for them to make their way through, Aaron knew that their campsite would be a little too close for comfort.

"We're running late but I'm confident that we'll get through the city with enough time to make camp," Aaron said, reinforcing his plans and pushing aside his doubts. He was not so much worried about getting into a fight as he was of being noticed before he arrived at the castle.

"Is this an evil city?" asked Quinn, curious as to why her partner desired to put Sharpsword behind them so quickly.

Aaron almost laughed. "What isn't evil these days?" he asked sarcastically. "No, Sharpsword is actually a very friendly place, but I did meet some people there who I'd rather avoid this time around."

"Are you going to tell me what happened or will it stay your little secret?" Quinn was getting weary from the long ride and needed conversation to wake her up.

"Byram and I got into a fight soon after we dealt with a thief." The memories of the alley still made Aaron sweat and he truly wished that his cousin were with him. Byram's skill to recognize trouble was priceless. "Also," he went on, "some of the people I met seemed a little too interested in my business, if you know what I mean."

Quinn chuckled. "I guess no matter where you are in the world, people will always be the same. Stovia is much like Sharpsword. Except that we have gorgeous mountain ranges while you have to look at flat land all day."

"What is wrong with this countryside?" asked Aaron, a little insulted. "These lands are more fertile than any place on Oneira. Plus, this flat land leads to the ocean where you can escape the stale air of the villages."

"Or drown," Quinn added.

"Either way, I would like to leave Sharpsword long before I am discovered by Dusk and his crew of thieves. Dusk is so sinister he probably has plots against his closest friends and relatives."

"Then why did you even go to him in the first place?"

"We thought we needed a map of Woodbyrne and Dusk said he could provide one. We really had no choice in the matter." Aaron was getting more nervous the closer they got to the guard towers of the small city. As he went over his game plan, he remembered that he and his new partner should prepare for the bothersome questions the gatekeeper would ask them.

"Should I use my own name, or can I make up a good one like Stephen Willows?" the spirited woman teased, causing Aaron to blush.

"I think that Quinn is as good a name as any," Aaron replied. "Besides, nobody around here has ever seen you before."

"And what will you call yourself today?"

"I think I should stay with Stephen Willows."

"Are you sure that it wouldn't be safer if we went around the city instead of going straight through it?"

"Sneaking around a place as shady as Sharpsword would probably draw more attention," Aaron explained. "Plus, it would take much longer and I want to get back to the castle as quickly as possible."

"Then why not state that you are the prince of Gower and have us escorted back to the castle?"

"Why would I want to bring that sort of attention to myself? Especially when everyone will ask me where Byram is and where you came from. I'll have plenty of time for that once the king and queen get a hold of me."

↗

"Please state your name and reason for entering the city of Sharpsword, good people," a well-armed guard demanded as soon as the two visitors dismounted their horses and walked forward.

"My name is Stephen Willows and this is Quinn Brainard," said the prince as he pointed to his companion. "We seek only passage through your lovely city, for our journey is not yet finished."

"Where do the two of you come from?" the guard asked.

"We both hail from the east and we are on our way to the coast of Gower," Quinn added, hoping to ease the situation. "Our boat is to leave at noon in two days' time and we are in a bit of a rush. If you want," she continued, "you can escort us until we reach the far gate to make sure that we behave ourselves."

The burly guard began to laugh. He opened the gates and walked over. "I could not imagine the two of you being able to afford a journey on a boat. You both look like you come from the wild, if you ask me."

Just then, Aaron realized how filthy and unkempt he and Quinn looked. Even if he were to state he was Aaron, Prince of Gower, nobody would believe him. His facial hair had grown in and he smelled no better than a drunken sailor who had been out at sea for several months.

"Our business is our own, good sir," Aaron said. "My companion and I have had a very hard road thus far and all we seek is passage through your city. As my partner said, you may have us escorted to the other side if you like. If not, step aside and let us be on our way."

"No, that will not be necessary." The guard was taken aback by the stranger's tone. "Your business is your own. That is, of course, as long as your business does not involve ill intentions."

"We wish only passage through Sharpsword," Quinn insisted. "Our looks may be foreboding, but our intentions are certainly not."

"All right, then. Please, stay as long as you like. Our bathhouses are very good and you could shed the dirt and grime from the road. And out taverns are filled with good ale, good food, and good people."

"Thank you for your kindness, brave soldier," Aaron said with a smile. "I will be sure to spread the word of your hospitality all through-out my travels."

The trek through the small city went as Aaron had hoped, with few people even looking in their direction. Most men and women were busy working or shopping for goods while their children apprenticed, learn-ing the skills necessary to follow in their parents' footsteps.

Unbeknownst to Aaron, somebody did happen to notice the two strangers make their way through the crowded streets. From his room at the Lantern Inn, Dusk was busy watching everybody, as was his job. Although Dusk was in charge of the most powerful crime guild in Sharpsword, he had made many enemies in far off places, and was fearful that they would someday pay him a visit. The masterful thief and assassin rarely traveled outside before sunset. In fact, since he refused to meet with anyone before dark, his colleagues began to call him Dusk. The old man liked his nickname. He also liked the fact that nobody knew his true identity.

The thief's eyes gleamed and a thin smile cracked across his face as he recognized the young man. "Well, well," he purred softly. "It seems that my friend has returned from Woodbyrne alive." Although his former customer looked worn down and had a small beard, he took only a second to remember the face. "Ah, it seems that you have made and lost a friend along the way," he concluded, realizing that the older of the two men was replaced by a beautiful young lady. Quickly, Dusk grabbed his cloak and tied the hood tightly around his head in order to make sure that his face was well hidden. He had much to do in a short amount of time. Thoughts of wondrous treasures deep within the thick borders of Woodbyrne crossed the evil human's mind. Dusk hated secrets just as much as he hated the sunlight, and he knew that the two travelers were hiding something.

⁓

Aaron became very uneasy as he and Quinn rode past the Lantern Inn. He remembered the strange and unusual people whom he met there and only hoped that they were too busy drinking and fighting to notice him as they went by.

"Is that where you got into the fight?" Quinn asked, pointing to a dark alley that crept around the back of the inn.

"Yes, that's where Byram and I got attacked just after our deal was finished with the thief." Bad memories of that unfortunate night made Aaron sick to his stomach. "The fight was mostly my fault for being stupid, though now I'd know better."

"Sounds like your inexperience got you and your cousin into the fight," Quinn said.

For the most part, she was right, but the truth did little to stop the flood of guilt that Aaron was feeling. He knew that he had raised too much curiosity when he spilled the bag of coins and gems onto the table. "I got us into more trouble that you could ever imagine," the prince whispered as he sulked in his saddle.

Quinn had hoped that their earlier chat would be enough to lighten Aaron's spirits but it seemed that she was wrong. "I think we should mourn the loss of your friend once we are within the safety of the castle."

"I agree. Let's just worry about getting out of this place before I screw things up again."

$\sim$

Quinn and Aaron were about ten miles from the edge of Sharpsword when it was time to setup camp. Still not comfortable with their distance from the city's dangers, Aaron suggested that they take shifts throughout the night, and that he would take the first watch.

As the young prince sat quietly in the darkness, he felt as if a thousand eyes were watching him. To his surprise, nothing came leaping out of the shadows, and he was able to enjoy the small clouds that drifted through the night sky. Aaron was a bit hesitant when it was time to wake Quinn for her watch. Quinn looked so peaceful. Aaron wondered how such a lovely woman could ever survive the horror of being locked up in Isidore's caves. Still, despite his feelings, the prince was a Gower and treated women as his equal. He was certain that Quinn would be insulted if he allowed her to sleep the night away. "Quinn, Quinn, get up. My turn to snore."

"I don't snore!" replied a sleepy Quinn.

"I apologize," teased Aaron, "must have been someone sawing down a tree." Quinn popped him over the head with her makeshift pillow.

The weary young man curled up in his flimsy blanket and promptly fell asleep.

❧

Quinn had been on watch for nearly two hours, when she felt some sort of energetic pulse throbbing inside her head. Although she was not sure what could have been causing the unusual sensation, Quinn was certain that it was no ordinary feeling. Quickly, she drew her short-sword and crept toward Aaron. When she arrived at his blanket, she was surprised to find the young man crouching down with his sword in hand.

"Do you sense it too?" he asked. "It's like one big heartbeat inside of my brain." When Quinn nodded in agreement, Aaron quickly gestured for her to follow him. In a matter of seconds, he led her to an old fallen tree that would provide plenty of protection in case there was trouble. Both partners had the same expression; neither of them could figure out why they felt so comfortable behind the safety of the tree.

Another surge entered Quinn's body, immediately causing her to pull out a dagger. Aaron also felt the energy and found himself crawling on his stomach toward a pair of pine trees with his dagger clenched between his teeth.

Quinn caught a strange scent coming from the direction Aaron was heading toward. Suddenly, her keen eyes picked out three dark figures making their way toward the campsite. Apparently, they were stealthy warriors trying to make their way toward the cover of the tree.

Aaron had caught the scent too, and was more than ready to take advantage of the situation. Moving faster than he thought possible, he made his way to the last person of the small party and readied for the strike.

Sensing the inevitable, Quinn slowly made her way to the blind side of the three intruders. The tall grass and thick shrubs did well to hide her location, and she was positive that they would be heading her way, although she could not explain why.

When he had a clear shot, Aaron sprang into action. His sharp blade quickly dug into the side of the intruder's neck, slicing a thin line that was followed by a gush of crimson fluid. The surprised killer hit the ground, choking on his own blood.

The men that were sent to attack Quinn and Aaron were much more than a bunch of thieves, they were assassins! In an instant, the two remaining attackers drew their long-swords and worked the prince against the back of a large tree.

Quinn suddenly became overpowered with battle rage. Silently, she crept up behind the cloaked figures and sprang into action.

Just when Aaron figured his luck had come to an end, one of the dark fighters howled in pain as he grabbed the back of his knee. When the second assassin turned to see what caused his partner to scream, he was met with the hilt of a heavy dagger in the side of his temple and died instantly.

Quinn turned toward the remaining killer still gripping his wounded knee, and raised her blade high.

"He is to be kept alive!" ordered the prince, realizing that Quinn was ready to strike again. Apparently, whatever caused the two friends to act in such a primordial way was still embedded in the woman's mind and Aaron had to calm her down.

"Alive, for now," answered Quinn. She cleaned and sheathed her blade before going to get some rope. By the time she returned, her adrenaline had burned out.

⌇⌇

Helinda O'Shan sat at her kitchen table and sipped the last of her tea. "A pity," she murmured to herself. "I didn't want them to need my blessing so soon." The kind priestess placed her empty mug into the sink, yawned a little, and went to bed.

The protection blessing, called Guardian's Watch, was used primarily on guard dogs to help keep them alert and wary of intruders. However, through experimentation, Mrs. O'Shan had learned that the blessing's effects on humans gave them animal-like instincts and uncanny fighting abilities until all immediate threats were gone. Once the dangers had left, so too were the enhancements.

Although she had hoped that the protective powers of the prayer would not be needed, Mrs. O'Shan was pleased to know that she helped out in some small way.

◇

The injured assassin awaited the punishment that was surely going to befall him. However, to his surprise, his captors sat down in front of him as if they were preparing to have a nice conversation.

"Who sent you to kill us?" Aaron demanded. He had witnessed many interrogations performed by the king's soldiers and was certain that he could get some information out of the lowly killer. "Who was it, and be quick in telling me or I promise you that your death will be a slow and agonizing one!"

"I don't know," answered the nervous young man. He was barely eighteen by Aaron's guessing, and the sound of his voice was that of a child's.

"You're lying!" Quinn exclaimed, raising her dagger, ready to strike.

"Why were you sent here to kill us?" Aaron pressed.

"I'm not in charge," he pleaded, "all I know is that we were sent to take you back dead or alive."

"I grow tired of asking you the same question, you little runt," Aaron boldly said as he picked the prisoner up by the collar and slammed him to the ground. "Who was it that sent you? One more foolish answer, and I set my partner loose." Aaron looked over to Quinn, who was still holding the dagger at ready.

"Dusk sent us." blurted the assassin, finally geting the message that his captors meant business.

"Well," Aaron responded, as he grabbed the lad's slender neck with his large hand, "now it is your turn to send a message back to that old buzzard. You tell Dusk that he should do better than threaten the likes of Prince Aaron Gower anymore. That is unless he would like to see himself end up like his pitiful toadies."

"I'll give—him—the message." croaked the henchman, trying hard not to pass out from the lack of air. When Aaron felt satisfied that the young man had learned his lesson, he loosened his grip and allowed him to breathe.

"I'm afraid I can't allow you to be let off so easily," interrupted Quinn. She walked up to the frightened young man pointing her dagger at his throat and said, "Next time I run into you, you piece of filth, it won't be so pleasant! Now get out of here!" As Dusk's henchman ran off into the night, Quinn looked at the amazed prince and smiled. "We still have a few hours before morning, why don't you go back to sleep while I continue my part of the watch?"

Aaron eyed the beautiful woman suspiciously, wondering if she had any intentions of following the henchman. She could take care of herself and then some. "I guess I'll see you in the morning," Aaron said as he prepared to go back to sleep.

Quinn was still full of energy and decided to climb one of the tallest trees near the camp to better survey the darkness. Her eyes occasionally wandered to a certain bright star in the evening sky. "That was for you, mom," she whispered, hoping that somehow the spirit of her mother would hear her and respond. Quinn had little patience for the dredges of society. Her father had been surrounded by them and Quinn swore that she would never associate herself with their kind.

The rest of the night passed by without incident. Aaron slept comfortably against the warm earth while Quinn reminisced about happier times with her family. She imagined talking with each of them long into the night and only stopped to get a drink of water or to listen more closely to an odd sound. By the time the sky began to glow orange, Quinn felt better than she had in months.

Chapter 15

By mid-afternoon, Aaron was making his way through familiar land. The young runaway was almost home and a feeling of security and familiarity almost made him cry for joy.

"Why are you so happy, Aaron?" Quinn asked, pulling the prince back into reality.

"We're almost home." A week ago, if someone had told the prince that one day he would be happy to see his homeland, he would have laughed in their face. However, after experiencing such loss and despair for what seemed like an eternity, Aaron was overwhelmed with happiness by the usual sights and smells of Gower.

After they had traveled another hour, the vast countryside became dotted with small cottages and farms. As with the merchants in Sharpsword, most of the farmers were too busy with their daily chores to notice the two travelers as they passed by. However, to his despair, Aaron noticed that those who did recognize him through his grizzly face and beaten clothes stayed out of his path. Some even went so far as to run into their houses until their prince and his companion had passed.

"I thought you said we were close to the castle?" asked Quinn, surprised by the way the people were acting.

Aaron's confused look did not help the matter. "We are only a few hours from the castle," he explained. "I know many of these people and I would have hoped for a warmer welcome." The prince thought long and hard for a moment before his eyes widened in shock. "The king likely sent his men out to look for me," he concluded, "and I'll bet they searched the surrounding homes and farms more than a few times looking for me."

"Ah, so they blame you for the violations," Quinn answered. "I guess I can understand that. I know I'd be angry if my home was invaded by a bunch of angry soldiers."

"Thanks for making me feel just a little bit better," Aaron shot back. Still, as usual, Quinn's words rang true. Aaron was to blame for the citizens' breach of privacy and he only hoped he could make it up to them one day, that is if the king and queen didn't kill him first.

Suddenly, a banner bearing the Gower crest appeared over a hilltop no more than half a mile from where the two friends were bickering.

"They found us," Aaron said miserably. "He sent them to get us."

In a moment, four soldiers dressed in the colors of the kingdom rode up on some of the most beautiful horses Quinn had ever seen. Ahead of them, a man dressed in clothes that identified his native heritage led the small search party. Although the much taller and much darker man appeared to be an outcast from the others, he held a powerful aura that could not be ignored. Self-confidence and pride radiated from his weather-beaten face, and his peaceful demeanor calmed all who surrounded him.

"Who is that odd-looking fellow?" Quinn asked bluntly.

"His name is Lennox Softfoot," Aaron answered, stunned that his father would call on such a person to find him. "He is a native to these lands and is the most respected scout in Gower. He and my father became friends long ago, when his ancient relatives still had some territories in these parts." Aaron remembered Lennox from when he was a boy. The peaceful and respected native had trained scores of scouts for the king's army, and had even taught Byram and Aaron a few things along the way. "When his family decided to head to the north, Lennox stayed behind." Aaron smirked at the thought of someone so willing to leave his old lifestyle behind. "Apparently, he felt that he owed my father his services for what the king had done for him and Clan Softfoot."

"What did King Dermot do?" Quinn was more interested in the prince's story than she was in the approaching soldiers.

"It's what he didn't do that earned the trust and respect of the tribes." Aaron dismounted his horse and tied it to a nearby tree, returning to Quinn's side to wait for the unavoidable meeting with his father's men. "The natives lived in these parts well before even my oldest relatives were born. When my ancestors, and the ancestors of our neighboring lands, came to settle in this area, they paid little attention to the tribes."

As the prince spoke, Lennox dismounted his horse and made his way over. Quinn and Aaron were so deep into their conversation that they did not even see him approach.

"However, not too long ago, medicines brought in from the east helped our populations explode and our lands needed to be expanded. Unfortunately for the ancient tribes, the kings and queens of those lands waged war against the natives. They were merciless, killing women and children like a bunch of savages. My great-grandfather, King William, took a much more peaceful approach with Clan Softfoot. Together, they helped the kingdom of Gower expand while allowing the natives to lead a peaceful and prosperous life. No Softfoot had ever been struck down by one of Gower's soldiers, plus they had our full support if they ever found themselves in the predicament of war."

Quinn felt something was missing. "Then why did they go north?"

"Twenty years ago, a treaty was signed by all of the kings in this part of the world to set aside a place for the natives to live if they so desired. The section of land had plenty of room for the beaten tribes to replenish their numbers and renew their spirits."

"My tribe was the last to take the offer and head north," a voice with a very thick accent interrupted. "It was a hard decision for the elders to agree upon, but in the end they thought it best for the tribe."

"Why did you stay behind?" Quinn asked, forgetting the more pressing matter of Aaron's return home after such a long absence.

"Because the man who stood behind the treaty and who would have died for the cause of Clan Softfoot was King Dermot. I felt that I owed my friend the same loyalty that he gave to me and my people. So, when my family headed north, I said my farewells and declared Gower my permanent home." The soft-spoken scout walked up to Quinn and bowed his head, his long and intricately decorated ponytail dropping forward. "I am Lennox Softfoot of the Clan Softfoot."

"I am Quinn Brainard from Stovia, good sir."

The seasoned scout turned his attention toward Prince Aaron, who was wishing that he was still with Isidore or lost somewhere in

Woodbyrne at that moment. "You have greatly disappointed your father," he said. "I do not even wish to know why you and Byram left the kingdom, nor do I desire to hear how one of the most skilled fighters I have ever known died on the journey."

"How did you know of Byram?" asked Aaron.

"My people have very close ties with the spirit world, Aaron Gower." Lennox walked up to the prince and grabbed both of his arms. "Your cousin's soul has been lost to us, young one. He will never know the true meaning of life." Lennox looked up into the sky and shook his head.

The tall scout instructed the prince and Quinn to follow him and his men back to the castle. Their pace was fast, and just as the sun was setting, Aaron saw the banners of his kingdom flying proudly over Castle Gower. The red sky added to the beautiful backdrop of the ancient structure. "How many times I would walk through those huge halls and not even stop to think about the history behind my heritage," Aaron said to Quinn. Soon the archery range came into sight and the prince was overcome with grief. "Why did you leave me?" he whispered to himself. "Why?"

When the small party reached the front gates, they dismounted their horses and stretched from the long ride. Lennox ordered the soldiers to take the beautiful mounts back into the stables where they could relax and eat. He led Quinn and Aaron through the courtyard and to the large front doors.

Quinn could not believe where she was. She knew that Aaron was a prince, but would never have guessed what that really meant until she witnessed the splendor of the castle for herself. Even the stables put her in awe. "The horses live a better life than most people," she said. Only the edges of the Royal Garden could be seen from the front entrance, yet Quinn could smell the sweet pollen and nectars from the thousands of bulbs and flowers that occupied it. The castle itself seemed to grow in size as she approached it, with its main entrance adorned with huge double doors made of solid oak and stained to a dark auburn. No special decorations were engraved upon their massive bulk, but their plain appearance only enhanced the powerful structure of the rest of the castle.

"I think it would be best if the young lady is led to one of the guest rooms while you see your parents," suggested Lennox. "They will want to speak to you first."

"I guess that would be best," agreed Aaron reluctantly. "See to it that she is given a hot bath, food, and some better clothing."

"Of course, Prince Aaron," replied the noble scout. Lennox led her down the hall, leaving the prince behind.

How do I do this? Aaron asked himself. Can I do this? Aaron had stood in the hallway for only a few seconds when he heard the boom of his father's voice echo off the stone walls and into his heart.

"Aaron!" the king shouted. "Get in here now, before I come and get you myself!"

The prince headed up the spiral staircase that led to his parents' private bedchamber. The doors of the beautifully decorated room were left open, adding to the prince's discomfort. From the inside, the young man could hear his mother trying to calm his father down from his rage. "This is not going to be pleasant at all," Aaron whispered as he tried to calm down. After a deep breath, Prince Aaron stepped inside his parents' room, expecting nothing but the worst.

As soon as he entered the room, the doors closed behind him, creating even more tension. King Dermot and Queen Audrey were dressed in their casual clothing and it looked as if they had not slept in a very long time. The queen's hair seemed a bit grayer than he remembered.

"There is much to explain, young man," scolded the queen, who, at that point, was fighting the urge to embrace her only son. How could she be so angry when the day before she feared she had lost him forever.

"Your mother and I," interrupted King Dermot, who was more angry than anything else, "have been in a state of shock over the past few days. I pray that you have a good enough reason for running off with Byram. Your note did not tell us where you went or when you'd be back." The king slammed his fist down on the nearby server table sending a tray of cups and plates crashing to the floor. "Running off like some fool! Do you have any idea what you put us through? Your mother and I have not been able to sleep or eat since that morning you ran off!"

"How do I begin to explain? So much has happened." Aaron hung his head, his grief and shame evident.

"Why don't you start from the beginning?" suggested King Dermot after a few deep breaths.

For the next couple of hours, Prince Aaron went over his entire story with his parents. He left out no detail and even explained the death of his cousin, albeit with great remorse and emotion. King Dermot and Queen Audrey had to stop and console one another for a long time when they heard of their nephew's untimely death. Afterwards, Aaron spoke of Quinn and their experiences with the elves and the struggles they had to overcome in order to escape from the darkness of Woodbyrne.

"My son," the queen said as calmly as she could, "I am not angry at you for desiring an adventure and some independence. However, how you accomplished those goals is inexcusable."

"I cannot believe that Byram is lost to us forever," grieved the king. "I had come to love that boy as a son."

"It is a loss for the entire kingdom," added the queen. "A part of me has truly died along with Byram."

"I know that the both of you probably blame me for all of this," Aaron said. "I am sure the entire kingdom will look at me as my cousin's killer!" The emotions that were swelling inside the prince suddenly erupted in uncontrollable sorrow. Aaron fell on his knees and began to cry. Audrey ran to his side and tried to console him, but to no avail.

Dermot also came over to his lamenting family and placed them in a loving hug. "We will overcome this," he said. "Byram's spirit will live in each of us, forever."

"I killed him," Aaron lamented, "I killed my own cousin! I coaxed him into entering the forest! I begged him to enter the cave! It was me who should have died by the hands of Isidore!"

"True, Byram's loyalty to you clouded his judgement. But, each person has control over their own lives. Byram made the choice to follow you," explained the king. "Byram, like yourself, desired the excitement from confronting unspeakable dangers. He could not have asked for a more noble death, Aaron. The two of you put yourselves at great risk for a stranger, and that is commendable." Dermot sat down on his bed and looked upon his wife and son.

"There is one other thing," the prince said. "I promised the wood elves of the forest that I would tell you of their plight."

"And what of their plight?" asked the king with a confused look on his tired face.

"They are a dying race. The demons are too powerful and too numerous. Soon, they will wipe out the wood elves forever."

"I'm afraid I don't follow you Aaron," King Dermot replied. "What exactly did you tell these elves?"

"I told them that you might be willing to send troops to Woodbyrne to aid the elves in their cause."

"That is an overwhelming task, Aaron. You should have thought twice before making such a bold statement."

Aaron was having mixed feelings on the matter. Part of him wanted to push his father further along the topic while the other part wanted to forget Woodbyrne forever.

The king got off of the bed and stood behind his son. "Aaron, it is not that I want the demons to wipe out the elves, it is just that I have a responsibility to the people of this kingdom. I will not send out my army to fight and die for the causes of the elves when it is none of my business to do so. The people of this kingdom will not understand why I would send their loved ones off to fight a war that has nothing to do with Gower. Besides, I have heard from many people that the wood elves are not to be trusted."

"But they saved my life. They got me out of Woodbyrne. What more do they need to do to prove themselves?"

After a long pause, the king continued. "I will talk this over with my advisors, Aaron. But I will not make any promises. It is a sensitive matter and one that may take some time to resolve."

"Don't worry, Aaron," Queen Audrey whispered into her son's ear. "Things happen for a reason. All of this is part of a larger scheme, which we just don't understand yet."

The queen was right. Aaron did not understand.

Woodbryne: The fallen forest

◌

Quinn had taken a warm bath and had changed into the fresh, clean clothes Lennox had given her. Although she only intended to relax on the huge bed, its comfort was overwhelming, and she quickly had fallen asleep.

Like the sound of a hammer, a loud knock startled Quinn out of her slumber. "Who is it?" she asked, after a good stretch.

"The king and queen call for your immediate presence, Quinn Brainard," replied a stern yet friendly voice from behind the door.

Quinn jumped out of bed and swung the door open, revealing a well-dressed Royal Guard. "They want to see me now?"

"Yes, King Dermot and Queen Audrey are waiting for you in the main audience chamber."

"Am I dressed properly?" Quinn asked. "Shouldn't I be wearing a gown or something a bit more respectful?" Although her clothes were made from the finest materials, they were no more than a simple pair of pants, a plain blouse, and leather boots.

"I would not worry, my lady," replied the guard with a soft chuckle. "Besides, you are wearing the queen's clothes."

"The queen's clothes?" Quinn suddenly felt a little lightheaded.

"I wouldn't be so nervous if I were you," the guard assured. "The royal family are some of the friendliest people in the world. I have yet to meet someone who had anything sour to say about them."

◌

It took a few minutes to reach the main audience chamber and Quinn was glad for that. Not only did the lengthy walk give her more time to calm down, but Castle Gower was truly one of the most beautiful places she had ever seen, with tall cathedral ceilings and enormous tapestries and paintings that dated back hundreds of years. One painting in particular caught Quinn's attention. It was a beautiful painting of the sun setting behind a cluster of snow-capped mountains. The painting reminded Quinn of her homeland.

"The Gowers like their nature, don't they?" Quinn asked, realizing that most of the decorations hung on the walls were scenes of great mountain ranges and lush forests.

"Yes, King Dermot is quite the nature lover," replied the escort. "He has spoken to many druids on how best to care for the land. He even set aside many acres of the kingdom that are never to be touched. Many believe Lennox Softfoot and his tribe had convinced the king and queen that open land is as precious as gold and jewels."

"Is the queen as kind as King Dermot?" Quinn wanted to get a better idea of how to act in front of Gower's royalty.

"Queen Audrey is to the people what King Dermot is to the land. She cares deeply for Gower and would die for its people." The guard quickly became silent as he turned a corner that led to the audience room.

"I guess this is it?" Quinn asked, feeling very nervous.

"Yes, this is it. I'll open the doors and escort you in front of the king and queen. I will introduce you and you will curtsy. When I leave, you are on your own, but don't worry. I am sure you will be just fine."

"What if I faint?"

"Don't faint."

The guard pushed open the large doors and led Quinn down a long, carpeted aisle. King Dermot and Queen Audrey sat patiently on their thrones as Quinn slowly made her way toward them. It felt like she was walking for miles and her legs became like jelly. Quinn could not believe the majesty of the audience chamber. It was adorned with giant statues made of imported marble from far off lands across the Frosty Sea and paintings that were at least fifty feet high and fifty feet wide. Hundreds of stained glass windows adorned the walls and cast down a prismatic sphere on the polished marble floor below.

"Quinn Brainard, as you requested, your majesties," announced the guard.

Quinn curtsied as best she could in front of her royal hosts.

"That will be all," said the king, sending his servant out of the room.

"Please relax, my dear," insisted Queen Audrey. "You are among friends here, so there is no need to be nervous."

"Like my wife said," added the king, as he stepped down from his throne and approached the nervous woman, "you are among friends." He bowed and kissed Quinn's hand. "Welcome to Castle Gower, Quinn Brainard of Stovia. I am Dermot and this is my wife, Audrey."

The queen stood up from her chair and nodded her head. "A pleasure to meet you, Quinn Brainard."

"A pleasure to meet the both of you," the flustered young lady blurted. "I am sorry if I seem a bit nervous, but I have never met with royalty before."

"Not to worry," assured Audrey, as she sat back in her plush throne. "I am sure you will feel at home in no time."

The soldier that had escorted Quinn to the audience chamber came back into the room carrying a small, cushioned chair. Maids carrying silver plates laden with fresh fruits and breads and a butler carrying a small table followed him. The chair was placed next to Quinn and the plates of food were put neatly on top of the table.

"I hope you understand why we are so anxious to hear everything that happened." said the king, as he went back to his wife and sat down. "This is your time, and I hope that you can find the strength to tell us your story."

Quinn poured herself a glass of fresh orange juice and ate some bread before beginning her story. Then, after some deep breaths, she told the king and queen her entire life's story, eventually leading to her rescue from the demons by Aaron and Byram. It was well into the evening hours when the young lady finished her side of the story.

"Thank you, Quinn," said Dermot. "You must be tired. Why don't you retire to your quarters and get a good night's rest."

"Thank you both for listening," replied Quinn who bowed and made her way out of the hall. When she closed the large doors behind her, the same guard who brought her there was waiting patiently to escort her back to her room.

"Thank you for waiting, but I remember the way back," Quinn said.

"As you wish. The king has informed us that you are permitted to walk freely among the castle as an honored guest. I understand your desire for privacy so I'll let you find your way back to your quarters alone." He saluted Quinn and left to attend to more urgent matters.

After the guard had left, Quinn walked slowly and silently to her room. Once she had entered her quarters, Quinn slid under the covers that adorned her bed. In a matter of minutes, she was fast asleep.

⌒

The next morning, Quinn awakened to the sound of exotic song-birds welcoming the new day. She felt energized; her night's sleep had gone completely uninterrupted and the walls of the large castle helped give her a sense of protection from any outside dangers.

"Quinn," a voice from behind her locked door called. "Quinn, it is time for breakfast."

Quinn put on a robe that she found hanging in her closet and opened the door. Prince Aaron, looking less refreshed than she did, stood miserably in the hallway with a blank expression on his face. "Good morning," she greeted.

"Did you rest well?" the prince asked, after a long, drawn out yawn.

"Yes, very nicely." Quinn noticed the dark circles under Aaron's eyes and realized the prince had not slept well at all. As she followed the young man to breakfast, she decided it would be best to remain silent.

"Good morning, Quinn," greeted the Queen, who was sitting next to the king at the head of a rather humble table. The room they had entered was quite small in comparison to the rest of the castle. Little vases filled with flowers decorated the walls, and the one window, which looked out over the Royal Garden, helped bring in the plentiful fragrances from the outside. Quinn had been expecting a more luxurious-looking banquet room and her surprise was easily read by her hosts.

"When we eat alone," the king explained, "I find that this room fits us quite nicely." Dermot helped himself to another generous portion of scrambled eggs and ham from a large plate. "The queen and myself feel that we should keep a more family-oriented atmosphere when there are no guests to entertain."

"Am I not a guest?" asked Quinn, as she sat and grabbed a large muffin from the table.

Audrey looked at her family with a smile on her beautiful face. She had taken a liking to Quinn, and the strong woman's spirit reminded the queen of herself when she was younger. Audrey used to get into many fights with other girls when she was in finishing school because she did not fit in with their elaborate upbringing. Apparently, she enjoyed playing war more than she did learning proper etiquette. Quinn was a diamond in the rough and Audrey wanted to reveal her power to the world.

"Well, you are a guest today, but a very special one." The Queen gave Dermot a swift kick in the shins in order to stop him from stuffing his face with food. "But," she continued, "you are welcome to stay here for a while longer if you like."

Quinn could not believe her ears. How could she say no to such an opportunity? "I would love to stay longer. How long would you like me to stay?" she asked.

The king and queen both stood up at the same time. Audrey walked up to Quinn and took her by the hands. "We would like you to live here with us," she answered.

"I—I don't know what to say," Quinn stuttered, almost choking on her raspberry muffin. She had wondered many times where she would go once she reached the castle, and the very thought of returning to Stovia never settled too well in her mind.

"We could train you and teach you skills in whatever your heart desires," added the king, making the offer that much more tempting.

"What if my heart shouts for the life of a fighter?" asked Quinn with a doubtful tone in her voice. "What if I want to learn about fencing or archery?"

"Well, then we will train you in all of those things plus more," answered the queen.

Quinn's smile spread from ear to ear.

Even Aaron, sulking in his misery, could not hide his happiness over the idea of having Quinn stay with them. He enjoyed the strong woman's will and the way she presented herself. As pretty as Quinn was, Aaron saw a good friend with a heart of gold and a spirit like the wind. He had needed her sense of humor and reality during their recent journey, and he was sure that he would need it again, in the future.

"Well," asked Audrey, "what do you think?"

Quinn turned to the prince and saw that he, too, was smiling. How could she resist? "I'll stay."

Interlude

D amek soared through the familiar halls of Isidore's dungeon
with great remorse. It seemed that only the day before, Isidore
had granted the demon scout permission to take an extended vacation
from his master's services. Damek began to drool when he thought of
the feasting that he had enjoyed while away from the constrictions of
the cave. The hogs and venison outside of Woodbyrne held a much
better flavor than the diseased ones that still hung around the evil forest.
The vile scout laughed as he remembered the torture he placed on the
unsuspecting people he encountered throughout his explorations. "Pitiful humans," the fierce creature growled under its foul breath, "they
hardly put up a fight at all."

"Damek, I swear I will kill you if you delay me one more second!"
an angry voice boomed from down the dark corridor. The Demon Master of Woodbyrne was a very impatient ruler. It had been nearly one
week since the humans entered his domain and had stole Quinn Brainard,
his most prized possession. Since then, the evil master planned on the
many ways in which he could act out his revenge. Still, whether he liked
it or not, Isidore needed the help of his favorite scout and second-in-
command. Only Damek, with his ability to blend in with the shadows,
could spy on the prince and Quinn without being discovered. Only
Damek, with his leathery wings and lightning fast reflexes, could stand
the chance of infiltrating one of the most heavily guarded castles on
Oneira.

In seconds, the huge doors swung open and the demon scout flew
into the large room. "You called for me, my master?" Damek asked, as
politely as he could, although disgust was written all over his face. Damek
hated the fact that he had to grovel to Isidore.

"I hope that you had a relaxing vacation?" Isidore asked with a smile,
although he truly couldn't have cared less.

"Yes, I did—"

A knee to the groin and a head-butt to the face cut Damek in mid-sentence and threw him across the large room. As it did many times in the past, decrepit black blood oozed freely from the scout's nose and mouth, staining the floor and covering his dark scales.

"While you were away," Isidore began, "we have had a bit of a problem with our security. It seems that you are not capable of training my legion of fighters to keep watch of my home!" Isidore picked Damek up by his throat and flung him hard against the wall. The demon master frequently vented his frustrations on his followers.

"I am more than capable of training your men, my master," Damek assured his enraged master. "I shall punish those responsible without delay!"

Isidore laughed at the very thought of letting his servant off so easily. "I have already taken care of that, you fool." He snapped his fingers and a puff of smoke popped in the center of the room. When the cloud vanished, at least two dozen corpses were lying on the floor. The encrusted blood stains and foul stench suggested the murders had taken place more than a few days before.

"Mercy!" pleaded Damek. "Mercy, my master! I swear that I shall never let you down again!"

"You sicken me!" Isidore bellowed. Then, remembering that he needed Damek, an evil smile found its way onto his face. "Now, Damek, you and I will go over some plans that I have come up with over the past few days."

"What plans, Isidore?" the demon asked, wiping the blood from his nose and mouth.

"Plans for revenge!" Isidore drooled at the very thought of making Prince Aaron suffer for what he did to him. "Revenge for the two humans who made it out of my dungeon alive!"

"I hope that I have a part in all of this?" asked the scout.

"You do, my friend. You have the best part of all." Isidore reviewed his plans with Damek and gave him his assignment.

Dismissed by Isidore, Damek headed back to his own chamber. On the way, he dreamed of his recent vacation. How he wished he were back out under the night sky! The demon scout knew that his master would never give him the freedom he desired. "Someday I'll rule my own section of this rotten world," Damek swore, "someday."

✬

It was a cool night in Gower. Not a cloud was in the sky and the harvest moon shined its light upon the land like a small, sun. Quinn Brainard walked through the Royal Garden with a sense of peace that evening, something that she had not felt since her mother was alive. The past two weeks at Castle Gower did much to flush the memories of Woodbyrne out of her mind. Weapons training and scholastics had kept the young woman very busy. Yet, no matter how hard Quinn tried to forget the dark forest, she could not forget the wood elves. The thought of their sufferings made her weep every time, and Quinn longed for the day that she could visit the wood elves under more peaceful conditions.

"Aaron?" the young woman called into the darkness, remembering her true purpose for that evening's walk. "Aaron, where are you?"

The prince had not been present at dinner and was not in his room. Quinn thought he might be at the memorial in the garden and promised the King and Queen to look for him at once. When she came to the open circle in the middle of the garden, she spotted Aaron kneeling under the large marble statue of the now-famous Byram Edelmar. Quinn decided to stay back for a few moments in order to give her friend his privacy.

The statue stood over ten feet tall and was carved out of marble. Quinn was amazed at how fast it had been constructed. Some folk even said that the king's wizards and priests had a hand in its creation. The statue's platform, made entirely of polished onyx, read:

IN MEMORY OF BYRAM EDELMAR
MAY HIS SPIRIT LIVE AS FREELY IN THE
AFTERLIFE AS IT DID ON ONEIRA

After a few minutes, Aaron stood up. "I guess my parents were looking for me," he said suddenly.

"Yes, they were." Quinn replied. "I told them I'd find you."

"Thank you, Quinn." Aaron turned around and approached his new friend. Fresh tears still clung to his cheeks. "Thank you for everything you said to me. I have talked to my cousin for a long time this evening and I feel as if I made my peace with him. Your words of friendship and understanding helped me in my time of sorrow, and now I have true meaning in my life, a goal to accomplish."

Quinn was glad that Aaron had come to terms with his sorrow, but what were these new feelings he had? Why was he acting so peculiar? "Do you still have some unsettled business to take care of?" she asked.

The queer look on Aaron's face changed again. "I need help, Quinn. I find it very hard to forget Woodbyrne."

Quinn understood all too well how he felt.

"On one hand, I want revenge for Byram. I want to charge into that cave and kill Isidore with my bare hands." Aaron approached Quinn and held her shoulders. "But on the other hand, I am not ready to go back just yet. To tell you the truth, I am afraid."

"I'm finding it hard to forget them too, and I want to go back and fight, but we have to be ready first. Woodbyrne was a horrible experience, but you made a promise to the elves," Quinn said. "You need to think long and hard about your responsibilities to the kingdom and to the elves." Quinn placed a gentle kiss on Aaron's forehead and grinned.

"Soon," the prince reasoned. "When my father comes up with a plan, then we will return."

Aaron accompanied Quinn back to the castle feeling relieved that she faced the same difficulties. "Our enemies will know what it is like to be hunted down and murdered," he assured his friend as they faded into the darkness of the garden. "They will dread ever entering this world in the first place."

Chapter 16

"**A**aron!" Byram shouted as a demon tore the liver from his open torso. "Save me, Aaron!"

The prince picked up his sword and ran after the demons that were murdering his cousin. "Byram, stay alive!"

The nasty creatures were now tearing the flesh off Byram's exposed face, yet the brave archer was only focused on his cousin. "Aaron, help me!"

Aaron ran up to the demon attacking Byram and raised his sword. Just as he was about to strike, something blasted the air from his lungs. Once Aaron regained his bearings, he found himself in Quinn's arms.

"Byram is already dead, Aaron," she reasoned. "Save yourself!"

"Please don't leave me, my cousin!" begged the archer. He was now covered in thick gore as the demons continued their work.

"I can't leave my own cousin!" argued the prince, but to no avail. Quinn's arms turned into giant chains, their metal links digging deep into Aaron's arms. "What good is he to us?" she asked. "He is but fodder." Her eyes became yellow orbs and blood poured from her mouth. "Save me instead!"

"I'm dying Aaron!" Byram pleaded. "How can you just stand there?"

"There is nothing I can do!" Aaron shouted to his cousin, who was missing an arm and a leg. The prince turned his attention to Quinn, whose entire face was covered in blood. Two ram's horns grew from the side of her head. Her arms, still gigantic chain links, tightened painfully around Aaron's muscular arms with each passing second.

"Help—me—Aa—Aaron!" Byram began to choke on his own blood as the demons began to work on his neck.

"Your friend is mine!" The creature holding Aaron said in a deep, unearthly tone. "You're next!"

Aaron knew only fear at that moment. He turned to Byram only to see a demon drinking the blood from his decapitated skull. He could take the punishment no longer. "The hell with you!" Aaron shouted at the disfigured monster. "Get off of me!" The prince desperately bit into the chained arm of the monster and somehow drew blood...black blood.

The monster released its hold and howled in agony. Aaron, knowing that his luck was not going to last much longer, stumbled to his feet and began to run for the exit of the cave.

"Aren't you forgetting something?" teased an all-too-familiar voice.

Aaron turned around to see Isidore standing before him. In his hand, the demon held the head of Byram Edelmar. "How could you leave without your beloved cousin?" asked the beast before hurling the head at Aaron.

Byram's head flew through the air but its eyes never left the prince. "Aaron! How could you do this?" it screamed horribly before it slammed onto the ground with a sickening crunch.

"Now it's your turn, Prince!" shouted Isidore, who was holding an unusually large double-headed axe. The demon master ran toward the prince at full speed.

Aaron tried to run but found himself chained to the floor by two large braces. He tried desperately to break free of the bonds, but to no avail. When he looked up, Isidore was no more than a few inches away.

"Your time has come to an end, foolish mortal!" taunted the demon, whose voice promised nothing short of death.

Aaron was a fighter, however, and refused to die easily. Miraculously, the braces snapped free and he fell on his backside, allowing the deadly axe to sail dangerously close to his neck. He turned to face his assailant, but to his surprise, Isidore had vanished. Only the eerie head of Byram was present, its eyes still focused on the prince. Still far from safety, Aaron got to his feet and made his way down the long corridor. A blood-red light seemed to emanate off of the walls and the floor began to get very soft. Aaron tried hard to keep his calm and make his way toward the exit of the cave.

"Do you really think I am going to let you escape?" asked a voice that surrounded the prince.

"Leave me alone!"

"I am going to feed on your bones like I did your cousin's," the voice continued. "You know, Aaron, I am glad that you and your friend entered my little home. It had been a while since one of you spoiled brats entered Woodbyrne."

Aaron began to run faster through the caves, frantically turning at every corner as if it would lead to the forest. At one of the dozens of turns that Aaron took, the ground gave way and he started to sink into a warm, bloody muck. Just as the vile mud was about to close over his mouth, Aaron stopped moving. In front of him, the ground began to bubble and a figure slowly rose out of the slime. When the body was fully out of the ground it stood at least six feet over the prince, but it made no movement. The muck and gore that covered it began to slide off onto the floor, revealing little by little who was trapped in the ground.

"No!" Aaron screamed. "You fiends!"

It was Henry Dermot. The entire left side of his head was caved in and his arms and legs were twisted and broken. Still, Aaron remembered the picture of his uncle that hung on the library wall.

"Why have you come here?" Henry asked, his voice sounding as if his throat had been crushed. "Why have you come to Woodbyrne?"

Aaron began to cry. "I wanted to see what was in here," he explained. "I wanted to be like you!"

"Well, now you are like me, Aaron." The large man grabbed the prince by the hair, lifting him straight out of the ground. "Now you are dead!" Henry smiled wickedly and slammed his nephew's head into the soft ground, almost snapping his neck in the process.

Aaron tried hard to hold his breath but the slimy, red mud made its way into his mouth. He could still feel his uncle's hand pushing him deeper and deeper into the mud. The mud made its way to his throat and he began to choke.

"No!" the prince screamed, his voice echoing off his bedroom walls. "No!"

Aaron sat up in his bed and took a deep breath. It was all a dream, he reasoned to himself. The young man got out of bed and nervously walked around the dark room. It had been over a month since Aaron told his father about the elves. Since then, the king put together a small committee to discuss the matter. But, like so many committees before them, no definite plans had been made. And with no firm deadline to work by, there was no telling when a plan would be finalized.

"When will this madness end?" the prince asked himself. Aaron had seen who the person in the mud was, and it disturbed him greatly. Were the dreams he was having a call for help, or a warning of things to come?

Aaron yawned and walked back to his bed. Just as he was about to lie down, he heard a noise from outside his window. Quickly, Aaron ran over and looked outside.

The moon was in all its glory that evening. Not a cloud dotted the sky and the constellations could easily be seen from the castle. However, despite the beauty of the night, something did not feel right. A pair of bright red eyes stared at Aaron from behind a tall shrub, not moving, not blinking. Aaron rubbed his eyes. When he focused back on the shrub, he saw that the eyes were no longer there. A wave of panic flooded the prince's mind and he frantically looked in all directions for the frightening orbs.

Suddenly, not fifty feet away from their original site, the two red eyes peered at the prince. Aaron had but a mere second to spot them before they disappeared from sight. Aaron grabbed his sword and rushed out of his bedroom. When he was outside, he ran directly to the spot where he last saw the spectacle.

"Come out, you coward!" Aaron called into the night. His only response was the noise of a few startled birds. "Come out and face me, one on one!"

"Who's down there?" asked a startled guard. "Is that you, Prince Aaron?"

"Where is it?" the prince asked his servant.

"Where is what?"

"The demon!" Aaron began to run through the garden, cutting his legs on the sharp thorns and branches. "Where is Byram's killer?"

The guard knew better than to wake the king and queen so late into the evening, so he ran for Quinn's private chamber.

Aaron continued his tirade on the Royal Garden and he had no intentions of stopping his mad hunt until he either passed out from exhaustion or if he found the creature that was spying on him.

"Aaron!" called a familiar voice. "Aaron, where in the blazes are you?"

"One of them made its way to the castle!" he shot back. "I saw it with my own eyes!"

"There is nobody here, Aaron," Quinn assured as she approached her panic-stricken friend. "It's just you and me."

Aaron knelt to catch his breath. Quinn had become the voice of reason over the past month. "I guess you are right, Quinn. Still, I saw something out here."

Quinn knelt down next to her friend. "I am sure you saw something," she agreed. "But maybe you made it out to be something that it isn't." The reasonable woman looked at Aaron and sighed. "Did you have another one of your dreams?"

"Yes, I did," Aaron snapped defensively. "But that doesn't mean that I didn't see a pair of eyes staring at me from the outside my window."

"You could have been walking in your sleep."

"I was awake!" Aaron shouted. "I was awake, I swear."

Quinn put her hand on the prince's shoulder and eased him off his knees. She gave him a much-needed hug and a kiss on the cheek. "Two fireflies can look a lot like a pair of glowing eyes if one has just come out of a deep sleep," she explained, trying to ease Aaron's mind.

The prince chuckled and began to walk back to the castle. After a few short moments, his chuckle became an unstoppable laugh.

"What's so funny?" Quinn asked.

Aaron turned to his companion and gave a weak smile. "I never saw fireflies that glowed red," he said flatly, and walked back to the castle.

Quinn shuddered. She knew of a creature that had a pair of the most frightening red eyes she had ever seen. Quinn even thought them to be far more piercing than Isidore's yellow orbs. "It couldn't be," she said to herself, trying to wipe out any thoughts of the foul creature that killed her father and took her to Woodbyrne.

A chilled breeze made its way through the trees and froze Quinn's very soul. She walked Aaron back to his room, and then quickly ran to her room and locked the door. Yet even Quinn, who had a heart of steel and a mind like a wizard's, could not help but give one quick glance into the dark night. "Damn fool," she cursed under her breath. "Now I'm even getting spooked over this."

❧

Circling high above Castle Gower, Damek stretched his wings out to meet the welcome breeze from the north. It had been a hot summer and the demon welcomed the fresh, crisp air.

The demon scout did not enjoy being spotted by Prince Aaron, and he was angry with himself that he had let his guard down just to kill a mouse out of boredom. The demon wondered how far his explanation would have gotten in front of Isidore.

"So, my little princess has found a new home," the creature hissed under his hot breath. "Isidore will enjoy this little tale."

Damek soared up into the sky just a few hundred feet more before he flapped his mighty wings and glided back toward Woodbyrne. He smiled at the fact that the prince was having horrible nightmares about his experiences in the caves. Damek was also busy thinking about Quinn. Such a wonderful specimen, a pity she escaped. But that can be rectified.

In mere seconds, the stealthy demon soared past the more populated section of Gower and made his way over the open farmland. He smiled when he thought of his master's plans for the peaceful community. "A pity," he mused.

❧

Aaron awakened late the next morning. The sun was out and a warm ray of light shone on his bed, warming his body and rejuvenating his spirit. The prince got out of his bed and made his way to the window where the bright autumn flowers that decorated the Royal Garden were in full bloom and their sweet scents drifted lazily in the morning breeze. Aaron took in a deep breath and yawned. Maybe I was just walking in my sleep, he reasoned, before he put on some dirty clothes and headed to the kitchen for a late breakfast.

Quinn walked through the garden lazily as she enjoyed its beautiful sounds and smells. She had been up since sunrise and she had already performed her morning exercises. Her personal trainer was amazed at how determined the feisty young woman was. Her skills had developed amazingly in just one month's time. Quinn had one underlying motive that helped her to push herself to her limits. "I told you I'd come back, Cathmore," she whispered. "I haven't forgotten you or your people." The young woman was almost ready to return and aid the elves of Woodbyrne, but there was one person holding her back.

Aaron had become somewhat of a disappointment to Quinn. He had an inner strength that the entire world could see, but he did not see it for himself. The recurring dreams that he had been having, she thought, were due to his unfulfilled promise to the wood elves. She decided to give Aaron and the king's committee one more week. And then, with or without Aaron, she would go to help them. "The elves need us now, not later," the frustrated woman mumbled under her breath.

Quinn continued her stroll through the garden until she came to where she had found Aaron the night before. She could not help but smile when she saw the cut trees and broken plants that had been in the way of the prince's frenzy. "Those flowers never stood a chance, my hero," she chided. Quinn looked up to the castle and focused on Aaron's window. She began to think of how perilous it would be if he were ever to fall out of it. As she made her way closer to the side of the castle, she tripped over a root and fell to the ground. The annoyed woman picked herself up and dusted off her clothes while cursing her luck. Just then, Quinn's keen eyes picked up a rather strange pair of footprints pressed in the rich soil. Her humility from tripping was quickly replaced with horror at the sight of the large lizard-like imprints in the soft earth.

"He was right." Quinn looked up at Aaron's room and looked back at the large bush. "Aaron was right!"

‹⁊›

Isidore waited impatiently for his servant to report back with an update. "Where is that uncontrollable freak," muttered the edgy demon. Damek had a way of shortening Isidore's already tiny fuse.

Suddenly, the doors of the main chamber flew open and a little demon soldier ran into the room. "Damek has arrived!" the excited servant shouted.

"Then where is he, you fool?"

The young messenger stumbled back when the roar of his master's voice slammed into him. "He is coming, my liege."

Isidore thought about decapitating the fool, but then Damek walked in and the frightened servant escaped behind him.

"Where have you been?" Isidore demanded.

Damek cautiously approached. "I was completing the task you had assigned me."

Isidore stood up and walked down toward Damek. "What have you to report?" he asked in an uncomfortably pleasant tone. Then, without warning, the demon master vanished into thin air, leaving Damek to turn about frantically in search of his master.

"I'm waiting," chided Isidore, who reappeared on the other side of the room, holding a very large morningstar in his clawed hand.

Damek began to sweat profusely. "I saw many things, my master."

"Tell me." Isidore was walking back across the room, his powerful weapon swinging easily at his side.

"First," began the scout, "Prince Aaron has apparently been having a hard time forgetting about Woodbyrne. Also, Quinn now lives with the rest of the royal family. It seems that she has taken up a taste for battle and she has been practicing with many teachers since she arrived at the castle."

"Anything else, Damek?" Isidore disappeared again without a trace.

"Yes," Damek answered quickly. "A shrine in honor of the man we killed was erected. Prince Aaron can be found talking to it at least three times a day, when he isn't busy dreaming of us." Another cocky smile crossed the demon's face but the sweat on his forehead revealed nothing short of fear.

"What else?" Isidore's voice seemed dangerously close.

"The king and queen try to comfort the prince but to no avail. Other than that, nothing seems to be happening at the castle."

"The king hasn't done anything?" howled the demon master, his voice cutting deep into the heart of Damek.

"Nothing, I swear!" pleaded the scout, who tried hard to hold his head together. "The prince must not have told his father about us."

"Anything else?" Isadore reappeared right in front of Damek, swinging the morningstar dangerously close to the scout.

"Like what?" asked Damek, unsure what his master wanted.

"Were you seen?" asked the mighty demon.

"Only for a second," he squeaked, "but nobody believes the prince's story. Not even Quinn!"

"One second too long, you insolent scum!" roared Isidore. "You fail to understand how important it is for my plans for revenge to go unnoticed."

In an instant, Isidore struck Damek across the skull with the spiked weapon. Black blood flowed out of a large gash left on top of the demon's head, but he tried hard not to show his agony. Isadore was enraged and came at him again, this time with a blow to the stomach, blasting the air from his lungs. Damek fell to the ground in agony. Damek tried hard to sit up but the pain was too overwhelming; the pitiful demon vomited all over the floor and began to choke.

The disgusted leader threw his bloody weapon across the room and returned to his throne.

Isidore always enjoyed teaching Damek a lesson but the demon master realized that he would need this stealthy scout if he wanted to take revenge on Gower. Isadore allowed sufficient time to pass, to make sure that Damek learned the errors of his way. Then, the demon master commanded a few words. A silver cloud surrounded Damek, covering him with a mysterious silver dust. Isidore said a final word and a blinding flash of light exploded where the dust had settled. When all was clear, Damek was kneeling on the ground looking as healthy as he did when he first entered the chamber.

"I have healed you, my friend," Isidore explained. "I apologize for my harsh treatment, but you did bring it on yourself. Hopefully you have learned your lesson."

"Yes my master. What do you wish me to do?" Damek knew that the wounds inflicted by his master were too serious to survive, yet he knew that Isidore only healed him because he was needed.

"I need you for an even greater task," explained Isidore. "Tomorrow at midnight, I will unleash my revenge on all of the people who live in Gower! Tomorrow I will begin my revenge on Prince Aaron Gower and all of the Gowers who stood before him."

Damek rose to his feet and anxiously approached his master. "What role shall I play in this great organization of chaos?"

"You," replied the confident ruler, "will be given a very special and sacred task." Isidore leaned forward and smiled at his servant. "You are to enter Woodbyrne and return to me with an elf."

"An elf?" croaked Damek, queasy after hearing his orders. The demon feared the wild wood elves just as much as any other demon did, but the fact that he had to face one of them alone made the scout pale. "Why not use one of the elves we have in the dungeons?"

"I want you to capture one from the forest because it has been too long since we sent the wood elves a message. They need to be reminded again that their time here is coming to an end. And I am also sending you out on this mission as a punishment for your failure at the castle. It has been a while since you've seen a good battle and this mission will help you get back in war mode. You will leave now and return within three days."

"I will not fail you, Isidore," promised Damek, hoping to win back his master's favor. His task was indeed a dangerous one, but Damek had lived for two hundred years with the elves of Woodbyrne. He felt that he had enough time to formulate a proper plan of action.

"Remember, I will not stand for another failure."

Damek turned to face his master one last time. "I will not fail you, Isidore." Damek opened the doors of the chamber and flew out at full speed; he had much to plan that day.

Isidore paced about his chamber for many minutes after dismissing Damek. The demon master had a very intricate plan to put into place and he knew that every detail had to be covered. "By midnight tomorrow," he whispered under his breath, "the pathetic people of Gower will tremble from the folly of their prince." Isidore stormed out of his chamber hurriedly. He had to speak to the commanders of his army in order to make sure that all of the details were clear. Isidore would not tolerate failures.

Chapter 17

In the farmlands just to the east of Headburrow, Jonathan Brown awakened a few minutes past midnight. It had been a very hard day on the farm and he needed a good night sleep. Jonathan was not sure what it was that had awakened him, but the old farmer had a strange feeling that something was awry. Slowly, so as not to disturb his wife, Jonathan crept out of his bed and headed for the front window of his small farmhouse. The creaking noises that came out of the old wooden floor sounded ten times as loud in the middle of the night as they did during the daytime. In just a few seconds, Jonathan was in front of his livingroom window looking out into the dark night.

"I must be going crazy," the old man whispered to himself. Just then, the sound of an animal's screams tore through the silence. Before Jonathan even turned back toward the window, another scream burst through the air. "Thieves," he cursed as he made his way over to his weapon rack and pulled his very old, and very worn, broad-sword off the dusty handles. Not quite used to carrying the weight of his steel weapon, Jonathan accidentally knocked over an old flower vase from a table. The fragile decoration fell on the floor and shattered into hundreds of pieces. Cursing under his breath, the old farmer ran over to his bedroom and checked to see if his wife had heard his folly.

Kimberly was still fast asleep, apparently undisturbed by her husband's clumsiness. Satisfied, Jonathan headed for the front door; his face like the steel he carried, was firm and cold. Although he was in his early seventies, he still remembered what it was like to be a soldier of the Royal Army. Slowly, Jonathan opened his front door and stepped outside.

Another horrible cry from a suffering animal ripped through the night, sending a surge of anger and revulsion through the farmer's heart. The very thought of someone hurting one of his beloved animals made the old man shake, especially when he thought of Freedom out in the barn. Freedom was his beautiful gray steed, the offspring of Jonathan's old war-horse. Over the years, the old farmer had grown fond of his large pet and he could not picture a day where he did not rely on the trusty steed to help him in daily chores with the farm and the fields.

Another horrible squeal came out of the barn where Jonathan kept most of his livestock and Freedom. The enraged farmer walked cautiously toward the barn with his sword raised for battle. "Freedom?" he called to his favorite pet. "Something the matter, fella?"

A large thump came from the barn, followed by laughter.

"Get out of there now!" Jonathan demanded, figuring some local thieves were trying to steal animals for the black market. "I am armed so you had better listen, you vile scum!" The old man had not felt so alive and yet so vulnerable in many years. As the cautious fighter got closer to the barn, a bright red light began emanating from the inside. The light was so intense that it spilled out of every opening, every crack in the wooden frame. It almost looked as if the inside of the barn was on fire, but Jonathan did not see or smell any smoke.

"What the hell is going on here?" Jonathan walked to the front of the barn in confusion. "Get out of my barn!"

The red light remained intense for a while as more screams and shouts from the animals filled the air. A very unearthly laughter accompanied the symphony of evil. Then, just as fast as it began, the light vanished. Darkness took the inside of the barn and all noises died off as well. Still, the laughter could be heard. It was less vocal than before, but unmistakably there.

"I'm coming in, you little pieces of garbage!" The outraged old man ran up to the doors of his old barn and flung them open with all his might. To his dismay, Jonathan saw nothing but impenetrable darkness. The smell of death hung heavily in the air and not one of the animals could be heard. "Freedom? Where are ya, boy?"

Without warning, two creatures burst out of the open barn, knocking the old farmer on his back. He could not make out what they were, but he heard their wicked laughter as they ran into the darkness of the night, vanishing in a matter of seconds. After a few uneasy moments, Jonathan was able to bring himself to enter the barn and face whatever it was that the two trespassers had done. The darkness of the barn was too much for the old warrior and he needed light. As he searched the side of the barn for his lantern, Jonathan noticed that the walls were wet with a sticky substance. Frantically, the farmer grabbed for his lantern, almost knocking it over when he finally found it.

"You better beware!" the wretched farmer shouted, figuring that there might be more people still hiding inside the barn. Finally, Jonathan struck a match and lit his lantern. The soft light from the wick let off a yellow glow in the barn. "What the hell is this?" he asked in disbelief, referring to the blood that was lathered on his hand and the entire wall of the barn. When he turned his light toward the barn, he began to scream uncontrollably.

All around, dead animals lay with their bodies torn to pieces. Sheep lay in corners covered in blood and gore while two cows lay on top of one another, their legs broken and their necks slit. In the far corner, Jonathan could see three of his pigs hanging from the loft by their tails. Their necks were also cut open and their blood flowed into pools under their corpses.

Jonathan began to shake and a small pain began to make its way into his left arm. "Freedom?" he called out, knowing that his favorite pet lay in the largest stall of the barn. Stepping over dead sheep and mutilated goats, Jonathan slowly made his way to Freedom's section.

"No!" The pain in his arm made its way up to his shoulder. "Freedom!" The farmer's favorite horse was lying in the stall. It still moved a little but the poor beast had wounds that were fatal. All four of the horse's legs have been gnawed into bloody stumps and the creature's neck lay eerily to one side. When the old man entered the stall to comfort his pet, he realized that Freedom's stomach was open and only his weight was preventing his innards from spilling onto the ground. "Who did this to you?" he asked his dying friend. "Who did this?" The horse nuzzled his owner one more time before it drifted off into death.

"Jonathan?" called Kimberly. "Where are you?"

"Stay in the house, Kim!" Jonathan did not want his wife to see the horror of the barn. "Stay in the house!" The old man got up and ran for the barn door. However, when he made it half way, the pain in his left side was too overwhelming.

"Where are you, Johnny?" Kimberly called. She saw the doors of the barn open and she made her way over.

"No, Kim! Stay in the house!" Jonathan made one last effort to reach his wife, but he tripped over a slaughtered sheep and fell to the ground. The lantern flew out of his hand and shattered, sending oil and flames on himself and the dry hay that covered most of the floor.

Kimberly arrived at the barn just in time to see her husband and the bloody massacre go up in flames. She fell to her knees and called to the heavens for help, but the barn burst up in a roaring inferno and Kimberly was forced to go back toward the house. It only took a few minutes before the barn collapsed. It took even less time for her heart and soul to follow.

"My poor Jonathan," she muttered. Kimberly turned her head to the ground and saw something very peculiar. She saw two sets of footprints leading away from the barn and into the cornfields. What puzzled the old woman was the fact that both sets of prints looked like the feet of a very large dog. Fearing for her life, Kimberly ran for the house. Before she slammed the door shut, she looked up and noticed more fire and smoke in the night skies just a few miles down the road. Her heart sank even deeper when she realized that the fires were heading her way, cutting off all routes of escape. The old widow went to her bedside and kneeled down to pray. She prayed that she would join her husband in death so that they might spend eternity together.

The smoke got thicker as the fires closed in on the small farmhouse.

Meanwhile, just a few miles northeast of Lake Campbell, Peter Hethington was up late with a nasty stomachache. "Next time, you try the stew first," he said to Maxine, who was curled up in her overstuffed straw dog bed in the far corner of the kitchen. Peter's wife, Alicia, was not a very good cook, but he could never muster up the guts to tell her. That evening Alicia had prepared a "special" stew, which included some mushrooms she picked out of the garden.

"I can't believe I've lived this long," Peter chuckled as he took another sip of his cider and looked over to a picture of his son, Kemp, a muscular young man who had tried foolishly to join the Royal Army at the age of fifteen. Peter laughed as he remembered how silly his son looked when the recruiters had rejected him. Now, seven years later, Kemp was a powerful soldier and a true leader. "He's probably eating better than me," kidded the old farmer. At times, he would tease his wife by telling her that Kemp ran off to join the army in search of a good meal. Her response was usually a threat with a rolling pin. Peter took another sip of his cider and smiled as he reminisced.

Unbeknownst to Peter, outside the farmhouse, a creature silently made its way toward the bedroom window.

Peter finished his third glass of warm cider and went to the sink. Suddenly, Maxine popped her head up and flattened her ears. She got up from her bed and walked to the front door, growling the entire time.

"What's the matter, girl?" Peter asked nervously, but Maxine just continued to growl at the door.

All of a sudden, the sound of glass breaking sent Maxine into a barking frenzy and caused Peter to drop his mug on the floor. "Alicia!" he called, realizing that the sound came from his bedroom. Frantically, he ran to the bedroom door in time to see a very tall, dark beast jump through the broken window with his wife strapped over its shoulder.

"Peter!" the horrified woman called out. "Peter, save me!"

The terrified farmer ran to the broken window as fast as he could, but the beast that had kidnapped his wife was too fast. Maxine ran past, jumped out the window and pursued the intruder into the tall wheat fields.

Peter tried to climb through the window to chase after the demon and save his wife. Unfortunately, he was not wearing any shoes and a wicked piece of glass sliced its way into the arch of his foot.

"Peter, help me!" the desperate woman shouted, her voice fading as she was carried further from the house.

After Peter painfully yanked the shard of glass from his foot, he limped over to his dresser and pulled out his hunting knife. "I'm coming, Alicia!" he called, hoping that his wife could still hear him.

Peter was only a few yards from the fields when he heard his dog yelp. "Alicia!" he called into the darkness of the vast farmland. "Honey, where are you?"

In a few seconds, Maxine limped out of the wheat field and lay on the ground in pain. She looked into her master's eyes as if to apologize for failing him.

Another call from Alicia rang out through the darkness, but it sounded far off in the distance. Peter, completely enraged, ran into the fields calling for his wife every step of the way. The very thought of her being murdered was more than enough to quell the pain in his injured foot.

Minutes passed like hours while Peter searched for his wife. "Alicia!" Tears of frustration and anguish began to swell in his eyes. "Alicia, answer me!" All that he heard were crickets and a gentle breeze slicing through the crop. After a quick breath, Peter began to search for a possible trail the kidnaper might have made. More and more running and searching led to nothing and Peter was exhausted. Sweat covered him from head to toe in a sticky lather. Completely unnerved and disheartened, the distraught farmer kneeled to the ground and began punching the soil with his bare hands, screaming for his wife all the while.

"Why is this happening?" Peter's knuckles turned bright pink. "Why is this happening?" Blood began to ooze out of tiny slits in the broken skin. "Why?"

Suddenly, a burning sensation made its way through the open cuts on Peter's knuckles as if they had been dipped in lemon juice. As the farmer inspected himself more closely, he picked up on a familiar scent, one that caused him to turn pale.

Confirming his suspicions, a red flare lit up the night sky. Peter looked in horror as a burning arrow sailed in his direction. "I love you, Alicia," was all Peter could say as the arrow slammed into the fields around him, igniting the crops and sealing his doom.

Tied and gagged, Alicia Hethington sat on the ground near her house and wept for her husband. Maxine crawled over on her stomach and rested her head on the woman's lap. All around them, the wheat fields burned out of control.

The sound of the front door of the farmhouse opening caught Alicia's attention and Maxine began to growl, although she was not in any condition to react. When the horrified woman turned around, she saw a horrible, dog-like creature walking toward her. Overcome with fright, she began to scream through her gags.

The hideous demon simply walked over to his prisoner and grabbed her by the hair, bringing the two of them face to face. "You all die," it hissed in a broken tongue before tossing the poor woman back on the ground. As the demon sped off toward its home, smoke began to pour out of the once-beautiful farmhouse. In a matter of minutes, the entire house was a blazing inferno.

Overwhelmed by exhaustion and grief, Alicia Hethington passed out, Maxine by her side.

ॐ

"Alicia!" a voice cried out. The crops were still on fire and the Hethington home was nothing more than smoldering cinders. "Alicia, where are you?"

Maxine popped her head up and yelped. The dense smoke from the fires made the night seem dozens of times darker, but the brave dog knew who was calling out from its inky blackness.

"Alicia!"

After a few moments of unease, Alicia awoke and began to choke on the gag that was still stuck inside her mouth. The ashes that fell out of the sky only added to her difficulty in breathing.

"Alicia!" The voice was getting closer. Maxine, unable to walk, began to bark. Soon the dog wagged her tail as if she was being reunited with a long lost friend.

Out of the burning wheat fields, Peter Hethington staggered over to his wife and dog. Half of his face was badly burned and most of the rest of his body was covered in blisters and red scabs.

"I made it," he said as he knelt down beside Alicia and untied her hands and feet. "You don't know how I feel to see you alive, my sweetheart!" Peter's voice sounded very weak and raspy. Still, his embracing hug felt as good as any medicine Alicia could have received.

"Who did this to us?" she finally asked, once her gags had been removed and she had taken a few deep breaths.

Peter looked into his wife's misty eyes and smiled. "We made it, Alicia." He began to cough up blood and bile. "We made it, my dear."

Trying hard to be strong for her badly injured husband, Mrs. Hethington looked him in the eyes and asked again. "Who did this to us?"

Peter began to cough again. Blood spewed from his mouth with every horrible cough, but he finally managed to control his pain. "It was no person," he responded. "We were visited by a demon this evening."

Alicia could not believer her ears. What were demons doing in Oneira? Why were they attacking her and her husband? The tired woman almost swooned again as her husband explained the nature of the beast that attacked their farm. "We should tell Kemp," she declared. When she looked to her husband for a response, Alicia found him on the ground with his eyes closed. Peter was still breathing, but he sounded awful. The severity of the burns on his body reinforced the fact that he was in critical condition.

Alicia, dragged her husband over to the water well where she tended his wounds as best she could. All around them, the fires continued to roar out of control. The heat was so unbearable that Alicia thought it would burn her and her husband away.

Maxine stayed close by her two masters. She took water when offered and she even seemed to keep guard while Alicia comforted her husband.

After Alicia cleaned as many of the burns as she could, she looked around to see what was left of her life. The home that she and her husband built when they first settled in Gower was no more than a black spot on the singed earth. The crops that fed her and provided money to live were a tower of red and yellow flames. Maxine, the family dog that was raised and trained by her only son was terribly hurt.

"The sun will be up soon enough, my husband," Alicia whispered. She placed Peter's head in her lap and gently stroked his hand. She could barely keep herself from breaking down into tears, but Alicia was strong. She would make it through the night; she knew that her husband's life depended on her ability to survive. How could she fail him? After all they had been through, how could she give in? "We will make it, Peter."

The roaring fires closed in around the three captives. All the while, Alicia thought of her son. She wished that he could have been there to kill the foul demon when it dared to break into her home. She had to survive in order to tell him of his father's fate. She had no choice.

The flames closed in.

࿐

It was a few hours before sunrise when a small demon soldier made his way hastily toward Isidore's main chamber. The vile creature could barely cover the smile that crept across his ugly maw. He had always wanted to speak to his master personally and now he had the chance. He was, however, curious as to why his comrades did not put up much of a fight for the honor of delivering the message. Full of pride and ignorance, the young demon rushed up to the large doors and knocked loudly. On cue, they swung open, allowing the little monster to hurry inside.

Isidore was sitting on his throne and he too wore a large grin on his goat-like face. "What do you have to report?" He seemed to be in a very good mood that evening, which made the messenger feel at ease.

"I have good news, my master. Your plan is working perfectly! All of Gower is aflame and its people are suffering!"

Isidore got up from his throne and walked down to his loyal subject. "Anything else?"

The young demon was confused. He only knew what he was told

by his superiors! How could Isidore want more than what he knew? "I don't understand, my lord," replied the messenger. Sweat began to bead on his forehead.

Isidore quickly grabbed the little soldier by the neck and threw him to the ground. "Did you hear any news from Damek?" the demon master asked.

The poor soldier got up to his knees and begged for mercy from his cruel master. "I swear that I have heard of nothing from my superiors! Damek has not been heard of since he left the cave!"

Isidore grabbed the creature by the neck and lifted him up in the air. The messenger knew all too well why none of his superior officers delivered the message. The truth became painfully clear when he felt the heat from his neck being broken by Isidore's powerful hands.

Chapter 18

Damek cursed under his breath as he flew over Woodbyrne in search of an elf for Isidore. His eyes glowed bright red as he used his infrared vision to scout out the land below. Damek made sure he was high enough in the air so the ever-alert elves would not detect him. Still, despite his precautions, the demon felt that the entire forest was aware of his presence.

"Maybe the green scum ran off as soon as they heard the thunder of Isidore's army," Damek thought, although he knew too well that the wood elves feared nothing. Suddenly, Damek spotted an outline of a tall, lean creature perched in a tree one hundred yards away. The demon's experience in such tasks confirmed his suspicions that the creature was truly an elf and not one of his kindred. Damek quickly flew downwind from the elf in order to keep his presence hidden.

"Either this one is a fool or I am the luckiest demon alive." Usually, the wood elves traveled in small packs and Damek was certain that he would wind up fighting five formidable elves just so he could capture one of them alive.

After a few more minutes of scouting, Damek was positive that the elf was alone. "Must be a scout or hunter," he figured before approaching his prey, while making sure to keep his element of surprise. Satisfied with his distance, the demon climbed higher into the night sky where he would wait for the elf to leave the cover of the trees.

As Damek waited, he reached down and pulled out a black dagger from a sheath made of elf skins. The nasty weapon was a gift from the smithies of his evil plane of existence. They wanted him to take the dagger to Oneira and kill as many of its inhabitants as he could. The knife itself was made of black steel, but it had a very magical aura to it. When Damek held it in his clawed hands, the weapon felt alive, as if he was holding on to a snake. Once the dagger entered its victim, it would inject a poison than could easily kill a war-horse. Over the centuries, Damek learned that the knife could actually read his intentions and would inject just enough poison to do what the scout desired. The vile demon had the power to kill or stun his victims simply by thinking.

"This one had better get out of there soon or I'll burn the damn tree down." Demons, in general, were not a patient bunch.

❧

Lorn matched the silence of the forest with patience and poise. Like the rest of his kin, the young wood elf dreamed of the day when he could go hunting and not have to worry about being attacked. This particular night was Lorn's turn to 'sit,' the job of sitting in a tree the entire night hoping that some wild game, preferably a deer, comes along. Sitting was the least favorite type of hunt for the wood elves. They all dreaded the night they were assigned that dull and wearisome task.

Lorn was wild and free at heart. Still, despite his disappointment, Lorn understood the importance of his task. He was hunting for the survival of his tribe and, if he failed, the children would go with out food to eat. Deer meat would provide nourishment, while the bones and skin would provide clothing, shelter, and weapons.

It was to the young elf's great surprise that his pointed ears picked up the sound of a large animal. Without hesitation, Lorn readied his longbow for a shot. In minutes, a large buck made its way to a small patch of grass and began feeding. Like most of the remaining animals in Woodbyrne, this deer was rather thin and sickly. Still, to the wood elves, its meat tasted better and lasted longer than that of a rabbit or squirrel. As silent as the night itself, Lorn took a few steps forward to assure a clean shot.

The deer did not even flinch when the razor sharp arrow sliced through its skin and pierced its heart. Lorn, sure that his shot was true, turned his head and let the buck die in peace. Afterwards, the elf jumped out of his hiding place and kneeled down by the deer to examine his accuracy. The arrow was so deep in the deer's chest that Lorn was barely able to find it.

"May your soul continue to run free in our forest, my friend." Lorn placed some of the deer's blood on his chest as a symbol of respect.

৵৲

Lorn stood up from the dead deer and waited for his companions to arrive and help with the carcass. A smile crossed his face when he thought of how the others would be speaking of his perfect shot.

Suddenly, a quick breeze rushed by and he felt a searing hot pain in his right shoulder. In a panic, the injured elf raised his horn in order to warn the others. However, the poison worked quickly and the elf was passed out on the ground long before the instrument ever touched his lips.

"I got you, you little vermin!" Damek growled as he landed next to his fallen prey. Before the other elves ran into the clearing, Damek flapped his mighty wings and soared into the dark sky with the sleeping elf safely in his arms.

৵৲

"Lorn!" a female elf called out into the silence of the night. When she and two other males entered the clearing they saw only the fallen deer and Lorn's horn.

"Do you think he's playing a game with us?" one of the males asked.

"Not likely," replied the female as she bent down to examine the ground. "He wouldn't leave his horn behind or leave the deer." Closer examination told the elf that there was something wrong. "His prints end here." She pointed to the spot where Lorn was standing when he was struck by Damek's dagger. "I see no other footprints and I am sure Lorn cannot jump that far." The three elves shared an uneasy chuckle with each other.

"Where did he go then?" asked the third elf, his mind creating horrible scenarios that were fed by the darkness of the forest.

"What is that?" the second elf asked, pointing to the area where Lorn's footprints ended. When he bent down to smell the damp area on the ground, his green complexion went pale.

"What's wrong?" the female asked. "What is it?"

"It's blood."

"Well, the deer is bleeding and I am sure it didn't just collapse on the spot," the more optimistic male assured them.

"It does not smell like that of a deer." The elf got up and pulled out his sword. "It is the blood of an elf!"

~

"My lord, come quick!" cried one of the king's messengers as he frantically ran through the halls of Castle Gower. "The kingdom is under siege! Awaken, King Dermot! The people are in peril!"

Dermot jumped to his feet and ran to meet his loyal servant. "What is the matter?" he demanded.

"The kingdom is under siege!"

"Are you crazy, man?" King Dermot ran to the balcony in order to get a look at the countryside. "We are at peace! We have been since ..."

The sight of a thousand fires and thick smoke stopped the king in his tracks. "What in the name of hell is going on?" Dermot turned to see his wife, Aaron, and Quinn all standing in the hall with their mouths agape.

"Who could have done this?" the king asked. "I want a full report as to what is going on," he said to the messenger. "Send out my best scouts along with sentries to overlook the chaos and find its cause. I am sure there will be injured and dead so have the Royal Priesthood prepare a camp for the wounded. I want this to be a smooth operation and tell my men to remain calm."

"Yes, my lord!" responded the messenger as he turned and ran out of the room.

King Dermot looked to his wife and son. "I don't know what is going on here, but I am going to need both of you. Audrey, see to it that the priests have enough supplies, and that the tents are erected quickly. Quinn, go tell Lennox to have his scouts report in immediately and find out how far the fires have spread. Lennox should report back to me as soon as his scouts return with that information."

In seconds, Queen Audrey and Quinn were off to tend to their duties leaving Prince Aaron to help his father and learn how to handle an emergency.

"I am hoping that you may help me find the logic behind this madness," the king implored.

Aaron had a good idea as to who was behind the chaos, but it frightened him too deeply to tell his father. Still, the young prince tried his best. "I think this could be a response from Isidore. The demons might have done this."

"Or the elves," the king added.

"Father, I truly doubt the elves did this. How many times do I have to tell you, the elves are the victims."

"Regardless of who did this, Aaron" the king declared, "now the citizens of my kingdom are the victims. It seems that whatever you left behind in Woodbyrne has come out and wants us to play."

⌘

Kemp Hethington, along with the rest of his fellow soldiers, jumped out of his cot, put on his armor, and ran outside to meet his commander. Although Gower had been at peace for as long as he could remember, Kemp knew the emergency drill as well as anyone and was the first to line up and await his orders.

"The kingdom is under attack!" the commander shouted. "King Dermot wants to send some men on horseback to accompany our scouts in assessing the situation. You are to survey damage and help return any wounded to the castle. You are not to engage the enemy forces unless instructed to do so. Our immediate goal is to escort the scouts and tend to the wounded."

Although the commander's orders were loud and clear, Kemp's mind was miles away from Castle Gower. The young warrior was thinking of his parents. His father was not that young anymore and neither was his mother. The very thought of them trapped in the fires made the powerful soldier angry, he had to do something. The second his platoon was dismissed, Kemp saddled his horse and sped off toward his home.

～

The road leading to the farm was full of chaos and destruction. Heavy smoke and haze blocked out the morning sun, which cast an eerie shadow over the land. All around, burned fields and rubble lay where once lush crops and humble homes stood. Men and women from the Royal Army did the best they could with the injured and dead. Those who had survived the ordeal were in such a state of shock and horror that they could barely function. The scars in their minds and souls would last much longer than their burns and bruises.

When Kemp arrived at the small path that led to his home, he saw that the destruction had not passed by his family. Black smoke and ash still rose high in the late-morning sky and the smell of burning wood and leaves hung heavily in the air. Kemp had to try very hard not to loose his nerves as he guided his horse toward his parents' farm.

"Mom! Dad!" he called into the gloom. The sight of his destroyed home was too much for Kemp to handle. The crops that sustained his parents with food and money were no more. The barns and pens that held precious livestock were gone. "Mom, where are you?" The hope in the young warrior's eyes was fading fast. "Dad? Where are you?"

"Kemp?" a familiar voice responded. "Kemp, we're over by the well! Come quick; your father is hurt!"

Suddenly, Kemp was no longer a stern and disciplined soldier. Instead, he was the young man who left his family behind in search of a better future. That young man ran as fast as he could to the well where he found his mother holding his dad in her arms. Maxine wagged her tail at the sight of her long lost friend, yet she was unable to get up and greet him due to her broken leg.

Kemp ran over and fell to the ground next to his mother. The sight of his father was overwhelming. Alicia had done the best she could to cover the wounds with torn pieces of her nightgown, but Peter's burns were already becoming seriously infected.

"It's good to see you, my boy," Peter wheezed when he laid eyes on his grieving son. "Get your mother out of here!" he demanded, coughing up blood as he spoke.

"I'll take care of the both of you," responded the proud soldier.

But, before Peter could respond he passed out.

"If we can find something to drag your father out of here, we could make the castle by nightfall," Alicia suggested.

Kemp agreed and quickly searched for the necessary supplies to make a portable bed. In less than two hours, Peter Hethington was safely strapped to a large plank tied to the back of Kemp's war-horse. Maxine gladly accepted the ride next to her injured master while Alicia and her son rode atop the horse.

"We'll have to go slow so as not to tire the horse," Kemp explained, "but we should make it to the castle before the sun sets. Priests and other healers were setting up a camp for the injured while I was leaving."

Once everything was set, Kemp led his family down the long road that led to the castle. However, it was not nearly as desolate as it usually was. Dozens of farmers, townspeople and soldiers were making their way to the safety of Castle Gower. Anyone who was not injured was happy to help those who were.

Amidst the confusion, an old bruised and battered woman gave Peter a soft pillow to rest his head on.

"Your father needs immediate attention," Helinda explained to Kemp. "The pillow will help relax his body during the journey, but I can't cure his injuries."

"Thank you for your concern," responded Alicia. "You are very kind."

Helinda smiled warmly and gestured for her escort to pick up the pace to the castle. She had very important business to discuss with the priests of Gower.

⟳

Quinn rushed into King Dermot's private meeting room where he had been most of the day waiting for an update on the situation. The sun had begun to set and the king was concerned for the safety of his people and the kingdom of Gower itself.

"All of the scouts have reported to me as you commanded, Sire," Lennox said with a great deal of respect.

"What had they to say?"

"It seems that most of the farmlands along the countryside have been burned and destroyed. Farmhouses were not spared and neither were the animals. Most of the crops that sustain Gower have also been set on fire."

The king cringed at the news. "What of the towns?" he asked.

"Both Headburrow and Sharpsword suffered losses and damage. Most of Headburrow was set on fire along with its surrounding countryside. Many people were killed but some have survived the plunder. Sharpsword was also set ablaze but its losses were far less tragic than Headburrow's. Many buildings were lost but nothing that can't be replaced." Lennox cleared his throat again before continuing his report. "Most of the survivors of the attack are heading for the castle. Your soldiers are helping with the injured."

"What of Mead?"

"It seems that Mead and its surrounding farmland were untouched in the siege. Many soldiers were left behind to help in its defense against any attacks this evening. The lords and ladies who keep guard there are awaiting further orders."

Headburrow burned! Sharpsword attacked! The farms and other small communities destroyed! "Who did this? Who set fire to my kingdom?"

"Your soldiers found no signs of an enemy," said Lennox. "Most of those who witnessed the attackers seem to be dead."

"You said most of them were killed," shouted the king, his voice like thunder. "What of the ones who survived?"

"They say that the creatures who attacked Gower came from the forest."

"From Woodbyrne?" asked the king in disbelief.

"It seems that the demons came last night under cover of darkness and attacked Gower." Lennox's words were like searing hot knives to the king.

"It seems my son was right all along." Rage found its way into the king's body and his face became as red as the blood that raced through his heart. "You are dismissed, Lennox."

Once Lennox left the room, King Dermot went to the balcony that overlooked Gower. The sunset did little to comfort him as he looked to where his priests had set up the camp to help the injured. The smells and sounds of death and pain spilled out from every tent erected. Priests ran about like field mice as they tried to pray and heal whomever they could. Dermot knew that many of his people would not make it through the night and many more would die defending Gower in the upcoming days.

"Why were innocent people targetted for this outrageous attack?" he asked the wind. Dermot called for his son.

Aaron rushed in to see his father. "What is it, father?" he asked.

"You were right all along Aaron. It seems that the demons of Woodbyrne have come to Gower," the king said coolly. "Tell me son, how many enemies did you make in that forest?"

Aaron hung his head in shame. He had no answer and was certain that his father was not expecting one.

"We must react to this violence before it is too late." King Dermot approached his son and placed an unexpected hand on Aaron's shoulder. "I need you to assemble the war committee immediately. See to it that none of my advisors are left out." Dermot looked onto his son with the eyes of a true leader. "Aaron, it is time for you to take on your inherited responsibility to these people." The king pointed a finger toward the injured that were lined up to receive treatment for their injuries. "Now, go and assemble the committee!"

Aaron ran out of the room to gather all of the people needed to aid his father while the king continued to look upon his land with woeful eyes. Rage filled his soul the more he looked at the carnage and suffering. Dermot welcomed rage as his ally; he would use it to focus on his enemy.

Chapter 19

In two hours, the entire committee gathered itself in Castle Gower's strategic room. The committee's main representatives were the war council, which included the Head of Archers, Sir Bickford Browne; the Head of Cavalry, Lady Allison Churchill; and the Head of Infantry, Sir Henry Goodwill. In addition to the war council, Dermot had chosen other members whom were experienced in more alternative approaches.

Brother Frewin Romney, who was considered the most powerful and most respected priest in the kingdom, had been chosen for his uncanny ability to reason. It was said that the young priest could turn a wild wolf into a lap dog, if given the chance.

Delwyn Westbrook, a mage of considerable power, was also an integral part of the committee. Delwyn was an absolute mystery to most, if not all, of the people in Gower. When he was not locked away studying, which was most of the time, Delwyn enjoyed traveling the countryside in search of tales from bards and various sorts of drunken fools. Not a single person in Gower, including the king, knew how old the mysterious wizard was. Some people said that he was as old as the giant trees in Woodbyrne while others said that he was the one who created all of the lands. The long white beard that covered his thin face could almost confirm either suspicion. Still, Delwyn had always been loyal to the Gower family and King Dermot would not have held the meeting without him.

Lennox Softfoot, the most respected scout in the kingdom, sat quietly in his chair as the other members of the committee walked in and discussed the attacks. The king cherished the native's demeanor and valued his opinions. Lennox was known to sit and think for long hours before speaking his mind. It was a custom of his tribe and one that usually produced rational results.

In addition to the usual members, Queen Audrey was present, as well as Quinn. Dermot respected the ideas of his beloved wife more than he did anyone else's and he hoped Quinn could shed some light on the demons that attacked Gower.

"I call this meeting to order," the king said. "Our kingdom was raided and our people slaughtered the past evening. My sources report demons running around killing and burning anything that stands in their path!" Dermot let his words hang in the air for a while in order to assure that his mood sunk into his audience. "I called all of you here because we must act soon or I fear that these filthy beasts may strike again."

Immediately, Lady Allison Churchill stood up and slammed her fist onto the large oak table. "I can have my people armed and ready to march by this evening, my lord!" Allison was a very tall woman in her late fifties whose red hair was as fiery as her spirit. She was always the one to suggest battle before reasoning out any other options. King Dermot was actually happy to have someone with so little patience because it made the rest of the council think and come up with more reasonable options.

"But we don't even know what they want," Delwyn interrupted. "These creatures are nasty and evil, but they never act without purpose." The old man looked at the prince with his pale gray eyes and winked. "There must have been some reason why they suddenly came out of their homes."

"But how long do we have to figure that out?" Sir Bickford Browne asked. "Last night could have just been a prelude of things to come."

"Or maybe it was just a cowardly reaction to a smaller dispute," added the queen. "Finding out the reason for the attack will help us decide which course of action is the best to take."

The committee went on for almost one hour. Everybody seemed to have their own idea of how to take care of the situation but not one of them could agree with the other. Finally, Dermot stood up and drew everyone's attention. "Perhaps my son and Quinn could enlighten us with a brief synopsis of their recent experiences in Woodbyrne." He gestured for Aaron and Quinn to stand in front of the committee.

Quinn and Aaron told their story while the entire room sat quietly and listened. Delwyn, as usual, was the exception. The ancient wizard immediately pulled out his personal notebook. He scribbled down as many notes as he could with his scratchy pen, while saying "ohh" and "ahh." Occasionally the old man would laugh and even snort while he recorded the words of the two youths. Aaron, along with the rest of the small party, was quick to notice that the wizard's pen never dried out although he never stopped to dip it in ink. On more than one occasion, Delwyn would blow his nose or scratch his beard, yet the pen moved on the paper without the help from either of the wizard's hands.

"So there we have it," said Brother Frewin, who spoke for the first time since he had sat down at the large conference table. "Our prince seemed to make some unheavenly enemies while he and the late Byram Edelmar courageously rescued Quinn." The young man looked to his king with a sheepish grin. "What are we to do about it?"

"Well, that's the purpose of this meeting. I was hoping we could all come to an agreement on a plan of action." Dermot was a warrior at heart. His entire family before him charged battlefields and defended kingdoms. Politics were not his canvas. In fact, Dermot was ready to suit up his horse and march straight into the heart of Woodbyrne with his army behind him. However, he had to be political. The future of Gower was in his hands.

"What if we were to erect better defenses against the intruders?" suggested Sir Henry Goodwill, the Head of Infantry. Henry was about the same age as the king, yet he looked as if he was twenty years younger than the king. His cleanly shaven face and long blond hair did well to conceal his age. However, despite his youthful looks, Henry's constant complaining and nagging made him sound like he was twenty years older than Delwyn. "Our architects are among the best in the land," he continued. "I'm sure they could develop a proper deterrent against these vile monsters."

"I am sure they could, my dear Sir Goodwill," answered Delwyn, who shut his notebook and placed it in a bag that seemed much too small for the bulky item. "However, that would take months of planning and even more time to set up."

"I agree with the wizard," interrupted Lady Churchill. "Gower will be burnt to the ground by the time your little plan could be finished. I say we act now before it is too late!"

Sir Goodwill sat back in his chair to take in his colleague's words.

"That too could prove to be a foolish plan," explained Lennox Softfoot. "That could be exactly what the demons want. If we run in like blind fools, we could be ambushed or worse."

"What could be worse than sitting and waiting for death?" The powerful warrior's face was turning bright red. "I am a fighter!" Lady Churchill roared. "Your Cavalry is ready to fight!"

"We must think of a way to get inside Woodbyrne and spy on our enemy," suggested Brother Frewin. "If we could find out what they are thinking we could devise a plan of action." The priest's suggestion seemed to make sense to the entire room.

"How are we supposed to do that?" asked the queen. "Should we send in our scouts to do the task?"

"I am not sure how we could spy on our enemy, my lady. I am sure they are patrolling all of the borders of the forest by now." Brother Frewin jumped out of his seat and pointed to Delwyn. "Delwyn could cast a spell to see what our enemy is up to."

The odd wizard looked at his friend. "I am afraid that Woodbyrne is beyond even my powers," he explained. "For years I tried to crack the defenses of that wretched forest, but to no avail. Besides, even my crystal ball could only see what is going on, I would not be able to hear anything."

"How many years?" mumbled Quinn, not realizing that Delwyn could hear her from across the room.

"Since it all began, my dear," Delwyn answered, causing the young woman to stir uncomfortably in her seat.

Prince Aaron stood up and cleared his throat. "What if we were to contact the wood elves? I am sure they would be willing to help us if we returned the favor." The suggestion caused much commotion.

"I am sure that the few stragglers you met would be of little use to us," said Sir Bickford Browne.

"Why not give it a try?" added Brother Frewin. The powerful priest did not like the looks of the rest of the room. "We have nothing to lose, yet everything to gain."

"Elves are a strange lot," barked Sir Henry Goodwill. "I say keep away from them by all means." The frustrated warrior looked to the queen for recognition. "Besides, who would be foolish enough to travel the countryside while our enemy is so close to our lands. We would never even make it to the forest."

"I could make it!" Aaron declared. "Just give me a day to assemble a proper party and I'll make the journey."

Audrey jumped to her feet and shouted at her son. "That is out of the question! Your business is in the castle, not out in the field!"

"This man will one day lead by actions," said Delwyn. "Besides, he has the most noble reason of all to return to the forest."

"And what might that be?" asked the king, scratching his beard as he pondered the idea.

"Justice. Justice for the loss of a true friend," Lennox answered for the wizard.

"I think we are forgetting the reason why I put this meeting together," argued Dermot. "We need an answer to our predicament. We must come together with a solution and act on it quickly!"

"Well, you know what I am thinking, my lord," said Lady Churchill, as if her opinion was the only one that the king should consider.

"Yes," added Delwyn with a thick coating of cynicism, "you want us to charge in like a bunch of pigs to the slaughter. Very good idea, if you ask me."

"Well, nobody was asking you, wizard!"

"I suggest you watch your tone of voice when speaking to me!" shouted the old mage. Delwyn lost his patience on very few occasions, and his outburst startled everyone. "I could easily turn you into the ass that you are acting like today."

"I think we should all take a break from this chaos," Frewin said, quickly holding up his hands as if to calm down a raging mob. "I think the stress is getting to us all."

King Dermot rose from his plush throne and paced around the large room. The gigantic king looked as if he was about to explode. "I cannot believe that we are turning on each other like this. I am truly ashamed to be here right now. "It took Dermot a few seconds to regained his composure. "Now, let us take a break and regroup this evening."

In a matter of minutes, the entire committee had left the room to get some food and fresh air. Only the queen remained behind to speak with her husband.

"You want to attack, don't you?" Audrey felt for her husband's dilemma. "I can see it in your eyes."

"I do, my darling. My people need a leader, not a lecturer, but I'm forced to be responsible so I let my finest men and women help me make the right decisions."

Audrey smiled and started to rub her husband's large shoulders. "That is very noble of you. You truly are a king of the people."

"But I feel like I am wasting my time. I know the course we are going to have to take, so why must I go through all of this nonsense?"

"Because you are fair and just. Only fools rush in blindfolded."

Dermot turned around quickly and embraced his wife in a hug. "At least I am not alone on this," he confessed. "I like it when you are around to watch over me."

"Well, at least you know who is really in charge of the kingdom."

The king laughed and kissed his wife on the lips. "You better believe it, my queen."

༒

Isidore sat on his throne and looked at the pitiful creature before him. The elf that Damek captured was still heavily drugged from the poison, and dried blood covered his arm and clothes. After a few moments of what Isidore considered patience, he approached his new captive and gave him a kick in the ribs with his booted foot.

"Get up, you pathetic scum!" the demon master ordered, although the elf was in no position to respond. Again, the vile demon slammed his boot into the side of the prone elf. Lorn began to get up.

"My people will come for me!" Lorn promised in his native tongue, though he knew it to be a hollow threat. "My people will kill you!" The drained elf almost collapsed from exhaustion.

"And how do you expect them to kill me?" mused Isidore, who spoke elven fluently. The centuries of total domination and success boosted the demon's confidence to the point of foolish pride. "Your people have tried before and failed!"

"But we have new allies to strike at you and your kind."

"I hope you are not speaking of the humans." The elf's surprised expression made Isidore smile. "Yes, I am now in the process of making sure that the elves of Woodbyrne are forever my prisoners."

"The humans are more powerful than you estimate, you stupid fool!" Lorn had just overstepped his bounds and was in grave danger. "Prince Aaron infiltrated your cave and rescued Quinn, from your very grasp."

A quick punch to the jaw sent the elf flying across the room. Blood spewed from split lips and crunched bones. Although he was drugged and had no chance of escape, Lorn would not surrender so easily.

"I am but one of many, Isidore. My people have gotten strong over the years that you failed to finish us off. The humans are our allies and that is just the beginning."

"The beginning?" asked Isidore, who stormed over to the elf with closed fists. He had dealt with the wood elves for centuries, yet he was always amazed by the strength of their will and pride. Although he would never admit such a weakness, Isidore wished that his followers were so brave and loyal. "Who else do you think you could get to aid your people's hopeless cause? Do you think the dwarves give a damn about your people? The dwarves are happy in the mountains mining like little moles and, quite frankly, I hope they stay there and rot for all eternity!"

Without warning, Isadore jabbed his claws into Lorn's stomach.

"My people have more allies than you think, demon!" The pain was too much for the wood elf. He could actually feel his stomach rupture and his diaphragm rip open. In a matter of seconds, Lorn was writhing in agony.

For now," Isidore continued, as he tore the innards of the elf, "I have an ally in you, my dear elf." Isidore picked the tortured creature up by his hair and gently caressed the side of his slender face. "I need you to lend an ear for my cause." Isidore grabbed Lorn's pointed ear and ripped it off, letting the elf fall onto the hard ground like a sack of rocks.

"Damek!" Isidore wailed. "Damek, get in here!"

In seconds, the demon scout was kneeling in front of his master with open hands. "Did I please you, Isidore?" the slippery worm asked. Damek could not help but smile when he saw the elf tossing and turning on the floor in its own blood.

"You performed adequately, my friend, and now I have another mission for you."

Damek's face dropped to the floor. Not another simpleton task. "I would be honored to serve you, my master," He lied.

"I want you to deliver a message to King Dermot." Isadore gave Damek the message to be delivered and instructed, "You are not to be detected. This is your final mission before the war."

Damek looked confused. "What war?"

"Do you think my plan was to simply burn a few crops and kill a couple of farmers?" Isidore walked up to his throne and sat down. "Prince Aaron and Gower are my targets—time to expand my own kingdom."

Isidore's words worried Damek. Woodbyrne was full of magic and power but Gower was just a piece of land with little value to demons.

"Why do you want Gower?"

"Because I want to be a Demon Lord someday soon, you stupid fool!" Isidore looked at his subject with amusement. "Conquering one of the most powerful kingdoms on Oneira would make the lords of the Lower Planes look favorably on me."

Damek took his master's words with a grain of salt. He knew that Isidore was full of himself and would eventually slip up. When that happened, he would become demon master of Woodbyrne. Until then, best to play along. Damek left to deliver the message to Castle Gower.

Seconds later, the flailing elf died and Isidore placed another glowing jar on his shelf. "I thank you for the entertainment, elf," Isadore chuckled. The demon master retired to his private quarters where he could plot his revenge on Prince Aaron of Gower.

❧

After a quick dinner, Aaron and Quinn gathered the council and headed back to the strategic room.

"I think we should get to the matter at hand without delay," began the king. Dermot rose from his seat and began to pace about the room. "Do we defend or attack? It is a simple question, yet the decision is very risky to the people and future of this kingdom."

Brother Frewin was the first to speak up. "I believe I have a solution that may satisfy both sides of the committee," the priest began. "I propose that we prepare for the attack on the demons without delay."

"I thought you were going to settle the dispute?" asked the prince.

"Aaron, let Brother Frewin finish," urged the queen.

"As I was saying," continued Frewin, who gave a quick smile to the blushing prince, "we should prepare to attack the demons as soon as possible but we must prepare for an all-out attack by our enemy. If last night was all the demons had in mind to do, then we will have plenty of time. If the worst is still to come, we best be ready to defend our land to the bitter end."

The room went silent for a very long time after Frewin's suggestion. Soon after, it was agreed that all measures should be taken to remove the demons' element of surprise.

"Lennox," said the king, "your services will be needed this evening." Dermot looked to his war council. "The three of you will create small scouting parties that will be led by Softfoot. Together, you will set up strategic locations around the countryside where the demons would most likely enter Gower. Aaron, I want you and Quinn to help in these plans since the two of you have recently been in the forest."

"What else should we do to ensure the safety of the people, my lord?" asked the queen.

"I would like you to gather all of the smithies and carpenters in town and have them begin to make weapons. Most of the citizens are farmers and their sickles won't do much against a well-armed enemy.

"My dear king," interrupted Delwyn, who looked very disappointed, "what about the elves? Should we not try to establish some sort of communication with them? After all, they have survived the demons for centuries."

"Delwyn, my first concern is for the safety of the people of this kingdom. After I feel that we are safe from any outside attacks, I will speak with you about setting up a meeting with the wood elves."

There was a loud knock that startled the entire committee. A messanger entered, holding a small box in his shaky hands. The servant's eyes seemed glazed over and his face was expressionless.

"What is it?" demanded the king.

"I have a message for the hero."

"Who is the hero?"

"I was told to give this package to the hero of the elves, my lord."

All eyes turned to Aaron, who was looking at Quinn. He reluctantly got out of his seat and took the package. After dismissing the messanger, he placed the package on a table by Delwyn. Delwyn then cast a spell that would reveal any traps or ill-matter in the box.

"It seems to be safe," the wizard concluded. "You can open it."

Aaron took a deep breath and pulled the ropes off the package. Slowly, he opened the box and revealed a severed green ear covered in dried blood. Instantly, the prince's face went pale and he took a few steps back.

"My god!" Quinn shouted as she turned her head. "What does this mean?" asked Audrey in revulsion. "Who did this?"

Brother Frewin closed the box up quickly. "It means that the demons are acting out of revenge for the insult that our prince has created." The priest put a cloth over the box and said a prayer for the unfortunate soul that had been tortured for the sake of evil.

Delwyn went over to Quinn and placed a calming hand on her shoulder. "It seems that the kingdom has made some terrible enemies, my child." The wizard turned to the king with a concerned look on his aged face. "Enemies that will not stop until none of us are standing."

"I think we all know what this means," said the queen.

Dermot heard his friends clearly, yet he never took his eyes away from the large window where he could see the sorrow his people were going through. Men, women and children were walking about crying for the loss of loved ones. An older man could be seen consoling his wife. Her head was caked in dried blood and her left arm was in a sling. The suffering of his subjects was indeed unjust and it had to be avenged. How would his people look upon him if he did nothing to stop their sorrow? What kind of ruler stood by and watched as murderers and thieves raped his land?

"My lord," Delwyn called from across the room. "I think we have no choice in the matter. The demons want to play."

King Dermot turned from the window with a look on his face that silenced the entire room. "We will attack these villains and drive them out of Woodbyrne forever!"

Tears rolled down the queen's cheeks.

"Who are we to determine the value of the elves? Don't they deserve the right to walk freely in the forest that was rightfully theirs to begin with?" Dermot's voice rose with every passing word, charging up all that heard him. "How could we let the demons drive us into hiding like mere cattle? This day I declare war on all of the demons of the forest!"

The entire room exploded into cheers for the king. All knew that the war was not going to be an easy one to win, but with King Dermot leading the way, they knew it was possible.

"You will be avenged, my people!" King Dermot shouted from the balcony. "The blood of our enemy will soon be shed in the memory of your loved ones!"

Outside the castle, in the emergency camps, all that heard the declaration of the king both cheered and wept.

Chapter 20

The committee met again early the next morning to discuss the plans of attack against the demons. The night had passed uneventfully, which put King Dermot in a slightly better mood. He would not admit it, of course, but he was glad to go to war against the demons. The Gower name was filled with great warriors, and Dermot was no exception.

"Time is against us, my friends," began the king. "If we are to wage war against our foe we must do so within the next few days." The king's words surprised the committee, especially the war council.

"Excuse me, my lord," interrupted Sir Bickford Browne, "but isn't that a very short amount of time to plan and execute an attack?"

"It is a very small window, I know, but what other choices do we have?" King Dermot stood up and opened the curtains of the meeting room, revealing the charred countryside of Gower. "The demons could attack at any second. We have no choice!" Dermot's harsh tone put everyone's doubt to rest. "Now, what is our best route of attack?"

The entire morning was spent going over the details of the upcoming battle. The war council agreed that preparing would be difficult, but not impossible. By early evening, the king and his advisors had plotted the best route to take for the march on Woodbyrne.

"What about the elves?" asked Quinn, who was relatively silent throughout the day. "Wouldn't they be a great ally to us?"

"I thought I made it perfectly clear that the people of Gower are our main priority," explained the king. "We do not have the time or the resources to create a treaty with a group of elves that we've never dealt with before."

"Well," continued Quinn, "My experiences in Woodbyrne make me feel that teaming with the elves would enhance our chances for victory, my lord. Their numbers are small but their hearts are great. With recent events, it appears that we need them just as much as they need us."

Delwyn sat back in his chair and smiled at the young woman. "You are indeed correct, Quinn. The elves of the forest would make a very powerful ally."

"How are we supposed to get there in time for the march?" asked Audrey, who really had mixed feelings about the wood elves. "Besides, the demons are probably scouting the countryside in search of any human activity. If we were to get caught, it could be devastating."

"I think it is best to leave those creatures alone," suggested Lady Churchill, whose negative thoughts of the wood elves still remained.

"I can't believe this," shouted Quinn, finding it very difficult to control her anger. "They saved us!"

"I do believe you are out of line, young lady," said Sir Henry.

Aaron had finally heard enough. "I believe it is the three of you who are out of line!" he corrected, his booming voice forcing the head of infantry to sit back in his chair. "The elves of Woodbyrne saved Quinn and me from certain doom. Every day for the past two hundred years the elves, whom you disrespect so easily, have died in the name of honor and freedom! When I left the forest, I made a vow to my new friends that I would bring their case before the king. Aaron walked around the table while he thought of another argument to support his plan. Fortunately, Delwyn was way ahead of him.

"I recall hearing tales that the lead demon is invulnerable to man-made weapons."

Aaron's eyes widened in surprise. How could he be so forgetful? "That's right! Byram and I struck Isidore several times but to no avail. Our swords didn't even hurt the monster."

"What of the rest of the demons?" asked the king. "Do they posses this ability?"

"No," replied the prince. "I know they can be killed but I am certain our blades will do little to wound their master."

"Even if we can get past these demons, how are we supposed to kill their leader?" asked Sir Henry in frustration.

"Maybe the elves know of a way to defeat this Isidore fellow," suggested Brother Romney. "Even if they don't know how to destroy him, they might know where to look."

Aaron had to keep pushing. "A large party would most likely get caught roaming the countryside; however a small, elite group could get past the spies and enter the forest undetected."

"Who is going to lead this 'elite' party?" asked Sir Henry.

"I could lead it," Aaron snapped. "I entered the forest before and I am certain that I could do it again. Besides, the elves are sure to be looking for us."

"And who will be brave enough to go with you?" the queen asked. "You can't simply force anybody to go into Woodbyrne on a hunch that the elves are looking for you." She agreed with her son, but she feared losing Aaron to the demons.

"The elves are too few in number to make such an attack," replied Quinn, who had calmed down considerably since her outburst. "Isidore's cave is heavily guarded and the demons outnumber the elves by too large a margin. But Aaron is right. The elves are victims. I saw first hand what happened to any of them if they were captured and brought back to the caves. We owe it to them to help them."

As the debate carried on, the king looked deep within himself to when he was a young man. Dermot had always dreamed of ruling a kingdom. He pictured himself conquering the evil of the land and winning over the respect of the people. It came as no surprise to the king that his own son's heart seemed to lie in the same direction.

"My lordship!" shouted Delwyn for the third time, finally snapping the king's daydreaming. "Who is going to lead this small band if we are to venture into the woods?"

"It would seem that only someone with experience in these matters should lead my best people to Woodbyrne," Dermot answered. "Prince Aaron is the one I feel would best lead the party to the home of the wood elves."

Aaron almost passed out when he heard what his father said. "I— I—I will not fail you, father."

"I know you won't, my son."

Aaron looked back to his mother and was even more astonished when he saw that she was smiling despite the fact that tears were rolling freely down her cheeks. "It seems to me that the time has come to begin your preparations as a ruler of this land," she said. "Still, your ability to persuade any other volunteers may prove more difficult than you think."

"I volunteer," announced Quinn. "I left many demons behind in Woodbyrne that I knew I would have to face again." Quinn walked up to Aaron and grabbed his hand. "I am just happy that I won't have to return alone."

"Then it is decided," said the king, who again wore a look of great concern. "Prince Aaron will have his party meet here tomorrow night and set out the next morning. We will give them four days time to return with an answer or we will set out to attack the demons alone." Dermot looked to his son with pride. "You will return to me in four days, my boy. With or without the help of the wood elves."

The meeting ended and Aaron was left to come up with a plan to set out for Woodbyrne in less than one day's time. "I have ideas of whom we should ask," he said, his voice quivering from nervousness, "but I think we'll need some help from the outside."

"Well, if you know who to ask," said Quinn, "then we should ask them tonight. In the morning, we can get more volunteers from the village, if necessary."

"Good idea. Several people are here in this room, but," Aaron explained, "I do not want to pressure anyone into volunteering by asking them in a room full of people. Let's give them a few minutes to disperse."

☙

By three o'clock in the morning, Aaron and Quinn had spoken to all of the people they thought would be appropriate for the mission. In the end, the party consisted of five people, including the prince and Quinn.

Delwyn Westbrook was still lingering about the castle when Aaron asked him to volunteer for the mission. In a matter of seconds, the old wizard was out the door and heading toward his home where he would gather the necessary items for the journey. Aaron chose Delwyn not only because he was a powerful mage, but also because he seemed to know much about the elves.

After the wizard agreed to join the party, Aaron approached his friend, Brother Frewin Romney, and asked him if he would like to accompany him to Woodbyrne.

"I would be honored to do anything I could for the sacred cause of cleansing Woodbyrne," was the priest's response. Aaron sigh in relief. Brother Frewin was a very talented priest and Aaron thought it might prove valuable to have some sort of protection against the evil of the forest. Brother Frewin also had the ability to heal injuries, which would be invaluable in a battle.

The most peculiar of those asked to join the party was Lennox Softfoot. It took a while for the proud native to agree with Aaron, but in the end he chose to go. "I know very little about the wood elves," he said, "but if you feel that my skills will prove useful, then I shall go." Aaron was a little embarrassed by Lennox's loyalty, but he could not help but feel happy that the scout agreed to join the mission.

"We still need another person to join us," Aaron said to Quinn. "Our only true fighters are Lennox and myself."

"I beg your pardon?" asked Quinn, insulted by the comment. "I've become a very good shot with the bow since I've been here and I would like to see you defend yourself against my sword."

Aaron blushed. "I'm sorry. I was just saying that I think we still need another member of the party who can fight. Frewin hasn't seen a fight since before he was a priest and who knows what good the wizard will be in a battle."

"I agree that we need another fighter, Aaron, but I don't agree with the way you see the other members of the party." Quinn yawned and rubbed her irritated eyes. "I'm tired. Why don't we call it a night and begin again in the morning?"

"I guess nobody in their right mind would be willing to join us if we wake them so late at night," joked the prince. "I'll get up in the morning and see what I can do."

"Agreed," answered Quinn. "Now shut up and let me go to bed."

The two friends retired to their respective quarters and drifted off to sleep. It took Aaron a while longer to relax since his mind was full of ideas and plans for the meeting with the elves. "I guess I'll just have to do it and pray for the best," he said to himself. "What's the worst that could happen?" He laughed. Then his smile faded as he thought to himself, I could get killed and never see my friends and family again.

❧

Kemp held his sobbing mother close to him as they stood in front of the freshly packed grave that held his father's body. Fall's morning wind spoke of a harsh winter to come.

Peter Hethington did not live long after his arrival at Castle Gower. Priests and healers tried their best to save the brave man from death, but his wounds were too grave.

"Everything is going to be fine, Mom," said the gentle soldier as he rubbed his mother's tense shoulders. "Dad would want you to be strong for him; strong for us."

"He didn't deserve this! He and I were supposed to live together forever!" Alicia walked away from her son and called for Maxine. The brave dog limped over to her side lay down on the ground next to her. Maxine wore a makeshift cast on her injured leg that looked too big for her body.

Kemp let his mother weep in peace as he tried to control his own emotions. The warrior did not want his mother to see him upset. The cool air off the ocean actually helped Kemp breathe better. All around the gravesite, men, women, and children mourned for the loss of loved ones. Kemp tried hard to forget the terror that had struck the countryside, but it was all too real to be ignored. The soldier wanted revenge for his father and mother.

"I had enough time to myself, Kemp," said Alicia. "Thank you for your patience with me."

Kemp held his mother's hand as he led her back to the camp where she would try to rest.

Not far from the base of the campsite, a messenger from the castle was blowing the horn that was used to call military persons to attention. Alicia instructed her son to leave her and Maxine and find out what was going on. Kemp quickly kissed his mother on the cheek and patted Maxine before running off to join the gathering crowd of soldiers.

⌁

The messenger allowed a few minutes for the soldiers to calm down before he spoke. "The king has ordered me to tell you that he is planning for a swift reaction to the attacks the other night." Again, the messenger waited for the soldiers to quiet down. "However, before you set out to avenge your loved ones and your kingdom, Prince Aaron Gower is in need of a brave soul to join him on a mission that will take place this very evening."

"Kind of short notice don't ya think?" asked a rowdy soldier from the large crowd of men and women.

Kemp gave the man a stern look that shut him up before he could get anyone else into the argument.

The messenger continued, "this is a most dangerous mission that will take you into the depths of Woodbyrne!"

"Is he a madman?" shouted a female archer.

"The prince has really lost it!" declared another.

Many of the soldiers simply walked away. Others talked to peers and discussed the importance of the mission, while a few more pondered their worthiness for such a task.

"Any who are interested are to go to the front gate of Castle Gower no later than noon. Remember that this is a mission that the king and queen have backed!"

Kemp made his way back to see his mother soon after the messenger left. He had a great decision to make, but one he could not make alone.

"What was that all about?" Alicia asked. The woman was resting on her bed with Maxine at her side. Many of the other people in the tent were either asleep or out for the day so the big tent was relatively quiet.

"Prince Aaron is looking for a soldier to accompany him on a covert mission."

"And you want to go, don't you?"

"Yes."

"And you are worried by the thought of leaving your poor old mother at the mercy of the king's priests and doctors."

"Sort of," replied Kemp. "It isn't the mission that concerns me, but where it would take me."

"Where are you to go?"

Kemp swallowed hard before speaking the name of the legendary forest. "We are to leave for Woodbyrne this very evening."

"I see," replied Alicia. "Why would you do that to yourself?"

"Because I have to." Kemp stood up and let his large size hover over his mother like a warm blanket. "I must avenge my father. I must avenge the people I was trained to protect. Whatever killed Dad came out of those woods. Now it is our turn to breach their borders and slaughter them like defenseless sheep."

"Will you go even if I ask you not to do so?"

Kemp looked down at his mother and smiled. "No. I will not go unless I have your blessing."

Alicia sat up in her bed and grabbed her son's large hands. She knew what she had to do but she tried to fight it. "How I wish you could be a small child again, my son. Then I could hide you from all this evil." As she looked around at the people who occupied the tent, the protective mother began to have new feelings about the mission.

"I go only with your blessing," repeated the young soldier.

"How can I say no to you? So many people are suffering and you have the ability to save them. Keeping you here with me is a selfish act that I would not feel comfortable doing." The battered mother began to cry once again. "Go, Kemp. Go and avenge your father. Avenge me and all of those you see here with me." Alicia tried hard to fight her tears. "Just promise me you will return."

"I promise you that, Mother." Kemp her mother a huge hug and kissed her forehead. "I will make it out of that wicked forest and I'll come back for you."

"You have my blessing."

"Thank you. I have no intention of leaving you here with only this smelly hound for the rest of your life." Kemp shook Maxine by the neck and got a playful bark out of her. One last kiss on the cheek and a loving smile was Kemp Hethington's last gesture toward his mother before he left the tent.

Alicia lay back in her bed and closed her eyes. "Take care of him, Peter," she whispered. "Take care of our boy."

⟳

Prince Aaron and Quinn were sitting in the empty meeting hall when a soldier entered the room.

"There is a volunteer waiting outside. Should I let him in?"

"A volunteer?" asked Aaron, surprised to have a response so soon after the announcement was made. "Sure. Send him in immediately."

"Who would be so eager to follow us into Woodbyrne?" Quinn asked.

"I think it would be best if I spoke to this soldier alone, Quinn. I would like to see how I handle myself in such situations. I think I am going to have to get used to all of this. Would you mind?"

Quinn understood and headed out one of the side doors. "I'll go check and make sure our supplies are being readied and that the horses are prepared."

It was not long before the messenger returned with the volunteer. Aaron quickly opened the door and showed the massive soldier in. "Please, sit down and make yourself comfortable." Aaron was very impressed with the size of the soldier. Even the prince, who was one of the best fighters in all of Gower, felt intimidated in front of the large man.

"Thank you, Prince Aaron." Kemp was very nervous. Usually he took orders from men who were much older than he was; men who had seen battles and killed enemies. Prince Aaron, on the other hand, looked only a few years older than he was, if he was older at all.

Aaron closed the door behind him. "Tell me a little bit about yourself and why you responded to our call to arms so quickly."

Kemp introduced himself and gave the prince a brief, yet thorough, history of his background. Afterwards, he explained why he chose to volunteer his services. "The demons that came out of Woodbyrne attacked my home." Kemp looked Aaron straight in the eyes. "They attacked my family and injured my father beyond help. My mother is a widow now and I am all that she has in the world." Kemp rose to his feet and presented himself like a true warrior. "I seek revenge, Prince Aaron. Revenge for my mother, for my father, and for the people of Gower."

"If you are all that your mother has in the world, why go off and risk your life?" asked Aaron, having a new understanding and respect for such responsibilities.

"My mother gave me her blessings. She knew that my destiny was not to sit and wait for an attack from the demons. She knew that I was meant for a greater purpose."

Aaron was impressed with the soldier's determination. However, he could not simply accept Kemp's offer. Too many lives were at stake, and Kemp seemed young and inexperienced. "Now I must tell you the entire truth before accepting your services, Kemp Hethington," said Aaron. "The party you desire to join is on a quest that will hopefully give the king's campaign against the demons the upper hand. We are to travel light and fast across the countryside and into the forest where we will meet with the wood elves. I am hoping that they will have some knowledge of how to destroy the demons' ruler, Isidore."

"I accept the mission, Prince Aaron, and I am ready to join your party."

"Understand that this is not some simple task, Kemp. There is a very good possibility that we will die before we even get to Woodbyrne. Once we set out, there is no going back. If we are in trouble there won't be any help. Do you understand me?"

Kemp though for a while before giving his answer. "Yes," he said. "I understand that this is a very important and dangerous mission. I am a soldier of the Royal Army and I was trained to face death for my country. I am willing to do so now." The soldier looked at Aaron with his clear blue eyes. "Will you take me with you?"

"Yes. Welcome to Castle Gower, Kemp Hethington. There will be a final meeting here after dinner tonight," added the prince. "You will meet the rest of the party and we will all get to know each other. Until then prepare yourself for the journey."

"Thank you, Prince Aaron," answered Kemp. He bit his lips to hide his smile and left the room.

"I guess the party is complete," said Quinn as she walked in from one of the other doors decorating the large room. "You handled yourself perfectly, Aaron."

"Thanks, Quinn. I guess you heard the entire conversation?" Aaron looked at his friend and smiled. "What about the supplies and the horses?"

"Taken care of." Quinn opened the window. A cool breeze entered the stuffy room. "When's tonight's meeting?"

"My father wants to speak to us after dinner. I guess he'll want to go over the plans before we leave in the morning."

"This isn't going to be easy, is it?" Quinn asked.

"It never is." Aaron opened the door of the meeting hall and escorted Quinn outside. "We still have all day before the meeting. "We should get our own gear and clothes ready for this trip. I don't want to wait until it is too late to realize that I forgot an extra pair of pants."

"Sounds good to me," muttered Quinn, who sounded as if her mind was hundreds of miles away. She was thinking of Woodbyrne. Memories that were buried deep in her subconscious began to make their way back to the surface.

Chapter 21

"What have you to report?" Isidore asked Damek. "Has our hero begun his campaign against us yet?"

"I am sad to say that he hasn't done anything at all, my lord." Damek flinched in anticipation of a strike from Isidore. "Actually, other than the refugees fleeing to the castle, I don't think much more is being done."

Isidore rose from his throne and began to pace back and forth in the large chamber. "I never asked you to think, Damek. That would put us all at great risk. Gower's king is said to be very apt at the art of war. I should have guessed that he would not foolishly rush to Woodbyrne the second my servants sacked the towns. I want you to send more of my soldiers out to patrol the borders of *my* forest."

Damek looked confused. "Why waste the time? It's apparent that the humans are cowards."

"Why don't I believe that?" asked Isidore, standing threateningly over his favorite scout. "I am sure a plan is being formulated, and I will not be caught unprepared!"

"I will obey your command, my master," Damek said.

"I know you will, Damek. I want more scouts on the borders and I want spies sent into Gower to try and muster up whatever information they can get." Isidore sat back on his throne of bones. "If there is any activity to report, I want to know first! Do you understand?"

"Yes, my master."

"Tell your fools not to take matters into their own pathetic hands. Nothing happens unless I say so!"

"Yes, Isidore." Damek stood up and hurried out the door.

Isidore had become nervous over the past day. Why hadn't the king responded to his raids? He was sure that something was going on, and felt vulnerable not knowing what it was. "I must get Dermot's attention once again," the demon decided.

❧

It was late afternoon when Aaron and Quinn made it to the stalls to look over any list minute details. To their surprise, Lennox Softfoot had already prepared the horses for the journey.

"Well met, Prince Aaron," greeted the loyal scout.

"The same to you, Lennox," replied Aaron. "We came to see that all was going well for this evening."

"All is finished with the supplies and horses, my prince." Lennox truly outdid himself. Every mount had the appropriate supplies to go along with their rider. Delwyn's horse was the only one that had no weapon attached to it. Some books and maps were spotted, but nothing with which the wizard could defend himself.

"What about Delwyn?" asked Quinn. "Isn't he going to need something for self-defense?"

Lennox chuckled. "Delwyn himself is the best weapon he will ever need, my lady. Probably all that any of us will need."

Quinn was very curious about the strange old man. "Just how old is that one?"

"My dear Quinn, if the mage hasn't yet told you about himself, then it isn't my business to speak for him."

"I guess the main road will be the fastest way to go in the beginning," the prince said to Lennox. "Once we get to Mrs. O'Shan's farm house, we can make our own path."

Lennox continued to pack up Kemp's horse while he listened to Aaron. "I think we should take a different route from the main road, Prince Aaron. I am certain it is going to be the one watched most by the demon spies."

"You think the demons are still roaming throughout Gower?"

"I've seen a few of them this morning." Again, Lennox did not stop his work while he spoke to the prince. "I tried to pursue one of them, but it was too fast for me to track. I think the beast had wings or I would have had it."

Quinn left the stable and headed toward the Royal Gardens.

"It seems that your friend is feeling a little nervous," Lennox pointed out as he finished his work on the horse.

"How can you tell?" asked Aaron.

"I can sense it. Quinn went through a horrible ordeal in those caves. I am sure there are memories pushed so far back that even she forgot them herself."

"You are right, my friend, it has effected us both. I've been having horrible dreams of Woodbyrne since I arrived back at the castle."

"We are finished here," Lennox said. "The plans are set and we still have the final meeting tonight. I think there is somebody else who might need your company more than me and these smelly beasts."

Lennox's horse neighed in response to his sarcastic remark.

Aaron understood what Lennox was telling him. "I will see you tonight at the meeting then," Aaron said and turned toward the garden.

*

Quinn had seated herself on a stone bench that faced a small fountain. A carved figure of a woman bending over to fill her jug was one of the dozens of small statues in the large garden.

"I thought you bathed this morning?" Aaron kidded as he sat down.

"Very funny, Aaron."

"You seem a little unnerved today. Is it this mission?"

"I haven't been feeling the same since you spotted the demon in the garden that night." Quinn's eyes filled with tears. "I haven't been the same since my father was murdered."

"I am so sorry, Quinn." Aaron gave Quinn a gentle kiss on the forehead and a soft hug with his muscular arms. "If you feel you aren't ready to go back to Woodbyrne, I would understand. The entire kingdom would understand."

"Thanks," replied Quinn as she composed herself, "but I feel as if I have no other choice. The demons turned my life upside down and I plan to repay them tenfold." She got up and walked to the fountain. "I just can't help but think of what will happen to me, and to us, if we're captured."

"You can't think like that," Aaron insisted. "If you do, then our chances are that much worse. Quinn, we are going to make it to Woodbyrne and we are going to make it back out. In our wake will be scores of those demons with their throats slit open!"

Quinn understood her friend. Her attitude had to change or she could bring down the entire party with her.

"I am not saying that you don't have the right to feel the way you do," Aaron assured her. "I'm just saying that we are going to be doing our best to avenge everyone who suffered from those monsters. That includes you, Quinn. Part of my reason for wanting to go back to Woodbyrne is to avenge your sufferings."

Quinn was taken aback by the prince's words. "Why mine?"

Now it was Aaron's turn to feel uneasy. Over the past few months he had actually become very fond of the powerful woman. Still, despite his feelings, he knew that Quinn had more important things on her mind.

"Because you are too kind and wonderful to have been put through such torture." Aaron tried hard to suppress his feelings. "You didn't deserve such an awful fate."

Quinn was blushing by the time Aaron had finished his sentence. "That is very sweet of you, Aaron, but I don't think any of the demons' victims deserved what they got." Aaron nodded. "However, I'm honored that you are willing to return to that awful place for my sake." Quinn walked up to the prince and kissed him on his cheek. "Thank you, Aaron. Thank you for listening to me this day. I feel much better having said all those things." The light in Quinn's eyes began to brighten. "Let's go and make sure everything else is ready for the meeting tonight."

"Sounds good to me," Aaron croaked. "Lennox seems to have everything under control here. I say we have a nice lunch and maybe practice some swordplay afterwards. We should even hit the archery range for a little while. If you don't mind me saying, I think you need all the practice you can get."

"I can brush my hair with one hand and shove my sword in your backside without even skipping a beat, my dear."

Aaron did not know what to say. "You are such a lady. With words as well as with appearance."

Both friends shared a much-needed laugh and headed back to the castle with renewed spirits. Aaron was enjoying his new feelings for Quinn and felt very alive. Quinn, on the other hand, felt more relieved than happy. She needed to vent her fears and frustrations and she was grateful that the prince was willing to lend an ear. However, she could see something in Aaron's eyes that she had never seen before. Even his words seemed a little different to her.

"I meant what I said about the swordplay," Quinn teased as they entered the castle.

"That's what frightens me so much."

It was two hours past dinner when the final meeting took place. Delwyn was wearing a rather gaudy robe. The long garment nearly hit the floor when the old man walked and it shined a magnificent gold. The seasoned mage was so out of place, the rest of the party members, even Brother Frewin, could not help but smirk when he walked in.

"I thought this was a formal meeting," remarked the wizard. "In the past, these sort of things were very formal."

"Those meetings were for grand wars on a scale that even I cannot remember, old friend," answered King Dermot as he and Lennox walked into the meeting room. "This mission's main purpose is stealth." The king sat himself at the head of the table while Lennox remained standing by the door like some sort of sentry. "This meeting is the final one before I bid all of you farewell."

For nearly one hour, Dermot and Lennox discussed the course of action the party members were going to take. By the end, everyone had a clear idea of their mission: to get to Woodbyrne and back as fast as possible and establish some sort of treaty with the wood elves.

"Now that we have finalized our goals, my friends," the king continued, "let us introduce ourselves to the party's newest member so he can learn the names of the people he will be protecting."

Delwyn was the first to stand up and speak. "My name is Delwyn Westbrook, my good lad. I am a wizard to the king and I am hoping to get to know you better by the time this campaign has ended."

"It will end very soon if you wear an outfit as outrageous as that one," Lennox called from across the room. The unusual outburst from the quiet scout received many laughs. Even the king could not help but chuckle.

"I am more than aware of what will be appropriate, Lennox," defended Delwyn. "If you are not careful, I might turn you into a horse so I can ride in style on this trip."

When the laughter died down, the introductions continued. Lennox gave a brief history of his background, as did Brother Frewin and Quinn. By the end, Kemp felt a little less nervous about the great task for which he had volunteered.

"My name is Kemp Hethington," the young man started. "I am a soldier in the Royal Army. I come from a family of farmers and common folk. The other night's raid on Gower hit my home, and ended in devastation. My father received mortal injuries trying to rescue my mother from the hands of one of those demons everyone's talking about."

Brother Frewin made a holy gesture in honor of the young man's father.

"I am sorry for your loss, Kemp," softly said Quinn.

"I feel for your father as I feel for all of the fathers and mothers who were lost to us that evening," added Dermot, his voice full of sincerity. "Now is the time to take action for those losses. This party serves one of the most bold and important roles of the campaign. I wish I could journey with all of you; however, I have to stay here and take care of the second part of the plan." Dermot rose and made his way to the door. "I wish all of you speed and success." The king looked to his son with misty eyes. "I have complete faith in you, Aaron. I know you shall fail neither me nor your future kingdom." With that said, the king left the silent meeting room and headed down the halls.

"That went smoothly," Quinn said to Aaron. The young woman followed her statement with a huge yawn.

"I think we're all tired," said the groggy prince. "I'm going to bed since we'll be leaving before the sun rises."

Quinn wished her friend goodnight and closed the door to the large room. There she stood alone for a very long while in front of the window that looked out on the kingdom. She saw many priests, healers, and volunteers running from tent to tent as they tried to comfort those who were injured. Then, Quinn remembered Kemp's story. His parents were simple folk leading normal lives. Fate had dealt them a dark hand and now their son was running off with a bunch of strangers into a forest he had never seen before.

It was not long before Quinn felt very weary and decided to go to bed. The halls of the castle shone a dim orange from the candles on the walls. Quinn entered her quarters and changed into a beautiful red nightgown. In mere seconds, exhaustion overtook the strong woman and she fell into a deep sleep. A sleep filled with sad memories of her childhood followed by terrifying memories of Woodbyrne. Dreams a young woman did not deserve to have.

Chapter 22

The night was silent. All around the castle, an uncomfortable silence lay heavily in the air. The moon peeked in and out of small clouds that were being pushed along by the autumn winds. Most of the villagers who had suffered from the demon raid were either sleeping or in a daze from the herbal pain relievers. Even the priests and healers found time to catch up on some much needed sleep.

Aaron Gower was the exception. He had a hard time falling asleep since he left Quinn in the meeting room earlier that night. What was his problem? Aaron was not feeling nervous about the journey and he was quite comfortable in his overstuffed bed. Still, the prince could not find any rest, no matter how many times he tossed and turned.

"Aaron," a voice whispered through the darkness of the bedroom.

"Who's there?"

"Aaron."

The startled prince thought he recognized the voice but he could not place a name as to whom it belonged to. "Dad?" he asked. "Dad, is that you?"

"I'm here, Aaron." This time the voice was so close that Aaron could feel the cold breath on the back of his neck.

Aaron turned around and almost fainted when he saw Byram standing menacingly over his bed. The once formidable archer looked anything but alive. Rotting skin was falling off his face and arms in huge chunks that landed on the bed. Byram's clothes were also torn to shreds and dried blood matted his hair to whatever skin was left on his face. The stench of death was overwhelming for Aaron and he had to fight hard to prevent himself from vomiting.

"What do you want?" cried the prince as he tried to divert his eyes from the horrible creature.

"We need you, my cousin."

"Leave me alone!" Aaron stood up in his bed and lashed out with clenched fists. However, Byram was too fast and he grabbed Aaron by the throat.

"Look what they did to me," the archer demanded.

Aaron could not answer since the powerful creature was slowly squeezing his throat. Still, the fighter in Aaron did not give up; he tried to kick and bite himself free.

"Avenge us!" Byram screamed. "Avenge us all!" With one quick movement, Byram threw his cousin across the room, slamming his head on the wall just below the bedroom window.

Aaron fought hard not to pass out. His head was throbbing so badly that he could hardly hear what the creature was saying. Once the prince turned to face his assailant again, he found that there was nobody in his room. Nothing except total darkness.

Moans and screams of sheer terror began to pour through the window. Thinking the emergency tents were under attack, Aaron grabbed his sword and looked out onto the encampment. But, it was not the death cries of innocent farmers and merchants that the prince heard, instead hundreds of bodies, like Byram's, were crawling on the ground toward the castle. Little elven children with missing limbs cried out in terror. Women and men alike were crawling on broken legs; some were without eyes and limbs as they made their way through the Royal Garden.

"Avenge us!" cried a voice. "Save our souls!"

Aaron focused in on one person in particular who stood just outside his window. The ghastly creature was missing his left arm and his eyes were gouged out of his head. Whip marks and large sores covered his body. To Aaron's amazement, the person looked very much like his own father.

"Uncle Henry?"

"We need you, Aaron Gower!" the dead man called. He slowly levitated up the side of the castle wall. "I need you!" The stench of death began to grow as the unholy creature grew nearer to Aaron.

"Why are you doing this to me?" the prince asked. "What have I done?" Aaron quickly turned around to flee from the evil sights but Byram was there to intercept him.

Too quickly for Aaron to react, Byram grabbed his cousin and cried, "Do it! Release us!"

All went black.

⌇

Aaron woke up in his bed and panicked. It was still dark outside but he could tell that the morning was not far off. As he checked himself, Aaron noticed that his room was still organized and his sword still hung on the wall. Even his head seemed to be fine. He remembered his encounter during the night, but questioned if they had been just part of a horrible dream or if he had really been visited by his dead cousin and uncle. Eventually, Aaron got out of bed and got ready for the mission. As he made his way to the stables, he realized that all of the others were up and about.

Kemp and Delwyn, who was actually wearing proper traveling gear, were going over last minute checks on their horses while Brother Frewin discussed some details with Lennox.

"Have either of you seen Quinn this morning?" the prince asked Brother Frewin and Lennox. "I thought she'd be here by now."

"She came to me earlier and asked where the temple was," the Priest answered. "She looked a bit upset."

"She is battling inner demons," said Lennox. "But, Quinn is a very strong woman and if anyone can overcome those obstacles it's her."

Aaron waited a minute more and headed to the castle's temple.

⌇

Quinn had just risen from the altar when Aaron arrived. Her cheeks were wet from tears and her eyes were very red. When she saw Aaron enter the room, she tried without success to cover up her emotions. "How did you know where to find me?"

"Brother Frewin." Aaron replied.

"I needed to speak to my parents before I ran off to Woodbyrne. I needed to tell them a few things. Things I never got to say while they still lived."

Aaron understood. After his return to the castle, he had spent many days either in the gardens or in the temple speaking to Byram.

Quinn wiped away her tears and walked past the prince, giving him a tender kiss on the cheek before she left. "Thanks for being concerned, Aaron."

Aaron turned and followed Quinn outside, where the rest of the party was already atop their mounts and waiting.

"The sun will be out soon," Lennox said with much haste. "I want us to be off the main road before that happens."

Aaron and Quinn mounted their horses and followed the scout out of the castle's quarters. "I'd rather our departure be witnessed by as few people as possible," Aaron stressed to Lennox. "The last thing I want is a mob of people cheering us on as we leave."

Before they got too close to the emergency tents, Lennox stopped the party and called for Delwyn. The old mage brought his horse next to the scout and began moving his hands in a specific pattern. In seconds, little sparkles of purple light began to swirl in front of the old wizard. Those lights made their way into the tents and disappeared. Satisfied, the wizard fell back in line with the rest of the party.

"What did you do?" Quinn asked as Delwyn passed her on his horse.

"A simple sleeping spell," the odd man answered with a wink. "By the time they wake up, we'll have been on the road for many hours."

"Does that sort of spell harm them?" Quinn could not trust those who dealt in magic since her time in Isidore's caves.

"Of course not," answered Delwyn. "I only harm those who plan on harming me or my friends." The quirky old man paused for a few seconds and smiled.

Lennox led the party while Aaron and Quinn stayed close behind. Delwyn rode behind Quinn, followed by Brother Frewin. Kemp Hethington, who was extremely nervous and excited all at once, brought up the rear.

The morning went by in a blur. Lennox ran the horses at full speed, only stopping to rest and water the horses as needed. By the time noon came, the small band of friends were in the middle of the farmlands and further away from Castle Gower's protection.

"I think we should stop and rest a moment," Delwyn suggested. "I didn't even get to watch the sun rise, we were going so fast." The old wizard knew and appreciated Lennox's plan and his complaints were just his way of speaking.

"We will stop for lunch soon enough, old one," Lennox answered. "I think we'll be leaving the comforts of the main road soon and the horses will need to regain their strength for the rough terrain ahead."

Although some of the members of the group were not looking forward to the harsh surface of Gower's open grasslands, they could not argue with the fact that they would be much safer the farther from the road they went.

Kemp Hethington did not agree. "The thought of hiding amongst the trees and bushes does not sit well with me," the warrior announced as he drew his sword. I thought we were here to kill demons?"

"Trust me, Kemp," Frewin explained, "you are going to have your chance to kill those nasty creatures soon enough."

Kemp put his sword back in its scabbard. "I just want to prove myself to the rest of the party." The warrior gestured to the others who were busy speaking to Lennox.

"Prince Aaron would not have been so quick to choose you if he hadn't deemed you worthy of accompanying him to Woodbyrne," the priest answered.

Kemp smiled.

"Just be patient, is all I'm saying to you, Kemp. Your greatest enemy on this mission could be your emotions, if you let them get out of control. Remember, revenge can blind even the greatest warrior, causing him to make fatal mistakes." Brother Frewin gave his horse a gentle kick in the sides and rode off to the rest of the party.

Kemp nodded at the priest's wisdom. A well-trained soldier of the king's army should have known better. Angered with himself, yet glad that he had such wise allies, Kemp fell in place behind the rest of the party.

After a few more moments on the main road, Lennox led the horses away from the prying eyes of the demons and into Gower's vast open plains. Fortunately, the land was level enough to push the horses into a full run. So excited was the scout that he forgot about Delwyn's plea for a quick meal and a rest.

By late afternoon, Quinn and Brother Frewin suggested that they should look for a proper area where they could spend the night.

"Yes, we are all overdue for a rest," agreed Prince Aaron. "Besides, at the pace we are taking, Woodbyrne isn't too much further."

Soon the scout's keen eyes found a suitable area to set camp. The small clearing was big enough for the entire party and surrounded by plenty of large oak trees and thick shrubs. Before Lennox approved the site, he, Aaron, and Quinn went ahead to check for signs of an ambush.

"I don't think they need to worry so much," Brother Frewin said. "I know we're far from the castle but if there were any demons nearby I should be able to detect them with this." Frewin pulled out a charm from the inside of his tunic. It was a simple looking crystal that was attached to a leather strap. "I blessed this before we left to detect any of the creatures."

"Demons aren't the only thing that we have to worry about, I would guess," reasoned Kemp, who was left behind to guard the priest and the wizard. "With almost everyone in the countryside retreating to Castle Gower, this is the best time for thieves and looters to do business."

"I told you he was a smart one," Delwyn said to his friend. "You said that he was just simple fodder, but I always knew different."

The three companions enjoyed a laugh together just as Lennox and the others came back out of the clearing. Apparently, the area was free from anyone or anything with devious intentions.

As the sun went down and the moon made its way into the sky, the party shared a cold meal together and a few good stories of days long past. They spoke of tales about men and woman who fought in grand battles and lived to tell their tales. People who overcame the odds and now were remembered in every bar and tavern across Gower.

It was decided that Delwyn would take the first watch and Quinn the second. As the others rolled out their blankets, Delwyn told them what he knew of Woodbyrne and the wood elves.

"The forest was once a place of amazing beauty and treasure. Woodbyrne used to be home to one of the most powerful and respected breeds of elves on Oneira. However, once the demons came, the forest turned black. The creatures from the Lower Planes knew only how to destroy the forest and its beauty. Wanting the magical power of Woodbyrne all for themselves, they massacred the wood elves too."

Much to Delwyn's disappointment, the party fell asleep before he finished the story. "So much to learn and so little stamina," sighed the old mage. He knew that this history lesson was essential to the survival of the party, and that in order to beat the demons, his friends must learn their unnatural behaviors. Ah, well, tomorrow is another day, he thought to himself. The old mage loved to spin tales and lecture on historical events. He would pass on a lifetime's worth of knowledge to anyone who would listen.

Sighing once more, Delwyn propped himself up against a huge oak and cast a spell on himself that would enable him to detect any warm-blooded animals in the vicinity. Immediately, the wizard's eyes began to glow a dark red from the spell's power. No matter how stealthy, no one was getting past the watchful eyes of Delwyn Westbrook.

مص

The night was calm and cool. The magnificent lights from the half moon and the countless stars shed a dark blue light on the earth. Creatures of the night were out in all their glory. The smell of autumn was in the air and it mixed wonderfully with the sweeter scents of summer.

The four demons crawling around in the bushes, however, did not care. They did not even notice.

Out on patrol along the main road that led into and out of Gower, the small party diligently watched for any signs of the humans that Damek had described to them. They were given specific instructions to capture the two friends alive and permission to slaughter anyone else who was foolish enough to travel during the evening.

"I see sompin'," shouted one of the demon soldiers, a shout that was too loud for the likes of the party's leader, who quickly silenced him. "I see sompin'," the fool whispered instead.

The demon soldier did in fact see a set of horse tracks that led off of the main road and toward a thick cover of the trees in the far distance. Quickly, the leader of the small party instructed his subordinates to follow him as silently as possible.

As they followed the horse tracks, the leader noticed how deep the horse tracks were and surmised the beasts had been running at a gallop. Just then, they heard the neigh of a horse in the distance, no more than fifty yards away.

"We need a plan," instructed the leader. "Ichel will scout ahead and see if anyone is keeping watch." The leader of the party pointed to the only one of the group who had any capability of being silent. "The rest of us will follow behind slowly and quietly."

"What if we see the prince and that nasty wench?" growled another demon as he unsheathed his poorly crafted saber.

The leader smiled wickedly and drew a rusty sword. "Damek instructed that we are to capture them alive, if possible." The demon's grin turned into a nasty smile that showed its rotting teeth. "I say that we have no choice since they put up such a fight."

Understanding what their leader was hinting at, the remaining demons fell into place while Ichel disappeared into the darkness of the night. Soon, Ichel doubled back and reported that the woman Damek had spoke of was keeping watch while the others slept.

The leader knew that luck was with them. They could attack the humans while they slept! When he reached the campsite, the leader crept out of the bushes right behind the unsuspecting woman. Slowly and quietly, he made his way toward her.

⨍

Quinn was enjoying the night's peace. The stars were beautiful and the autumn air was fresh. Suddenly, a powerful hand slapped across her face, snapping her out of her trance and dragging her to the ground. The surprised woman tried hard to break free and call for her companions but it was a futile attempt; the creature that held her was too powerful. Quinn saw three more figures approaching her sleeping friends with swords ready to strike, and grins that covered their dog like faces from ear to ear.

The three demons positioned themselves for a quick strike. One demon stood over Kemp, while the second went to Aaron, and the third covered Lennox. On cue, the demons struck down at the sleeping humans with all of their might. To their surprise, the swords swept right through the bodies and slammed into the ground, one even breaking his sword when it hit a rock. The sleeping humans vanished into thin air, leaving the demons in utter confusion.

Quinn smiled when she saw the outraged monsters curse and spit as they searched the campsite. Then she became completely still. She did not even blink her eyes or breathe.

An arrow whizzed through the air from the top of one of the large oak trees and slammed into the demon holding on to Quinn. The missile dug deep into the creature's shoulder and forced him to release his hold on the woman. The rest of the party emerged from their hiding places and attacked the demons with ferocity and cunning.

Delwyn quickly said a word of command and Quinn's long sword suddenly appeared in her hands. Without hesitation, the young warrior struck the injured demon in the chest, piercing his heart. The creature died long before his convulsing body ever hit the ground.

Brother Frewin approached one of the demons with his mace still attached to his belt. The demon smiled and lunged forward for the kill.

Unfortunately for the demon, Brother Frewin was prepared for the attack and quickly stepped to the side and snapped his fingers. Immediately, tiny sparks flew from his open hand and slammed into the demon's face; each one exploding into a ball of light as they hit. Capitalizing on the opportunity, Brother Frewin grabbed his mace and struck the blinded creature in his canine head until he dropped to the ground.

Kemp was seething with anger as he sped toward the demon closest to him. The creature knew he was in trouble and decided to throw dirt into the fast approaching human's eyes. Kemp ducked and shouted, "This is for my father!" and swung his two-handed sword down at the stupid creature. The massive blade cut flesh and bone alike, leaving the monster headless and with one less arm than with he came.

Aaron went after the leader of the scouting party, but the cowardly creature ran off into the night.

Still perched in his tree, Lennox Softfoot saw the demon try to flee and he quickly aimed his bow.

Two arrows streaked out of the sky and slammed into the fleeing demon's chest and neck. The injured creature grabbed hold of his bloody wounds but to no avail. Slowly he dropped to the ground, choking to death on his own blood.

When the fight was over, the corpses were hidden under fallen branches and leaves. Afterwards, the party reassembled at the campsite where Delwyn was already puffing on his pipe and giggling like a young boy. "Not a bad spell," he said, referring to his illusion spell that lured the demons out from hiding. "I had a feeling that the hands of Isidore stretched further than the woods." The old man plopped himself back into his blankets and drifted to sleep while the others tried to make light of their situation.

"A good thing you heard them yelling to each other, Quinn," congratulated Kemp as he cleaned black blood from the edge of his large sword.

"A good thing they had no idea on how to surprise anyone," added Aaron. "We would have heard them attacking Quinn long before the wretches got near us."

"Still, it was good that Delwyn had his spell ready in such a short amount of time," Quinn praised the old wizard. Although Delwyn was strange, the party could not deny his value.

After a brief absence, Brother Frewin returned to the party as they prepared to go back to sleep. The priest had been busy casting spells on the dead demons, that would prevent anyone from finding their rotting corpses.

Lennox told Quinn he would guard for the remainder of the night. Since it was only a couple of hours before sunrise, Quinn did not give any argument and went to bed.

"How are we to destroy this scum?" Quinn asked aloud to anyone who was listening.

"There is always a way to destroy evil, Quinn," answered Brother Frewin, who detected fear in the woman's voice. "We just have to find out how. Perhaps the elves will have some idea."

"Why is this evil so determined to come after us?"

"I was told by my elders that evil was here to test us. As long we have faith and hope, evil can never win. However, evil becomes stronger the more weak one becomes. If you or I were to loose faith, the demons would overtake us all and bring us back to the pits of Isidore."

"Do you think we have a chance to kill this demon master once we find him?" Quinn continued.

"We need allies in this fight," Frewin explained as he rested his head on his lumpy pillow. "The elves are our best chance for survival. I only hope that they see the need for us as much as we see the need for them."

"There is always a way to destroy evil, as Frewin explained," added Delwyn. "We won tonight because we were prepared and steadfast. The demons tried to flee the second the tides were turned and that is where their weakness is."

"What do you mean 'weakness'?" asked Kemp

"Creatures who do no good in this world have no true purpose," explained the priest, since Delwyn had fallen asleep. "Once they see that their mission of terror is starting to fall apart, they flee because they lack any morale. Isidore is the glue that holds the demons of Woodbyrne together."

"And you think we have a chance to beat him?" Prince Aaron asked from under his covers.

"With the help of the elves and the backing of the king, I know we can beat him." With that said, the men drifted to sleep.

It took Quinn more time to drift off, however. She could not get the image of the vile Isidore out of her mind. The terror she had experienced raised her doubts; doubts that Isidore could be killed so easily. Nor was she certain that the demons would flee once their master was dead. Quinn remembered the horrible winged creature that had slain her father. She knew that the hideous beast was more than just a follower of the demon master. Quinn quickly shook her head and tried to forget. Eventually, and with only one hour before dawn, she drifted into an unsettling sleep.

Lennox, watching the forest carefully, enjoyed Frewin's uplifting speech, but doubted the fight against the demons would end quickly. The seasoned veteran had seen his share of battles over the years, but never had he faced so formidable an enemy. No, Lennox did not agree with the priest at all. This will be a difficult and dangerous battle, he thought, never taking his eyes off the surrounding darkness.

Chapter 23

The party awakened early the next morning to a gloomy day. Thick gray clouds had moved in from the north overnight and left a chilled mist over the land.

Lennox, who had remained awake the entire night, wanted to leave as soon as everyone was up and fed. "We should stay off the road for the remainder of the trip," the scout announced as soon as they all were on their horses. "There will probably be scouts looking for their lost companions this day."

As the morning wore on, the gray clouds seemed to thicken and a dense fog made it tough for Lennox and the rest of the party to see more than a few yards ahead of them.

Aaron slowed his horse so that he could ride next to Quinn for a while. The two friends remained silent for most of the journey.

It was early afternoon when the companions made their way to a small rocky hilltop with very little grass and even fewer trees. The entire party got off their horses and stared in awe at the sight in front of them.

Woodbyrne, stood in all its glory, like a gray wall of despair. The gray clouds had turned darker over the thick canopy of the forest. An eerie fog wove slowly in and out of the immense trees.

"It almost seems that the sunlight simply refuses to shine there," said Kemp, breaking the silence. "What ever made you decide to go in there?" he asked the prince.

Aaron shrugged his shoulders. "Believe it or not, the forest looked a bit more inviting the last time I was here."

"It is hard to believe that any good can possibly exist in there," Brother Frewin said, shivering.

"Our mission is to find out if that is true," answered Lennox as he pulled out his map from one of the saddlebags. As he and Aaron discussed where they would have the greatest chance to 'find' the elves, the rest of the party spoke amongst themselves. All of the members, except for Delwyn Westbrook.

Delwyn remained silent, reminiscing of days long past. Days when he was no more than a youth in search of knowledge and adventure. "So long since I have seen your beautiful world," the old wizard said to the forest. "I come back now to free you from the evil that infects you." Delwyn sat and tried hard to emember when he and his friends would run through the forest with the elves and laugh aloud. "Those were some of the best times I had ever lived through," the old mage whispered, as if to some unseen spirit. "Before the demons came and destroyed everything."

ॐ

"What have you to report?" Isidore asked Damek. He had become edgy over the past couple of days, mainly because King Dermot had not yet reacted.

"My men have reported no army activity from our enemy, your lordship." Damek shuffled uneasily as he spoke to his master. The demon scout knew that Isidore was on the edge of a major eruption and the lesser demon did not want to be around to see it.

"Have you heard from all of your men?" Isidore asked in total disbelief.

"All of my men have reported to me just as you demanded." Damek was aware that one of his troops had not come in yet, but he decided to keep it a secret for the time being. One beating a week was quite enough. "The outskirts of Gower have been completely evacuated. Anyone left is either too badly hurt or too frightened to do anything."

"What are you doing with these stragglers?"

Damek smiled. "My men grow tired and hungry throughout the day. I gave them permission to do as they please to the weakling humans."

"You had better make sure that your troops are following orders, Damek," warned Isidore. "If I find out that your control is lacking in any way, I swear that you will wish you were dead."

"I understand, Isidore." With that said, Damek flew out of the room at full speed, leaving Isidore to ponder his dilemma.

"I know you are up to something, Prince Aaron," growled the angry demon as he paced the large floor of his chamber. "What else could I possibly do to make you react?" Suddenly, a wicked smile broke across Isidore's face. "Maybe I have been too idle since my last attack," decided the demon master."

⟡

Isidore shivered as he stood in front of his huge cauldron that was filled with the thick, rich blood of the wood elves. The spell he had in mind was going to drain him, but the result would be well worth the effort.

"I will have nature itself attack you where you live, Prince Aaron," the demon barked as he prepared to ask the Lower Planes of existence for the powers needed to accomplish his horrific task.

Isidore began his spell with a few simple prayers to his homeland and to the demon lord who reigned supreme there. As Isidore prayed for power, his head rolled from side to side and his yellow eyes turned backwards, making him look blind.

The spell began to take shape as the lord of the Lower Planes answered Isidore's calls. The red blood in the cauldron began to turn black and a dark mist began to swirl inside. Isidore shouted even louder when he realized that his spell was beginning. He rolled up the sleeves of his ceremonial robe and pulled out a simple black knife. The hilt of the blade was made out of the bones of the elf that had forged the blackened steel.

Another shout of command ripped through the chamber and Isidore slashed the blade across his forearm, letting his own black blood drip into the cauldron. Immediately, a huge clap of thunder roared through the room; its powerful force knocked Isidore to the floor and shattered some of the large statues into fragments. Isidore quickly got back on his feet to complete the spell. Again he stood in front of the cauldron and raised his huge arms high above his head. The demon shouted the final word of command. A powerful wind tore through the chamber knocking him to the ground and blowing out the candles.

Isidore watched a small black cloud rise out of the cauldron. Small snaps of thunder could be heard inside the pulsating form. Isidore smiled as the magical storm made its way through the small cracks in the ceiling and out into the forest. Exhausted, the mighty demon master of Woodbyrne laughed weakly before falling into an unnatural slumber.

⨋

Brother Frewin was the first to notice the dark red cloud form behind Woodbyrne's thick cover while the rest of the party was busy with the next stage of the plan. "I think we're in for some trouble!" Quickly, the wise priest said a few prayers to ward off evil.

The others looked up to see the massive cloud heading toward them.

"What an unusual storm," commented Kemp as he went over to calm his horse. The beast was acting as if a ghost had spooked it.

"I have a feeling this is not a natural occurrence," said Delwyn, receiving a nod from Brother Frewin and Lennox.

As the party discussed what should be done, the storm grew. By the time the sinister clouds reached the edge of the forest, they blocked out the rest of the sky. Red lightning shot from its innards and huge blocks of hail began to slam into the earth.

"Under the trees!" Lennox shouted as he and Brother Frewin led the horses under a thick patch of oaks not fifty feet from Woodbyrne's edge.

As the party ran for cover, the massive storm intensified. Gusts of wind from all directions ripped trees from the ground and tossed them hundreds of feet away. The hail became like small blades that cut through branches and pounded into the soft earth. The red lightning hit the ground frequently and splintered anything that was in its path.

"We have to do something before we are killed!" Aaron shouted as he was pelted by a shard of ice.

Just as the trees that covered the party began to slip apart, Delwyn stepped forward and instructed his friends to gather into a close huddle with the horses. When everyone was ready, the old wizard spoke the words of an ancient spell. In a matter of seconds, a thin blue light surrounded the party and acted as a shield from the horrible weather outside. Hail slammed into the magical wall and the red lightning tried to break its surface, but to no avail.

"This will only last a few hours!" Delwyn shouted over the sound of ice slamming into his protective cover.

"The storm is moving fast!" Lennox said. "I am hoping that it will pass us soon!"

As he waited for the unnatural storm to pass, Aaron studied its movement.

"What are you thinking?" asked Quinn, who was actually enjoying the spectacle around her. She felt safe enough and figured that she might as well enjoy the experience while she could.

"I am thinking that this storm is alive," answered the prince, stealing the smile right off Quinn's face. "It grows every second and it's moving toward the west.

"You are right," Quinn agreed. "Storms of this nature usually come in from the west and move eastward with the winds."

Aaron looked gravely at his friend. "It's moving toward Castle Gower. I am guessing that this storm's purpose is to pummel the rest of my father's kingdom."

"Prince Aaron is correct," added Delwyn. "This storm is an attack on Gower. I feel its energy and I know it to be evil."

"We can't let it reach the castle!" shouted Quinn. "All of the wounded are set up there and they have no other place to run!"

"We are going to stay here for as long as we can!" barked Lennox. "We cannot stop this storm. We have a mission to finish and my job is to make sure it is accomplished!"

"What about the king and queen?" Quinn asked desperately. "Will they have protection for themselves?"

"That is not our concern." Lennox answered. "We can only pray that the lookout at the castle sees this coming before it is too late."

After a few brief moments, the frightened woman went over to the horses where she joined Brother Frewin and Kemp in calming them down.

"We have a while before this storm passes us," said the priest. "I said a prayer that will settle the horses' nerves for the remainder of the storm. I think that all of us should try to get as much rest as possible."

Although Brother Frewin was right, nobody in the party got any rest. The pounding of the hail and the bolts of lightning did little to comfort anyone. All around them, trees were leveled and the ground was chewed up.

All the while, however, Prince Aaron's thoughts were back at the castle with his mother and father. He silently prayed that Castle Gower would be able to stand up to the raw force of the hailstorm.

After a very long hour, the hail began to diminish, and the lightning became more infrequent.

"It looks like the storm slowed just in time," Kemp commented as he pointed to the small cracks in the blue shield. "I guess it was more powerful than we thought."

"I guess it was," agreed Delwyn, who was not at all happy with what he saw. The spell he had cast could survive an avalanche. How powerful was this Isidore if a simple conjured storm could rattle even his powerful enchantments? The thought did not rest easy in the old man's mind, and he decided it would be best if he kept those thoughts to himself. "I guess it was," he repeated miserably.

After reorienting themselves, the small party approached the edge of Woodbyrne. In the background, the storm continued to rage on, slowly making its way across Gower's beautiful landscape. Although nobody mentioned it, the storm sounded like it grew in intensity the further it got from the forest.

"From here on, we walk," announced Lennox Softfoot, breaking the mood. "The horses will have too difficult a time navigating through the dense forest and I will not put them under such a risk."

"If we leave them tied up, they will be slaughtered," Quinn retorted.

Lennox understood the woman's concern and assured her that the horses would be placed in a safe area. After all necessary supplies were taken, the scout took the reins of the horses and led them away from the group to a secluded area with plenty of grass for them to feed on.

After a quick check on supplies, the small group made their way to the designated entrance of the forest.

"We should make our destination in just over two hours, if all goes well," said Lennox.

"I somehow doubt that is going to happen," Aaron said.

Isidore awakened from his unexpected slumber thinking that his head was going to explode into a million pieces. However, the agony was well earned. Isidore dragged his body off the ground and slowly stumbled out to his main audience chamber where he crawled onto his throne and called telepathically for Damek.

The evil scout flew into the room less than five seconds after hearing his master's call. A huge grin covered the creature's lizard-like face.

Isidore did not share Damek's joy. "What do you have to report?"

"A storm is ravishing Gower's land!" Damek said.

"Gower is getting pummeled from hail and chaotic lightning bolts!"

"Excellent." Isidore was truly happy to hear that his spell was successful. "Report back to me when you hear of any activity from the castle. This storm has to stir the king's emotions or humans are made of tougher stuff than I could have possibly imagined." With a wave of his hand, Isidore sent his scout out of the room.

Isidore sat in his throne for a long while and contemplated his next move. Unfortunately for the impatient demon, he was going to have to wait for some sort of retaliation from the king before he could properly plan out a course of action.

"How I hate waiting!" the demon master cursed.

Chapter 24

The forest was relatively dry with the exception of a few chunks of hail left from the powerful storm. For the most part, the dark woods had not been affected by the mysterious anomaly, which came as no surprise to the prince and his band of adventurers. Centuries of decay and neglect had caught up with the ancient forest, making it very difficult to traverse.

Delwyn, the wizard who had been a very valuable asset thus far, was the only one with a smile on his face. As he picked his way through the rough terrain, the old mage sensed the magic that Woodbyrne held. "Can the rest of you feel it?" he asked time and time again. However, the expressions of the party showed that they did not share the same feelings.

"Do you think we're heading in the right direction, Aaron?" Lennox asked. The veteran scout seemed unsure of his bearings.

"We are heading to where Byram and I ran into the ambush set by the demons." Aaron's stomach turned as he remembered the scene. "After the fight, we were led into a trap by the elf, Cathmore Stardust."

"Just keep your senses with you, Aaron," said Lennox as he placed a reassuring hand on the prince's shoulder. "I fear that bad memories may be your greatest obstacle in this mission. Perhaps retelling the details of the events will help you face the memories, and at the same time we may pick up on a detail that will point us in the right direction."

As the second hour of wandering in the forest passed, Aaron retold the events in detail. Along the way, he recognized a familiar clearing surrounded by brush. "This is where Byram and I were attacked by the demons."

"Are you certain that we are at the right spot?" Brother Frewin asked. "I've been trying to detect the beasts since we entered these woods, but have not detected anything."

"I am positive this is the spot. We fought the demons and hid their bodies under a thick patch of fallen leaves and branches."

"Where did you place them?" Frewin asked.

Aaron brought the priest over to where he remembered hiding the corpses. "Over here," he said, pointing to the section of earth that looked more disturbed than the rest of the area. "I actually thought we did a better job than this."

"You did a fine job," Lennox said as he knelt down to inspect the shallow grave. "It seems that something else has been here in the last few days." Lennox motioned for Kemp and Aaron to help as he moved the debris from the makeshift grave.

"Dear Lord!" Quinn shouted as a waft of pungent stench slammed into her face. All three men in the hole covered their faces and tried not to vomit.

"Smells like the prince was right," Delwyn laughed, finding all of his partners' reactions amusing. "Why don't we just put the dirt and sticks back on the corpses and leave this area?"

"Because these are not the corpses of demons," explained Lennox as he held up a hand that seemed to be humanoid. "There are two elves in this hole. From the looks of them, I would say that they have been here for a while."

"But I am positive that this is the place where I buried the bodies," insisted the prince. Aaron was so sure that he covered his face with a cloth and jumped back into the grave. He pushed the bodies to the side and felt around in the soil for any signs of the demons. Just as Aaron was about to give up his search, he felt something cold and sharp. The prince pulled up the object and wiped it off, revealing a sinister looking dagger.

"That surely isn't from the forge of any elf that I've known," declared Delwyn. "Even a dwarf with ten gallons of mead in him would make a better blade if he used his head for a hammer."

"Why would the demons go through such a time-consuming task in order to hide a few bodies?" Kemp asked.

"Revenge," answered Delwyn. "They killed the elves for payment of their own kin." Again, Delwyn tried hard to remember the days where the forest was filled with creatures pure of heart and of spirit.

Lennox and Kemp gently replaced the bodies of the slaughtered elves. When the grave was properly covered, Brother Frewin said a few prayers for the fallen creatures' spirits. Afterwards, Aaron suggested that the party move deeper into the woods. "The elves would hide from the main roads for fear of being detected."

High up in the trees, far away from the eyes of the humans, Cathmore Stardust wiped the tears away from his eyes. The bodies that the humans found were friends of his who had been sent out on a scouting mission and never returned. When the small group of adventurers had left the burial site, the wood elf leapt from his perch and landed on the soft earth without a sound.

"Your death will be avenged, my brothers," Cathmore swore in his native tongue as he knelt down and said his own prayers for his murdered kin. When he had finished, he thought long and hard about Woodbyrne's newest visitors. The elven scout remembered Prince Aaron and Quinn, but he questioned those who followed them. Where was the king, and why had Aaron brought such a small party with him? Still, Cathmore was truly impressed with the other humans. Not many outsiders would have guessed why the bodies were replaced and even fewer would have the respect to make sure the grave was properly reset.

Quickly, and without sound, Cathmore Stardust ran off to meet with his leader. The elf could not help but smile when he thought of the possibilities of ridding the forest of the demons once and for all.

So determined was the elven scout that he did not stop to catch his breath or take water. By the time he returned to the main campsite, it was hours past sunset and most of the elves were asleep. Only a few guards remained awake as they focused their keen senses on the surrounding forest.

Cathmore was brought to a halt when two of his kin jumped from a treetop and threatened to strike unless he yielded.

"Not bad," Cathmore said, congratulating two elves that had already replaced their swords in their scabbards.

"We didn't hear you coming until you were already inside the camp's perimeters," confessed one of the guards, a younger elf that was in training with his companion for the title of scout.

"I still congratulate the two of you for hearing me at all," replied the scout. Cathmore knew that he had to give his two students as much positive reinforcement as possible. However, the seasoned veteran wondered when it would be best to tell them that he saw them fifty yards before they even knew he was moving through the woods. Something for their next training session. "Time and training will create two of the finest elven scouts ever seen in this forest."

"Second only to Cathmore Stardust," replied the second elf in a playful tone.

"Of course I have to exclude myself since I am the best ever." The three comrades shared a much-needed laugh. "Tell me, my pupils, where can I find our leader this fine evening?"

"In the main tent, of course," the first elf replied. " Probably going over more plans."

Cathmore thanked his pupils and hurried over to the main tent.

A single candle lit the tent. Forrester was alone inside, busy constructing a new map to be used by his patrol parties. Forrester had an intelligence that was undeniable. Some even believed that he would have become a great mage if it were not for the fact that magic had been banned once the demons arrived. Others said that Forrester was related to a powerful wizard and that he practiced the forsaken craft when he was alone in his huge tent. Of course, the rumors never threatened Forrester's rule, so the wise elf let his people speak freely about their suspicions.

"Enter," Forrester called when he heard Cathmore ask to come in. Quickly, the powerful elf lord stood up and covered his map work.

Cathmore entered and bowed to his leader.

"Cathmore, tell me you have some good news for a change." Forrester smiled gently and patted his friend on the shoulder, instructing him to rise and be at ease.

"I have some information that may be of use to you," said Cathmore as he reached for a bladder full of water that was hanging on the wall of the tent. After a few heavy mouthfuls of cold water, the elven scout sat down at the elf lord's worktable.

Cathmore smiled. "I was near where I first met the prince and his cousin, Byram," the scout began. "It was there that I saw Prince Aaron Gower return with five powerful allies. One of the humans was the woman, Quinn, who Aaron and Byram rescued from the caves."

Forrester was truly overjoyed with the news. He and Cathmore spoke for hours formulating a plan that would lead the humans to a safe place to meet. The main campsite was out of the question. Forrester did not want any foreign eyes to see where he and his people took refuge from the chaotic struggle with the demons.

"I am sure the prince would never tell our location to anyone, my lord," stressed Cathmore, somewhat surprised at Forester's lack of trust.

"I am sure that none of the humans would speak," said Forrester, "no matter what torture they were put through. However, humans are not as protected against mind probing as we elves are. I fear that if any of them were captured, Isidore might use one of his spells to read their minds and find out where this camp is."

"Then where should we take them?"

"The Forest's Heart. That is the safest place for us to meet the humans."

"I do have one last thing to tell you, my lord."

"Out with it, Cathmore," Forrester said bluntly.

"Prince Aaron has brought a wizard with him to Woodbyrne. I have watched the mage closely and he seems to wield great power. I know that magic has been banned, and for good reason, but he could prove vital to our cause."

Forrester took a long time before answering. "I know our people look at magic as a source of evil but the demons are powerful. And a good magic user could prove most valuable in destroying Isidore." The elf lord had never truly agreed with his people's decision to ban all use of magic. "Go and meet up with the humans," Forrester instructed. "Bring them to the Forest's Heart."

"What of the wizard?"

Forrester took a beep breath and scratched his head. "Bring everyone. I will be responsible for telling the others of the wizard, when the time is right." The honorable elf despised having to keep secrets from his people, but in the case of the human wizard, he felt it to be the lesser of two evils. "I am sure that the others will understand once this is all over."

ᴧ

"Would anyone like some food this wonderful morning?" asked a melodious voice from high up in one of the trees.

Quickly, Lennox pulled out his bow and readied an arrow while Brother Frewin grabbed his mace and held it ready to strike. The party had decided that it would be safer to have two people instead of one keep watch while the others tried to sleep in relative peace. It had been a quiet evening and a slight sense of ease had found its way into the small campsite.

"I assure you that I am here to help," Cathmore explained as he slowly made his way down the tree with his weapons still in place. "I am here to speak with Prince Aaron. He has informed all of you about his happenings in my forest?"

Lennox eased up on his bow and instructed the priest to lower his weapon with a raised hand. "Go and wake the prince and the others."

"I am Cathmore Stardust," said the elf as he bowed.

"Well met, Cathmore Stardust. I am Lennox Softfoot. I have been traveling with Prince Aaron on our quest to find you. I was beginning to suspect that the elves were not interested in the help of we humans."

"Quite the contrary, Lennox Softfoot. The elves of Woodbyrne have been in dire need of powerful allies for over two hundred years." Cathmore grinned slyly. "I only pray that I have chosen the right person to come to our aid."

Before Lennox could answer, Aaron and Quinn ran over to greet their friend. "It is good to see you again, Cathmore," said the prince. "I apologize for how long it has taken me to make good on my promise."

"I understand such things can take time. Woodbyrne is not a place of joy and happiness," said the elf. "You and Quinn have been through much in a very short time." Cathmore bowed his head toward the beautiful woman. "Woodbyrne can scar a person's soul as a dagger can scar one's flesh."

Once the rest of the party introduced themselves to the friendly elf, they all sat down and enjoyed the breakfast Cathmore had brought of various breads and dried fruits. The exotic foods were a far cry from the dried meats and stale bread the party had eaten ever since they left the castle.

"Forgive me for asking such a nosey question," said Brother Frewin, "but once the demons came and ravished your people, why didn't the elves leave the forest and make their home elsewhere?"

Cathmore stood up. He wore a proud yet sad look on his chiseled face. "Woodbyrne is and always shall be the home of Cathmore Stardust, and all of the wood elves. This is my forest as well as the forest of all of my kin. The demons are but a disease to my home. They are my people's plague and we have yet to find the cure."

Aaron stood up and walked over to the elf. He embraced Cathmore's hand with his own and stared directly into his deep brown eyes. "I have returned to help you in your cause, Cathmore Stardust. The demon plague has now spread to Gower, and I fear that unless our people unite, we have no chance for survival."

"We have seen much activity lately in the forest, but I had no idea that Isidore was striking back at you and your kingdom," Cathmore responded, surprised at the news. He had figured that Isidore was merely sending out more patrols to search for the elves' main campsite.

"It seems that the powerful demon master is bent on revenge, Cathmore Stardust," interrupted Delwyn.

"So it does, my dear wizard," Cathmore replied.

"How did you know he was a wizard?" asked Quinn.

"I have been following your every move since you and your friends stepped foot into this forest," admitted Cathmore. "I truly wanted to greet all of you the second I saw you; however, I too must follow the orders of my superiors." The stealthy wood elf continued to explain that he had witnessed some of Delwyn's spell casting and noticed that Brother Frewin was a holy man of great power.

"I can guarantee you that your trade will remain a secret, Delwyn. Only myself and my leader shall know, and we agreed that it will remained concealed for as long as possible."

"I'd trust the word of a wood elf any day," replied Delwyn.

"We have only been granted a few days to set up a meeting and come to some sort of arrangement," explained Aaron. "I hope you understand that I am in great haste and that we must speak with your lord as soon as possible."

"I do understand, my friend. That is why I am here." Cathmore walked up to Quinn and kissed her hand. "You look much better since I last saw you," the elf complimented, causing the young woman to blush. "My lord is Forrester Silverbow. When we are done here, I shall take you to him."

The party quickly packed up their supplies and followed Cathmore into the forest. They only stayed on the main road for a few minutes before the young elf led them into a thicker, wilder section of the woods; to a place never before seen by non-elven eyes.

Chapter 25

The journey through Woodbyrne was not an easy one, but it did prove to be uneventful. Along the way, Cathmore spoke to Aaron and Quinn about the demon activity since they had left the woods. The other members of the party kept silent and continuously scanned their surroundings for any demon activity.

Lennox was the only member of the party who seemed distracted. Although the scout knew he could trust Cathmore, he did not enjoy the fact that the silent elf was able to sneak up on him so easily. When his patience had ended, Lennox Softfoot walked up to Cathmore and interrupted his conversation with the prince.

"Is there a problem?" Aaron asked. He had come to trust his father's friend and was concerned when the scout rudely made his presence felt. "You look worried."

"I am afraid that I must speak with our new ally," the scout said dryly. "If you could possibly give us a few minutes to get to know each other better, I am sure it would be beneficial to the party."

"Of course, Lennox," the prince answered, although he had no idea why the scout was acting so strangely. "I'll go inform the others where we are heading."

"You don't trust me, Lennox," Cathmore said the second the prince and Quinn were out of range.

"I need to know how you were able to surprise us like you did."

"The wood elves of this forest have the ability to speak with its trees," the elf explained.

"I thought this forest was all evil."

Cathmore looked at his new companion with pity in his deep brown eyes. "You are wrong, my friend. The trees of this forest are very much alive and are very much against the demons. Like the rest of the creatures that used to live here, they pray for the success of the elves."

"I meant no insult to you, good elf. It is just that I was raised to keep away from this forest. I have heard stories that would keep even the boldest fighter awake at nights."

Cathmore understood his human counterpart. He not only heard of the demons' horrible doings, he witnessed many of them first hand. Still, it hurt whenever he heard of the stories being told outside of his home.

The rest of the morning went by without incident, and by mid-afternoon, Aaron decided that his friends should rest and take lunch. While they sat and ate, Cathmore explained his abilities in greater detail. He explained that all of the elves of Woodbyrne were capable of speaking with the trees as well as the more intelligent creatures of the woods. The humans were also made aware that some elves had the ability to blend in with their surroundings.

"My ability to blend," explained Cathmore, "far surpasses most of my kin, since I have the most opportunities to practice. The elves of these woods, along with all other elves, have the ability to see in the darkest of nights."

"No wonder you came upon me with such ease," Lennox said.

"I also know these woods better than most, my friend. You and the rest of the party are all foreigners here."

"Cathmore, how much further is our destination?" Aaron asked while he packed up his supplies and readied himself to get back on the road.

Just as the wood elf was about to answer, he raised a hand to silence the rest of the group. He dropped to the ground and placed a pointed ear on top of a large tree root. After only a few seconds, he instructed Aaron and the others to take cover behind a large fallen tree. Then, like a cat, Cathmore ran up the side of a gigantic oak and disappeared behind its thick cover.

The humans quickly concealed themselves behind the fallen oak. After a few minutes of silence, Kemp and Brother Frewin began to question their guide's actions.

"I don't hear anything," Kemp whispered to Aaron.

"Cathmore would not react so quickly if he didn't think it was absolutely necessary," scolded Quinn.

After a few more long and agitating minutes, Lennox informed Prince Aaron, through hand gestures, that he heard noises heading toward them. Not long after the scout's discovery, the rest of the party heard what seemed to be the voices of two creatures speaking rather loudly. As silently as possible, Lennox readied his bow while the others unsheathed their weapons.

In a matter of seconds, two wretched looking demons stepped into a small clearing no more than twenty yards from the fallen tree. One of the beasts carried a dead rabbit while the other swore and waved his hands wildly about his head.

"You had the legs the last time!" the foul creature argued in his unearthly tongue. "It's my turn to have them!"

The larger of the two demons, the one holding the dead rabbit argued his side just as angrily. "I killed him! You just sat there and picked your nose!"

As the small band of humans watched the fools argue over food, they were appalled by the appearance of the evil creatures. Although they had encountered demons before, Kemp and the others never had the chance to gaze upon them. The demons looked like some sort of half-breed spawn between a human and a gigantic wolf. Their faces and bodies looked as some horrible fire had charred them. Each creature wore some sort of green leather armor and torn pants, and they both carried a long sword and a crossbow.

Lennox readied his arrow for a shot.

Aaron, aware that he and his friends had the upper hand, also readied his bow. The prince instructed Quinn and Kemp to leap out with their swords once the surprise was over.

Suddenly, just as Lennox was about to stand and fire his bow, two arrows whistled out of the treetops and slammed into the demons with a loud thud. One of the arrows flew into the larger demon's neck, causing him to drop the rabbit and fall to his knees while the other arrow found its way into the chest of the second demon where it lodged nicely in the lining of his heart. Both creatures fell dead to the ground in seconds, neither making a sound as they drifted into eternal darkness.

Cathmore jumped down from his perch and went over to inspect the dead bodies. Satisfied with his marksmanship, he called for help to hide the carcasses.

"How did you move so quickly?" Quinn asked, her eyes never leaving the dead demons. "Are all wood elves as fast as you?"

"In Woodbyrne," explained Cathmore as he covered the bodies with dead leaves and branches, "you are either fast or you are dead." The elf found the rabbit that had been killed by the two demons. Gently, the elf placed the small creature in his food bag and said a small prayer.

"I will be happy to get off this trail," Kemp stated as he slung his pack over his massive shoulder. "I never thought I would get to see an elven village."

"Alas, you will not be seeing the village, my friend," Cathmore corrected. "I am taking you to a sacred area no human has ever laid eyes on."

"Isn't the village the best place to hold the meeting?" asked Brother Frewin.

"It wouldn't be very safe to lead us to the elven campsite," said Aaron. "If we are followed, it won't be long before Isidore sends his entire legion of soldiers after us. And from the look on Cathmore's face, I would say that even he didn't expect to see any demon activity in this part of the woods."

"You're right, Aaron," agreed the elf. "The trail we are on hasn't been used for years. It disturbs me greatly that the scum of Oneira found their way here."

"All the more reason for us to get a move on," urged the old wizard.

ॐ

Damek flew high above the countryside in search of his missing patrol. The sunlight made the demon scout an easy target but he did not care. It was almost time for action and he was certain that he could take care of any humans who might have stayed. Damek was also certain that Isidore was aware of the missing patrol, and that it was only a matter of time before another cruel punishment was delivered.

As Damek flew over an abandoned farm, the idea that his patrol had looted and slept there entered his distrusting mind. Quickly, he flew down to the farm and landed between the farmhouse and the barn. He was certain that one of the two structures would hold his missing party. Occassionally, demon patrols go off on a tangent and completely forget their mission.

It only took the scout a few minutes to check the farmhouse. It was a small home with no signs of any activity. Satisfied, Damek headed outside where he would inspect the large barn. "Maybe those fools decided to dine on the livestock," he thought as he got closer.

Suddenly, Damek heard a noise come from the inside of the barn. Quickly, he pulled out his black dagger and kicked open the doors. When Damek entered the barn, he was surprised to see that some of the livestock had survived the attack. Two horses lay on their sides dying from lack of food and water while numerous chickens ran about in search of the smallest bites to eat. Rats could be seen eating away at the livestock that had not survived the attack.

"Such a pity," said the demon. "How I would have loved to be here a few days ago when all of you were in better health."

Another noise from the hayloft snapped Damek back to attention. As he narrowed his eyes, he noticed dust fall from the ceiling of the loft. Damek smiled wickedly as he unfolded his wings and levitated above the bails of hay.

"I know where you are," said the demon as he tried to be bold and menacing like his master. "You have no chance of survival so you might as well reveal yourself." Damek concentrated his heat vision and found a large form hidden under two stacks of hay.

Unfortunately, Damek underestimated the resourcefulness of the hidden creature. Before he could react, the creature jumped out and threw a fistful of dust into his eyes. Damek tried hard to clear up his vision but a searing pain in his hip told the demon that he had been injured by a very sharp object. Screaming in rage, Damek beat his wings hard and flew straight through the roof of the barn. When he felt that he was out of harm's way, Damek cleaned his eyes and checked his wound.

A deep gash ran from his hip to his lower thigh, which allowed black blood to ooze freely down his leg and off his webbed foot. Damek cursed under his breath. From up above the broken barn, Damek saw a man run into the farmhouse carrying an axe, an axe that was coated in black blood. The demon also noticed that the human ran with a very bad limp.

With the speed that only the unnatural possessed, Damek swooped down on the house and smashed through its front window. The human, who hid behind a large couch, knew that he was in terrible danger. Damek advanced on him without hesitation, his sharp black dagger leading the way.

"Don't come any closer, you murderer!" the farmer demanded as he stood in front of Damek with his axe held ready to strike. "I bled you before and I will not stop until you are dead!"

"You stupid fool," said Damek as he snapped his fingers, causing all of the candles in the room to ignite. "My wound is superficial at best." As the demon readied himself to strike at the unfortunate human, a devious plan entered his sinister mind.

"Keep away you beast!"

"You don't know how lucky I am to have found you. You are going to help me explain a few things to my boss."

The man dove at Damek with a wild strike that would have chopped an oak in half. Damek, able to see the move in plain sight this time, stepped aside and grabbed the farmer's arm, causing the axe to hit the ground with a resilient bang. Damek pulled the farmer's head back, exposing his delicate neck. "You are the best thing that's happened to me all day." Damek's dagger slit the farmer's throat, killing him instantly. The victorious scout gathered up his loot — the dead farmer and the battle-axe. After tying some dirty rags around his injury, Damek soared into the sky with his bag of excuses neatly tucked under his arms. The demon flew as fast as he could back to Woodbyrne.

⌒

"I've been very busy planning the inevitable battle with King Dermot and I am not in the mood for your stupidity," warned Isidore as the demon scout glided into the chamber.

"I brought you an answer to your question, my master." Damek knelt on one knee in front of Isidore.

"What happened to your men?" Isidore asked. "You had better have come to me with proof this time, Damek."

"I was flying high over one of the abandoned farms," began the devious scout, "when I spotted an equipment bag that our soldiers carry when they travel outside of Woodbyrne."

Isidore got off his throne and approached Damek with clenched fists.

"I found the man who killed our missing patrol," Damek said as he quickly opened the bag and revealed the corpse of the farmer. "It took me a while to do it, but I slew him for killing our brothers."

"How could one weak human kill a troop of demons single-handedly?"

"He carried this axe." Isidore pulled the heavy battle-axe from a blood-stained bag and threw it on the floor. "He used it against me and was able to score a hit." Damek showed Isidore his wound, which was caked with dried blood.

"Where are the bodies of my minions?"

"I couldn't carry them all, especially since I was injured." Another quick lie entered Damek's head. "I burned their corpses in order to cover up any proof that our forces were back in Gower."

Seemingly satisfied with Damek's story, Isidore dismissed his servant and ordered the farmer's body to be cut up and given to his men for dinner. The demon master returned to his private quarters where he sat and contemplated the actions he should take against Prince Aaron and the rest of Gower.

Chapter 26

By late afternoon, Cathmore had led his friends to an even more secluded trail. It had so many twists and turns, every human except for Lennox had lost their sense of direction. Fresh grass covered the forest floor and a refreshing breeze made its way through the thick canopy of pines. An unusual sense of peace and calm wafted over the party and even Aaron began to smile and absorb the beauty of his surroundings. Delwyn simply sighed in relief as he pulled out his notepad and began jotting down a few thoughts.

After a small climb up a mossy hill, the trail ended at a natural barricade of a few gigantic pine trees and some smaller oaks.

"Forrester Silverbow is near," Cathmore announced nervously. "Behind these trees lies one of the most sacred places of my people. In the last two hundred years, very few elves have had the opportunity to come here. And never before has an outsider stepped foot on that holy ground."

Brother Frewin smiled and said a few blessings under his breath. The young priest knew he was near something precious.

Cathmore walked to the very end of the trail and began to recite an old elven verse, one that even Delwyn Westbrook had a difficult time understanding. The trees that blocked the path began to bend outward, revealing an entranceway.

"Before you enter, all weapons must be left behind," said the elf as he placed his gear alongside one of the large pines. Cathmore set aside his magnificent long bow and the quiver full of arrows.

Without hesitation, Aaron lay down his sword and bow next to Cathmore's weapons. The prince gave an assuring smile to the rest of the party as he stood by the wood elf, waiting to enter the holy ground.

Kemp Hethington, still wary of the foreign creatures, was reluctant to lay down his weapons. "What if some thieving demon finds our weapons?"

"These are some of the most sacred grounds I have ever been in," Brother Frewin explained. "There is some sort of spell that radiates from all parts of the land surrounding us. It is a spell that deters any evil from entering. I could only hope to cast such a powerful spell a hundred years from now, if I could live that long. Your weapons are safe here."

With a reluctant sigh, Kemp lay down his massive sword and a few daggers he kept hidden in his boots, behind his chain mail, and up the sleeves of his tunic.

Cathmore laughed at the arsenal the young human carried with him, but he understood what it was like to feel that at any moment, your life could end in a horrible death. "We are now ready to enter the most sacred and peaceful section of forest in all of Oneira." The elf continued to walk through the tree-gate.

Once again, Aaron gave his friends a nod and followed Cathmore through the gate.

"We're all safe from harm," explained Quinn. "If that were not the case, Cathmore would have left one or two of us behind to stand guard." With that said, the young woman followed Cathmore and Aaron through the gate.

The rest of the party members followed the female warrior. Delwyn gave a chuckle when he saw how far each tree bent in order to allow them passage. It was almost as if they were alive, he thought. Delwyn could also tell that the trees would be able to stop any unwanted visitors from entering the sacred ground if they had to. "A powerful deterrent," he whispered.

❧

The land behind the giant trees was a large clearing that stretched for two miles. Lush grass and wildflowers decorated the ground, and the purest lake anyone had ever seen lay peacefully in the center. Insects of every type and color flew overhead or hopped in and out of hiding in the tall grass as beautiful birds landed near the lake to take a drink of water. A large stone altar stood at one end of the lake. Next to it was a small stone building that Frewin recognized as a church. On the other end of the small body of water a stream flowed lazily away from its source and headed off into the woods. Apparently, the pristine lake had an underground source that fed it.

Cathmore allowed his guests to absorb their surroundings for a little while before he approached Aaron. It had been decades since the wood elf had visited the special place and he too needed a moment to catch his breath. The raw beauty and serenity of the Forest's Heart helped rebuild his morale. It was a shame the rest of his people could not witness such beauty, he thought. On many occasions, it had been suggested that the Forest's Heart be used as a place for the elves to escape their life with the demons for a while. But, Forrester and other noble elves felt that the traffic back and forth would bring unwanted curiosity from Isidore and his minions.

Prince Aaron took a deep breath of air when he noticed someone exit the stone chapel. The person had the same features as Cathmore, yet there was something very different about him. Aaron saw the elf wore traditional traveling gear but there was something hidden under the green and brown clothes.

"Greetings, Prince Aaron!" the elf lord said as he made his way effortlessly toward the humans.

"Greetings, Forrester Silverbow," Aaron replied, matching the elf lord's politeness. The rest of the party smiled and nodded in response to the friendly greeting.

"Forgive me for having you and your friends travel such harsh roads, but I felt that this meeting was too important to have anywhere else." Forrester grasped Aaron's hand and shook it as if they were old friends.

"We had no problems coming here," the prince said awkwardly. "Especially since we had such capable protection." Aaron pointed to Cathmore, who was busy refilling his deerskin with fresh water.

Forrester introduced himself to the rest of his guests. However, when he got to Quinn, the elven lord knelt on one knee and took her hands. "I am very happy to see you back in Woodbyrne, Quinn Brainard. Coming back to this place proves that you are a person of great strength and compassion."

Quinn kissed the elf gently on his forehead. "Thank you for your words. But if it were not for the elves, the prince and I would never have left Woodbyrne alive. For that, I am forever grateful."

After the pleasantries had finished, Forrester invited Aaron to follow him into the old stone building where they could speak in privacy. In the meantime, the rest of the party was invited to refill their water skins and make themselves at home.

⁓

"My people have been in a quandry for over two centuries," began Forrester, after he and Aaron shared a drink of elven mead. "We know how to destroy our nemesis, but our numbers are too few."

"If the wood elves joined the humans of Gower, our two forces could easily push the demons back to whatever hole they crept out of."

"What do the humans ask in exchange?"

"I am afraid I don't understand what you mean, my friend."

"For centuries, the elves have watched the progress of the humans. At first, they were simple nomads and farmers who stayed close to the coastline where they could fish. However, as the human population grew, they spread over the land and layed claim to its abundant resources. King Dermot does have an excellent reputation, yet I fear an alliance with the humans would mean giving up at least part of Woodbyrne's majestic forest, something the elves would never agree upon."

Prince Aaron stood up and placed his drink on the table. "I swear that the wood elves shall forfeit none of their home to the humans."

Forrester smiled. "Then it is agreed. My people will join the humans in a single effort to overthrow Isidore. The elves will send scouts to search the borders of Gower for any trouble."

Prince Aaron also smiled. "In return for your help, the humans will not step foot inside Woodbyrne until the wood elves grant permission to do so. In addition, we will open a trade system that will benefit everyone. Gower has an abundant supply of grains and meats that the elves could enjoy, while Gower's people could benefit from some of your fine weapons and armor."

Once all of the agreements and promises were made, Forrester and Aaron went outside and invited the others to come join them for the finer details of the upcoming campaign.

⌇

After a few hours of discussion, a battle plan was made. It was rather simple, yet the humans and the elves felt that it would be the most effective way to conquer the demons.

"King Dermot will lead his army to the western entrance of Woodbyrne," explained Forrester. "The demon spies, who would have spotted the king's movement, will inform Isidore of the army's progress. Isidore will then send his minions to intercept the humans at the edge of the forest. However, the demons won't be expecting an attack from the elves. Our people will hide in strategic locations where they will shower Isidore's forces with arrows and attack from behind, cutting off any chances for escape. The humans will rush in from the front and, if all goes well, we will meet in the middle."

"The elves will also strike fear into the demon army," explained Delwyn. "They have been afraid of the native forest dwellers since they first stepped onto our plane of existence. If it were not for their greater numbers, the demons would have been destroyed centuries ago."

Delwyn's words caused the rest of the party to give him a strange look. Even Cathmore and Forrester looked at the old wizard with more than a bit of curiosity. Elves could live up to five hundred years, but neither had ever heard of a human who could match such a feat.

"I think we are forgetting one small detail," interrupted Brother Frewin. "Prince Aaron and Byram both fought Isidore in hand to hand combat. Byram scored a hit or two with his sword and it did little to slow the demon. Apparently, Isidore has powers that exceed even those of his minions'."

Aaron shivered with fear and frustration. In his mind he saw Byram score a powerful hit against Isidore but to no avail. How could they hope to destroy Isidore even if they succeed in killing the rest of the demons?

"I know of a person who might be able to help us," said Forrester, which brought an odd smirk from Delwyn. "He could shed some light on the situation. For now, we should make camp. It will take us a few hours to reach our destination and we have only a brief amount of sunlight left."

Before the sun had set over Woodbyrne, the party had set up a small camp alongside the lake. A fire was made and Kemp and Brother Frewin began to cook the rabbit that Cathmore took from the demons. Cathmore explained that the surrounding trees and ancient magic would prevent any outsiders from noticing the blaze and smelling the cooked food.

After dinner, Forrester sat in front of his new friends and allies. The powerful elf went over how the demons had entered Woodbyrne. He told the story of two young wizards who had decided to play with magic that was far beyond their capabilities. Those two elves had opened a gate to another plane of existence and called forth a demon that even the most powerful mages dared not call.

"When Isidore realized that he was summoned by two bumbling, adolescent elves, he easily stepped right through the portal. One of the wizards was killed instantly, but the second wizard, the fool whose idea spelled ruin for Woodbyrne, escaped from the cave and ran into the forest. Some rumors say that the wizard killed himself when he saw the horror unfold before his eyes." Forrester turned his brown eyes toward the small campfire. "Others say that the wizard went back to the demons and offered his services to Isidore, who, in return, allowed the foolish elf to live. For these reasons, the elves of Woodbyrne banned the use of magic and all who dwelled in its secrets forever."

"Are you all right, my lord?" asked Cathmore when he saw tears begin to roll down Forrester's cheeks.

"It is hard to push back such sad memories, my friend." The emotional elf took a few deep breaths in order to calm himself. "The wizard who escaped those many years ago was named Wynn—Wynn Silverbow." Another brief pause allowed the small band of friends to absorb what he just said. "Wynn Silverbow is my father, and the one person who I pray has an answer to our dilemma."

The entire party remained silent. Cathmore, who had come to love Forrester as a brother, could not believe his ears. "I cannot believe that the one person responsible for the survival of our race is the son of the one person responsible for its demise."

"Alas, it is true Cathmore. I am the son of the magic user who opened the gate to the Lower Planes of existence. Please understand why I have kept it a secret for so long."

"Your father had no idea of the chaos that would follow," said Aaron, who placed a comforting hand on Forrester's slender shoulder. The prince understood all too well the burden of guilt that the proud elf had carried for so long. Aaron thought it was very brave and noble of the elf to confess to the group.

"I would love to speak more of my father's past, but I feel that is for him to do once he is ready to face his people." Forrester never understood why his father chose to remain hidden deep within the woods, making Forrester swear to never tell a soul his whereabouts.

"Please," insisted the elf lord, "get yourselves to bed and rest." Forrester went over to his blankets and took off his boots and tunic, revealing a beautiful, delicate chain mail armor. "It will be dark soon and all of you deserve a good sleep. I assure you that this section of Woodbyrne is safe. Even Cathmore, my most trusted scout and friend, needn't worry about falling asleep on the job this night."

"I only fall asleep when I am keeping watch on you, my liege," kidded Cathmore as he too removed his traveling gear and lay on his soft blankets.

Aaron instructed his companions to organize their gear and supplies and get some sleep.

"I am really proud of you, Prince Aaron," Quinn whispered playfully before she closed her eyes. "Your father is going to be very proud of you."

"I just wish Byram were around to witness my achievement."

"I'm sure that wherever he is, he is very proud of you too." Quinn shut her eyes and fell asleep.

In a few minutes, the entire company of humans and elves were sound asleep under the watchful eye of the Forest's Heart. There, they enjoyed a night's sleep the likes of which they had not had for a very long time.

Chapter 27

The party left the safety of the Forest's Heart early the next morning after a quick breakfast of dried rations and water. Forrester took the small group through a different opening so no one would remember the location of the clearing. Once they had crossed back into Woodbyrne, the gigantic trees that protected the land shifted back to their original position, completely covering any signs of the clearing.

The elf lord eagerly led his companions through the thick and unkempt forest. There were twists and turns every few yards and even Cathmore and Lennox had a difficult time maneuvering. Despite the tricky terrain, however, the leader of the wood elves kept a steady pace. In just a couple of hours, the trail led into a small clearing. It was not nearly as large as the Forest's Heart, and there seemed to be little protection from intruders. Tree stumps and manicured walkways proved that the clearing was far from mystical. In its center stood a small cottage made out of stones and wood. White smoke gently puffed out of the stone chimney and over the grass roof.

"There is powerful magic at hand," said Delwyn with a huge grin. "I think Wynn has come a long way since his times as an apprentice."

"My father has spent most of his life trying to find a way to rid Woodbyrne of the demons. In that time, he has come across many new spells and enchantments." Forrester asked the party to wait outside while he ran up the stairs and entered the cottage.

"I would never have guessed that Forrester had such an unusual background," Cathmore admitted as he sat on the ground and waited for his leader to return.

"Many people have some sort of past that they refuse to confess," said Quinn. She looked at Delwyn. The odd wizard was busy scribbling down sentence after sentence in his small notebook. Every few minutes he would stop and laugh at some private thought.

"Delwyn is right," said Brother Frewin. "There is a feeling in the air that almost equals the sacred circle we were in yesterday."

"How come I don't sense a thing?" Kemp asked in frustration. All the talk of magic and spells had worn thin on the young warrior. The mysterious art was a coward's way to most warriors, and Kemp Hethington was no exception.

"It would be foolish to insult the one person who might hold the answer to our ultimate mission," said Aaron. "I am sure that the wizard would rather have spent the past two centuries singing and dancing among his people. However, I find him noble for devoting so much of his life to righting a wrong."

"I certainly don't want to spoil our mission, my prince. It's just that I am getting edgy out here in the wild. We have seen very few demons, and the ones that we came across were cut down so fast that I didn't have time to blink."

"You will get your chance to fight," Cathmore promised. "Be glad that our journey has been dull. In time you will be up to your head in the foul creatures."

Forrester opened the doors of the cottage and bid his guests welcome. As they got closer, Delwyn noticed many runes engraved in the stones that made up the house. Some of them glowed red as they passed.

When the party went up the stairs on the front porch, they felt as if they had passed through some unseen barrier. For a second, the guests felt weightless. Then, just as fast, the sensation left and they were standing in front of the open door.

"My father is waiting for you inside," explained Forrester. Once all had entered, the front door automatically closed and locked itself.

The inside of the cottage had a very warm and welcoming feel about it. The scent of spices and baked goods hung heavily in the air while candles that decorated the tables and shelves, let off a soft, yellow glow that was gentle on the eyes.

Delwyn, the most knowledgeable of the party when it came to magic, was not fooled by the warm decorations and humble appearance of the elven mage's home. Protective spells had been cast on every section of the house. The old human understood many of them to be gates and portals for escape. Other incantations would disintegrate even the most enormous giants. "Wynn is a powerful wizard, indeed," the wizard said under his breath.

"Much of the magic I have learned came to me in only the past few decades, Delwyn Westbrook," came a pleasant voice from another room. Wynn Silverbow slowly entered and gestured for his guests to take a seat. The wizard looked more like a big brother to Forrester than he did a father. His handsome face had few wrinkles and his dark brown mane had very few gray hairs.

Quinn was a little disappointed by the mage's appearance. Wynn's simple earth-toned robes and dark green cape were a far cry from the elaborate gowns she had seen on Delwyn. No wands, books, or other common wizard paraphernalia were apparent either.

"I recently stumbled across some ancient elven books where I've found new and more powerful magic." Wynn gave each of guests a warm smile and sat in a soft chair. "I have found ways to harm the demons, my son. I do believe that is why the humans have come to Woodbyrne?"

"We were sent by King Dermot to make an alliance with the wood elves," said Aaron as he bowed. "Together, our forces will drive the demons out of Woodbyrne, and off Oneira forever." Aaron knelt on one knee and introduced himself. "I am Aaron, Prince of Gower. It is an honor to meet with you, Wynn Silverbow."

"It is an honor for me to see that respect and valor still have a place in these dark times, Prince Aaron."

After the rest of the humans had made their introductions, Wynn turned to Delwyn and gave him a coy smile. "I hope that there comes a day where the two of us can share in the art of magic again, my friend," he whispered to the old human.

"As do I, Wynn. It has been too long since we have shared our secrets."

"I have been very busy these past two centuries," the elven wizard said loudly, grabbing the attention of the entire room. "I have learned many new magics and have even created a few spells of my own."

"With the help of the humans, the elves of this forest will be able to take back what is rightfully theirs," explained Aaron. "Our only concern lies in the destruction of the demons' leader."

"Perhaps I know of a way to destroy that vile creature," Wynn said. Horrible memories of nights long past began to flood the mage's mind; memories of his poor wife, killed by the very creatures he and his friend brought into the forest. He shook his head, trying to rid himself of the memories, however briefly.

"I have devised a plan," Wynn continued as he began to pace around the room. His guests waited as the old mage organized his thoughts. "First you must capture a demon and make sure it lives. A holy man must sacrifice it under the open skies of the Forest's Heart. While the demon is dying, its black, polluted blood must be collected and returned to me so I can cast a spell to purify the blood. In essence, turning evil to good."

"Capturing a demon will not be an easy task," explained Cathmore. "They never travel alone and I fear that we may bring unwanted attention to this section of forest."

"Elven smiths will create the sacrificial dagger," continued the powerful mage, putting the scout's concerns to the side. "This blade will be hollow, allowing us to place the purified demon blood into it. I can easily make the blade magical, but a priest will be needed in order to make it holy. Once the dagger stabs Isidore, it will pump its cargo into his bloodstream. I hope that when all of this is over, the demon master will regret ever entering Woodbyrne. Hopefully, he will be cast off this plane of existence forever."

"Shouldn't we try to destroy Isidore?" Kemp asked, not fully understanding why the wizard simply wanted to banish the terrible demon. "It seems silly to just remove him from Woodbyrne."

"Demons of that power can only be killed in their own world," Forrester explained. "Unfortunately, there is no reasonable way we can accomplish that task."

"If we beat Isidore back into his own world," added Delwyn, "he may never again return to Oneira." The old wizard lit up his pipe and began to puff on it. "Demons can only be called to this plane by a summoning. Finding the name of a creature as powerful as the one we all face is unlikely."

"Then it is settled," said Aaron. "We will set out today. I am sure we can find one of those savages in no time."

"The trees will help guide us to our victims," said Cathmore. The young elven scout had a gleam of hope in his eyes and excitement in his voice.

"I will go and instruct our finest smithy to forge the hollowed dagger," Forrester said. "I have complete confidence that our new friends will have little trouble in tracking and capturing a demon." The elf lord gave his new allies a quick farewell and sped out the door.

The next hour was spent preparing for the hunt. Aaron and Lennox instructed their companions to leave behind whatever provisions they brought with them into the forest.

"We will need only our weapons and our wits," the prince said. Cathmore nodded his approval.

Wynn assured his guests that their supplies would be safe inside his cottage. "Not even a moth can pass my wards," he promised.

Delwyn and Brother Frewin spent their time memorizing and reviewing the necessary spells that would be needed to capture an unholy creature. When all was ready, the makeshift party met in the front of the cottage and waited for Cathmore to lead them into the forest.

"We shall return only when we have succeeded in our mission, Wynn Silverbow," said Cathmore in his native tongue.

"Good luck to all of you. I will remain here and prepare for the ceremony." The elf mage closed his front door and smiled. "You will regret not killing me, Isidore. You will regret it for all eternity."

༈

After an hour of westward travel, Cathmore suddenly fell to the ground and placed an ear to the base of a gigantic fur tree.

"Fifty yards that way," said the elf as he pointed to the west. "It seems that we have three unwelcome visitors this day." A troubled look found its way onto Cathmore's handsome face. "The demons have gotten closer than I expected."

Aaron decided that surprise would be the best course of action. "If we kill two of them fast enough, the third will be subdued more easily."

"I have a spell ready that will freeze one of the monsters long enough for the rest of you to finish taking care of them," said Delwyn. The old wizard smiled evilly and rolled up the sleeves of his brown traveling cloak. "I am not sure how long it'll last so please be quick."

Silently, Cathmore and Lennox scouted ahead until they came upon their intended victims. Using hand motions, Lennox instructed Cathmore to climb up a tree and wait for a signal to attack. The wood elf eagerly ran up the side of a large oak and found a perch where he could select four arrows from his quiver.

Lennox returned to his friends and gave them a brief description of the situation. In a matter of minutes, the entire party was hidden twenty yards from the demons.

ᴣ

Three vile creatures from the Lower Planes of existence lay on their backs around a poorly constructed fire pit. Bones of large and small game littered the campsite along with various other pieces of trash, including rotten body innards, torn clothes, and excrement. Each demon seemed to be asleep; their rusty swords by their sides and their crossbows against a fallen tree.

Cathmore slowly positioned himself where he could take an easy shot with his bow. Quinn hid behind a large tree and waited patiently with her sword in hand while Brother Frewin pulled out his polished mace.

It had been decided that Kemp was to occupy one of the demons while Delwyn cast his spell. The young fighter was proud that he had been given such a responsible position. However, not being able to kill all of the evil monsters did not sit well in the warrior's stomach.

Kemp was uncomfortable with his chosen spot. The tree he was behind had many low branches, which made it difficult for the fighter to see clearly. Kemp tried his best to move to a better location, but in his search, he stepped down on some fallen branches with his heavy, leather boots, sending a loud noise throughout the silent forest.

Immediately, the three demons jumped to their feet and armed themselves. Red badges engraved on their leather tunics informed Cathmore that they were an elite scouting group and each could easily kill one or two elves with little trouble.

"Check the perimeter!" one demon shouted in his unearthly tongue. "We will not fall victim to any more elves!"

Lennox and Cathmore acted the quickest, both loosing a barrage of arrows at the leader who had barked the orders. To their delight, not one of the seven missiles missed their target.

The demon leader tried to pull the arrows from his body. In the process, the evil creature fell to the ground which forced one of the razor sharp arrowheads deep into his black heart. Choking on his own blood, the evil creature passed off into the realm of darkness.

Aaron and Quinn jumped out of their hiding spots and charged the second demon from opposite directions. They knew it would spell disaster if the creature were able to escape into the woods and inform his superiors.

Kemp pulled out his two-handed sword and quickly charged the remaining demon. He merely wanted to occupy the creature long enough for Delwyn to cast his spell. The situation changed, however, when the demon before him pulled out another sword and began spinning two deadly blades in his face.

Quinn and Aaron had a tougher time than they had imagined with the second demon. Apparently, the foe was trained better than most of his kin. The demon was able to keep the two humans at bay for a long while, and he even managed to score a few hits on both Quinn and Aaron. Still, despite his training, the evil creature was no match for the skilled humans. After a while, he grew sluggish and his muscles began to feel numb and lifeless. The outmatched demon decided that he would take out at least one of his enemies with him before dying. Ignoring the prince, the demon swung with all his might at the beautiful woman with hopes to cleave her head right off her shoulders.

Quinn saw the strike coming and easily ducked under the sharp steel. Aaron quickly took advantage of his position, dropping to one knee and thrusting his sword into the back of the demon's hamstring, causing the creature to fall to the ground. Quinn smiled and jabbed her sword into the creature's neck, severing arteries and causing an overwhelming amount of blood to spew into the air. Almost instantly, the demon ceased to move.

Kemp was in a fair amount of trouble when Brother Frewin noticed that he needed help. The highly skilled creature outmatched the young warrior; both blades came dangerously close to him with every attack. "I'm coming, Kemp," he called as he started toward his friend. However, the young priest arrived just in time to see the demon stick its short sword into Kemp's stomach.

Delwyn quickly finished off his spell just as Brother Frewin and the two scouts arrived. A streak of green light shot from the wizard's fingers and slammed into the demon, paralyzing the creature where he stood.

"Don't pass out on me!" Frewin shouted to his injured friend.

Kemp tried hard to concentrate on the priest's words but the pain was too overwhelming. How could he have let that piece of crap hurt him? How could he fail his father so soon?

"We're losing him!" shouted Quinn. "He is losing a lot of blood!"

Brother Frewin quickly pushed Quinn and the others aside and knelt down next to the fallen soldier, placing a hand under his armor to asses the severity of the injury. "The wound severed arteries," the priest decided. "I need room to work!"

"Everyone clear away from Frewin!" ordered Prince Aaron.

Frewin's hand remained on the open wound. He could feel the warm blood pulse out of Kemp's body. As he remembered a very powerful healing prayer, Brother Frewin closed his eyes and began to pray to his god. In seconds, the priest's hands got warmer and the heat grew to a very uncomfortable temperature.

Kemp snapped out of his delirium to see his friend standing over him. The heat from the spell made him cry out for help. "It burns! Leave me alone!" Kemp tried to move away from the priests strange prayer, but there was no strength left in his body.

It only took Brother Frewin a few seconds to finish his prayer, but it seemed like hours. When he finished, he collapsed in utter exhaustion.

"Good work, Frewin!" congratulated Delwyn, who went back to his journal. "Good work indeed!"

Just as the others walked over to their fallen friend, Cathmore appeared from the trees with strange looking fruit and plant roots. He quickly knelt down beside Kemp and went to work on dressing the wound. "These are ancient herbs and fruits that my people have used for eons. Our brave fighter here will be feeling better in a few minutes."

Frewin recovered from his exhaustion just as fast. The young priest was very pleased with himself when he saw that Kemp was going to live. "I won't be able to heal a paper cut for the next three months," the hero said jokingly.

"I can't believe you were able to do that for me," Kemp said to Brother Frewin. "I am forever in debt to you, my friend."

Frewin turned red, but he had to admit that the prayer had worked perfectly. Kemp now stood on his feet and was ready to travel, although each step he took was a very painful one.

Lennox worked quickly to tie and gag the paralyzed demon before the spell wore off and the demon became aware of his hopeless situation.

"We must head back to Wynn as soon as possible," Cathmore urged. "I am sure that tonight will be ideal for the ritual."

After they had hidden the dead bodies, the band of adventurers was back on the trail that led to Wynn's cottage. They had blindfolded the demon, preventing him from learning the way to the house of the elven mage. An occasional punch in the back of the head from Kemp reminded the foul creature that he had better behave.

"How are you feeling?" Frewin asked as they began their return trip to the cottage.

"I feel very strange, Frewin." Kemp took a moment to feel the scar that would remind him of his brush with death for the rest of his life. "I should have died back there, right?"

"If we hadn't acted quickly, you could have passed away."

"Dying felt very strange. I felt no pain and I could only see my memories." The warrior began to grow pale again. Kemp was thinking of his father. He wondered if at the end his father had felt the same way. Suddenly, tears began to flow from his eyes.

"It is a hard thing to lose a family member," Quinn said as she fell into step with Kemp.

"I shouldn't be doing this," said Kemp as he bit his lip and took a deep breath through his nose. "I will have plenty of time to mourn once I return safely back to my mother."

"You may be right," Quinn agreed. "Just try to focus on the mission. Our success in Woodbyrne will play a most important role in avenging the people of Gower, including your father."

"We all share your sorrow," Brother Frewin agreed. "When this is all over, I would be happy to help guide you through your times of mourning. You are my friend, Kemp Hethington, and I would not think of leaving you out in the cold once we accomplish our mission."

Kemp could not believe the loyalty of the other members of the party. Although he had met them just a few days ago, Kemp felt that every single one them would do anything for him. "I can say with confidence that I have made the most loyal and loving friends anyone could ask for."

Kemp regained his strength faster than imagined. It was an hour or so before sunset when the lights of the magical cottage were seen through the thick brush of the forest. Inside, Wynn prepared his supplies for the ritual that lay ahead.

"This evening will prove to be a magical one," the elf said to his companions. "I hope that it proves to be a success as well."

Chapter 28

Wynn rushed out of his cottage the minute he detected Cathmore and the humans. After a quick greeting and congratulations, the powerful wizard cast a spell that transported the demon to a secret dungeon located somewhere beneath the cottage.

"We must act quickly," said Wynn with great urgency. "Tonight shall be full of magic and my son has assured me that the dagger will be ready."

"We are all prepared to help you in any way possible," said Brother Frewin. The young priest knew that he was going to have a role in the evening's enchantments and he could not help but grin.

"My father should know of our progress," Aaron said, breaking the excitement of the moment. "We have succeeded in creating an alliance with the wood elves, and the Royal Army should move out of Castle Gower as soon as possible."

Thus Aaron decided that he, Quinn and Kemp would return to the castle and instruct the king to ready his army. Wynn needed Brother Frewin and Delwyn Westbrook (to their delight!) to assist with the ceremony that evening. The powerful elven wizard assured the prince that all would be ready when the king's army marched up to Woodbyrne. Lennox Softfoot was also asked to stay behind to help with the security and safety of the ceremony. "I would be honored to stay behind with the elves," the scout replied. "Maybe Cathmore could even teach me some of the secrets that made the elves such a stealthy race."

"I have a spell that will send you directly to your horses," Wynn said with a smile. He presented two small vials full of a red liquid to the prince. "Once you are with your horses, rub some of this onto each of the beasts' legs. It is a powerful potion that will enable your mounts to run at three times the speed of the fastest horses on Oneira. I gave you one for the trip to the castle and one for your return."

"Thank you for all that you have done for us," said Aaron as he and his partners huddled together so that the wizard could cast his spell.

"How will you know when the army is near?" Kemp asked.

"Have faith in us, warrior" Delwyn assured. "We will be able to detect the army's progress faster than you will."

Wynn said his last farewell and began to wave his hands in a fluid motion above his head. Suddenly, a bright flash of light stunned the three travelers. Just as fast, the light was gone and they stood in front of their horses.

"That was incredible," said Quinn. "Too bad the old wizard could've sent us directly to the castle."

"I guess he had to conserve energy for tonight's activities," said Kemp.

As before, Prince Aaron found that the horses had been cared for in his absence. Fresh bales of hay lay at their hooves and they even looked as if they had been groomed. Sitting atop a very large tree branch, two male elves with powerful looking bows and swords sat quietly.

Aaron approached the two guards to thank them, but they simply nodded and gestured for him to be on his way.

Quickly, Aaron opened the vial given to him by Wynn and splashed the magical liquid onto each of the horses' legs. When he had finished, Aaron still had a few drops of the potion left, which he decided to keep hidden under the safety of his chain mail armor. Then, as fast as a cheetah in pursuit, the three horses sped off toward Castle Gower; their passengers making sure to hold on tight for fear of falling to the ground. Quinn looked behind her to see the remaining beasts, as well as the two elves, simply vanish into thin air, leaving only some sparkling dust behind where they once stood.

"I can't believe this!" Quinn shouted, although the pounding of the horse's hooves easily outmatched her shouting.

It mere minutes, the three friends were miles away from the border of the gloomy forest. Still, despite their progress, the ride back to the castle was filled with sorrow. All along the main road, houses and buildings had been destroyed. Some of the destruction had been from the first raid, but most came from blocks of hail and powerful lightning.

Almost all of the buildings in Sharpsword were damaged beyond repair and not one single person remained to tell the tale. Farms, both large and small, fared no better. They too had either been leveled or burned to the ground.

By early evening, when the autumn sun lit the sky a most beautiful orange, Aaron spotted the flags that flew over his home. Quickly, Aaron brought his three companions to a halt.

"What's wrong?" Kemp asked the prince. "We can be there in less than an hour."

"I am just trying to prepare myself for what we are about to see," Aaron explained. "That storm the other night was magical indeed. Isidore himself must have summoned it and sent it toward our countryside."

"How can we even think of beating this demon if he can summon a storm like this?" Quinn asked. "How could we dream of winning?"

"Because," yelled Kemp, "there isn't anything else to dream! I have a promise to keep for my father, Quinn. We all have promises to keep!" Kemp gave his horse a swift kick and sent it speeding down the road.

"I am afraid, Aaron. I am afraid of the demons and their leader." Quinn began to cry. "I miss my mother and father, Aaron. I miss them dearly!" Quinn got off her horse and began to weep uncontrollably.

Aaron jumped off his mount and embraced his dear friend. He did not say a single word. All Aaron did was show Quinn that she was not alone, an action that made the young woman feel loved, something she had never truly felt before.

"We are going to win! You have to trust me, Quinn."

Quinn looked up at Aaron, his strong blue eyes pierced her very soul. "I believe you, Aaron," she said in a whisper. "I believe you and I will follow you always."

"Then let's go speak to my father. I am sure he and my mother are anxiously awaiting our return." Aaron escorted Quinn back to her horse, and the two friends sped down the road.

To their surprise and delight, Kemp had decided to wait for them a few hundred yards away. After a quick apology, the three companions pushed their horses to their unnatural limits.

⌁

The grounds around Castle Gower were busier than Aaron had expected. The tents that had been erected outside the castle wall had been leveled. Priests and volunteers tried desperately to repair the torn canopies that provided shelter for the wounded. Scorch marks and small craters covered the ground, reminding everyone of the deadly hail and lightning that had accompanied the storm. Many trees and shrubs were splintered by the onslaught from the skies. Patches of dried blood littered the ground, a painful reminder that trees and buildings were not the only victims of the storm.

"These are truly sad times," said Kemp.

When the prince saw what had happened to his home, he was aghast and yet relieved. Castle Gower had taken considerable damage from the hail and lightning, but it still stood proud in defiance to Isidore and his minions of evil. Unfortunately, the entire eastern side of the castle had no roof and sizable holes and cracks pocked the once beautiful tile. The stables were equally damaged and Quinn had to turn her head when she saw what had happened to some of the horses inside.

Everyone was so busy helping each other that they did not even see the return of their future leader. Aaron was glad for the lack of attention, however, and he and Quinn made their way to the front gates of the castle.

Kemp explained that he had to go and find out what had happened to his mother but would return to the castle at the crack of dawn.

"I am sure your mother is alive and well," assured Quinn, who could see the fear in Kemp's eyes. "Go and be with her. Tell her that her son proved to be worth a thousand soldiers in the forest of Woodbyrne." Quinn gave the warrior a gentle kiss on the cheek and returned to the prince's side.

"It is a blessing to see you, Prince Aaron!" called a stout guard as he ran up to greet Aaron and Quinn. "We were beginning to believe that you were not coming out of that cursed forest."

"Rest assured, my friend, that we are all safe and sound for now.

Everything is going according to plan. Where are the king and queen?"

"King Dermot is in his private quarters," the soldier replied.

"Why is the king in his private quarters when all of this is going on?" Aaron pointed to the tents.

"King Dermot is tending to the queen, I'm afraid," the soldier said. "Queen Audrey was injured during the red storm the other night."

Aaron jumped off his horse and ran into the castle.

"Where are the others?" The guard asked.

"The others are fine, my friend," Quinn assured the guard as she dismounted and followed Aaron into the castle.

ॐ

"What do you mean they left the forest?" Isidore asked in his un-earthly voice. "They should have been detected long before they even entered!"

Damek was at a loss for words. He only recently heard the news of three riders speeding off toward Gower at remarkable speeds. "They must have used some magic to conceal themselves from us."

Isidore stepped down from his chair and began to pace up and down the large chamber. He knew that Damek was not the one to blame, yet he could not believe that the humans were powerful enough to enter Woodbyrne undetected. "Go to the castle, Damek. Keep a close watch on King Dermot's army. I have a feeling that the elves are in on this, so send out some scouts to try and capture one of those green degener-ates."

"I will act immediately, Isidore." Damek bowed his head and walked out of the room.

"Damek."

"Yes?" The winged demon knew that he had gotten off too easy.

"Fail me again and I'll kill you a thousand times."

"I understand," was the only response the surprised demon could give. Damek knew that one more failure would surely result in a fight to the death with Isidore.

⌒

"How did it go with our master?" one of the demons on patrol asked. "Was he pleased with our efforts?"

Damek approached the pathetic fool with clenched fists; an evil snarl on his reptilian face bared his jagged teeth. Damek did not even explain what had happened with Isidore before he struck out at the lesser scout.

"We did only as you instructed!" the smaller demon cried as a powerful fist slammed into his snout.

"You failed me for the last time, Rathan!" shouted the scout as he kicked his subordinate to the floor. He took out his black dagger and said a word of power. Quickly, the tip of the evil weapon turned bright red.

"I won't fail you again!" Rathan pleaded. The lesser demon knew about Damek's weapon. He knew that it was capable of releasing varieties of poisons simply by words of command, and although he had no clue as to what kind of poison Damek just called for, Rathan knew it to be more that a simple sleeping potion.

Damek jumped on his victim and slid the dagger between his ribs. The knife injected the searing hot liquid into Rathan, causing him to shake and spasm uncontrollably. In seconds, the skin on the demon's bones began to melt away into a smoking pool of gelatin and ooze. Rathan screamed in agony until his very head dissolved and fell apart. In the end, there was nothing more than a horrible stench and a pile of smoldering bones.

"Now you will never fail again," Damek said to the steaming pile of rot. He knew that he was wrong in killing the useful demon, but he had to show Isidore that he had nothing to do with the failure. Quickly, Damek opened the door to the enclosed chamber and entered a less secluded room. The three other demons who had witnessed the humans escape stood huddled in the far corner. Fear was in their eyes and they knew that Rathan, their scout leader, would never come out of the small torture chamber.

"I have a new mission for you three incompetents," Damek spat as he sheathed his dagger. "The three of you are to scout the forest and capture an elf. You must bring him back here alive. My orders come directly from Isidore. Our master is very displeased with your lack of success so the three of you had better come through this time or it will be the end of your miserable existence!"

"We understand, Damek," one of the demons answered.

Quickly, the unfortunate scouts shuffled their way out of the empty room, keeping an eye on Damek and his dagger all the while.

When the soldiers scurried away, Damek sat down and sighed. Although he was just as cruel and rotten as the rest of his kind, Damek felt that Isidore's rule was too barbaric. Damek did not want to kill one of his best recruits, but he wanted to know what it felt like to be as cruel a leader as Isidore. To his surprise, Damek felt empty. True, he enjoyed using the dagger on his victim and felt no remorse for taking the life of another, but Damek felt that lessons of death were not the right path to take when trying to assert command.

"Isidore is a fool for his actions," muttered the scaled demon. Damek rose from the ground and unfolded his powerful, leathery wings. He had a very important mission to accomplish but he wanted to succeed for reasons other than Isidore's. If the humans defeated Isidore, Damek would never have the chance to succeed the unpopular demon master. All of Damek's hopes and dreams rested on the fact that the demons had to be successful against the king's army.

Quickly, Damek flapped his powerful appendages and soared through the twisted halls of the demon caves. It was a beautiful night, with not a cloud in the sky, when the winged creature made it out of the cave entrance. The moon shone brightly and its soft light reflected eerily off Damek's shiny black scales. Damek did not pause to absorb the beauty that surrounded him. Instead, he fantasized about killing humans and elves in the upcoming battle.

༺༻

Aaron was amazed to see so many people inside his parent's quarters. Priests were busy calling to their gods for their ability to heal and bless while healers cut fresh bandages that were placed in a white salve. The room was so crowded that the prince did not even see his father.

"Father!" Aaron called out searching for his Father in the crowd. "I have returned to you with news from Woodbyrne!"

King Dermot rose from his wife's bedside and looked upon his brave son. Tears of joy and anguish quickly filled his eyes. Dermot had horrible thoughts about sending his only son on such a dangerous mission. If anything had happened to Aaron, he would never have been able to forgive himself. The king chased everyone but the healers from the room.

Once the crowd had left, Aaron shut the door and embraced his father for a very long time.

"We were concerned for you, my boy," the king said, once he was able to compose himself. "Your mother will be overjoyed to see you."

"What's happened to Mom?"

"A flying piece of hail or debris from that violent storm the other evening hit her on the head." King Dermot led his son to the queen's bed where she lay quietly on her back; a clean bandage covered the top of her head. "Once the storm came I ordered all of my men to escort the people into the castle for protection. It was chaos. Men and women were being mowed down from huge hail, flying debris and lightning. In all of the mess, your mother saw a little girl calling for her mom. Thinking only of the child's safety, she ran outside and grabbed the child. A piece of debris hit her in the head just as she turned back toward the castle. I thought she was dead when I saw her lying on the ground." Dermot had to wipe many tears from his bearded face.

"Is she going to be alright?" asked Aaron. "How bad is she?"

Just as the king was about to answer his son, Queen Audrey opened her eyes and smiled weakly when she saw that her son had returned to her. "I am going to be fine, Aaron," she whispered. "I just need some rest before I am up and about again."

"Rest easy, my love," King Dermot whispered to his ailing wife. "Our son is safe and you can now concentrate on getting well." After he kissed her gently on the lips, Dermot led Aaron from the bedroom so they could speak more openly.

⟡

Quinn was already waiting as the king and prince arrived in the strategy room.

"It is so good to see you back at the castle," King Dermot said to Quinn as he crossed the room to embrace her. "It relieves me to see you both in good health, Quinn."

"Thank you, your majesty. It has been a long and weary road."

The king looked around the room. "Where are the others? Did they not make it out of Woodbyrne?"

"Kemp is with his mother right now," Aaron answered, "and the rest of our party members are still with the elves in the forest." The prince explained to the king about the plans for the magical dagger.

Dermot was pleased. "Then the wood elves are willing to aid us in our cause?"

"Yes," said Aaron. He and Quinn explained all of the finer points to the king telling him the elves were willing to help if the humans agreed to not enter Woodbyrne until the elves were ready to welcome outsiders.

"What is our plan?" Dermot asked. "If the elves are going to be hiding in the trees, I guess it would be best for my army to march directly up to the boarders of the forest."

"That is pretty much what Forrester suggested we do," replied Quinn. "The elf lord is a seasoned veteran and a noble warrior."

"Are they ready for a fight?" King Dermot thought of his war council's warnings.

"The elves have been fighting for the past two centuries," Aaron answered. "We can trust them completely."

King Dermot paused for a moment to collect his thoughts. The veteran warrior knew that the upcoming battle with the demons was not going to be an easy one. Many men and women would die and many others would be maimed or severely injured. Still, Dermot could not think of any other answer for his kingdom's situation. "Then I guess it is settled," he said. "We will begin our march in the morning."

Aaron looked at his father with respect and love. He realized that the decision to send men and women to do battle was probably the hardest decision one could ever make.

Later that night, bells rang throughout the castle and the surrounding countryside. All who heard the bell knew it was a call from the king to all of the members of the Royal Army and anyone who would be willing to volunteer services for the good of Gower.

Soldiers dropped whatever they were doing to gather their weapons, armor and traveling gear. Since enrolling in the king's army, each soldier had prepared for the day when they would hear the call of the bronze bell.

It was time for war.

Chapter 29

Wynn Silverbow slowly stepped back from the sacrificial altar and smiled at his friend. Both he and Delwyn had been very busy preparing for the evening's ceremony, and the night was perfect. The sky was clear and it seemed as if every star in the heavens shone down upon the pristine lake. Brother Frewin, Lennox, and Cathmore watched patiently as shooting stars streaked across their line of sight.

"Somebody is coming," Cathmore declared. Quickly, the stealthy elf and his human counterpart readied their bows and hid behind a pair of boulders.

Forrester Silverbow ran out of the thick forest. The powerful elf carried a wooden box that looked as if it could hold a long dagger rather comfortably. Quickly, the elf lord approached his father and opened the small compartment.

Gently, Wynn placed his hands in the box and lifted the finely crafted weapon for all to see. The dagger looked rather simple, no etchings or decorations were upon it, but its keen edge and high polish made it obvious that it was forged by the hands of a highly skilled smithy. The dagger had a small hole in its tip, giving the weapon the appearance of a snake's fang.

"I need both of you to come with me," Wynn said to Brother Frewin and Delwyn. "The rest of you will prepare the demon for the ceremony. Have everything ready in one hour's time."

After the two wizards and the priest entered the ancient chapel, Cathmore, Lennox, and Forrester headed for the basement where the demon prisoner was held. All three men knew that it was going to take a lot of muscle to subdue to creature, but the thought of sacrificing the monster did not weigh too heavily on their consciences.

"Don't you worry about me," Alicia said. "I have all the faith in the world in you and your abilities."

To Kemp's delight, his mother had survived the terrible storm. Maxine also made it through that horrible night without a scratch. Still, despite his mother's luck, Kemp did not feel comfortable leaving her again.

"I am not afraid to leave you alone, Mom. I now know where my courage and strength comes from. Both you and Dad are true warriors." Kemp's words made his mother blush. "This time, I'm afraid that I'll never see you again because I am going off to war."

Alicia held her son's hand and kissed him on the cheek. "You are going to be fine," she insisted. "You are one of the best soldiers in the army. I am certain that you will come out of this as a general or even higher." Alicia gave her son a playful nudge. "Maybe King Dermot himself will hand his crown over to you because he'll come to realize what a true leader is."

The powerful warrior embraced his mother in a huge hug and kissed her on the forehead.

"When you return," Alicia whispered, "I want to hear about everything, especially about the elves."

Brother Frewin took a huge breath before beginning the ceremony. The priest had exchanged his traveling gear for a simple yet pure white robe provided by Wynn. The demon, stripped of its clothes, lay silently on the altar. Frewin looked up to the heavens and raised both of his hands and called for a blessing from the gods above.

While their friend continued his prayer, Forrester and Lennox each knelt on opposite sides of the small altar. They were to prevent the demon from breaking his bindings and escaping into the woods. Like the priest, both warriors wore simple white robes. Their only weapons were small daggers hidden beneath the delicate fabrics.

Brother Frewin's chants became louder as he went on. The more the priest spoke, the more uncomfortable the demon became. Eventually, the holy man was in a trance.

Lennox quickly placed his hand on one of the leather bindings. To his relief, they were as tight as when he and Forrester had first secured the wretched creature.

The demon soon became frantic when Frewin reached under his robe and presented a dagger for all to see. The deadly weapon gleamed brilliantly under the night sky, as the dagger seemed to absorb every beam of light from both the moon and the stars. The chapel glowed, illuminating the marvelous colors in the stained glass windows.

From behind the altar, Cathmore, dressed like the others, appeared with a silver bowl in his hands. Quickly yet silently, the elf approached the altar and knelt next to the priest.

Brother Frewin suddenly stopped his prayers and looked at the terrified demon. He raised the dagger above his head.

"Tonight begins the penance for all the vile creatures who dared to step foot on our soil!" cried Frewin as he drove the tip of the dagger deep within the beating heart of the wretched demon. The sharp blade dug deep into the demon's chest as it tore through skin and flesh to find its mark. Not even solid bone was strong enough to slow the dagger's flight. Black blood spewed from the mortal wound. Frewin stepped away from the altar and allowed Cathmore to collect the blood in the silver bowl.

Once the blood was taken, and the demon stopped breathing, Delwyn and Wynn appeared, wearing identical white robes. As rehearsed, Brother Frewin took the bowl of blood from Cathmore, allowing the elf to leave the priest and the wizards alone. Forrester and Lennox also rose and followed the scout out of the magical circle.

Brother Frewin knelt on the ground with the silver bowl placed firmly in his hands. Wynn struggled for a moment to remove the dagger from the demon corpse. Then, he and Delwyn stood in front of the priest and began to recite an ancient spell.

"Do you have any idea what they are saying?" Lennox asked Forrester, now a safe distance away from the altar.

"The two wizards are calling for the power to enchant the dagger," explained the elf lord. "The priest has already blessed the blood and made it pure. Now it is up to my father and Delwyn to make the blade powerful enough to enter Isidore's body."

"With the two of them at the helm," Cathmore added, "I am sure the dagger will be powerful enough to kill the most ancient of dragons."

After what seemed to be hours, the two wizards had finished their enchantment. To the onlookers' disappointment, there were no balls of fire or strange lights to be seen. Still, the two powerful wizards looked very pleased with themselves.

"Are you ready, old friend?" Delwyn asked his counterpart.

Wynn winked in response and knelt with Brother Frewin. He slowly dipped the point of the dagger into the blessed blood.

An enormous clap of thunder rocked the entire forest, followed by a flash of light; the second the deadly tip of the blade touched the demon's lifeblood, sending all but Wynn and Frewin on their backs. When the surprisingly disruptive moment had ended, Wynn noticed that no blood remained in the bowl; the dagger itself throbbed as if it had a beating heart.

Quickly, the three onlookers rushed back into the circle to make sure nobody had been seriously injured. But Delwyn Westbrook was already standing and writing something down in his traveling notes. The odd wizard was even chuckling.

Brother Frewin and Wynn were not affected by the thunder. The two friends were busy inspecting the dagger.

"We have succeeded in our mission," Delwyn said. "Now we have to wait for our friends in Gower to come to the rescue."

"I should leave tonight," said Forrester, with a little bit of disappointment. "I want to see how our people are preparing for the upcoming battle. They have been patient with me thus far, but I need to be present for my followers."

"Good luck, my son," Wynn whispered as he watched his heroic offspring sprint into the dark woods. "And thank you for this second chance."

౨౦

Prince Aaron took a deep breath of the evening air. His heart raced ten times its normal speed and beads of sweat ran down the young man's forehead.

"Will you be accompanying me tonight?" King Dermot asked his nervous son. The king had on glorious battle armor that covered him from head to toe. The ancient metal was highly polished and connected with dark red leather. Since the enemy was far away, and since it was considered disrespectful to display weapons to his subjects, the king of Gower refused to brandish his deadly blade until it was time to march.

"But what if they blame me for all of this?" asked the prince. "What if they blame me for the pain and suffering?"

"Don't be ridiculous, Aaron." King Dermot turned to one of the many large mirrors in his preparation room and checked himself to make sure that he was presentable. "We have only ourselves to blame for not helping the elves two hundred years ago." Satisfied with his appearance, Dermot opened the doors that led to the main audience chamber and stepped outside. Aaron followed, close behind him.

Queen Audrey and Quinn were waiting for the king and prince to arrive. The queen, still recovering from her injury, was dressed for battle. She preferred the flexibility of chain mail to the stiff, heavy plate mail her husband wore. Although her attire was not as bold, Queen Audrey looked as much a warrior as did her mate. Like King Dermot, the Queen of Gower did not show her people a weapon.

"We are ready, your majesty," said Quinn as she bowed her head in respect for the king.

"Let's get this over with. We have a long night ahead of us and I doubt a long speech is something we need." With a loud clearing of the throat, King Dermot ordered the many guards in the room to clear a path to the balcony where he would speak to his public. Queen Audrey walked next to her husband with pride. Following the royal couple, Prince Aaron and Quinn stepped out onto the balcony.

Unlike the king and queen, however, Aaron felt nervous as the huge double doors were flung open and the roar of the crowd slammed through the marble room.

ᘓᕽ

King Dermot acknowledged his army before he started his speech. All of the king's soldiers stood at attention and saluted the king. Men and women who were not enrolled in the Royal Army stood by them with their own swords and axes in hand. Many of the volunteers were farmers who had lost their homes and property when the demons set fire to the countryside.

The three divisions of the Royal Army stood apart from one another. To the left of the courtyard stood Sir Bickford Browne and his Royal Archers. Lady Allison Churchill and her cavalry unit lined up on the right side of the courtyard. Sir Henry Goodwill stood proudly in the center with his infantry unit, the largest division of King Dermot's army. All of the volunteers stood at the edges of the courtyard.

"Our demon enemies will torment us no longer!" Dermot began, his deep voice echoing clearly off the stone walls of the castle. The king waited for the cheers to calm.

"We humans have made a pact with the elves of Woodbyrne to crush the demons once and for all!"

There was total silence in the courtyard.

"The people of the woods have been fighting for over two centuries to rid the demons from Oneira!" The king continued, dismissing his people's silence as fear of the unknown. "With our powerful army, plus the elves' knowledge and stealth, we will be able to rid Oneira of the demons once and for all!"

Again, the people cheered.

"We have little time to prepare. We must be ready to march at the break of dawn."

"Quinn Brainard," the king motioned for the woman to come closer, so the people in the courtyard could see her, "is in charge of volunteers. We will gladly take any men and women who are capable!"

Quinn bowed and excused herself from the balcony. She immediately reported to the recruitment tent to begin processing volunteers.

"I leave all of you now," King Dermot concluded, "in the hands of the army's leaders. With their guidance, we will be ready to march at dawn!" A hearty cheer followed the king's speech as he left the balcony for the main audience chamber.

⌇

The courtyard remained crowded and there was constant commotion on the castle grounds throughout the evening. Men and women said their last farewells to loved ones while tired smithies tried to pound out a few more weapons for the volunteers. The entire kingdom of Gower worked as a single unit. Strangers offered a hand to each other as everyone prepared for the march.

"I am very proud to be a part of this," Aaron admitted to his father as the two men watched the commotion from the castle. "I feel that I have grown up these past few days."

"Indeed you have, my boy. We have all matured a little from this. I just hope everything turns out as expected."

Aaron did not respond to his father, knowing that the king had much at stake on the alliance with the elves. Instead, he thought of his friends whom he had left behind in Woodbyrne. He thought of the task they had to accomplish in order for the campaign to be successful. Aaron truly wished he were back in the dreaded forest so he could help with the preparations. "Please come through, old wizard," he whispered under his breath. "Isidore cannot continue to exist in our world."

⌇

Many of the preparations were finished as the night wore on. Volunteers unable to go to battle helped by watering and feeding the horses. Others gathered and packed rations and other supplies needed by the soldiers. Smiths pounded away at slabs of steel, working to the brink of exhaustion just to get another blade into a volunteer's hands. Although the weapons were made quicker and with less precision than normal, they would no doubt work better than a garden hoe or horse whip.

Quinn had one of the tougher jobs of the evening. She was overwhelmed when a wave of farmers and merchants almost tore down the front of the recruitment tent. A few soldiers were ordered to keep the crowd in check and Queen Audrey occasionally stopped in to lend a helping hand. By the end of the night, Quinn had recruited almost two hundred new soldiers into the Royal Army. Each new volunteer was outfitted with makeshift armor and new swords.

⇒

Dermot and Aaron were busy the entire evening going over battle plans. Aaron, Quinn, and Kemp were to break apart from the army during the first night under the cover of the Royal Army.

"The sheer size of the army should cause enough noise and commotion to take away any attention from the three of you," the king said. "With a little luck, by the time the army is standing in front of the dark forest, the elves will be ready and waiting in the treetops and thick brush."

"Isidore will certainly hear you coming miles before the army reaches the border," Aaron said with a hint of nervousness in his voice. He had never taken part in such vital plans and he was not sure how he felt about the responsibilities given to him.

"You know, Aaron, I am very proud of you right now," the king said with a warm smile.

"Of me? I thought you'd be angry with me."

"You know, my boy, you have been living in a world of self-pity ever since you returned from Woodbyrne the first time. Did you hear me? The first time. No one has ever entered that wretched place and lived to tell about it. You, on the other hand, entered and returned twice. For that, I am most proud of you."

"If it weren't for me, all of this would not be happening," insisted the prince.

"The people of Gower would have eventually suffered once the demons became restless. If it were not for you, Quinn would be dead and the forest elves would be spending the rest of their long lives fighting a futile battle." King Dermot placed a hand on his son's shoulder. "The people of this kingdom consider you a hero."

Aaron laughed. "That'll be the day."

"The day has come, Aaron. You have already begun to build an honorable reputation whether you like it or not."

A loud knock at the door interrupted the conversation. "All the preparations have been made, your lordship," a messenger called from the other side of the oak door. "Your horses are being saddled and readied. Quinn and Kemp await our prince in the stables."

"We'll have plenty of time to finish our discussion once this campaign is over," the king said. "There are many people who love you and care for you very much, Aaron. I only hope you realize that before they are gone."

"Father, I do. These past few weeks have helped me to realize how precious life is."

King Dermot and Prince Aaron walked out of the audience chamber. Aaron realized as five soldiers escorted them down the long corridor that each soldier would gladly die for his cause.

Chapter 30

Gray clouds and a dense fog greeted the prince as he made his way out of Castle Gower. He, along with the rest of the kingdom, had not been able to get any sleep.

Outside, men, women and children were still busy running around as they desperately tried to outfit the soldiers with enough supplies before the march. In the distance, away from the chaos and loud noise, the magnificent war-horses were already lined up and checked by the knights who would ride them into battle. In the far distance, Aaron saw the archery division reviewing last minute preparations with their commander, Sir Bickford Browne. It seemed that the last section of the Royal Army that remained in the compound of the castle was the infantry unit. Those men and women needed less time to prepare and had been ordered by Sir Henry Goodwill to stay behind and help reinforce the tents where the wounded were being treated.

As Aaron watched the people of Gower work, he smiled. Gertrude, the dwarven barmaid, was busy running about the castle grounds shouting orders to men who were carrying lumber and canvas for the tents. She sported a very large double-sided battle-axe slung over one shoulder, apparently familiar with the ways of battle. The deadly blade reminded the other volunteers that they had better keep in line if they did not wish to see it used.

"The second I saw her I knew she would make an excellent leader," said Quinn, as she walked over to Aaron. "I don't think I really had much of a choice, anyway. Do you see the size of that axe? It could cleave a bull in two with a single stroke."

꒰꒱

"Is your mother all right?" Quinn asked Kemp as she and Aaron mounted their horses. "I've been worrying about you ever since we returned from the forest, but I've been so busy with the new recruits that I never had the time to check in on you."

"She's fine," the massive warrior replied. "I just hope that I'll return a second time from that wretched forest."

"We'll return," Aaron assured him. "Just have some faith in the alliance, Kemp. For now, I think we should be moving out."

The three friends checked their supplies one last time before they headed toward the king. As they passed the castle, Aaron looked up to see his mother standing on a large balcony. It warmed his heart to see her up and about.

"Be safe, all of you," Audrey called. "I'll be expecting all of you to return soon."

⁂

"This will be a day to remember!" Dermot called to his loyal soldiers. "Tomorrow, we will look upon the forest that has concealed a very dangerous foe for over two centuries! For the next two centuries, that very forest will remember the humans and elves who willingly put their lives at risk in order to rid Woodbyrne of the demons forever!"

Every man and woman cheered for their kingdom and its ruler. They called for justice to be served to the demons, and they pledged their allegiance to Gower.

After giving his troops a few minutes to calm down, Dermot motioned for the lead scouts to start off before the rest of the army.

The four royal scouts, all trained by Lennox Softfoot, kicked their horses into motion and headed out of the castle grounds. On the other side of the large wall protecting Castle Gower, cheers rang out from those who had chosen to stay behind, and those who were unfit to march in support of their kingdom.

"It's a funny thing, Aaron," the king whispered to his son.

"What's that?"

"I still get butterflies in my stomach from all of this." After a long pause, the king chuckled.

After a few minutes, Dermot decided that his scouts were far enough ahead of the army to begin the march. "To battle, my friends," the king said to his three advisors. "Aaron, you may begin the march."

Aaron, with Quinn at his right and Kemp at his left, started his horse through the castle's gates. Behind him, King Dermot rode next to Sir Bickford Browne, Lady Churchill, and Sir Henry Goodwill.

Behind the king marched the archers, whose sole job would be to shower the demons with deadly arrows from afar, dropping or injuring many of the creatures as well as breaking their spirit in the process.

Following the archers, the cavalry rode tall and proud on top of their steeds. The cavalry would charge the demons after the barrage of arrows. The massive war-horses, with their battle armor, could easily mow down scores of men with a single leap.

The infantry brought up the rear of the long line of soldiers. Those brave men and women would follow the cavalry and hopefully meet up with the elves for the beginning of the melee. The soldiers were concerned about facing such strange and evil creatures, but they all had faith, in themselves and in their king.

Gertrude Stonegully had been given the honor of leading the volunteers behind the rest of the army. "Don't ye all get too nervous 'bout this fight!" the dwarf called out over the farmers and merchants. "Miss Brainard wouldn't have picked any of ya if she didn't think ya could fight a bit!" Gertrude waved her hand and kicked her pony into motion. With pride and confidence, the volunteers of Gower fell in behind the rest of the Royal Army.

Damek was impressed with the army's progress. He had followed them for most of the morning and all through the afternoon. By the time night had fallen, the Royal Army had traveled more than half the distance to Woodbyrne. King Dermot demanded a quick pace and his followers were more than willing to please their king.

"This king is quite the leader," the winged demon said to himself as he hovered hundreds of feet above the camp. "I think Isidore could learn a thing or two from that one." Damek cautiously flew lower in order to get a better view of the army. Although the soldiers had been ordered not to use any fire, Damek's ability to see heat in total darkness allowed him to spot their camp easily. But, to his dismay, the powerful spy was unable to pick out Prince Aaron from the rest of the army.

What bothered the demon even more, was the fact that King Dermot had a very formidable cavalry division. Damek counted eighty war-horses feeding lazily on the hillside.

"Isidore underestimated the humans," Damek said as he beat his leathery wings and soared back up to the safety of the night sky. After a few curses and fits of anger, the demon scout decided that his master would have to learn about the war-horses in order to make preparations for the coming battle. Besides, if Damek had failed to inform Isidore of every detail, the more powerful demon master would unleash a fury never before seen by the winged scout.

⤳

"The clouds are coming in from the north," Dermot said to his son as the two sat and ate a cold meal. "Winter is fast approaching."

"I always thought autumn was a beautiful time of year," Aaron replied.

"Remember when your mother and I would take you on those hay rides?"

"You mean the ones at the Fall Festivals?"

"You were petrified of those ponies," said the king as he tried to conceal a slight giggle. "The first time you went on one of them you cried so loud that people ran from all over the festival to see what was wrong."

"Why is that so funny?" Aaron asked.

"When the man in charge of the stable ride pulled you off the pony, you wet yourself and him!" Now the king roared into laughter.

"Very funny, Dad."

"I miss those days, Aaron."

"I sure don't."

"No, I mean I miss doing all those father and son things with you.

Even your mother wishes she could spend more time with you now that you are grown up."

"Dad, why didn't you and mom have any more children after I was born? Was I that difficult?"

The king paused before answering his son. "While your mother was giving birth to you," he began with a shaky voice, "she started to have convulsions. When I asked what was wrong, they said—" Tears began to form in the king's eyes. "They told me she would probably die."

"What happened?" pressed Aaron.

"Healers were able to save your mother's life, but the result was that she'd never be able to bear children again." King Dermot took a long drink of water before he finished. "It was months before she could even get out of bed. I learned quickly how to take care of you, so your mother could rest."

"How come you never told me this before?" asked Aaron, shocked at his father's grim news.

"Because there are some thing that a husband and his wife keep between themselves."

"I'm sorry for asking such a personal question, Dad."

"You have every right to know, my boy," the king answered. "When your mother was feeling better, she practically kicked me out of our quarters so she could catch up with mothering you to death."

A long time passed while they ate their cold rations.

"Excuse me Prince Aaron," called Kemp from the darkness. "The horses have been fed and Quinn is eager to get going."

"I'll be right there, my friend," Aaron responded as he smiled at Quinn's eagerness to get to the elves. "Tell Quinn that I am on my way."

"Be safe this evening," King Dermot said to his son. "If it gets too treacherous, make camp and begin in the morning."

"We will go as far as we can this evening. At daybreak, I'll give the horses the second potion and we should make the forest by mid afternoon."

"Is there enough time for the elves to get ready?" the king asked.

Aaron laughed. "The elves have been ready for two hundred years."

Aaron, along with the rest of his band, planned on going to the cave where he and the others would ambush Isidore when he returned from the battlefields. It was a gutsy move, but the prince knew he would have the upper hand with surprise on his side.

"Isidore will certainly be drained from the battle," Aaron said. "And, I'll be in the company of the finest warriors in Gower."

"Just stay close to the wizard," Dermot instructed. "He is much more powerful than you can imagine."

"I think Quinn shares those feelings."

"As well she should. I don't even know the full extent of the old man's capabilities, but he has been my trusted advisor for most of my life." The king stood up and stretched. "I should be getting over to my council."

"I guess I'll see you tomorrow," said Aaron as he also stood up and stretched his weary muscles. "The elves will be able to lead you to the cave."

Dermot embraced his son and kissed his forehead. "Be safe, my son."

"You too, dad," Aaron whispered before he grabbed his supplies and ran off into the darkness of the night.

✧

When Aaron got to his horse, he was not surprised to see that Quinn and Kemp were already on their horses waiting for him. Quinn's arms were crossed, and the prince knew she was running out of patience.

"I had some things to go over with the king," Aaron explained, trying hard not to show his amusement toward Quinn's rather cute expression.

"I know," Quinn said dryly. "I just want to get all of this over with as soon as possible."

Aaron quickly untied and mounted his horse. "We should keep a slow and cautious pace until the morning. When the horses can see better, I'll give them the second potion."

"I wish the entire army had some of those potions," remarked Kemp.

"We could have won the battle this morning and been back to the castle for the celebrations already."

Quinn and Aaron nodded in agreement and urged their steeds away from the large campsite. A few soldiers were littered along the back of the camp and they all wished the companions a silent farewell with a nod of their heads. Aaron returned the gestures with a faint smile and a nod of his own. Together, the three friends made their way back to Woodbyrne for what they hoped would be the last time.

⤸

"You worry too much, my loyal friend," Isidore assured his favorite scout. Damek had told his master about the king's progress and his fear that the humans had proved themselves to be a worthy adversary. The demon horde would have to use all of their resources if they planned on beating the Royal Army of Gower.

"I counted eighty horses geared with armor and heavy lances," Damek stressed, hoping to encourage Isidore to do something.

"Did you see Prince Aaron or my lovely lady from Stovia?"

Isidore's lack of interest angered the scout. "I was unable to see. King Dermot must have ordered a ban on campfires."

"A pity," said Isidore. "I am certain that she is with them."

"The army should make our borders some time tomorrow afternoon," Damek said as he tried to get Isidore to focus on the more serious matter. "My soldiers will be ready to meet them with open arms."

"You have done well this time, Damek." Isidore lifted his massive frame off his throne and began to pace around the huge hall. "You said you saw eighty war-horses?"

"Yes, eighty of the beasts." A huge weight lifted off Damek's shoulders as he watched the twisted mind of his leader work.

"That shouldn't be a problem," said the demon master.

"But our army will be run down like ants in a stampede," Damek stressed, hoping he wasn't over-stepping his boundaries. "We won't stand a chance against them."

"You dare to doubt our capabilities?" Isidore roared.

"No!" Damek lied.

"Have one hundred of my bravest and most worthy soldiers gathered in front of the cave by morning!" Isidore called out before closing the door.

"They will be awaiting your every command, Isidore," Damek answered.

Chapter 31

Outside the entrance to the cave, four demons watched the sunrise burn through the dense overcast. Damek had told them that the humans were on their way to Woodbyrne and there would be a battle by the day's end. Not wanting to anger their master, or get killed before the battle, the four servants guarded the cave without a word of complaint.

"What's that noise?" one of the creatures asked.

"Shut up or Damek's gonna' get mad!" scolded a second demon.

"I said I heard something coming this way!"

"Shut up! Both of you!" a third demanded.

"Wait a second," the fourth said. "I think I hear it too."

Now all of the demons felt a subtle rumble from beneath the earth. The dull rumble grew to a small quake. They nervously looked about for the cause of the disturbance.

"I see something!" shouted the third guard.

A dense, black cloud began to seep out of the ground around the cave's entrance. At first, it seemed nothing more than a small puff of pipe smoke, but in seconds the mysterious mass exploded and engulfed the entire clearing.

"I can't see anything!" the first demon shouted. "Where are you guys?"

Loud hissing noises followed by screams were the only answers for the frightened guard.

"Damek?" the demon whispered. "Is that you?"

The hissing noise grew louder, as did the size and density of the black cloud. The guard could barely breathe, the air had become so thick. In sheer desperation, the demon unsheathed his sword and began to swing wildly at the blackness that surrounded him.

"I'll kill you, I swear!"

As the guard swung his blade, the black cloud began to heat up. Now it seemed that burning ashes from a volcano filled the demon's lungs every time he tried to take a breath of air. Then, without warning, a large jolt from beneath the earth knocked the helpless demon to the ground.

"Damek—where—are—"

Just before the guard died, something from out of the blackness jumped on top of him and began to tear him apart.

Isidore awakened on the hard stone floor with a violent shudder. Beads of sweat covered his red skin and he breathed heavily. In front of the powerful demon stood the black cauldron he used to pray to his gods of evil and chaos.

"Damek!" the demon master shouted as he dragged himself off the floor and peered into the cauldron. To his delight, all of the black, putrid liquid that occupied the pot was gone. His prayers had been answered, one way or another. "Damek, get in here now!"

"You called for me?" the winged demon said as he entered.

"My army will now be able to trample King Dermot's forces!"

"What do you mean?" Damek asked.

Suddenly, shouts and calls from inside the cave broke their conversation.

"Come quick! Come quick!" shouted a foot soldier. "We are under attack!"

"Go out there and tell those stupid fools that we are not under attack!" ordered Isidore, pure anger and hatred fueling the recovery of his strength. "Those are our mounts!"

Damek quickly rushed to warn his troops.

"Stupid fools," Isidore muttered under his breath as he grabbed his cloak and followed Damek to the cave's entrance.

"My most humble thanks for answering my call," Isidore began as he knelt down on one knee in front of the one hundred terrible creatures that lurked about the mouth of the cave.

Zaaghs, the dark steeds that looked like a cross between a horse and a panther, roamed the Lower Planes. Just as tall and as fast as war-horses, zaaghs had many of the more deadly traits of the powerful cat. Deadly clawed paws replaced the less harmful hooves, and razor-like teeth replaced the worn molars of equines. What disturbed most demons were the lifeless, white orbs where the eyes should be. Since the coats on the unnatural creatures were pure black, their eyes seemed eerily out of place.

"We are here only because Ulric wishes it to be so, Isidore," one of the creatures answered in its unearthly tongue. "We will aid your cause only for the pleasure of killing humans and elves!"

"You have my word that there will be plenty of humans and elves to kill and feast upon! As we speak, a large army of humans marches toward us with thoughts of war and victory."

"The only victory will be ours," another zaagh answered, causing more than a few of its kind to shout and scream in ecstasy.

"It is settled then," declared Isidore. "You will permit my soldiers to ride you into battle. When victory is ours, you are free to leave this plane, and return to your hellish domain."

"Not so, Isidore," answered another of the powerful creatures. "We stay as long as we feel that victory is ours. If the tides turn, and the humans take the upper hand, Ulric has informed us that we may leave you to your failure."

"Agreed then. You stay as long as you deem fit."

Damek whistled and called for the demon soldiers he had chosen to come out into the open. "Here are the soldiers you asked for, Isidore," the scout said.

"Remember," Isidore said to his own demons, "your job is merely to lance and kill as many humans as possible. Let the zaaghs make all other decisions for you."

One by one, each soldier approached a zaagh with caution and fear. The zaaghs knelt and allowed their temporary allies to sit on top of their muscular backs. Satisfied that they were not about to be eaten, many of the demons cracked smiles simply because they had never dreamed that they would one day ride a creature with such power and ability.

Isidore turned to his scout. "Damek, I am going to retire to my quarters for a while. Begin the march for the borders one hour after the sun has reached its climax. I have a feeling that the king will not waste time in attacking the forest. Make sure the foot soldiers are briefed and given proper weapons."

"As you command, my leader," replied Damek as he bowed in respect.

Isidore went off into the cave and headed for his private chambers. The demon lord of Woodbyrne would not have much time to rest before the march began.

ॐ

When morning first shone its light, Aaron quickly distributed the last of the magical potion to the three horses. Then, he and his friends mounted their steeds and sped off toward Woodbyrne to meet Cathmore Stardust.

The small group was barely an hour into the ride when they reached the hilltop that overlooked the forest.

"I never wanted to see this place again," Quinn said. "Now, I've become a regular visitor."

"After this war," Kemp responded, "we all might be able to visit Woodbyrne as friends of the elves."

Suddenly, someone jumped down from a nearby oak tree, startling the small party and causing Aaron and Kemp to draw their swords.

"At ease, Prince Aaron," called Cathmore Stardust as he brushed back his long, brown hair. "I did not mean to startle you, but I thought it best for me to stay out of sight."

Quinn could not help but laugh as she noticed the coy smile on the elf's face.

"How did the ceremonies turn out?" Quinn asked. "Where are Lennox and the others?"

Cathmore smiled. "Everyone is safely resting in Wynn's cottage. We will be there in a matter of minutes." Cathmore presented a small, clay disk from under his green cloak. "All I have to do is break this and we'll

304

all be teleported back to our friends."

"What happened to the dagger?" Kemp asked.

"It is being kept safely in a box in the wizard's cottage. You will all see it when Delwyn gives it to the prince."

"I'm getting the dagger?" gasped Aaron. "I thought either you or Forrester would take it."

Cathmore shook his head. "You stood up to Isidore and lived, Aaron." Then the elf broke the magic disk and released a powerful teleportation spell. In the blink of an eye, elf, humans and horses disappeared.

᠊ᢌᠵᠥᡝ

"The king's army will arrive no more than two hours after midday," Aaron said after he had greeted his friends in Wynn's cottage. "They are making good time and will have sunlight to begin the attack."

"I am sure Cathmore told you that the ceremony was a success," said Wynn Silverbow.

"May I see the dagger?" Aaron asked, no longer able to contain his excitement.

Delwyn and Wynn said a few quick words of power that dispelled the many wards and curses cast upon the coffer. When the protections had gone, Wynn opened the box and revealed the magical blade inside.

Aaron trembled when he saw the magnificent dagger. Its high polish and keen edge reeked of power.

"And now the blade has an owner," added Cathmore.

Aaron wiped his sweaty palms on his pants and picked the dagger out of the box. Immediately the handle of the weapon shaped itself to fit the prince's grip. The dagger's subtle pulse made it feel as if it were alive.

"Do you think it'll work?" asked Kemp. "I mean, wouldn't a sword be better for this sort of thing?"

"It'll work just fine," Brother Frewin answered. The priest approached Aaron and locked eyes with the young leader. "Are you ready for this responsibility, my prince?"

305

Aaron gazed at the dagger in his hand. What would happen if he failed? What if the demon army overtook the king?

"This isn't the time to ask yourself such questions," said Delwyn, startling Aaron. "Isidore will not give you another chance."

Aaron looked at his friends and looked back at the dagger. How could he fail when he had such powerful allies to back him? Allies who would easily die for his cause? "I am ready, my friends. After this day, Isidore will be no more!"

"Then it is done," said Forrester. "I'll leave and order the elves to head toward the rendezvous point. We will be ready to strike before the demons even unsheathe their pitiful blades." The elf lord turned and headed down secret trails that even his father did not know.

"I have taken the liberty of preparing our supplies while you were back at the castle," Lennox said to Aaron after Forrester had left. "We should probably head out to the cave as soon as possible."

"I agree with you, my friend," Aaron answered. "I just hope that very few demons remain behind."

"The demon with the wings," said Quinn, "saw the Royal Army before it left the castle."

"Isidore has many eyes," Wynn added. "He will certainly be sending his entire horde to meet your father at the forest's entrance."

"Why would he leave the cave unguarded?" Kemp asked. "Would it not make sense to have minions waiting for a plan like ours?"

Wynn shook his head and laughed. "I never said that Isidore will leave his home unguarded. The demon master will not want the king to even enter the forest, that is why he will be moving all of his forces to the border. If the humans were to entrench themselves within the thick brush of Woodbyrne, it would almost be impossible to remove them."

"Then what should we be expecting at the cave?" Cathmore asked.

"Even Wynn cannot be sure," Delwyn answered. "We will probably run into few, if any, demons at the caves. However, my brave bunch of soldiers, I do know that we will encounter creatures never before seen by human or elven eyes."

"Then I should get moving," Aaron decided. "I cannot ask any of you to join me."

All but Wynn insisted that they were ready to aid the prince until the bitter end.

"What sort of beasts do you think we'll run into?" Kemp asked after wiping the sweat off his brow and from his upper lip.

"Don't get yourself so worked up, Kemp," insisted Brother Frewin as he placed a relaxing hand on his friend's shoulder. "You are fighting for the forces of good. Together, there is nothing we can't accomplish. Besides, I have many prayers that will help keep us safe from some of the more common wards and traps." Frewin could tell that Kemp was still a bit shaken. "You have proven yourself very skillful and most reliable in battle, Kemp. We will need your skills when the fight begins."

"I know we are going to need you," Quinn added. "We would not have gotten this far if it weren't for your valor and courage."

"Well," croaked Kemp, "I certainly can't argue with that. You can count on me, Prince Aaron. I would not think of letting you or any of my new friends wander off into the abyss alone."

"Then it's settled," Lennox said, "We leave in an hour."

"Wynn, we could use your knowledge and power, if you are interested," said Prince Aaron to the silent wizard. "You could even help us keep Delwyn quiet when we are close to the cave."

Wynn laughed and cleared his throat. "I would be honored to come journey with you, my lad, but I'm afraid that adventure and combat are no longer in my veins. I'm no longer able to keep up with even the slowest of demons."

"Well, Wynn Silverbow, there is a look in your eyes that tells me you are not being totally forthcoming, but you have aided me and my friends more than a simple thanks could ever repay. I only hope that we will meet again when all of this is finished."

"You are just as Delwyn had said," Wynn said. "A powerful warrior with the heart and sense of a true leader."

Aaron opened his mouth, but Wynn held up a hand. "Go now and prepare for today's events. As you said, hopefully we will be able to talk again once this is over."

Aaron bowed and left to be with his friends. He had much to do before the hour was over.

ఌఌ

In less than an hour's time, the small party of friends left Wynn alone in his cottage while they headed off toward Isidore's caves. Wynn wished all of them farewell and said a few prayers for them.

"Now, what do I do first?" the elven mage asked himself, once he was alone. Wynn quickly took off his common robes and flung them carelessly onto a chair. Then, with the haste of a mad man, he opened a large closet and began fumbling around in the darkness. "Where did I put it?" the old mage asked the spiders and ants. Suddenly, he remembered where he had left his traveling gear. Wynn recited an ancient spell that revealed a hidden door on the far side of the walk-in closet. He quickly approached the door and kicked it open. He proceeded to enter the darkness without a second thought. After only a few short moments, a wizard geared up for heavy travel re-entered the daylight.

"I thought I gained more weight than this," remarked the wizard as he checked his dark green traveling robe and supplies. Like the few other elven wizards that had once existed, Wynn did not wear any type of hat or hood. Instead, he pulled his hair back as tightly as he could and placed it safely in a ponytail to keep unwanted hair out of his face while he cast spells.

Satisfied, Wynn Silverbow shouted a command and disappeared from his living room in a puff of smoke, reappearing in a secret laboratory with a large book in his hand.

After flipping through the ancient pages, Wynn sat himself in the circle of power he had created for memorizing spells. In just a few minutes, Wynn was in a trance that Isidore himself could not disrupt.

ఌఌ

Isidore emerged from the depths of his cave with a look that would frighten the grim reaper. If the demon master was worried about the outcome of the battle, it did not show on his stern face. Isidore wore midnight black armor that covered his entire body, making his red skin and yellow eyes look all the more sinister. A black cape hung loosely off his massive frame. No helmet adorned the demon's head since his black ram horns could easily deflect the biggest war hammer.

"Is everything as I demanded?" Isidore asked Damek, who waited at the cave's entrance. Damek wore no armor since none could be made that provided the protection and mobility of his reptilian scales. On his hip, the famous black dagger hung neatly in its elf-skin sheath.

"We are ready to leave on your command!" announced the demon scout. Damek knew that his master was at his best when his mind was focused on the destruction of his enemies.

The demon master climbed on top of his zaagh and rode to the head of his army, which was lined up neatly around the cave entrance and into the woods. The demons atop the zaaghs were to ride first followed by the foot soldiers that respectfully, and wisely, stayed out of the way of the strange and chaotic creatures.

Isidore gave his army one more look before he unsheathed his blackened sword. Rumors said that the sword was once as shiny as the purest silver, but centuries of slaughter had tarnished the evil blade. "Today we march to set claim to our territory!" the terrible leader began. "Woodbyrne has been ours for over two hundred years! The elves could not rid us, the humans will not rid us!"

The evil army of demons shouted in unison for their leader. Today we will extend our land into the humans' territory!" Again, cheers rang out throughout the forest.

"It will not take long to destroy the people of Gower and gain control of new and richer lands!"

Cutting off the next round of cheers, the demon ruler gave the order to march. While Damek flew in front of the army, Isidore and his minions headed down the trail that would take them to meet King Dermot and the Royal Army of Gower.

Chapter 32

"What an awful looking place," Sir Henry Goodwill said as he and the rest of the army looked down at Woodbyrne from a rocky hilltop no more than two hundred yards from the forest's borders.

"They will have a terrible time battling uphill," Sir Bickford Browne said. "Our archers should be able to thin out their ranks long before we have to engage in hand-to-hand combat."

"Remember one thing," reminded the king. "The demons have only to stand their ground and prevent us from entering the forest."

"Do you think the elves are in position already?" asked Sir Henry with doubt in his tone. "I mean, how could all of the wood elves be hiding in those trees?"

"It seems impossible to me too," added Lady Churchill. "Are you sure these elves can be trusted?"

"If Prince Aaron said they would be waiting in the trees for the most opportune moment, then I am certain that they are there right now looking at us."

"Sire!" called one of the scouts. "There is something coming out of the woods!"

A thick fog-like mist had begun to seep out of every section of the forest, covering the ground and the surrounding trees for dozens of yards.

"I think our adversary is here," Dermot announced. "Get your people into position!"

The three advisors quickly ran to their respective divisions and began to shout orders.

"The archers are ready, my king," Sir Bickford Browne announced. "You have only to give me the command to attack."

"The fog is getting thinner!" shouted one of the scouts. "I can make out forms behind it!"

"Indeed it is," the king replied under his breath.

Just as it had risen from the forest floor, the mysterious fog began to recede. Although they could not see too clearly, the Royal Army began to notice large, dark shapes moving inside of the mists. Dark shapes that resembled large horses with armed riders atop their backs. Slowly and methodically, those dark, evil shapes made their way forward.

&

"Where did he go?" Brother Frewin asked Lennox as he and the rest of the party sat and waited for the elf to return. Cathmore had led his friends without incident to Isidore's cave. However, the fact that not a single guard stood in front of the entrance was more disturbing than if all of Isidore's soldiers had been standing guard. The elf had instructed his friends to wait while he scouted the area for an ambush.

"He is searching the area as he said he would," Lennox replied. The human scout was nothing short of fantastic at his trade, but even proud Lennox Softfoot had to admire the cunning and skill of the wood elves. "If you like, I'll call him for you."

"Silence, all of you!" scolded Delwyn as quietly as possible. "Now is not the time to be foolish. One more peep and I'll turn the both of you into slugs!"

Without so much as a whisper, Cathmore crawled back into the thick brush where he rejoined his nervous companions. "I can see no signs of demons outside of the cave."

"Nothing at all?" asked the prince in disbelief.

"I could not tell if anything awaits us inside the cave, but I could sense nothing in the surrounding area."

"What about the trees?" Quinn asked. "Did they tell you anything on the demons' whereabouts?'"

Cathmore paused for a moment. "That's what I find a little disturbing," he admitted. "The trees were not answering my calls."

"What do you make of that?" asked Aaron.

"I don't know. They have never ignored me before. "

"Well, we'd better act quickly before Isidore returns," Frewin said.

"I can sense spells and wards that will inform him of our trespassing."

Aaron quickly devised a plan that would enable the party to be concealed while they approached the cave entrance.

๛

Lennox and Cathmore started ahead of the rest of the group as the others hid behind a thick group of trees. If there were any traps to be found, everyone was certain that one of the two scouts would find them. Once all was clear, the rest of the party would follow their tracks.

Cathmore and his human counterpart were no more than five yards from the entrance of the cave when they heard a loud rustling noise from behind them.

"Look out!" Kemp called as three very large trees began to uproot themselves and head for his vulnerable friends.

"It's a trap!" Delwyn shouted as five well-armed and heavily armored demons rushed out of the darkness of the cave, all wearing confident grins on their bestial faces.

Lennox and Cathmore watched in horror as the three trees shifted and transformed into hideous beasts that stood twelve feet high. They had thick brown skin, and thicker legs and arms, which made them look like small trees. Their bodies were covered in small branches and leaves, and their faces resembled the large wooden cysts that grew on diseased trees.

"Forest trolls!" Cathmore shouted as he unsheathed his long-sword. "I thought they were but a tale to frighten children out of wandering too far into the woods."

"Apparently not," answered Lennox as he too readied his weapon for attack.

๛

Damek and Isidore watched as the king of Gower barked orders and charged through his ranks while mounted on his white horse. Isidore looked across the open field at his nemesis and laughed.

"What do you find so amusing?" Damek asked.

"It has been a very long time since anyone has opposed me." Isidore unsheathed his blackened sword and shouted for his cavalry to take their position.

While the zaaghs and their demon riders moved to the front of the army, Isidore asked that Damek approach the humans with an offer.

⨭

"The archers are ready, sire," announced Sir Bickford Browne. "We await your command."

King Dermot nodded but did not say a word. Something off in the distance caught the wary king's attention and he did not want to take his eyes off it. "I see something approaching us," he finally said. "It looks like some giant bat." Both of the creature's hands were held open to show the humans that it was unarmed.

"What do you think it wants?" asked Sir Henry Goodwill.

"It wants to waste more time so that Isidore can better set up his forces," answered the king as the unearthly creature landed in the middle of the two forces.

"I have a message from Isidore, Master of Woodbyrne, for King Dermot!" the winged beast called.

Two horses, followed by a smaller pony, broke away from the rest of the army and headed towards Damek. One of the riders was an older man whom seemed to be of some significance to the army. The second rider was obviously a guard and the third appeared to be a bearded child holding a very formidable battle-axe. When the three allies grew near, Damek was surprised to see that a dwarf accompanied the humans into battle. A female dwarf at that!

"What a strange bunch of people you humans are," Damek said when the three companions were within range. "I have not seen a dwarf in a very long time."

"And ye'll never see one again when I'm through with ya!" spat Gertrude.

"King Dermot wants to know what your message is," Sir Bickford Browne stated before the dwarf acted irrationally, something their kin was famous for.

"Isidore does not wish to shed blood this day," the evil demon began. "All that he wants is Prince Aaron and Quinn Brainard."

"I should have known this was a waste of time," cursed Sir Bickford. "I won't even bother conveying to the king such an asinine request, you vile creature!"

"Very well, human scum!" Damek said as he flapped his leathery wings and rose quickly into the air. "Then let us see whose forces are the most powerful this day!"

"Indeed we will!" answered Gertrude as she swung her axe wildly about her head. "Why not start with you, ya rotten blackguard!" The dwarf's words were loud and harsh, but Damek could care less.

"I guess that went as well as could be expected," sighed Sir Bickford.

The three messengers quickly turned their mounts around and headed back to tell the king what he could have guessed long before they even arrived.

~

"Sir Bickford," the king commanded, "you may strike when ready."

Immediately the head of archers called for his troops to line up in front of the rest of the army.

"Ready!" the seasoned veteran shouted, and his troops pulled back on their deadly weapons. "Take aim!" He continued. This time the archers raised their weapons above their heads to an angle that would send the volley of missiles directly at the demons. "Loose!"

In an instant, the twang of dozens of bows cut the afternoon air followed by the whistle of arrows as they screeched towards the front line of the demon army.

~

Damek, along with the rest of the demons, looked on in horror as the deadly barrage of missiles sped across the sky towards their ranks. However, despite their fear, Isidore had given strict orders not to move out of harm's way.

314

Isidore, the one demon who merely smirked at the king's first offensive, raised one of his red hands and spoke a word of command. In an instant, a white line broke across the sky where the arrows headed. Once the missiles reached the magical border, they vanished.

～

"What trickery is this?" King Dermot asked.

"Ready!" Bickford Browne shouted as he prepared his troops to unleash another barrage of arrows.

Just as King Dermot turned and ordered the archers to hold their fire, a loud crack of thunder caused the ground to shake violently. Sir Bickford and the rest of the army looked up just in time to see a white line appear over his division's heads.

"Take cover!" the king shouted as he jumped off his horse and raised his shield above his head, and the same arrows that had vanished before the demons reappeared before the archers.

Men and women ran everywhere in order to get out of the way of the volley. Dozens of men and women lay writhing in agony after the shower had finished. Many died from their wounds.

"What do we do now, my king?" Bickford Browne asked. Even he had not been able to escape the attack without injury. The shaft of an arrow stuck out of his left shoulder while another had lodged itself deep within his left thigh. Blood covered the old archer and he simply looked at his lord with a pitiful smile.

"We have no choice but to attack!" the angered king shouted as he watched herbal healers and priests carry his wounded friend from the front lines. "Ready the cavalry!" Dermot called to Lady Churchill, who was already doing just that.

"Charge!" King Dermot shouted, and his cavalry thundered down the hillside toward the demons. The infantry, led by Sir Henry Goodwill, followed their mounted counterparts down the hill with roars of anger and revenge.

"Make your kingdom proud!" Gertrude shouted as she led the volunteers down the hillside behind the infantry. Like the rest of the army, the volunteers screamed and shouted as they charged into a battle that none of them thought they would survive.

❧

"Attack!" Isidore shouted, ordering his soldiers to meet the king's force head on. Like the Royal Army, the demons on foot followed the cavalry unit with shouts and screams of rage.

While Isidore watched smugly as his army sped off to intercept the humans, Damek was busy looking towards the northern-most section on the hill that overlooked Woodbyrne. "Who is that?" the scout asked, referring to a lone, robed figure waving his hands in the air.

"What are you talking about?" Isidore asked.

"Is that a wizard?" Damek asked. "He wears robes and I don't see weapons of any kind."

Isidore peered at the lone figure. "I cannot believe what I am seeing!" he roared. "He's alive! That stupid fool still lives!"

"Who is it?" Damek asked, wondering why Isidore had not commanded him to go and kill the wizard.

"It's Wynn, I'm sure of it!" shouted Isidore. "I feel his aura as I did two centuries ago when the stupid fool invited me onto this pathetic plane of existence."

"What's he doing up there?" Damek asked as he unsheathed his black dagger.

Isidore turned back to the fray and watched as a thin line of mist began to stretch across the entire length of the battlefield. From where Isidore was stationed, he could tell that his troops would reach it long before the humans.

"Go and kill him, Damek!" Isidore barked as he watched the thin mist spread further and further across the battlefield. The charging demon army was so full of rage and adrenaline that they seemed oblivious to the danger they headed towards. "Kill him before he casts that spell!"

Damek was already on his way.

❧

Wynn saw Damek coming in plenty of time to finish his spell. Quickly, the elven mage clenched his green fists and shouted the final word that completed his casting. He then smiled and watched as his magic went to work.

On command, the thin line of mist erupted into a wall of fire that reached fifty feet into the air. Both zaaghs and demons were too close to the deadly flames to stop in time. Scores of the demonic creatures were incinerated on contact, although many of the foot soldiers were far enough behind to sustain only minor burns from the magical flames. Then, just as quickly as they appeared, the fires vanished, leaving behind a demon army with too few demons and zaaghs to meet the king's charging forces.

Isidore could only watch as the humans bore down on his unfortunate army.

⤳

"Die!" Delwyn shouted to the giant tree troll as a black bolt of energy soared from his outstretched hand and slammed into one of the five demons, killing it on contact. Although the spell proved deadly for the unfortunate guard, Delwyn had wished it to take down one of the giant tree trolls. However, Aaron had jumped into the melee and would have gotten killed if the spell had missed its target.

The remaining four demon warriors attacked Quinn and Kemp.

Delwyn rolled his eyes back and began uttering the words to his desired spell.

Cathmore found the lumbering troll's maneuvers to be lethargic and predictable. Unfortunately, he could not see an opening in the creature's thick defenses. All over the troll's bodies, little branches stuck out like quills waiting to stick some unfortunate victim.

"This is going nowhere!" Aaron shouted. He knew that if something did not happen soon, they would never enter the cave.

Lennox continued to thrust and parry with the third giant troll. He uniformly cut and shaved the small branches away from the creature's body as each thick arm swung over his head.

Cathmore saw a small opening where a larger branch had broken off the troll's body and left behind a nice-sized spot where the elf could stab. The powerful troll swung again with both arms so as to crush the elf from both sides but the agile scout was on the ground rolling long before the thick limbs even got close. Taking advantage of his speed, Cathmore stabbed the troll with all of his might, his sword digging deep into the troll's chest as a putrid, green liquid spewed out of the wound. However, Cathmore was unable to remove his blade from the creature's cavity and was left defenseless against another attack. The troll smashed Cathmore on the head and sent him flying into cave wall.

Quinn dug her sword deep into the neck of one of the demons she fought, bringing a grizzly end to its miserable existence. The second demon waited for the young woman to leave herself open for attack, then quickly ran over and directed his blade toward the woman's neck.

"Quinn, behind you!" Kemp shouted as he pulled his sword out of the torso of one of the demons. The powerful fighter smiled when he saw his friend duck safely under her attacker's swing. Still, the warrior's aid took his concentration off his own fight and had left him vulnerable. The second demon charged and dug his sword into Kemp's arm.

Brother Frewin stood back in the safety of the trees as he closed his eyes and called to his god. The wise priest knew of a prayer that might help against the trolls, but the slightest distraction could prove fatal to him and the rest of his party. All that Frewin could do was stay behind until he had finished.

"Aaron!" Delwyn called from across the clearing. "Lead it towards me!"

Aaron swung wildly at the troll and moved backwards towards the wizard. As expected, the massive creature began to advance on the weaker human.

"Run as fast as you can!" the wizard instructed, once Aaron was far away from the rest of the party.

Aaron saw that Delwyn held some sort of red orb in his hand and was aiming to throw it. Quickly, the prince ducked low and ran off toward the cover of the trees.

Woodbryne: The fallen forest

Delwyn Westbrook tossed the red orb at the advancing troll. The magical item smashed into its chest and exploded into a ball of fire. The doomed troll could do little more than scream as it was engulfed in the deadly flames.

"Go after Cathmore's troll before it kills him!" The wizard instructed while Aaron watched in amazement as the burning troll writhed in agony on the forest floor. Somehow, the flames stayed on the troll and did not spread to the rest of the forest.

Quinn and Kemp were having a difficult time with their remaining enemies. Apparently, those demons were among Isidore's finest warriors and would not bow easily to the humans.

Kemp tried hard to keep his attacker at bay while he swung his two-handed sword with one arm. His left shoulder continued to bleed freely and the noble warrior feared that he had to do something soon or he would not live to see his mother again.

Quinn was overmatched by the powerful demon. The creature was able to score several hits against the woman, gaining ground with every passing second.

Lennox saw Cathmore's troll approach him with an evil grin. The hardened scout tried to gain the upper hand with the monster he was already battling. However, despite his courage and physical prowess, the forest troll never stopped its barrage of attacks. One after another, its powerful fists slammed down with deadly force. Lennox's legs grew tired as cramps worked their way into his muscles. One last swing from the giant beast's heavy arm sent the fatigued scout to the forest floor. Then, just before the gigantic troll blocked his view, Lennox saw Kemp on the other side of the clearing fall to one knee as his demon kicked the sword from his hand.

The troll that struck Lennox had underestimated the powerful humans, however, and turned around just in time to see Brother Frewin slam his glowing mace into its thick chest. The creature screamed in agony from the magic-enhanced blow and swung at the priest with one of its powerful limbs. Luckily, the nasty mace stunned the troll long enough to allow Frewin to get out of the way.

Lennox quickly got to one knee and pulled out his powerful bow. With years of experience to back him up, the native took aim and, with blinding speed, set loose two arrows toward the demon attacking Kemp. The pitiful creature stopped as one arrow lodged into its chest while the other skipped off its neck and slammed into a nearby tree.

Kemp sprung at the stunned demon and pushed the arrow further into the creature's heart. In a moment, both Kemp and his enemy fell to the forest floor covered in each other's blood. Both warriors were still and lifeless.

The troll injured by the priest shook off the pain from the mace and turned back toward Lennox. However, before it could advance, something began to gnaw at the creature's legs. Thousands of ants and termites had found their way to the troll's wooden frame and had begun to feed relentlessly at its thick skin. In seconds, the forest troll was covered from head to toe in a deadly swarm and collapsed to the ground.

The remaining troll stepped over its dying comrade and lifted its huge arms to strike at the scout.

Brother Frewin and Aaron had other ideas and hacked at the tall creature from behind, each scoring powerful hits long before the troll could even turn around.

Quinn saw that her friends were taking care of the remaining creatures and fought back at her adversary with renewed strength. Still, despite her rage, the demon was a seasoned veteran and one of the leaders in Isidore's wicked army.

Delwyn saw that Quinn was in over her head and cast a simple spell that sent dozens of bright bolts slamming into the demons eyes, temporarily blinding the creature.

Quinn took full advantage of the spell and thrust her sword into the demon's neck. She had to duck one last time as the powerful warrior tried to take the young woman with him in death.

When the battle finally ended, Brother Frewin ran as fast as he could to Kemp's side. There the valiant warrior lay still on the ground as blood flowed freely from his horrible wound.

"The demon must have hit an artery," Delwyn concluded.

"He is still breathing," Frewin said. "There is little time to waste." The priest told the rest of the party to care for themselves while he tried to save his friend's life.

Aaron gently led Quinn away from the gruesome sight so he could tend to her wounds.

Delwyn and Lennox rested uneasily against a large oak tree.

"How did those insects know to go after the troll?" the scout asked. "I thought I would be next."

"Those creatures were summoned by our very own Brother Frewin," the mage explained as he pointed over to the priest. "He saved your life, my friend."

"Indeed he did. Just how powerful is that young priest?"

Delwyn could only shrug in response. "All I know is that my magic and his prayers are completely different. Perhaps we can speak to each other about it once all of this is over."

"Perhaps," Lennox said. "If this ends the way we hope."

Chapter 33

"We all thought you to be dead, Wynn," said Damek as he landed with a thud a few yards in front of Wynn Silverbow. Damek slowly pulled out his dagger and cautiously approached the wizard.

"I guess you were wrong," Wynn replied.

"Do you really think you can beat me?"

Wynn gave the advancing demon a quick wink and replied, "I guess we will just have to find out."

"Demon!" called a voice from behind a group of large maple trees. "I am feeling up to the challenge!" Forrester Silverbow stepped out and pulled out his magnificent silver bow. In his quiver, dozens of silver arrows awaited their master's call.

Damek looked enraged at his new adversary. "What sort of trickery is this?" he demanded.

Faster than the winged demon could react, Forrester moved into action and set loose four deadly arrows in quick succession.

Damek avoided two of the arrows, but the third ripped through his wing and the fourth scraped his leg, leaving behind a black streak of blood. The magical arrows forced Damek down on his knee, holding the open gash in frustration.

With such an opportune moment before him, Forrester dropped his bow and grabbed his sword. Quickly, the powerful elf charged in with all the speed he could muster.

Just as the elf was about to strike, the demon spun around and landed a heavy punch on Forrester's throat, sending the elf to the ground gasping for air.

"Nice try, elf," spat Damek as he raised his dagger for the killing blow.

Without warning, a bold of lightning slammed into the demon's chest, sending thousands of volts and immense heat throughout his body. Damek was thrown dozens of feet back before he crashed to the ground and lost his hold on the magical dagger.

"You did it, father," Forrester said as he regained his breath. The elf lord still clung to his throat as he lay on the hilltop. Damek lay smoldering on the ground.

Wynn, holding a blue wand, rushed to his son's side and tried to help him up. "Are you all right, my boy?"

"I'll be all right. Now, let's get back to the others. They will soon need our help."

"It'll take more than that!" Damek shouted from behind the two elves. The evil demon kicked Forrester in the ribs and grabbed Wynn by the throat. In an instant, the mage was being carried off into the sky by the demon scout. Damek had been badly injured from the bolt of lightning. His chest had been torn apart, bubbled flesh showed where once glimmering black scales were and his eye was closed shut and covered in blood. "You are going to pay dearly for what you did to me," the demon promised.

۲

Isidore set off his spell and watched in delight as the king's horses became spooked and threw their riders. Quickly, the demon soldiers swarmed in and cut down as many knights as possible before the king's infantry unit could come to their aid.

۲

As the two armies battled, Isidore meticulously searched for Prince Aaron and Quinn Brainard. "Where are you two?" the demon master questioned under his breath. "Why would the prince miss such an event?" Suddenly, Isidore realized his mistake. Quickly, he cast a spell that proved his suspicions. Fueled by anger and rage, Isidore jumped on his zaagh and sped off towards the cave, completely unaware of the scores of waiting elves hiding in the tree tops.

꒰ꗞ꒱

Although every elf that watched the spectacle wanted dearly to strike at the root of their sorrows, they were given specific orders not to touch the master of the demons. Their arrows would do him no harm but would jeopardize their plans.

꒰ꗞ꒱

"Is he going to be all right?" Prince Aaron asked Brother Frewin.

The young priest had finished his prayers and sighed. "He is going to live, I am certain. My prayer stopped the bleeding and closed the wound; however, there is no way Kemp's going to be able to continue this battle. And to make matters worse, I am getting very weak. Soon, I will need time to rest."

"Where's Cathmore?" Quinn asked, suddenly realizing that she had not seen the elf since the fight with the trolls.

Lennox ran over to where he had last seen his friend. There, he saw Cathmore tending to his wounds, which included a broken arm and a badly bruise head. "I am so sorry, my friend," he apologized as the others ran over to see the broken elf.

"No apologies needed," Cathmore insisted. "In the heat of battle it's hard to account for everybody."

"Can you walk?" Quinn asked.

Cathmore, with the help of Aaron and Lennox, stood and nearly fainted as the pain blinded him. Blood covered the elf's face and his luscious hair lay in matted clumps atop his injured head.

Aaron and Lennox carried Cathmore over to where Kemp had been treated. There, Brother Frewin quickly opened some salve and applied it to the elf's more serious wounds. Afterwards, he recited with what strength he had left to aid the elf's recovery.

Quinn made a makeshift brace that would be able to support the elf's broken right arm. It was crudely constructed but it would ease some of the pain.

"What do we do now?" Aaron asked Delwyn, who was busy scribbling notes in his increasingly larger notebook.

Suddenly, a strong wind swept into the clearing. It came from the path, which led away from the cave towards the borders of Woodbyrne. From the treetops, birds flew away and many other small animals headed for cover as the strong winds bent huge branches and whipped up dust and other debris.

"I feel something is terribly wrong with this," said Lennox. "We should get out of view as soon as possible."

"What about them?" Quinn pointed over to Brother Frewin as he quickly moved from Cathmore to Kemp, trying hard not to allow one of them go with out proper treatment.

The wind began to kick up, causing everyone to protect their eyes from twigs and dirt. Dark clouds began to form over the clearing and the cave, blocking the sun. From the path, a black cloud began to creep towards the small company.

"We have no time to waste!" Delwyn shouted. "Carry the wounded to a safe place; we *must* go inside the cave and wait for Isidore!"

There was no time to argue. Kemp and Cathmore were hidden by large trees and big rocks. "I must stay behind with these two or they will die!" Frewin shouted as the winds picked up.

The evil windstorm made it impossible to cross the clearing. The friends concealed themselves behind thick bushes and boulders as they watched the storm fling branches and rocks about.

Aaron held on tightly to the silver dagger. The magical weapon had begun to grow warm and it throbbed in the prince's hand like a beating heart. "Is Isidore casting another storm?"

"I'm afraid it is much more serious than that, my boy," replied the wizard.

"What do you mean?"

"Isidore is coming!"

⤷

"I heard your friend died screaming like a coward," Damek taunted as he tossed and turned in the air with his prisoner. "What was his name, wizard?" Another violent shake jolted Wynn's body. "Greentree, wasn't it? Yes, that's what Isidore told me. Salomon Greentree!" Damek broke out in an evil laugh as he rose higher into the afternoon sky. Soon, the battle below looked like two armies of ants fighting over their territory.

Wynn had his eyes closed the entire time. He tried hard not to listen to the demon's taunts. Instead, Wynn Silverbow thought of how things used to be. He thought of the sounds of children running through the woods while deer scampered about and birds sang their melodies. Wynn thought of the days before Isidore and his evil horde of followers crashed into Woodbyrne and stole its beauty and purity. Wynn also thought of the wand still clenched securely in his slender hands.

"Now you die!" Damek shouted as he dove back towards the ground at lightning speed. "I am going to use you to crush that stupid fool with the bow!"

Wynn held tight to the wand. "I am sorry," he whispered. "I was only a child and craved fame and power."

"What are you ranting about?" demanded Damek.

"Please forgive me."

"What are you saying?"

Wynn grabbed the wand with both hands and opened his eyes so he could see his son one last time. "I love you, my boy. I always will."

"No!" Forrester shouted. Quickly, the elf threw himself to the ground and pulled his green cloak over his head.

"Forgive me," said the wizard one last time, and then he broke the wand.

The explosion rocked the land. Both demons and humans stopped their fighting and watched as a gigantic ball of fire lit the late afternoon sky in a bright orange glow.

༄

Forrester got up quickly and checked himself for burns. Fortunately for the elf lord, Wynn had timed it so the explosion would go off safely in the air. Forrester picked up his silver bow and slung it over his shoulder. "You were supposed to see this end," he said. "You were supposed to be there when Isidore fell."

The sound of the battle re-engaging reminded Forrester that it was not over yet. "There will be time enough to mourn after this war has ended." After one more farewell to his fallen father, Forrester Silverbow, son of Wynn Silverbow, ran off into Woodbyrne where he would meet up with his kin and join the fight.

⌘

Although the demons fought with skill and cunning, they were no match for the sheer determination of the humans. The soldiers of the Royal Army fought for their wives and husbands. Thoughts of their children made them swing their swords with a vengeance. Memories of burned crops and killed loved ones pushed them beyond their limits. Anger filled their eyes and rage fueled their souls.

The fact that the second most powerful demon on Oneira died in a fiery explosion, and Isidore, demon master of Woodbyrne, had fled to the caves did little to encourage the demon army. Quickly, their defenses began to crumble around them.

"Into the forest!" a lesser demon leader shouted to his remaining troops. "If the humans want us, they'll have to hunt for us on our own grounds!"

"Back to Woodbyrne!" another leader called.

Quickly, the demons backed away from the humans and slowly made their way into Woodbyrne. It was not an easy task but many of the remaining demons made it into the thick cover of the trees and dug themselves in for battle. To their surprise, however, the king's army stopped a short distance from the forest's border.

⌘

"Are you sure about this, sire?" asked Sir Bickford Browne from the hilltop overlooking the carnage.

"I gave Sir Henry specific orders *not* to pursue the demons if they entered the forest," Dermot replied.

"What are we supposed to do then?"

Dermot smiled wickedly as he kicked his horse into a gallop. "We are only to prevent them from leaving, Bickford!"

"Why would they want to leave?" asked the Head of Archers as he too kicked his steed into a gallop.

※

"What are ya waitin' for!" shouted one of the impatient demons.

"Cowardly humans!" cursed another.

"For Woodbyrne!" shouted Forrester as he motioned for his companion to blow her horn and give the signal for attack.

With sheer hatred and desperation as their motivation, scores of elves shot hundreds of arrows down on the demon forces. In an instant, blood and gore covered the earth and screams of pain filled the air. Before the dog-like beasts could even react to the barrage, they were overwhelmed by a flurry of wood and steel.

Forrester jumped down from his perch to join his people in their hour of glory. "Do not let any of the beasts escape!" he shouted as he ducked under an axe that was aimed for his head. Forrester countered the move with a backward slash of his finely edged sword, taking off the demon's arm from the elbow down. Seeing another elf about to be attacked from behind, Forrester grabbed the axe and hurled it at the demon. The elf lord acted as a true leader, shouting commands and helping defend his people's lives.

In minutes, the demon army ran wild while the wood elves cut them down. Some of the vile creatures were actually stupid enough to kneel down and beg for mercy. Others tried their luck with the humans but found no sanctuary outside of the forest.

Although the ground grew thick with black blood, Forrester Silverbow had never seen his home look so beautiful. The enemy was not so powerful after all. "For Woodbyrne!" he cried, "For Woodbyrne!"

The elves were victorious. Not only had the demon army been destroyed, but elf casualties were limited to wounds that would heal. When the battle had almost finished, Forrester Silverbow made his way to the border where King Dermot waited patiently with the remainder of the Royal Army.

Aaron tried hard to relax as he and his companions waited for the demon master to arrive. The black cloud that had crept into the clearing mixed with the strong winds and made it almost impossible to see. He could barely make out his friends, but he could see Quinn, also ready for the confrontation, clenching her bow in anticipation of Isidore's return.

Suddenly, the ground began to shake violently as the pounding of a gigantic horse could be heard coming down the path towards the cave.

"Everyone ready themselves!" ordered Prince Aaron. "He is here!"

Chapter 34

The demon master rode proudly into the clearing. In his left hand, Isidore held his wicked two-handed sword.

"Hero," the demon called, "I know you are here! There's no place to hide!" Isidore turned his mount.

Aaron tried hard not to let his nerves get the best of him. He had been through much since the last time he had seen Isidore but his accomplishments seemed pitifully insignificant in front of so powerful a foe.

At the other extreme, the magical dagger that the prince held wanted to meet Isidore in the worst of ways. It wanted to enter the demon's body and lodge itself in the beast's heart. Slowly, methodically, the dagger began to take control of Aaron's thoughts.

"I am going to enjoy killing the two of you!" continued Isidore as his evil mount sniffed the air in search of the humans.

"Get him!" the dagger shouted into Aaron's mind. "Now is your chance!" Still, Aaron waited for the right time to strike. "Kill him now!" the dagger urged.

"I am going to kill you much more slowly than I did your pathetic cousin!" promised the demon. "At least Byram was a brave soul, unlike you, Aaron! Your cousin was not a coward!"

"Get him! Kill him!"

"Byram wouldn't leave his own cousin for dead!"

"Kill him!"

Aaron snapped. The young prince ran out from his hiding spot and charged Isidore head on. His dagger raised above his head, Aaron planned to jump up at Isidore and drive the wicked blade into his neck, one of the few places that Isidore's black armor did not cover.

Without warning, the zaagh snapped its powerful jaws and ripped into Aaron's shoulder, crushing bone and tearing flesh in the process.

The evil creature's violent bite caused Aaron to dropped the dagger.

"Release him!" demanded Quinn, as she and the rest of the party advanced towards Isidore. "I said release him!"

"One move and I kill him!" Isidore warned, stopping the companions in their tracks. "So nice to see you again, Quinn," he purred, a disgusting smile crossing his face.

Aaron, trying hard not to scream in agony, noticed that the wizard was about to cast a spell. Also aware of Delwyn's actions, the zaagh shook the prince's shoulder with its tooth-filled maw.

Aaron's screams and pleas were more that enough for Delwyn to stop his casting, and he dropped his hands.

"Release the woman to me and I will call off my army!" Isidore demanded.

"Surely you do not think us to be that foolish?" Delwyn asked. "You are surrounded by powerful enemies, Isidore. It would be wise of you to leave this plane and return to your decrepit world before it is too late!"

"Another wizard with a big mouth, huh?" Quickly, the demon master said the words to a spell that hurled a ball of fire towards the mage.

Calmly, Delwyn spoke a word of power and held out an outstretched hand. The fireball exploded into little snowflakes that landed harmlessly on the ground. Delwyn looked at Isidore and playfully winked at the enraged creature.

"Your prince will pay for that outrage," shouted Isidore, but before he could ask his zaagh to crush Aaron's neck, the large beast snorted and fell to the ground, freeing Aaron and throwing Isidore in the dirt.

The demon master looked over to see four arrows jutting out of the beast's neck.

"Cathmore!" Quinn shouted as the elf collapsed by the rock he had been hidding behind.

Isidore screamed in protest and sent a blinding flash of light throughout the clearing. When it diminished, he was nowhere to be found.

"He's in the cave," Lennox shouted as he ran up to aid his injured prince. "Can you go on, Aaron?"

Aaron's left shoulder was crushed from the vicious bite. The prince's powerful armor had prevented his arm from being severed, but the sheer power of the zaagh's bite had broken his collarbone.

"I'm afraid I don't have anything that could help," Brother Frewin apologized. "We need to get him out of here as soon as possible."

"I can go on," Aaron grunted as he forced himself back on his feet. "I must go on!"

"I agree with Aaron," Quinn added. "If we retreat now we'll never have the chance to get Isidore alone. He's afraid of us now. We have no choice but to continue."

The remaining party members agreed. Proudly, they picked up their weapons and headed for the cave.

"Stay behind and tend to the elf and Kemp," the prince said to Frewin as he picked up his magical dagger. "If my father has been successful then I doubt you will be alone for much longer." With that said, Aaron walked into the darkness of the cave.

↭

Dermot rode up to the kneeling elf and dismounted his horse. "It is I who should be kneeling before you, good elf," he said as he extended his hand in friendship. "You and your people helped save my son's life."

"You and your son helped rescue my people from certain annihilation," the elf responded. "I am Forrester Silverbow, son of the great Wynn Silverbow, the most powerful mage to have ever existed among my people."

"I am Dermot, King of Gower," the king replied. The two leaders approached each other and embraced.

"That was your father on top of the hill, wasn't it?" asked Sir Henry Goodwill.

"Yes it was. My father sacrificed himself for the good of our people," replied Forrester. The gallant elf lord raised his head and stuck out his chest. "He has made his peace with his people and with this land."

"I am sorry for your loss, Forrester," replied the king. "I only wish that we had the time to talk about his heroics. For now, we must meet my son at the caves. Can you lead the way?"

"Yes, and with the speed of the horses, we can be there long before the sun sets."

Dermot agreed to accompany the elf lord and the rest of the wood elves to the cave while the rest of his army waited for his return. He then ordered five of his men to give up their horses to the wood elves, and, within seconds, he and his new allies sped down the long trail that led to the cave. Behind them, the rest of the elves followed on foot. Although Dermot was concerned for his son, he could not help but smile as he charged down the dark path.

"It has been too long," the king whispered.

⁂

The small party had a difficult time as they meticulously crept down the dark corridors of Isidore's lair. There was insufficient light from the few candles that were lit on the wall and it seemed like every corner would have a creature waiting to greet the unfortunate trespassers. Aaron was unsure of how he and Byram had previously picked their way through the gloom and Quinn seemed to have forgotten her escape route.

"There is little I can go by," admitted Lennox Softfoot. Even the ever-alert scout could not decipher which way would lead to Isidore. "The beast left no tracks and it is impossible for me to tell if we are descending or ascending."

"These halls are magically protected against such things," said the wizard. "Isidore must have stepped up his defenses after the prince and Quinn got away with their lives."

Suddenly, the candles on each side of the wall burst into flame. Each member of the party, except for Delwyn, readied for battle.

"What's going on?" Quinn asked as she clung to her sword.

"He is leading us to him," answered Aaron.

"You are correct, my lad," congratulated the wizard. "It seems that Isidore doesn't want us to get lost in his maze of gloom and despair."

As the small company made their way down the cave, candles sparked to life, directing the humans to follow. Eventually, the candles led the party to a giant chamber with two large doors.

"This is it," said the prince, as he led his companions towards the gold doors. "These doors lead to Isidore's main chamber."

Before the companions could prepare, the massive doors swung open and a yellow light poured into the hallway.

"I bid you welcome," called a voice from inside the great hall.

Slowly, the companions made their way down the long corridor, stopping just before the bone doors, which were also open.

Without warning, a wall of fire burst into the hallway behind the humans, cutting off any means of escape. The heat from the fires intensified to the point where there was no choice but to enter the large room where Isidore waited.

The powerful demon master sat proudly on top of his throne in the center of the great hall. All around the massive demon, thousands of small vials decorated every inch of the walls.

"You have nowhere to run!" Aaron shouted. "Give up now or face our wrath!"

"My dear Prince," cooed the demon, "why would I do such a foolish thing when I am about to destroy all who oppose me?"

"What are you saying, vile spawn?" Delwyn demanded, twisting a blue wand in his hand. "How do you intend to crush the king's forces when you know they shall be the victors in this battle?"

"Why don't I show all of you?" Isidore snapped his fingers and a black orb appeared before the party. Terrible screams and shouts came from the darkness like children lost from their mothers. The horrible sounds caused Isidore to smile.

"You are listening to my homeland," explained the powerful demon. "As we speak, twice as many demon soldiers are preparing to enter this world." Isidore let his words hang in the air for only a moment's time. "Soon, like your precious king, all of you will be dead."

"Not if we can help it!" shouted Delwyn as he raised his wand and pointed it towards Isidore. However, when the wizard shouted the words needed to set off the magic item, nothing happened.

Isidore began to laugh loudly. "Your magic does not work here, old man. However, mine most certainly does!" Isidore barked a word that sent Delwyn to his knees. The powerful wizard tried hard to fight the magic but to no avail.

Isidore grabbed his sword from the side of his throne and jumped down to battle with the humans.

๛

"What is that?" asked Dermot as he pointed to a large black cloud that had formed just a few yards above the treetops. Although it was still far away from the ground, it was growing quickly. Even from their distance, the elves could hear screams and cries from within the depths of the magical cloud.

"It's forming over the caves!" answered Forrester. "Quickly, we haven't much time!"

Dermot thought only of his son as he forced his horse into a wild run for the caves. "Hang on, Aaron," he pleaded. "Hang on."

๛

Lennox Softfoot was the first to try to take on the demon master. The skilled human was completely overpowered by the large demon, but tried hard to hold off his attacks while the prince sought a way to use his dagger.

"Now is your chance!" the magical dagger shouted into Aaron's mind. The powerful weapon had grown very hot and Aaron found it very difficult to hold.

"Not yet!" Aaron yelled back. "Now is not the time!" Aaron reminded himself of his failure outside the cave in order to clear his head. He needed to trust himself, not rely on the dagger to choose for him.

Lennox's defense deteriorated quickly; Isidore's swings and chops were too powerful and accurate for the native scout. After one powerful blow, Lennox could feel his wrist start to break under the pressure of the two-handed sword.

Seeing that his friend was in great peril, Aaron sheathed his dagger and pulled out his sword. Quickly, Aaron joined his dear friend in hand to hand combat with the confident demon master.

335

Quinn remembered that none of her weapons would harm Isidore. She had to find something to use against the demon master. While Aaron kept Isidore busy, she started to look along the shelves of vials. The soul inside each jar looked like it was in some kind of hibernation. Just when she was about to give up and join her friends in certain doom, a friendly voice entered her head. Frantically, Quinn searched for the vial that seemed to be calling her name.

"Free me," pleaded a desperate voice. "Set us all loose!"

"Where are you?" Quinn asked out loud. "There are so many vials!" The young woman began to panic.

Isidore had little trouble attacking the prince and Lennox at the same time. His powerful swings and sheer anger drove both men back towards the far end of the hall. "I almost feel sorry for the two of you," taunted the wicked creature.

"You must act now, Aaron!" pleaded Lennox. Aaron knew the scout's strength ran low and it would be mere seconds before he fell. His left wrist was completely useless and it would not be long before his right one followed.

Isidore took deep breath and blew a stream of fire at Aaron. As soon as the nimble prince dove for cover, Isidore swung his sword at Lennox.

The quick scout did his best to deflect Isidore's large sword but his efforts fell short and the evil weapon drove itself deep into his ribs. Lennox simply dropped his weapon and grabbed his open wound. Spurts of blood flew in every direction as he tried to slow the flow of blood.

"Pathetic humans!" Isidore shouted as he gave the scout a powerful kick in the stomach that sent him into the bone doors with a sickening thud. He then turned back to the wizard. Delwyn still writhed on the floor in pain from his unseen attacker. "Now it is your turn to die, wizard!" the powerful demon shouted as he waved his hands in the air.

Quinn had given up hope when the voice called her again.

"Free us!"

"Where are you?" Quinn asked again. Suddenly she noticed, just a few yards away, one of the glass jars had begun to glow. Quinn ran over to the flask and picked it off the wall.

336

Isidore cast his spell and laughed as dozens of lizards appeared on the wizard's body. The wicked little creatures began to gnaw on the old wizard's skin, causing Delwyn to squirm on the floor with even more desperation than before.

"Die, you beast!" Aaron shouted as he lunged for Isidore's head with the dagger.

Smiling, Isidore turned and deflected the attack with a swing of his hand. The power of the strike spun Aaron around and left him prone. Isidore clenched Aaron's injured shoulder with his powerful hand. The demon master's black claws easily ripped through Aaron's armor and lodged themselves into his flesh. "Your time has come, hero!"

⁂

"It appeared just as soon as they entered," Brother Frewin explained to King Dermot and Forrester Silverbow.

A barrier of fire that seemed to grow in size and intensity whenever anyone got close to it completely blocked off the cave's entrance.

"Isidore wants to be left alone," Forrester explained.

By then, the large cloud had completely developed in the sky and slowly made its way towards the earth. The screams and shouts that came out of the darkness were now accompanied by scores of glowing eyes, all of which promised certain doom if allowed to enter Oneira.

"Our job is finished," King Dermot sighed as he watched the black cloud descend. "It is too late to warn the others. We can only pray that my son is successful."

⁂

"Does it hurt?" Isidore teased as he scraped one of his black claws into Aaron's collarbone.

Aaron did not answer. Instead he clenched the dagger in his good hand while he searched the room for Quinn. Where had she gone?

"Ahh, I almost forgot about that one," said Isidore.

"Quinn!" called Isidore as he turned around to look for the missing woman, dragging Aaron with him. "Where did you go, my sweetheart?

337

We can still be friends!"

"I'm right here, Isidore!" answered Quinn. The young woman stood far enough away from the demon to be relatively safe, yet she was close enough for Isidore to see that she held one of his glass jars.

"What do you have there?" the demon demanded. "Don't worry, Quinn, soon you will be calling one of those your home! Just as soon as I kill your prince!" Isidore raised his sword high above his horned head for a final strike at Aaron.

Quinn threw the jar to the ground and unleashed the soul inside. The gaseous form quickly sped towards Isidore and engulfed his entire body. Within the ghostly mists, the form of a person could be seen, hatred written all over his face.

"Byram!" called the prince as he saw what looked to be his cousin pounding on Isidore's face with ghost-like hands. Isidore swatted at the gaseous form with his monstrous claws.

Although the apparition did not seem to cause Isidore any visible injury, it somehow delivered enough pain for him to let go of Aaron's shoulder.

"Die!" shouted the prince as he lunged forward with all of his energy and drove his dagger into the demon's chest.

Isidore screamed as the magical weapon tore through his black armor and lodged itself into his heart. The dagger began to glow and pump violently as it injected the purified blood into Isidore's very soul. When the dagger lost all of its power, Isidore dropped to his knees.

"This isn't happening," the demon insisted. "This can't be happening!" The powerful demon master of Woodbyrne looked at Aaron and Quinn one last time before his yellow eyes shut and he fell to the ground. In seconds, the lifeless body exploded into a ball of fire and vanished.

All of the glass jars the adorned the walls exploded and shattered into thousands of pieces. The souls that had been prisoners inside began to fly throughout the room and circle above Aaron's head. One soul, however, remained on the ground next to his beloved cousin.

Aaron fell to his knees and began to cry as the soul of Byram looked down upon him. "Please forgive me," begged the prince. "I never meant for this to happen."

Byram knelt down beside him and gently caressed his face. Although no words were said, the glimmer in Byram's eyes told Aaron that all was forgiven.

"Please stay with me?" asked the prince. "Please come back to me?"

Byram shook his head at his cousin and then looked up to the ceiling where the thousands of other freed souls waited for their savior to join them.

Aaron looked up at his cousin and gave him a playful smile. "I guess we will be together soon enough, my friend. Go now and rest while I finish my job down here."

Byram winked and looked back up to the rest of the souls. He raised his hands, turned into a white mist, and joined the others. Instantly, the freed souls rushed out of the cave, leaving behind a silver trail for the humans to follow.

"We should be leaving, Aaron," called Quinn. "I'll take care of Delwyn. You go see about Lennox." When Quinn reached the old wizard, she saw that he was still alive but covered head to toe in cuts and bites.

"I'll be okay, my dear," Delwyn assured her. "Just help me back on my feet and we can get out of here."

"Lennox!" Aaron shouted as he ran over to aid his friend. The seasoned scout was barely alive and had lost a lot of blood. Aaron acted quickly and tore some cloth to use as a bandage. The evil blade had sliced right through Lennox's flesh and scratched bone. Aaron had no idea how the scout still breathed, but he did not have time to wonder.

Lennox seemed to respond to his leader's care and slowly rose to his feet. "Let's get out of here, my friend," he muttered. "I can make it."

Once the four companions were able, they meticulously made their way out of the dark caves. The silver trail still hung in the air to guide them safely to the surface.

Chapter 35

King Dermot watched in amazement as the black cloud burst into flames and vanished. The voices that had promised certain doom for Woodbyrne and Gower now screamed in terror as the world around them burned into hot gasses and deadly fumes.

"Look at that!" Brother Frewin shouted as he pointed to the cave entrance.

The protective wall of fire had vanished and a wave of mist poured out of the entrance. As eerie forms climbed into the twilight, their ghostly shapes became visible to all that looked upon them.

"They're free!" Brother Frewin shouted in joy. "Aaron must have beaten Isidore!"

Forrester, too, joined in on the celebration, as did all of the elves that had accompanied him.

"Where are you, my boy," Dermot whispered into the air. "Where are you?"

"Something is coming out of the cave!" a female elf shouted as she readied her bow for attack.

"Put your weapons down!" shouted Aaron from inside the cave. "We have had enough fighting for one day!"

Quinn and Delwyn exited together. Delwyn had suffered many cuts and bruises, but the resilient old mage was able to leave the lair on his own. Lennox Softfoot was too badly injured to make the long trek out of the cave. After only a few yards, he collapsed. Ignoring the pain from his injured shoulder, Aaron gladly carried his friend out of the cave.

"Aaron!" Dermot shouted as he dropped his sword and ran toward his son. "I thought I'd never see you again, my boy."

Aaron laid Lennox gently on the ground and embraced his father.

"Dad, my shoulder! Be careful!" Aaron almost passed out as his father gave him a huge bear hug.

Brother Frewin and the elves tended to Delwyn and Lennox. Although the priest was unable to pray for his friends, he was well trained in the art of healing. In the end, Brother Frewin, along with many special salves and bandages from the wood elves, was able to mend the open wounds and save the lives of both his friends. Afterwards, the exhausted priest tended to Aaron's injury so he could make it back out of the forest in relative comfort.

"When we leave here," explained the priest, "you may not see me for a very long time."

Cathmore and Kemp found the strength to join in the celebration with the rest of the humans and wood elves. The elven scout even managed to shed a tear for all of his fallen kin, many of whom he had never had the honor of knowing.

After his shoulder was bandaged and placed in a sling, Aaron ran over to Quinn and hugged her. "You did it!" he proclaimed. "You saved Woodbyrne and Gower!"

"No, Aaron. We all did." Quinn began to shed tears of joy and sadness. "You avenged the death of your cousin while I avenged my father. Together, we saved this beautiful forest, and Gower, from the shadow of Isidore."

꙳

A feeling came over Audrey as she helped the healers tend to the injured citizens of Gower. The queen had experienced many feelings since her husband and son left; however, none of those dark and terrible thoughts resembled what she felt at that particular moment. A feeling of peace came over her as if a gigantic weight had been lifted off her chest.

"Excuse me?" asked an injured old man whom the queen was tending. The poor old farmer had been gashed in the neck by one of Isidore's followers on the night of the raid and he barely made it to the castle alive. "Is there something wrong, my lady?"

"No, nothing is wrong, my good man. It's just that I think they did it but I can't be sure."

"You are correct, Queen Audrey," said an elderly woman from the other side of the tent. "Indeed our prince drove the killing blow into that wretched creature."

"How do you know that?" asked Audrey.

"I am Helinda O'Shan," said the woman as she bowed to the queen. "I met your son and his cousin before they went to Woodbyrne, and Quinn when they escaped its dark canopy."

"Are you certain that they are all right?" Queen Audrey could hardly hold back her joy.

"Throughout the years, I have been able to hone my abilities to serve me, and they serve me well. Your love for your family is as strong a bond as one could have. I am not surprised you feel it as well."

As soon as the healers and the injured heard of the possible victory of the king and the prince, the tents were overwhelmed with cries of joy and prayers of thanks. Soon, like wild fire, the entire kingdom ran about shouting praise for their victorious leaders.

All of the excitement overwhelmed the queen and she knelt and began to weep. She wept for her people and the lives lost to the demons. She wept for those who lost loved ones and for those who would wear the scars of war for the rest of their lives. Most of all, however, Audrey wept for her son. How hard it must have been for Aaron to return to Woodbyrne. How terrible it must have been to see his best friend die before his eyes.

"What is wrong?" asked Mrs. O'Shan. "Is my news not enough to lighten your spirits?"

"No, it's not that at all," explained the queen. "My son is coming home. I thought I'd never see him again."

"My poor dear," said the kind and understanding lady as she crossed the room and knelt down beside her queen. "You can be assured that you will see him again. He is going to make a very powerful leader one day."

"He already is, Mrs. O'Shan. Aaron is a powerful leader just like his father before him."

Woodbryne: The fallen forest

 ᘓ

The sun had turned the sky a deep orange by the time Forrester and his elves had led the humans back to Woodbyrne's borders. The elves had given back the horses so that the injured party members could travel in relative comfort.

"So it is agreed that no visitors shall enter this forest until further notice?" asked Forrester, reminding the king of the agreements made before the campaign had begun.

"As you and my son agreed upon, Lord Forrester Silverbow," replied Dermot with as much respect and admiration as he could muster. "I understand that you and your people have two centuries of work to catch up on."

"We have many ancient customs and rituals to relearn. This is something that we must do alone, King Dermot. I hope that you understand."

"You need not explain yourself to me, my friend," replied the king. "I can only say that I hope to live long enough to see your beautiful forest alive and well with you and your kin inside of it." Dermot nudged his horse forward and started back to the campsite. Many of his soldiers had fallen that day. The survivors deserved to know of the victory and that their comrades did not die in vain. "Until we meet again, Forrester Silverbow!"

"Farewell, good King Dermot of Gower!" called the elf lord. "And farewell to all of you, my friends," he said to Aaron and his party. "You have all done more for us than words can say."

"As did you and your people," Aaron stated. "We have learned much from each other and I look forward to when we shall meet again."

"Be assured that you and your friends will be the first ones to walk into the Woodbyrne of old. A magical forest where animals and elves live and play in harmony. A forest of life and beauty." Forrester then paid his last respects to the rest of the party and entered Woodbyrne accompanied by all but one of his warriors.

"I wish there was a way to thank all of you," said a saddened

Cathmore Stardust. "My people would be no more if it were not for your help."

"We wouldn't be here either if it were not for your kind heart and keen senses," Quinn Brainard replied.

"You have been a dear friend to us," said Aaron. Tears began to fill the young warriors eyes as he looked upon the tearful elf. "Byram is also thankful."

"Your cousin would be proud of you," Cathmore assured him. "Walk tall this day, Aaron. Know that none of our people died in shame."

Cathmore shook the prince's hand and gave him a quick hug. He then continued to pay his respects to the rest of the members of the party. "I will see you soon, Quinn Brainard. The agreement said nothing about me not leaving the forest to pay a visit now and again."

"I would love that," said Quinn as she wiped tears from her dirty cheeks. "It would mean a lot to us if you did."

After everyone paid their farewells, Aaron got on his horse and led his small party back to the main camp. The sun was no longer in view and the stars had made their entrance.

Delwyn Westbrook rode next to the young woman but was too busy scribbling in his notepad to even capture a little of the moment. He had been through much and refused to forget to write about any of his experiences. "Our tale will be sung in many taverns by many bards," he would pronounce every once in a while. "The legend of Prince Aaron and Quinn Brainard have already begun."

Lennox Softfoot held his head up high as he rode back to the camp with another victory under his belt. He also looked forward to Cathmore's visits. The elf was far superior in all aspects of scouting and Lennox truly wanted to learn more from the elf. He only hoped that his broken wrist would heal well so that he would still be of some use. The aging native still had many years ahead of him and he saw no reason why they should be spent in retirement.

Bringing up the rear, Kemp Hethington and Brother Frewin were busy as they talked about their experiences. "I can't wait to see the look on my mother's face when I return," said the young warrior. "King

Dermot has already assured me a noble position in the Royal Army."

"Just remember, my friend," said Brother Frewin, "you have powerful friends who will always be there for you, no matter what the situation may be. As for me, I simply want to get back to my order and rest. I want to renew my relationship with my god and with my prayers."

That night, up on top of the hill overlooking Woodbyrne, Prince Aaron and his friends celebrated with the rest of the Royal Army. Even Sir Bickford Browne was able to join in on the festivities. Unfortunately for the old warrior, his leg had suffered so much damage that he would never have full mobility in it again. Retirement sat well in his mind as he leaned back and reminisced over his long, successful career.

Aaron and his companions were labeled heroes by the rest of the soldiers and many songs were sung in their honor.

When the cheers and songs of victory died away, and when the rest of the camp was sound asleep, Aaron went up to the top of the small hill and stared westward. A feeling that the young prince never thought he would have washed over him like a wave of warm water. Prince Aaron of Gower was homesick.

Epilogue

Ulric, demon lord of the Lower Planes, sat on his throne in disgust. All about the massive creature, fallen souls screamed for the mercy and forgiveness of the one creature that could release them from their eternal suffering. The echoes of ancient ghosts and wails of horrible banshees cut through the darkness like claps of thunder.

As he looked up at Woodbyrne, and at the celebrations of the elves, Ulric felt sick to his stomach. He then looked up at Prince Aaron and his fellow humans as they rejoiced over their victory.

"How could Isidore allow the humans and elves to beat him?" The loss of Woodbyrne was a great loss indeed for Ulric's plans. "A pity," growled the gigantic demon. Ulric was not upset about the loss of one of his demon masters. Instead, he was upset that he lost control of Woodbyrne. "That forest was crucial to my expansion into the mortal world!" he cursed, his eyes glowing with rage. "I must get it back!"

More screams snapped Ulric out of his pitiful state. They were the pleas of a new addition to the fallen souls of the Lower Planes.

"Ahh, Isidore has come home," purred the wicked lord. "I have a million years' worth of anger to take out on you, my friend! I will never get over your failures! Never!"

Ulric jumped off his throne and stormed out of his black sanctuary. Just before he left, though, he took one more look up at Woodbyrne. "I will look upon that place every day to replenish my anger!" he promised. "Woodbyrne is far too important for me to let go. I must get it back before the elves grow strong again."